Nineteen Eighty

David Peace

A complete catalogue record for this book can be obtained from the British Library on request

The right of David Peace to be identified as the author of this work has been asserted by him in accordance with the Copyright, Designs and Patents Act 1988

First published in 2001 by Serpent's Tail

First published in this edition in 2008 by Serpent's Tail, an imprint of Profile Books Ltd
3A Exmouth House
Pine Street
London EC1R 0JH
website: www.serpentstail.com

ISBN 978 1 84668 707 5

Printed in Great Britain by CPI Bookmarque, Croydon, CR0 4TD

10 9 8 7 6 5 4 3

This book is printed on FSC certified paper

For the dead, a compass –
The living, salt.

'Ah, distinctly I remember it was in the bleak December;
And each separate dying ember wrought its ghost upon the floor.'

– The Raven
Edgar Allan Poe

Beg, Beg, Beg

The way I heard it, the nignogs just let themselves in.

Eric was sat there watching Songs of *fucking* Praise, *back to the door, and head nigger walks up behind him, pulls his hair back, and slits him ear to ear. Then they make themselves a sandwich, take a shit, and wait for his wife to come home –*

Just like that.

Part I
Saint Cunt

echo test transmission one a citizens band broadcast of pictures at an atrocity exhibition from the shadows of the sun out of the arc of the searchlight joyce jobson in halifax on friday the twelfth of july nineteen seventy four more life in a graveyard the rain keeping them in time for a look in the royal oak one more lager and then a fish supper with donald the lift home the chat the banter the chip shop shut out of the shadows the darkness he steps five foot four inches and quite good looking slightly wavy hair dark long sideboards he would not frighten anybody and says in a yorkshire way he says the weather is letting us down again and e know e am going to be in trouble severe cuts above both eyes and lacerations on the head her skull had suffered double fractures from an iron bar or hammer and for a moment the living soul is here among the dead who are suspended and soon will die get away from here intensive care just in case she had two small slashes in the small of her back each about six to eight inches long caused by a sharp instrument the clothing had first been lifted up before the marks were made then the clothing was rearranged where is kojak now he asks himself donald is it possible that you went out of the front door of your house and ran along the gardens around the side of the row of houses and waited in the dark for your wife is it possible donald it is you who out of the shadows the darkness step and attack your wife and say in a yorkshire way you say the weather is letting us down again was that you donald you have had your differences you and joyce we know and then you ran back along the gardens and sat back down in front of kojak that was you was it not the chopper man in a yorkshire way he says the weather is letting us down again and she is going to be in trouble severe cuts above both eyes and lacerations on the head her skull had suffered double fractures from an iron bar or hammer and for a moment the living soul is here among the dead who are suspended and soon will die get away from the silences in the shops the graffiti on the walls and doors the wet beds the days off work the days off school the days in the hospital the long days in the house the weather letting us down again and again and again the newspapers and the telephone calls the headaches and the pills the doctors and the police this is what the ripper has done to my wife the invisible man who put the dog hairs on her clothes who did not ladder her tights who left her white heels unmarked but still she sits in the house and gets depressed life pointless and crying out in a yorkshire way she screams the weather is letting us down again and they will put me away they will our sex life destroyed my daughters persuaded me to go out and buy clothes but e only did it to please them and they would laugh because e would never go anywhere to wear them and e used to enjoy cooking and cleaning but now e do it just to avoid sitting and thinking of chopper man a living soul here among the dead who are suspended and soon will die get away they say e could not be near a man or even look at one without feeling funny in a yorkshire way they all say the weather is letting us down again and e know it sounds horrible but sometimes e would look at my own husband sitting there the weather letting him down again and again and again my living soul here among the dead who are suspended and soon will die and e must get away from here from what ripper has done to me weather letting us down again the telephone call the silence before in a yorkshire way he says e missed you once but e will get you next time weather is letting you down again missed you once but not the next test

Chapter 1

A shot –

I'm awake, sweating and afraid.

Downstairs the telephone is ringing, before the dawn, before the alarm.

The LED display says 5:00, my head still full of murder and lies, nuclear war:

The North after the bomb, machines the only survivors.

I get out of bed and go downstairs and take the call.

I come back upstairs and sit in the cold on the edge of the bed, Joan still pretending to be asleep.

On the radio Yoko Ono is saying:

'This is not the end of an era. The 80s are still going to be a beautiful time, and John believed in it.'

After a few minutes I say: 'I've got to go to Whitby.'

'It was him then?' she asks, face still away.

'Yes,' I say, thinking –

Everyone gets everything they want.

I drive alone from Alderley Edge across the Moors, alone between the articulated lorries crawling slowly along the M62, the weather stark and grey, the landscape empty but for telegraph poles.

At 7:00 the radio breaks the news to the rest of the world:

'The Yorkshire Ripper has claimed his thirteenth victim, as police confirmed that Laureen Bell, aged twenty, was killed by the man responsible . . .'

I switch off the radio, thinking –

Murder and lies, lies and murder –

War:

It is Thursday 11 December 1980.

I arrive in Whitby at 11:00 and park in the drive of the large new bungalow, alongside three expensive cars.

There's sleet in the sea-spray, freezing gulls wheeling overhead, the wind screaming through a thousand empty shells.

I ring the doorbell.

A tall middle-aged woman opens the door.

'Peter Hunter,' I say.

'Come in.'

I step into the bungalow.

'Can I take your coat?'

'Thanks.'

'This way,' she says, leading me down the hall to the back of the house.

She knocks on a door, opens it, and gestures for me to go inside.

Three men are sat on the sofa and chairs, grey skin and red eyes, silent.

Philip Evans stands up: 'Peter? How was the drive?'

'Not so bad.'

'What would you like to drink?' asks his wife from the doorway.

'Coffee would be nice.'

'Have to be instant, I'm afraid.'

'Prefer it,' I say.

'Ever the diplomat,' laughs Evans.

'Everyone else OK?'

The other two men nod and she closes the door behind her.

'Let's get the introductions out of the way and then we can get on,' smiles Philip Evans, the Regional Inspector of Constabulary for Yorkshire and the North East.

'Gentlemen,' he says, 'This is Peter Hunter, Assistant Chief Constable of the Greater Manchester force. Peter, this is Sir John Reed, the Chief Inspector of Constabulary.'

'We've met before,' I say, shaking his hand.

'A long time ago,' says Sir John, sitting back down on the sofa.

'Of course,' nods Philip Evans. 'And this is Michael Warren, from the Home Office.'

'Nice to meet you,' I say, shaking the thin man's hand.

Evans points to a big chair with wide arms: 'Sit down, Pete.'

There is a soft knock on the door and Mrs Evans brings in a tray, setting it down on the low table between us.

'Help yourself to milk and sugar,' she says.

'Thank you.'

There's a pause, just the wind and Mrs Evans talking to a dog as she retreats back into the kitchen.

Philip Evans says: 'We've got a small problem.'

I stop stirring my coffee and look up.

'As I mentioned on the phone, there's been another murder. A nurse, twenty years old, outside her halls of residence. Leeds again.'

I nod: 'It was on the radio.'

'Couldn't even give us a day,' sighs Evans. 'Well anyway, enough is enough.'

Michael Warren sits forward on the sofa and places a small portable cassette recorder beside the plastic tray on the coffee table.

'Enough is enough,' he echoes and presses play:

A long pause, tape hiss, and then:

'I'm Jack. I see you are still having no luck catching me. I have the greatest respect for you George, but Lord! You are no nearer catching me now than four years ago when I started. I reckon your boys are letting you down, George. They can't be much good can they?

'The only time they came near catching me was a few months back in Chapeltown when I was disturbed. Even then it was a uniformed copper not a detective.

'I warned you in March that I'd strike again. Sorry it wasn't Bradford. I did promise that but I couldn't get there. I'm not quite sure where I'll strike again but it will be definitely some time this year, maybe September, October, even sooner if I get the chance. I am not sure where, maybe Manchester, I like it there, there's plenty of them knocking about. They never learn do they George? I bet you've warned them, but they never listen.'

Thirteen seconds of hiss, then:

'Take her in Preston, and I did, didn't I George? Dirty cow. Come my load up that.

'At the rate I'm going I should be in the book of records. I think it's eleven up to now isn't it? Well, I'll keep on going for quite a while yet. I can't see myself being nicked just yet. Even if you do get near I'll probably top myself first. Well it's been nice chatting to you George. Yours, Jack the Ripper.

'No use looking for fingerprints. You should know by now it's as clean as a whistle. See you soon. Bye.

'Hope you like the catchy tune at the end. Ha. Ha.'

Reed leans forward and switches off the cassette just as *Thank You for Being a Friend* starts.

'As you know that was June last year,' says Warren. 'What you won't know is that Home Secretary Whitelaw immediately approved the use of the Police National Computer to back up covert surveillance operations of vehicles in the West Yorkshire area, to use birth and school registers to cross-reference these against all males born in Wearside since 1920. He also secretly approved the release of DHSS records to trace all males who have lived or worked in Wearside in the past fifty years. So far they've interviewed and eliminated 200,000 people, done over 30,000 house to house searches, taken over 25,000 statements, and spent the best part of four million pounds.'

'And most of it on bloody publicity,' says Sir John Reed.

'*Flush out the Ripper,*' whispers Philip Evans.

Sir John snorts: 'Some bloody plan that was. 17,000 fucking suspects.'

'Some bloody plan,' repeats Michael Warren, putting in another cassette tape, pressing play again:

'*Every time the phone rings I wonder if it's him. If I get up in the middle of the night I find myself thinking about him. I feel after all this time, I feel that I really know him.*'

I look across at Reed, the grey skin and red eyes.

He's shaking his head.

'*If we do get him, we'll probably find he's had too long on the left breast and not enough on the right. But I don't regard him as evil. The voice is almost sad, a man fed up with what he's done, fed up with himself. To me he's like a bad angel on a mistaken journey and, while I could never condone his methods, I can sympathise with his feelings.*'

Warren presses stop.

'You know who that was?'

'George Oldman?' I say.

Philip Evans is nodding: 'That was Assistant Chief Constable Oldman talking to the *Yorkshire Post* last week.'

Warren: 'Thank Christ they called us.'

Silence.

On the dark stair, we miss our step.

Sir John Reed says: 'Sixteen hours a day, six – sometimes seven – days a week.'

I shrug: 'I'm afraid I don't know much about it.'

'What do you know?'

'About?'

'About the whole bloody farce?'

'Not much more than I've read in the papers.'

'I think you're being modest, Mr Hunter. I think you know a lot more,' winks Reed.

I start to speak, but he raises his hand: 'I think like most senior detectives in this country, I think you feel West Yorkshire have lost the plot, that the *Ripper Tape* is bollocks, that he's laughing at us, the British Police, and that you'd like nothing more than to have a crack.'

I return his stare: 'So is it bollocks? The tape?'

He smiles and turns to Philip Evans, nodding.

There's a pause before Evans says: 'There'll be a press conference later today and Chief Constable Angus will tell them that Oldman's out.'

I say nothing now, waiting.

'Peter Noble's been made Temporary Assistant Chief Constable with sole responsibility for the hunt.'

Again I say nothing, waiting.

Michael Warren coughs and leans forward: 'Noble's a good man.'

Nothing, just waiting.

'But there are already calls for outside help, a fresh perspective etc., so Angus is also going to announce the formation of a *brains trust, a Super Squad* if you like, to advise Noble's team,' continues Warren.

Nothing, waiting.

'This Super Squad will be Leonard Curtis, Deputy Chief Constable, Thames Valley; William Meyers, the National Coordinator of the Regional Crime Squads; Commander Donald Lincoln, Sir John's Deputy; Dr Stephen Tippet from the Forensic Science Service; and yourself.'

Waiting.

Sir John Reed lights a cigarette, exhales and says: 'So what do you think now?'

I swallow: 'We are to advise?'

'Yes.'

'For how long?'

Michael Warren says: 'Two or three weeks.'

Reed is staring at the end of his cigarette.

I say: 'May I speak frankly?'

'Of course,' says Philip Evans.

'As a public relations exercise I think we might have some success in diffusing the undoubted criticism the Yorkshire force is going to face over the next week but, as for any practical use we might have, I think we'll be distinctly limited.'

The whole room is smiling, grey skins and red eyes shining.

'Bravo,' claps Sir John Reed.

'We called you here today,' says Evans, handing me a thick red ringbinder. 'Because we would like you to head up a covert Home Office inquiry into these murders, working under the guise of this Super Squad. You'll be able to handpick up to seven officers to work with you; based in Leeds, you will be reporting only to myself here in Whitby. Your brief is to review the case in its entirety, to highlight areas of concern, should any arise, to determine strategies, to pursue all avenues.'

'And to catch the cunt,' spits Reed.

I wait, eyes on the prize.

Philip Evans says: 'Questions?'

Quietly: 'Why covert?'

Evans is nodding: 'The public is unlikely to accept two simultaneous investigations. Secondly, nor will the West Yorkshire lads. Thirdly, we don't want to wash our dirty linen in public etc., should there be any. Morale being what it is these days.'

I look around the room.

Sir John Reed says: 'So go on, ask?'

'Ask what, sir?'

'Why me? That's what you want to know, isn't it? That's what I'd want to know.'

'OK. Why me?'

Reed nods at Michael Warren.

'Primarily your work with A10,' says Warren. 'And the fact that you've previously been involved with investigations into the West Yorkshire force.'

'With all due respect, one investigation was over five years ago and failed to reach any conclusion, aside from making me possibly the most unpopular copper in the North. And the second one was over before it began.'

'Eric Hall,' Evans says to the other two.

I look down at the cup of cold instant coffee on the table before me, the light reflecting in its black surface.

'Hunter the Cunt, they call you,' laughs Sir John Reed.

I look up at him.

'That bother you, does it?' Reed asks.

'No,' I say.

'So there's your answer.'

'Thank you.'

'I make spies of them despite themselves,' he smiles.

'General Napier,' I say.

Sir John Reed has stopped smiling: 'You know your history.'

'Yes,' I say. 'I know my history.'

Outside it's snowing.

There is blood on my windscreen, a dead gull on the lawn.

I switch on the windscreen wipers and drive back alone across the M62, alone between the articulated lorries crawling slowly along, the weather stark, the landscape empty –

Just murder and lies, lies and murder:

'The Yorkshire Ripper has claimed his thirteenth victim, as police confirmed that Laureen Bell, aged twenty, was killed by the man responsible . . .'

It's after 8:00 when I get home.

Joan is watching *TV Eye*.

'They're repeating that *Mind of the Ripper*,' she says.

I sit in front of the TV, watching the faces swim by.

I am forty years old, Joan thirty-eight.

We have no children.

I can't sleep –

I never can.

My back bad, getting worse and worse, day by day.

Always awake, sweating and afraid, eyes wide in the dark beside Joan.

The radio on –

Always on:

Hunger strikers near death, thirty-two murdered in one LA weekend;

Gdansk, Tehran, Kabul, the Dakota;

The North of England –
No law.
I get out of bed and go downstairs.
I can hear the rain against the window pane, behind the curtains.
I go into the kitchen and put the radio on and wait for the kettle to boil.
The rain against the pane, a song on the radio:
'Don't be afraid to go to hell and back – '
I open my briefcase and take out the red ring-binder, the red ring-binder they gave me:
Murders and Assaults upon Women in the North of England.
The kettle's boiling, whistling:
Everyone gets everything they want.
I unlock the back door and take the tea and the red ring-binder out into the black garden and the rain. I walk down the side of the garage to the shed I built at the back. I take the key from my dressing gown pocket and unlock the door to the shed.
I am cold, freezing.
I go inside, lock the door behind me and put on the light.
My room –
One door, one light, no windows; the smell of earth and damp, old exhaust fumes and ageing gardening gloves; a long desk across the length of the back wall, two grey metal filing cabinets standing guard on each of the side walls. Between them, on top of the desk, a computer and keyboard, a black and white portable television, a CB radio, a cassette recorder and a reel to reel, a typewriter. Under the desk, across the floor, wires and cables, plugs and adapters, boxes of paper, stacks of magazines and newspapers, tins and jars and pots of pens and pencils and paperclips.
I perch the tea on top of the red ring-binder on the corner of the desk and I switch on the two-bar electric heater and the computer –
Anabasis:
The bastard bits of an Acorn with Memorex RAMpacks, pirated parts from Radionics and Tandy, an unopened ZX80 still in its box, the whole machine covered in cassette tapes and blu-tack.
I sit down at the desk and stare at the wall above *Anabasis*:

At one map and twelve photographs –
Each photograph a face, each face a letter and a date, a
number on each forehead:

Theresa Campbell	*a*	6–6–75	3.
Clare Strachan	*b*	20–11–75	2.
Joan Richards	*c*	6–2–76	4.
Marie Watts	*d*	28–5–77	0.
Rachel Johnson	*e*	6–7–77	0.
Janice Ryan	*f*	5/12–6–77	1.
Elizabeth McQueen	*g*	20–11–77	2.
Tracey Livingston	*h*	7–1–78	3.
Candy Simon	*i*	27–1–78	0.
Doreen Pickles	*j*	27–5–78	5.
Joanne Thornton	*k*	18–5–79	0.
Dawn Williams	*l*	9–9–79	0.

I take the tea off the red ring-binder and open the first page:

Contents:

Divided by the years:

1974:
Joyce Jobson, attacked Halifax, July 1974.
Anita Bird, attacked Cleckheaton, August 1974.

1975:
Theresa Campbell, murdered Leeds, June 1975.
Clare Strachan, murdered Preston, November 1975.

1976:
Joan Richards, murdered Leeds, February 1976.
Ka Su Peng, attacked Bradford, October 1976.

1977:
Marie Watts, murdered Leeds, May 1977.
Linda Clark, attacked Bradford, June 1977.
Rachel Johnson, murdered Leeds, June 1977.
Janice Ryan, murdered Bradford, June 1977.
Elizabeth McQueen, murdered Manchester, November 1977.
Kathy Kelly, attacked Leeds, December 1977.

1978:
Tracey Livingston, murdered Preston, January 1978.
Candy Simon, murdered Huddersfield, January 1978.
Doreen Pickles, murdered Manchester, May 1978.

1979:
Joanne Thornton, murdered Morley, May 1979.
Dawn Williams, murdered Bradford, September 1979.

He's already written the next chapter:

1980:
Laureen Bell, murdered Leeds, December 1980.

My chapter –
The last chapter.
I close the red ring-binder, the red ring-binder they gave me –
Nothing new.
I look up at the wall, the map and the photographs, the letters and the dates, the numbers:
Seven years, thirteen dead women, seven of them mothers, twenty orphaned children.
Reed's voice echoing around the shed:
'What do you know?'
My words echoing back:
'Not much more than I've read in the papers.'
Echoing back round my head, this shed, this room –
My room –
The War Room –
My obsessions:
Murder and lies, lies and murder –
See them, smell them, taste them.
The War Room –
My War:
Motherless children, childless mothers.
I am forty years old, Joan thirty-eight.
We have no children, we can't.
Somewhere back on the Moors, the visibility down to yards, I'd made that deal again:

I catch him, stop him murdering mothers, orphaning children, then you give us one, just one.

transmission two in cleckheaton on cumberland avenue attractive anita bird on monday the fifth of august nineteen seventy four day clive had hidden every pair of my shoes grabbed my head and plunged it into a bucket of cold water he was a mental man who had been advised to keep away from women for at least five years but he had bought me a colour television and we made up but e was frightened of him and feeling a bit tearful playing crying in the chapel as e brought in the sheets from outside and folded them in the kitchen the kitten missing so e went to look for it and out of shadows the darkness he steps well dressed he was and smelt of soap a good looking waiter italian or greek he wanted to come in for a cup of tea his racing eyes and dainty hands and in a yorkshire way he says do you fancy it not on your life e say and then the hammer comes down one two three times and he pulls down her panties and he raises her blouse and slashes her stomach and wants to stab but then the light goes on and the man is asking what is going on who is out there who is making all that noise come on what is going on out there nothing to worry about you go back inside everything is all right now are you sure yes nothing to worry about but she will need a twelve hour operation to remove the splinters of brain from her skull the last rites to live behind wires and alarms alone with her cats and her pictures of christ and david soul and khalid aziz the three inch dents in her head and the hair she cuts herself crying in the chapel e am in my own world the curtains pulled in a housecoat with her cats walking in the middle of the road scared of the shadows and the men behind her when six months before the mystery man had come to the corner shop and left messages every day for a week would she go out with him for an evening for a few drinks and spot of supper and he drove her into bradford to a city centre restaurant and she cannot remember which but she knows all waitresses wore black long skirts and he was friendly in a yorkshire way and he knew all about her even though they had never met before and he said his name was michael gill or was it gull a doctor gull he lived with his grandmother who was old and ill and that he also had a cat they finished their meal and he drove her home to cleckheaton and no he would not come in for a coffee because he had to go home to put grandmother to bed and he did not even give her a kiss on the cheek and she never saw him again and six months later she lay in the street the blows from cuban heeled boots and the lacerations across her stomach the kind that west indian boyfriends like her clive inflict upon girlfriends who have been unfaithful do you fancy it not on your life and then the hammer comes down one two three times he pulls down her panties and he raises her blouse slashes her stomach and she is not anita now she is anna and she will never be anita again cos anita died that night on cobblestones and times e wish e had not had that operation e wish e had died with her on cobblestones for then e would have known nothing but the blackness and nothing more for if e had known what lay ahead for me e would have refused what they term a life saving operation for my life is not saved it is lost so e have had fifteen thousand pounds compensation no amount of money can give me back my anonymity can give me back my boyfriends no money can remove the stigma of the ripper can give me back my doctor gull or was it gill michael gill fifteen thousand pounds compensation to live behind wires and alarms with my cats and pictures of christ scared of the shadows and the men behind me alone do you fancy

Chapter 2

7:00 a.m.

Friday 12 December 1980.

Manchester Police Headquarters.

The eleventh floor.

The Assistant Chief Constable's office –

My office.

I've got my suitcase by the door, the radio on:

'The early Christmas exodus is expected to continue from univer-sities and colleges across the North of England as the President of the NUS issued the following statement:

'Anyone who goes to any of the Northern Universities today will know immediately the pall this Yorkshire Ripper has cast over the whole student population . . .'

Going through the tray on my desk, the Christmas cards.

'And in other news, it was announced that 30,000 pigs are to be slaughtered in an attempt to stop the further spread of swine fever . . .'

I hear the door across the corridor open and close.

I put the last papers in their folders and go out into the corridor.

I stand before the door of the Chief Constable and knock.

'Come.'

I open the door.

Chief Constable Clement Smith is behind his desk.

'Good morning,' I say.

He doesn't look up.

I stand, waiting.

Eventually he says: 'So you took it?'

'Yes.'

The Chief Constable looks up; his close-cropped hair, full black beard and dark eyes giving Clement Smith one expression:

Orthodox.

'I've been asked to put together a team to assist me,' I say.

Silence.

'I'd like to take John Murphy and Alec McDonald, plus DI Hillman and DS Marshall from Serious Crime.'

'Helen Marshall?'

'Yes.'

'Is that it?'

'Yes.'

'You know you can have up to three more?'

'Yes.'

'Have you spoken to these people?'

'No.'

'Have you got a timetable in mind?'

'With your permission, I'd like to get everyone together this morning.'

Silence.

'I've got to be over in Wakefield for the afternoon press conference and I'd like to take John Murphy with me for that.'

Silence.

'I'm due to meet Chief Constable Angus, George Oldman and Pete Noble, and then make a start.'

Silence.

'If that's OK with you?'

Eventually he says: 'I've been instructed to give you whatever you need.'

'Thank you.'

A pause, then: 'I'll have them meet in your office at ten.'

'Thank you.'

Clement Smith nods and goes back to the work on his desk.

I walk to the door.

'Peter,' he says.

I turn around.

'You made up your mind pretty quickly?'

'Not something I felt I could refuse.'

'You could have,' he says. 'I would have.'

'I think it's an honour, sir. An honour for the Manchester force.'

He goes back to the work on his desk again.

I open the door.

'Peter,' he says again.

I turn around.

'Let's hope so,' he says. 'Let's hope so.'

10:00 a.m.

My office.

Detective Chief Superintendent John Murphy: Manchester–Irish, mother knew mine, early fifties, over twenty years' CID experience, a couple of tours with me in A10, direct involvement in the so-called Ripper Hunt having been in charge of the 1977 Elizabeth McQueen investigation.

Detective Chief Inspector Alec McDonald: Scots, Glasgow-bred, late forties, five years with Vice, five years Serious Crime, direct involvement with the Ripper through the 1978 Doreen Pickles investigation.

Detective Inspector Mike Hillman: mid thirties, five years A10 with me, extensive anti-corruption work, now Serious Crime.

Detective Helen Marshall: early thirties, ten years Vice and Drug Squads, now Serious Crime.

The best we have –

Their eight bright and shining eyes on me:

'Thank you all for coming and at such short notice.'

Nods and smiles –

'I'll get straight to it: I've been asked by the Home Office to head an investigation into the murders and assaults on women in the North of England publicly referred to as the work of the Yorkshire Ripper. Murders that as of yesterday now total thirteen.'

No nods, no smiles –

'The brief of the investigation is to review and to highlight areas of concern, to advise alternative strategies, and to pursue and arrest the man responsible.'

Eight eyes on me –

'I've asked you here this morning as I would like each one of you to be a part of this investigation. However, it is going to mean that you will be seconded from your present duties, that you will be over in Yorkshire a hell of a lot, that you will be away from your families, working twenty-four-hour days, seven-day weeks, limited time off.'

No nods, no smiles, just stares –

'You know the demands and I would not wish to presume upon any of you. But I have worked with each of you and I believe you are the best people for this job.'

Hard stares –

'So, if you cannot commit, say so now.'

Silence, then –
John Murphy: 'I'm in.'
'Thank you, John.'
Alec McDonald: 'In.'
'Thank you.'
Mike Hillman: 'I hate bloody Yorkshire, but go on then.'
'Thanks, Mike.'
Helen Marshall: 'I'll have to get someone to feed the dog, I suppose.'
'Thank you.'
I sit back down in my chair: 'Thank you, all of you. I knew I could count on you.'
Smiles again, the stares gone.
'In a bit, John and myself will get over to Wakefield for their afternoon press conference. Everyone else should take the opportunity to hand over their present duties. Chief Constable Smith's office will issue all the necessary authorisation later this morning.
'After the press conference, I have got a meeting scheduled with Chief Constable Angus and Assistant Chief Constable Oldman. John'll secure the offices and arrange hotels for us. But let's provisionally agree to meet in Leeds tomorrow morning at nine, location to be confirmed later today?'
Nods.
'Questions?'
Mike Hillman: 'They know we're coming?'
'Brass, yes; but not their lads or the press and we should keep it that way.'
Nods again.
Alec McDonald: 'You want us to start boxing up our files on McQueen and Pickles?'
'Not straight off. Let's see what they've got over there first.'
A nod.
Silence, then –
I say: 'OK? Until tomorrow.'
We all stand up.
'And thanks again,' I say, eight bright eyes shining back.
The best –
Mine.

*

Over the Moors again, between the articulated lorries, stark and empty, snow across their cold, lost bones –

John Murphy and myself, the memories neither cold nor lost –

Ours.

The football exhausted, my hands tight on the wheel, eyes on the road, silent.

After a few minutes I put the radio on, listeners phoning Jimmy Young about the death of John Lennon, about the hostages in Iran and the Third World War, about a factory in Germany that needs no people, just machines, and about the Yorkshire Ripper, mainly about the Yorkshire Ripper:

'We'll paper every surface with a thousand posters saying: The Ripper is a Coward . . .'

Murder and lies, war:

The North after the bomb, machines the only survivors.

Murder and lies, lies and murder.

Murphy says: 'When were you last over this way?'

'Yesterday.'

'No, I mean with A10?'

'Should have been Bradford Vice, 1977. Remember all that?'

He nods: 'All set to come right? Interviews, the lot, then – '

'Case closed.'

'Muddy waters, eh Pete?'

'You could stand your truncheon in it, John.'

He sniffs up: 'Before that would have been the Strafford then?'

'Yep.'

'Fuck,' whistles Murphy. 'Bloody Yorkshire.'

'Yep,' I say –

The Moors, Murphy, and me –

The memories neither cold nor lost:

The Strafford Shootings –

Christmas Eve 1974:

A pub robbery that went wrong –

Three dead at the scene, three wounded, one of them fatally –

Two of the wounded, coppers –

Suspects escaped, armed police and roadblocks on the streets of Yorkshire, possible links to Republican terrorists given the proximity to Wakefield Prison.

Twenty-four hours later and it was four dead, two wounded policemen –

Nothing adding up –

Inquiry ordered –

January 1975 and in we came –

A10:

Me and Clarkie –

Detective Chief Inspector Mark Clark, a friend.

Four weeks in –

A frantic phone call, a two-hour drive across these damned Moors again, home to bloody sheets and another miscarriage.

Clarkie took over, Murphy stepping in as his deputy.

Two weeks on –

Clarkie collapses: pains in the chest, brought on by exhaustion.

Murphy in charge, Hillman as deputy.

Two more weeks –

Clarkie dead: pains in the chest –

Everybody home –

Case closed.

The Moors, Murphy, and me –

Memories neither cold nor lost.

'Been a while since you seen George then?' says Murphy, back.

'Can't bloody wait,' I spit.

'Brought your phrasebook?'

'Phrasebook? No bastard speaks over there.'

'Bloody heathens,' nods Murphy.

I stare out at the lanes of lorries, the Moors beyond, the black poles and the telephone wires –

The North after the bomb, machines the only survivors.

Murder and lies, war –

My War:

Murder and lies, lies and murder.

'What kind of reception you think we're going to get?'

'Cold,' I say.

'Bloody Yorkshire.'

His.

Wakefield, deserted Wakefield:

Friday 12 December 1980 –

Nothing but the ill-feelings and bad memories of thwarted investigations, of the walls of silence, the black secrets and the paranoia –

Professional hells.

January 1975 –

Nothing but the ill-feelings and terrible memories of the thwarted, of the walls of silence, the black blame and the guilt –

Personal hells.

January 1975 –

Impotent prayers and broken promises, reneged and returned –

December 1980:

Wakefield, barren Wakefield.

West Yorkshire Metropolitan Police Headquarters, Laburnum Road, Wakefield.

We park our black Rovers amongst the other black Rovers and go inside out of the rain to be directed back out, across the road to the gymnasium of the Training College.

We are early.

But I can hear the press waiting on the other side of the building, waiting –

Early.

Another uniform sends us down another corridor to a small room beside a kitchen.

And here, in amongst the catering, we find the Yorkshire Brass:

Angus, Oldman, and Noble –

Hiding and already beaten, standing between their sandwiches and their better days, their Black Panthers and their M62 Coach Bombings, their A1 Shootings and their Michael Myshkins, those better days a long time gone.

'Chief Constable Angus?'

He turns around.

'Mr Hunter,' he sighs.

The room is silent, dead.

I say: 'This is John Murphy.'

'Yes,' he says, not taking Murphy's hand. 'We've met before.'

Some other men step forward from the back of the room,

familiar faces from conferences and old Gazettes, Oldman and Noble dropping back out into the corridor.

Angus introduces Murphy and myself to Bill Meyers, the National Coordinator of the Regional Crime Squads, to Donald Lincoln, Sir John Reed's Number Two at the Inspectorate, and to Dr Stephen Tippet from the Forensic Services, a man I've met a number of times before.

Leonard Curtis, the Thames Valley DCC, has been unable to make the trip and Sir John himself left for the Caribbean early this morning.

'Crisis, what crisis?' smiles Murphy as we're ushered out the door, towards the gymnasium, towards the waiting pack.

The Pack –

Yesterday's shock has turned to anger, outright anger.

They are baying for us, smelling wet blood and wanting it fresh.

Lots of it.

A suit from Community Affairs shepherds us through the double doors and into the fray, a sea of hate.

We wade down to the long plastic tables at the front, eight of us, Murphy waiting by the exit.

We take our seats; the pack sitting before us, photographers and TV crews standing over us, everyone jostling for an angle.

Outside the large gymnasium windows it's almost dark, a black ocean, the sheets of glass reflecting back the bodies of the press, their lights, their cameras, their actions.

Angus taps his microphone.

I am staring up at the ropes dangling from the ceiling.

'Gentlemen,' begins Angus. 'As you are aware, last night I attended an emergency meeting of the West Yorkshire Police Committee which was called in light of the confirmation of Laureen Bell as the thirteenth victim of the Yorkshire Ripper.

'I proposed a number of changes to the Investigation and the Police Committee have accepted them.'

'Your resignation?' shouts someone from the back.

Angus feigns deafness: 'We have invited a number of senior detectives from across Britain and a leading Home Office scientist to assist us in our hunt for this maniac.

'These men are Mr Leonard Curtis, the Deputy Chief Constable of Thames Valley, who unfortunately could not be with us today . . .'

'Bit like the fucking Ripper, eh Ron?'

'Mr William Meyers, the National Coordinator of the Regional Crime Squads. Commander Donald Lincoln, the Deputy Chief Inspector of Constabulary. Mr Peter Hunter, an Assistant Chief Constable with Greater Manchester, and Dr Stephen Tippet from the Home Office Forensic Science Services.

'These gentlemen represent the most experienced group of officers who could be mustered to assist our investigations. They will conduct a thorough review of past and present police strategy in the hunt for the Ripper. They will look critically at police action and advise their West Yorkshire colleagues as to appropriate strategies.

'Furthermore I would like to announce some internal operational changes which the Police Committee have also approved.

'As of today Peter Noble has been appointed Temporary Assistant Chief Constable and been taken off all other duties and given sole responsibility for the hunt for this man.

'Assistant Chief Constable Oldman will remain as head of West Yorkshire CID with responsibility for every incident except the inquiry into these murders and attacks.

'It is my sincere hope that, with the continued assistance and support of the public, these changes will bring about a speedy and successful end to these horrific crimes.

'Thank you.'

The sea of hate swells –

A deafening, roaring wave:

'Would the Chief Constable care to comment on allegations that valuable time was lost . . .'

'Was Laureen not reported missing as early as ten-thirty?'

'And comments from her flatmate that she called the police repeatedly to insist that a search be conducted . . .'

' . . . comment on rumours that she bled to death while officers failed to respond to the repeated worries of her friends and flatmate?'

'And that Miss Bell's bloodstained handbag was discovered some time . . .'

'That her bag was handed in and simply logged as lost property despite the bloodstains?'

' . . . and would it not have been possible for roadblocks to have been set up?'

'Have any suspects been arrested, any witnesses . . .'

Drowned, beached –

Oldman, a redhead resting in his left hand, glasses off, tears in his eyes.

Noble straining to pick questions from the torrent.

Angus, lips pursed, fingers in the dam.

The man from Community Affairs trying to keep afloat, sinking.

The rest of us, at sea –

Lost.

I look up at the ropes again, dangling –

Looking for a way out –

An exit –

An exit from:

' . . . suggestions in some reports that the so-called *Wearside Jack Tape*, the *Ripper Tape*, that it is in fact a hoax?'

Silence.

Oldman eyes closed, Noble mouth open, Ronald Angus on his feet and shouting: 'I would urge members of the public, all members of the public and the press to ignore suggestions that the recording is a hoax. I am 99% sure that the man on the tape, that the voice on the tape is genuine, 99% certain that this is the man we are looking for, that this is the Yorkshire Ripper.'

Looking up at the ropes, dangling –

On the dark stair, we miss our step.

A way out –

An exit.

'Fuck.'

Doors slamming, jackets off, sandwiches flying, cans cracking.

'Fucking cunts, the lot of them.'

In the back room, the Brass whipped.

'A bloody shambles.'

The recriminations and the blame, looking for lambs, a scape-goat –

Community Affairs to the slaughter, Angus wielding the knife:

His turn for blood.

Oldman off to one side, staring into space:

The Scapegoat.

I leave Murphy by the silver foil and the sandwiches and walk over.

'George,' I say.

He looks up, taking off his glasses, thinner than I've ever seen him.

'Can I sit down?'

He's staring straight up at me, his eyes black and tiny holes.

'George?'

'Fuck off Hunter.'

There's a hand at my elbow, Noble whisking me away.

'We'll meet in Millgarth at six,' he's telling me.

I'm nodding, staring back at Oldman, him back into space, black and tiny.

'He doesn't mean it. He's had a shock that's all,' Noble is saying.

Nodding, staring into my own space –

White and huge –

Lost.

'What was all that about?' Murphy is shaking his head, reversing out of the car park.

Radio on:

'*Big changes were ordered today in the hunt for the Yorkshire Ripper . . .*'

'He didn't know,' I say.

'You're fucking joking?'

'*Mr Ronald Angus, the Chief Constable of West Yorkshire, announced that a brains trust of senior detectives from around the country and a leading forensic scientist are being drafted in to the hunt for the man who has now claimed . . .*'

'They don't waste any bloody time, do they?'

'No.'

'*Mr Angus also confirmed that Mr George Oldman, Assistant Chief Constable and Head of West Yorkshire CID, has been relieved of his command of the inquiry.*'

We drive up the motorway, the M1, listening in silence as the stories eventually change, as they move on to two and a

half million unemployed, a job lost every two minutes, on to
the H Blocks and the Eastern Bloc, to a local woman who cut
her own throat with a pair of electric hedge clippers.

'Jesus,' mutters Murphy as we approach Leeds. 'What a
fucking place.'

Leeds –

Wakefield deserted and barren, Leeds twice that hell and
more –

A collision of the worst of times, the worst of hells –

The Medieval, the Victorian, and the Concrete:

The dark arches, black mists and broken windows of industrial decay, industrial murder, industrial hell –

Dead city abandoned to the crows, the rain, and the Ripper.

And today, this day:

Friday 12 December 1980 –

It looks no different than we remember, than we feared –

Dread spectre from a woken nightmare –

A past trapped in a future, here and now:

Friday 12 December 1980 –

Screaming in the wind –

A bloody castle rising out of the bleeding rain, a tear in the
landscape –

Leeds, the grim and concrete medieval:

Dead city –

The crows, the rain, and the Ripper –

The Ripper, King –

The King of Leeds.

In a cold and rotting café, in the shadow of an industrial estate,
we drink cold and rotting tea to kill the time, lorry drivers
eating the fish special, kids playing the slot machine.

It's pitch black as we pull into the underground car park beneath
Millgarth Police Station, Kirkgate Market closing up. Moments
later and we're running back up the ramp and into the rain, the
lift not working, the market gutters overflowing with rotten
vegetables and foul water, Murphy cursing Leeds and Yorkshire,
their coppers and their killer.

'Assistant Chief Constable Noble please.'

The fat sergeant on the desk, his face and hands covered in boils, he sniffs up: 'And you are?'

'Assistant Chief Constable Hunter and Chief Superintendent Murphy from Manchester.'

He wipes his nose in his fingers: 'Wait over there.'

'We have an appointment,' hisses John Murphy.

'Fat lot of bloody good that'll do you if he's not in.'

I lead Murphy over to plastic chairs under bright strip lights, the smell of wet police dogs rank and strong.

'Fuck him,' mutters Murphy.

'He's not worth it, John.'

And we sit in silence, staring at the boot marks on the linoleum floor, picking off the dog hairs, waiting –

Waiting for it to start.

And sitting here, staring into the black marks, the dog hairs, I realise how long I've been waiting –

Waiting for it all to stop:

Five years –

Five years to come back and right the wrongs, to make it right, make it all worthwhile –

The five years of marriage and miscarriage, of wet pillows and bloody sheets, of doctors and priests, of the drugs and the tests, the broken promises and plates –

Five years of –

'Manchester? You can go up.'

'About fucking time,' says Murphy.

The Sergeant looks back up from his desk: 'Just Mr Hunter that is.'

I've got my palms up between Murphy and the desk: 'You try and get hold of someone, see if you can sort out the hotel. I'll talk to Noble about the offices. Yeah?'

He's got his eyes on the Sergeant, the eyes and boils back on his desk.

'John?'

'Right, right, right.'

I say: 'Then I'll meet you back here in an hour or so. OK?'

He's still got his eyes on the Sergeant, but he's nodding: 'More good old-fashioned Yorkshire bloody hospitality.'

The Sergeant doesn't look up.

*

'I'm sorry about before,' says Temporary Assistant Chief Constable Peter Noble, sitting back down behind his desk.

'No harm done,' I say as I take a seat across from him.

'Well that's OK then,' he smiles.

He's older than me, but not by much –

Forty-five at the most; thick hair starting to turn grey, a moustache that gives him the look of a man still hard, still in the chase; and on a morning as he shaves he's thinking of Burt Reynolds, fancying his chances, still in the hunt.

'It's not going to be much of a picnic for you,' he's saying. 'Though I suppose you must be used to it by now.'

'Sorry? Used to what?' I say, staring at the photograph of two children on the windowsill behind the desk.

'Not getting the red carpet.'

'Don't expect it.'

'That's lucky then,' he laughs.

The door opens and Chief Constable Angus comes in: 'Gentlemen.'

'We were just getting started,' says Noble, standing up.

'Well I say we call it a night,' laughs Angus. 'After bloody day we've had, I say we extend some hospitality to Mr Hunter here and get him some dinner . . .'

'I'm afraid I've arranged to meet John Murphy in . . .'

'Don't worry about John,' winks Angus. 'Dickie Alderman and a couple of the lads are taking care of him. They've sorted you out rooms at the Griffin and they've gone for a pint or two. Or three.'

'The Griffin?'

'City centre. Be ideal.'

I pause, then say: 'I had wanted to make a start right away.'

'Course you had,' smiles the Chief Constable. 'And you will. But we can get just as much done over a steak and a couple of drinks as we can up here.'

They are both at the door, waiting.

'I need to make a call to Manchester.'

Noble points at the phone on his desk: 'Be my guest.'

The Draganora Hotel is a modern skyscraper near Leeds City Station, its third-floor restaurant dark and empty.

We take our seats in the window, the rain on the wired glass, city lights running in the wind and the night.

'It's one of them carvery deals,' smiles Angus. 'Help yourself to as much as you want and keep going back up until they have to carry you out.'

We order drinks and then head over to the long table at the back of the room, the food lying waiting for us under dim orange lights.

Noble and myself follow Angus along the line, piling on under-cooked meat and over-cooked vegetables until there's no space left on our plates.

And as we eat we make small talk about the poor seasons Leeds and Man U. are having, the jailing of Lord Kagan, the murder of John Lennon; the three of us careful to avoid the obvious, careful to avoid the fact that we are the only diners in the restaurant of a four-star Leeds hotel a week before Christmas, careful to avoid the reason we are here and no-one else.

Noble goes back up for more.

'Not much bloody loss if you ask me,' Angus is saying.

'You weren't a fan then?' I ask.

'To be honest with you Mr Hunter, I reckon they weren't that popular over this way. Be different for you mind, coming from over there I suppose. But on this side, we pride ourselves on not following trends.'

'Still talking about bloody Beatles, are you?' says Noble, back with a plate for himself and another for his Boss.

'I was just telling Mr Hunter here, how Yorkshire is always the last bastion of common sense. Like the bloody resistance, we are,' laughs Angus.

'Not much bloody loss if you ask me,' nods Noble, ploughing through his second-helpings.

I sip at my gin and watch the rain, wondering if Joan has gone to bed yet.

Angus is still piling it on his fork, still laughing: 'You're not on bloody hunger strike are you?'

'No,' I say. 'Why?'

'Thought you might be off your grub in sympathy.'

'What?' I say, smiling but not following.

Angus looks up from his cold pink meat: 'The Maze. You're a Roman, aren't you?'

'No.'

'Sorry, no offence. Heard you were.'

'No.'

'Well anyway,' he says, putting down his knife and fork and taking out an envelope from inside his jacket. 'If you're not eating you might as well have a butchers at this.'

I take the envelope and open it.

Inside is a memorandum from Angus to Sir John Reed, Philip Evans, and myself –

A memorandum outlining the terms of reference for my investigation into their investigation.

I look up.

Angus and Noble have stopped eating and are watching me. 'Another drink?' asks Noble.

I nod and go back to the memorandum –

The memorandum that in two sentences states that I have been invited by the West Yorkshire Metropolitan Police to review inquiries made into the murders and attacks attributed to the so-called Yorkshire Ripper, that I am to recommend any necessary changes to operational procedures, and that I am to make those recommendations directly to Chief Constable Angus. During the course of my review, should any evidence arise to suggest that any persons involved in the Ripper inquiry are themselves guilty or suspected to be guilty of any offences or negligence, then that evidence is to be immediately forwarded to the Chief Constable and no further or independent action is to be taken on the part of the review.

'I hope you don't feel that there's any attempt here to circumscribe or in any way limit the scope of your investigation,' smiles Chief Constable Angus. 'However, and Sir John and I are in complete agreement on this one, an open-ended investigation such as this, any open-ended investigation for that matter, well they can so easily develop into some kind of amorphous bloody mess that, in fact, serves only to obscure and hinder the initial investigation. Am I right?'

'Absolutely,' nods Noble.

I take a sip from my fresh gin, counting backwards from a hundred, and then say: 'You do know why I was brought in?'

'Yes,' says Ronald Angus, the Chief Constable of West Yorkshire.

'That's OK then.' I smile.

Ronald Angus and Peter Noble both take big swallows from their glasses, then Angus glances at his watch and Noble before turning back to me and saying: 'We've arranged for you to have an office right next door to the Ripper Room. That'll give you easy access to the people and the papers you need.'

'Thank you.'

Angus nods and then suddenly asks: 'How's your wife these days?'

'Well, thank you,' I say, lost again.

'I'm sorry,' he says. 'I didn't mean to pry but I heard she hadn't been so well, that's all.'

'She's fine, thank you.'

Silence –

Just the restaurant dark and empty, the rain on the wired glass, city lights running in the wind and the night.

Silence, until –

Until Noble suggests: 'Shall we go to the bar?'

'The Casino?' adds Angus.

'To be honest with you both,' I smile. 'It's been a long day and I'd rather just get to the hotel if that's all right?'

'You're the guest,' says Angus.

'I'll drop you off,' offers Noble, standing and signalling for the bill.

We take our coats and go down the escalator and wait for the cars to be brought round, the night cold and damp, the conversation dead.

'Thank you for the meal,' I say, shaking Angus by the hand.

'Good old-fashioned Yorkshire bloody hospitality,' winks Angus. 'You sleep tight now Mr Hunter. Make sure them Yorkshire bugs don't bite.'

The Griffin is an old hotel on Boar Lane.

I say goodnight to Peter Noble and dash for the door and the lobby.

Inside there seems to be some kind of renovation work underway, white sheets hanging from the walls, draped across the furniture.

It's almost nine o'clock.

I'm the only person here.

I ring the bell and wait.

'Can I help you?' asks a receptionist, coming out of a back room.

'Yes, I should have a reservation. My name is Hunter, Peter Hunter.'

He opens a book on the counter and goes down a list with his finger.

'I'm sorry. I don't seem to have anyone here by that name.'

'Murphy? John Murphy?'

'Ah, yes. Are you sharing with Mr Murphy?'

'I hope not. I think maybe the reservation was made through a Superintendent Alderman from the Millgarth Police Station?'

He's nodding: 'Yes, yes.'

'Has Mr Murphy checked in yet?'

'No, not yet.'

'Would it be possible to book me into a separate room?'

'If that's what you want.'

'Please.'

'Can you give me half an hour? We're a bit short and some of the rooms are being redecorated.'

'That's fine. Can you lend me an umbrella?'

'Bar's open if you're wanting a drink.'

'I need a walk.'

He goes back into the office and returns with a black brolly.

'Thanks,' I say.

'You know where you're going?' he asks.

'Yep,' I say.

'Course you do,' he laughs. 'You're a policeman, aren't you?'

Back into the rain, back into the night, through deserted city streets, under broken Christmas lights swinging in the wind, along Boar Lane, the shopping centres and the vacant offices dark and huge, black canyon walls looming, up Market Street, the queues of empty buses all lit up with no place or passengers to go, through the Kirkgate stalls, past the mountains of rubbish, the rats and birds feeding, back to Millgarth, back underground, and two minutes later I've reversed the car up and out of the garage and am away, following the signs out to Headingley.

*

Two nights on and everything dead now –

A *Leeds & Bradford A to Z* in one hand, I come to the place where Headingley Lane becomes Otley Road, to the Kentucky Fried Chicken, to where the bus stops, to Alma Road and Laureen Bell.

I back into a dark wide drive and turn the car around.

I drive back towards the Kentucky Fried Chicken and pull into the car park, positioning the car so I face the main road, then I go inside.

It's stopped raining but I am still the only customer.

I order some pieces of chicken and chips, a cup of coffee, and wait under the white lights for over ten minutes while the Asian staff prepare the order, staring at another light reflected in another cup of black coffee.

I take the food back out to the car and sit in the night, the window down, picking at the pale and stringy meat, watching the street.

No-one.

Two nights ago it must have been different.

I drink down the cold coffee, wanting another, the food salty.

I get out of the car and walk across the road to the bus stop.

It's 9:53, the Number 13 coming up Headingley Lane.

It doesn't stop.

I cross back and turn right onto Alma Road.

There's police tape and two dark cars waiting.

I walk down the dim tree-lined street, crossing to avoid the cordon, past the officers sitting in the police cars.

At the end of the road is a school and I stop at the gates and stand and stare back down Alma Road –

Alma Road –

An ordinary street in an ordinary suburb where a man took a hammer and a knife to another man's daughter, to another man's sister, another man's fiancée –

An ordinary street in an ordinary suburb where a man took a hammer and a knife to Laureen Bell and shattered her skull and stabbed her fifty-seven times in her abdomen, in her womb, and once in her eye –

And then, in this ordinary street in this ordinary suburb, he stopped –

For now.

it not on your life transmission one found by a milkman at six on friday the sixth of june nineteen seventy five on the prince philip playing fields scott hall leeds with multiple stab wounds to abdomen chest and throat inflicted by a blade four inches in length three quarters of an inch in width one edge sharper than the other severe lacerations to the skull and fractures to the crown inflicted by a hammer or an axe a white purse with mummy in biro on the front containing approximately five pounds in cash was also noted to be missing from the deceaseds handbag this is the world now containing approximately five pounds in cash all this and heaven too missing but e only have eyes for you in tight white flared trousers and a pink blouse and short blue bolero jacket at twenty to ten in the royal oak at ten in the regent at ten thirty in the scotsman fourteen whiskies and a tray of curry and chips at one ten AM stopping motorists at the junction of sheepscar street south and roundhay road leeds attempting to obtain a lift it is known from an eyewitness that an articulated lorry with a dark coloured cab and a tarpaulin sheeted load stopped at the junction of roundhay road and sheepscar street south this is the world now her handbag strap looped around her left wrist six buttons on the grass five from her blouse and one from her blue bolero jacket her brassiere pushed up her trousers pulled down about her knees her panties in their normal position there was a positive semen reaction on the back of her trousers and panties her head had suffered two lacerations one of which had penetrated the thickness of her skull there was a stab wound in her neck and fourteen wounds in her chest and abdomen although the murder weapons have not been found and no mention of the head injuries or of the weapon should be disclosed to the press all information to the murder room this is the world now a good time dead on the grass her children waiting at the bus stop for two hours for mummy to come home from shebeens the regent the white swan the scotsman the gaiety barbarellas room at the top friday night is crumpet night if you cannot pull tonight you will never pull buy the lady a barbarella legspreader this is the world e was driving through leeds at night e had been having a couple of pints and e saw this woman thumbing a lift and e stopped and asked her how far she was going and she said not far thanks for stopping and jumped in and e was in quite a good mood and then she said did e want business and e said what do you mean and she says bloody hell do e have to spell it out so we drove to the park in my green ford capri and before we started she said it cost a fiver and e was a bit surprised e was expecting it to be a bit romantic and e am not the type that can have intercourse in a split second e have to be aroused but all of a sudden she said e am off it is going to take all fucking day you are fucking useless you are and e felt myself seething with rage and e wanted to hit her and e said hang on do not go off like that and she said oh you can manage it now can you and she was taunting me e said can we do it on the grass and she stormed off up field and e took the hammer from my tool box and followed her and spread my coat on the wet grass and she sat down and unfastened her trousers and said come on get it over with and e said do not worry e will and e hit her with the hammer and she made a lot of noise and so e hit her again and then e took out knife from my pocket and e stabbed her fifteen times e think and her arm kept jerking up and down and so e kept at her until she was very dead and then e shot off home this is the world now containing approximately five pounds in

Chapter 3

There were people on the TV singing hymns –
  People on the TV singing hymns with no face –
  People on the TV singing hymns with no face, no features –
  And when I switched off the TV, when I pulled back the curtain,
everything outside was white and without feature, except for the parked
cars and the ugly gulls circling overhead, screaming –
  The North after the bomb, machines the only survivors.

I'm awake, sweating and afraid –
  The word *shreds* on my lips thinking, what face or no-face
does *he* see?
  I reach out for Joan but she's not there –
  I'm alone in cold hotel sheets, the radio on:
  Dirty protests, hunger strikes, three London policemen suspended
as a result of Operation Countryman, Helen Smith . . .
  I turn over and reach for my watch on the bedside table:
  It's 5:10 –
  Saturday 13 December 1980.

It's still dark and freezing outside, the rain gone –
  Just the Ice Age.
  I walk up the precinct beside the Bond Street Centre.
  I buy a *Yorkshire Post* and go back to the Griffin.
  I sit in the dining room, the first guest, and order breakfast.
  The smell of paint, the synthesizer rendition of Holst's *The
Planets* and the hiss of the speakers, the bad dreams –
  I've a headache.
  It gets worse:
  I open the *Yorkshire Post*, read their reports of the Ripper, of
yesterday's press conference –
  I read my name.
  The porridge comes and goes and I'm staring at a cold mixed
grill, the terrible colours running together, wishing I was back
home with Joan.
  'Just what the doctor ordered, that,' says John Murphy, sitting
down.

'Big night?'

'Ah, you know; building bridges, that kind of thing. And yourself?'

'Dinner with Angus and Noble.'

'No George?'

'No George.'

'And?'

'Not much; just defined the terms of our investigation for us.'

'What?'

I hand him the letter: 'Did you call the others?'

He nods, eyes on the piece of paper before him: 'Meeting us here at half eight.'

'Good.'

'What is this bollocks?' he says, finished reading.

'I don't know. I'll have to make some calls.'

Murphy's breakfast arrives and he sets about it.

I order a fresh pot of tea.

'How was Dickie Alderman?'

'Friendly enough. You know him?'

'Not really; just the face. Learn anything?'

'Morale's shocking. George going's about the last straw for most of them. We're not going to help.'

'That why they put us here?' I say, watching the workmen arrive.

Murphy smiles: 'Yorkshire hospitality.'

'Bastards, eh?'

I sit on the edge of the hotel bed and dial Whitby:

'Philip Evans speaking.'

'This is Peter Hunter.'

'Pete? How are you?'

'Fine, thank you.'

'Settled in?'

'We've got an office and the hotel's sorted.'

'Saw the press conference. Looked rough?'

'It was.'

'How are they treating you?'

'Not bad, but I am calling about Chief Constable Angus.'

'I see.'

'I was wondering if you're aware of a letter he's given me in which he's basically outlined the terms of reference for our investigation?'

'I see.'

'Have you seen it?'

There's a pause, then Evans says something I can't catch –

I say: 'I'm sorry, could you say that again?'

'Can you forward the letter to me? And I think it'd be wise if you did the same with any future correspondence pertinent to the Inquiry.'

'No problem. Is Sir John aware of the letter?'

'I couldn't say. He's on holiday until the New Year.'

'Yes, someone said. Should I contact Donald Lincoln?'

'No, I'll do that.'

'So I should just ignore the letter?'

'Don't worry about it, I'll sort everything out.'

'I'm a bit concerned that . . .'

'Don't be. Leave the politics to me and just concentrate on the investigation. Any hint of obstruction on Yorkshire's part, pick up the phone and I'll put a stop to it.'

'Thank you.'

'Keep in touch, Pete.'

'I will.'

'And remember, it was never going to be a picnic.'

'Goodbye.'

I hang up and dial Millgarth: 'Assistant Chief Constable Noble, please?'

'Who's calling?'

'Peter Hunter.'

Hold.

'I'm afraid the Assistant Chief Constable is in a meeting. He'll call you back.'

'But I'm – '

The dial tone.

In the lobby of the Griffin, in between the white sheets and the splattered ladders, they're waiting:

Detective Chief Inspector Alec McDonald.

Detective Inspector Mike Hillman.

Detective Sergeant Helen Marshall.

'Good morning.'

Nods and greetings, twitching and blinking.

I sit down next to John Murphy, the five of us round a low marble-topped table, a plastic bag keeping the paint off.

'Sorry about this,' I begin. 'We have been promised an office in Millgarth, but it's yet to be set up. I thought we might as well make a start here.'

'Better than bloody Millgarth,' laughs Mike Hillman, an eye to the décor.

'OK,' I say. 'This is what we're going to do.'

They're all leaning forward, notebooks out.

'I'm going to give you each a year or two of the investigation and twenty-four hours to get to grips with the files. First thing tomorrow morning we'll meet and start going over the files together. This way you'll have detailed and specific knowledge of certain cases and a good overview of the investigation as a whole.

'Each of the cases you're assigned, you're going to need to know inside out, to the finest detail, but – '

A pause, a beat:

'You need to pay special attention to the following and list:

'The names of all persons mentioned, be they witnesses, suspects, whatever, listed alphabetically.'

A low whistle from Alec McDonald.

'It'll be a long list, aye Alec,' I say. 'And I'm not finished; plus I want descriptions of all suspects, descriptions of all cars sighted or investigated, alphabetically by make, year, and colour. Finally the names of all policemen involved in the case, alphabetically.'

'Policemen?' repeats Hillman.

'Yes. No matter how minor their role.'

Silence –

'OK?'

Silence –

'Mike 1974 and 75, including Clare Strachan.'

A nod.

'Helen, 76.'

Another nod.

'John, you got the short straw: 77.'

'Liz McQueen?'

'Amongst others.'

Alec McDonald sighs: '78 and 79?'

'No, that'd give you five,' I say. 'Just 78. I'll take 79 and this last one.'

Notebooks open, already writing.

Me: 'OK, listen – '

Another pause, another beat, before I say: 'His name, the Ripper's name, it's in those files. They've met him.'

Helen Marshall says quietly: 'How can you be so sure?'

'Trust me,' I say. 'I've asked for the names of any person who has been arrested in connection with any crime involving prostitutes, again no matter how minor or insignificant. Because he's known.'

'George Oldman did say if he met the Ripper he'd know him instantly,' says Mike Hillman.

I close my eyes, hands together –

'Let me add that you're to list everyone irrespective of blood type or accent. Especially accent.'

'So we're not looking for a Geordie then?' grins Alec McDonald.

'No.'

A last pause, then –

'We're looking for the Yorkshire Ripper.'

One final beat –

'And we're going to find him.'

Back upstairs, on the edge of the hotel bed, dialling Millgarth: 'Assistant Chief Constable Noble please?'

'Who's calling?'

'Assistant Chief Constable Peter Hunter.'

Hold.

Murphy's leaning against a cheap chipped dressing table, snow falling on the roof of Leeds City Station, the windows rattling with the trains and the traffic, the wind and the draughts.

'You realise how many bloody names we're going to get?'

I start to speak, but put my hand up, listening –

'The Assistant Chief Constable is in a meeting. He'll call you back.'

I say: 'You tell him it's urgent.'

'I've been told to hold all calls.'

'It's an emergency.'

'But – '

'I am Assistant Chief Constable Peter Hunter of the Greater Manchester Police Force and I'm ordering you to put me through.'

Hold.

'Fucking hell,' mutters Murphy.

I take a deep breath.

'Peter Noble speaking.'

'Peter? Peter Hunter here. Sorry to disturb your meeting.'

'Yes?'

'The office? Is it available? What's happening?'

'What?'

'The Chief Constable said last night that an office on the same floor as the Murder Room would be made available for the use of me and my team, yeah?'

'And you want it now? This minute?'

'Please.'

Silence –

I look up from the grey carpet.

Murphy's shaking his head.

Noble asks: 'Where are you?'

'The Griffin.'

'It's nine – '

'Half past.'

'Whatever. An office will be ready by one.'

'That's the earliest – '

'The earliest.'

'OK if we come over now and start getting copies of the files we need?'

Another silence –

Noble: 'No-one's explained the system then?'

'What system?'

'Well, we obviously can't just let you take stuff willy-nilly.'

'Of course – '

'Not a bloody library.'

'Of course not. We're going to need to log – '

'Actually, no. Well, yes; you're going to have to log it, that's right. But you're also going to have to request the files first.'

'OK. We'd like to request access to copy all the case files pertaining to the Ripper Investigation.'

'Look – '

'Everything.'

'Look – '

'As soon as possible.'

'Look, that's not going to happen.'

'What do you mean?'

Another silence, longer –

'You better come over. I'll call the Chief Constable.'

'Fine.'

'Ten o'clock?'

'Ten it is.'

I hang up.

Murphy's looking at the dirty snow, watching a train pull out of the station –

'That'd be the Manchester train,' he says. 'Train home.'

Step inside –

Noble and I are sat in silence, waiting for Angus.

I'm facing the window and the snow, my back to the door, massaging my temple.

He's just sat there, waiting, watching the door.

Angus is on his way from Wakefield and again I'm wondering why the Chief Constable's office is over there and not here in Leeds, not here in his biggest city, not closer to his second largest, Bradford.

Then the door opens and here he is –

No knock –

Noble standing to change places, Angus sitting down in his seat, me in the same chair –

Angus: 'Gentlemen?'

Noble's gushing: 'There's a couple of things we need to get straight . . .'

Angus isn't listening, just looking at me.

' . . . an office next to the Murder Room,' Noble's saying.

Angus stands up: 'Let's have a look then.'

We follow him out of the door and up the corridor, up towards the Murder Room, the *Ripper Room*, the telephones ringing and the typewriters clattering, up to a small windowless room next door.

A couple of uniforms are carrying boxes and bin-bags out.

'Those are for you to use,' says Noble, pointing at two grey metal filing cabinets on the other side of a brown table.

'Do you have the keys?'

Noble sighs: 'I'll be sure to get them for you.'

'And for the office itself?'

He nods once.

'So this is OK?' asks Angus.

'Phone lines?'

'How many do you need?'

'Two. Minimum.'

'OK. Tomorrow.'

'Thank you. Now what about the files themselves?'

'What about them?'

'The procedure? How do we get access to them?'

'Just ask me,' says the Chief Constable.

Noble's closed the door, the three of us standing around the table, the bare bulb almost at eye-level.

'OK,' I say. 'We'd like access to copy each of the files that pertain to the Ripper Inquiry.'

Angus smiles: 'You know how much bloody stuff that is?'

'No, but I imagine it'd be a lot.'

'It is.'

'But I still need access to it all.'

'This is an ongoing active investigation. These files are constantly being updated and reviewed.'

'I would hope so. But the fact remains that I need access to them.'

'To a large extent, without a guide, they'll be meaningless.'

'Then if you can supply a *guide* that would be a great help. But obviously, without ready access to the files I can't do the job I have been asked to do by Sir John and the Home Office.'

Angus's face has changed, benign and kindly Uncle Ron gone: 'Obviously. And I appreciate that but, Mr Hunter, for your part you must also appreciate that I can't have these files just wandering off here and there.'

'Obviously.'

'And the copying alone'll be a huge undertaking.'

'Then just grant us the access we need.'

Noble's staring at Angus, Angus at me, me at him –

Eventually Angus says: 'We'll put you another desk in here, a couple more chairs. I'll provide you with a *guide*, a liaison officer. Your people ask him to get them the files they need; he'll provide, log and replace them as required.'

'Thank you.'

He looks at his watch: 'One o'clock?'

Noble and I nod.

'One o'clock,' repeats Angus and opens the door for me.

It's eleven by the time I get back to the Griffin.

They're sat there, waiting.

I lay it out.

They mutter, roll their eyes, and take an early lunch.

Upstairs, I dial Whitby:

Philip Evans is away for the rest of the day.

I lie down on the bed, my thoughts scrambled messages, a migraine headache sparring with the pains in my back, jarring with the radio:

Old science fiction and future histories, the news from nowhere, the screams from somewhere

Hoping for something more, I close my eyes.

When I open my eyes it's 12:30, the pain still here –

In my back, behind my eyes.

I get up, wash my face, and take the lift downstairs.

Outside it's stopped snowing but the sky is almost black with heavy cloud and premature night.

I walk through the sludge and the mud to the Kirkgate Market and Millgarth, freezing.

The rest of them are waiting for me by the desk.

I lead the way upstairs.

Noble is waiting outside the Ripper Room, waiting to introduce us.

'I believe you've actually met?'

Bob Craven has his hand out, half the Ripper Room crowding out into the corridor.

'What were you back then, Bob?' laughs Noble.

'Just a plain old Sergeant,' Craven smiles.

'Well, times change; Assistant Chief Constable Peter Hunter meet Detective Superintendent Robert Craven.'

We shake hands, the grip cold and tight:

The Strafford Shootings –

Christmas Eve 1974:

The pub robbery that went wrong.

Four dead, two wounded policemen –

Sergeant Robert Craven, wounded hero cop battles for life etc, etc, etc.

'You look a little better than the last time we met,' I say.

He laughs: 'You don't.'

'Bob's going to be the liaison,' says Noble.

I say nothing.

'Your guide.'

Nothing, waiting for Noble to keep on justifying it:

'Bob's been involved from day one. He's worked a lot of the cases, worked Vice, probably forgotten more than most of us'll ever know.'

'That would be a shame,' I say.

Noble stops: 'You know what I mean, Mr Hunter.'

'Yep,' I say. 'I know what you mean.'

'Well then, I'll leave you to it.'

'The keys?' I ask. 'Did you get the keys?'

'Bob's got them,' Noble says, walking off, leaving Craven dangling them from the end of his finger.

I ignore him and go to open the door –

It's locked.

'Can't be too careful,' smiles Craven. 'Allow me.'

By three the tables are covered in piles of files, Craven going back and forth to the Ripper Room next door, my team scratching and scribbling away for dear life under the low blue clouds of cigarette smoke hanging by the bare bulb.

'Telephone,' says Craven, coming back with another stack of manila folders.

'For me?' I say.

'Yeah, next door. Line 4.'

I get up.

'It's the wife,' he winks as I get to the door.

I walk next door –

Next door into the Ripper Room –

Into the photos on the walls, the maps and the faces –

The charts and the boards, the chalk and the pen on every surface –

The mugs on the desks, the cigarettes in the ashtrays –

Everywhere:

Repetition, tedium –

Indexes, cross-index –

Files, cross-file –

References, cross-reference –

Everywhere:

Process –

Repetitious, tedious process –

Second after second –

Minute after minute –

Hour after hour –

Fifteen, sixteen hours a day –

Day in, day out –

Six, seven days a week –

Week in, week out –

Four weeks a month –

Month in, month out –

Twelve months a year –

Year in, year out –

Year after year, month after month, week after week, day after day, hour in, hour out, minute in, minute out, second in, second out, for –

Five years.

A fat man in a sports coat's holding out the receiver –

'Joan?' I say, taking the phone.

'I'm sorry, love,' she says. 'But the Chief Constable's office just called.'

'The Chief Constable's office?'

'About tonight? They wanted me to tell you that they've arranged for the tux to be sent round in about an hour.'

'The tux? Tonight?'

'Yes. I said I didn't know when you'd be back so they wanted me to let you know.'

The Christmas Ball –

'I'd forgotten.'

'I thought you might have,' she laughs. 'Shall we cancel?'

'No, we can't. You're sorted out?'

'Yes. I'd completely forgotten too but . . .'

'Well, it'll be good. I'll be back in a bit, stay the night, and come back first thing tomorrow.'

'OK.'

'How are you?'

'I'm fine.'

'I've got to go.'

'I know.'

'I'll see you soon.'

'Yes.'

'Bye.'

'Bye.'

I put back the phone, conscious the whole of the room is watching me –

The photos on the walls, the maps and the faces –

The Ripper Room –

Him.

I drive back fast, over the Moors –

Fast over their cold, lost bones, the radio on loud:

Hunger Strikes & Dirty Protests –

Ripper, Ripper, Ripper.

Fast, over the Moors –

Over their cold, lost bones, the radio on:

Earthquakes & Hostages –

Ripper, Ripper, Ripper.

Over the Moors, radio gone –

Cold, lost bones:

The Strafford Shootings –

Christmas Eve 1974:

The pub robbery that went wrong.

Four dead, two wounded policemen –

Sergeant Robert Craven and PC Bob Douglas.

Driving, hating –

I hate Bob Craven and I don't know why –

Don't like the maybe why:

Hated him then, hate him now –

Hated him since the day I met him, stuffed full of tubes and drugs on a Pinderfields bed.

Hated him like it was only yesterday:

Friday 10 January 1975 –

In we came:

Me and Clarkie –

Detective Chief Inspector Mark Clark.

Two weeks on and they'd still got roadblocks across the county, the stink of an English Civil War, me and Clarkie walking down that long, long corridor, armed guards on the bloody hospital doors, Craven and Douglas on their backs in their beds, the only survivors.

Me and Clarkie, we shook hands with Maurice Jobson –

Detective Chief Superintendent Maurice Jobson, legend –

The Owl.

There were a lot of other faces about, that rat-faced journalist Whitehead from the Post *for one.*

They didn't know me then, but they would.

Douglas was sedated and Craven ought to have been –

Lying there, head back, calling out from the depths, eyes twinkling up from those same depths, screaming:

'Kill the cunt! Kill 'em all!'

But that was as close as we ever got –

Jobson wouldn't let us near him: 'Man's in no state. Took a butt to the head.'

And for all the promises we'd got coming, all the cups of tea up the Wood Street Nick, we never did get a good go at him.

Over the Moors, snow across their cold, lost bones –

Clarkie turned to me and said: 'It stinks. Fuck knows why, but it does.'

And I stared out at the lanes of lorries, the black poles and the telephone wires, thinking –

Murder and lies, lies and murder –

War:

My War –

'Bloody Yorkshire,' hissed Clarkie.

Over the Moors –

Cold, lost bones:

It stank then and it stinks now, that same old smell –

Bloody Yorkshire.

*

The house, my affluent detached house and two-car garage is quiet, dark, one light on in an upstairs room, the curtains open.

I push open the bedroom door and there she is, in front of the mirror in her dressing gown, eyes red.

'You OK?'

'You startled me.'

'Sorry. You been crying, love?'

'No,' she smiles. 'Just soap.'

I walk over to her and kiss the top of her hair.

'Didn't expect you so soon,' she says.

We're looking at each other framed in the mirror, something missing.

'I thought I'd put the tree up.'

'We've left it a bit late, haven't we? All the stuff's up in the attic.'

'I'll get the steps from the garage. Have it up in no time.'

'You'll get filthy.'

'Got time, don't worry.'

'Up to you.'

'Got to make the effort.'

She's nodding, staring back into the mirror, back into her own eyes –

'Those lights are so old,' she says.

The Christmas Ball, the Midland Hotel –

Saturday 13 December 1980.

Through the black city streets, the broken lights and the Christmas ones, down Palatine, Wilmslow, and the Oxford Roads, the official black car and driver taking us in towards the red and the gold, the money and the honey, the home of the loot, holding hands in our rented clothes on the back seat of a car that is not our own, through dominions of disease and depopulation, the black streets that would have you dead within the hour, taking us in towards a thousand hale and hearty Manchester folk, drunk in the seclusion of the Midland Hotel, the castle of loot, an abbey to the anointed and self-appointed City Fathers, with their city mothers, wives and daughters, their secret lovers, whores and sons.

Without no one –

Through the black city streets to the place where the red

carpet meets the street at the doors to the Midland, these gates of iron in these strong and lofty walls with no hint of ingress or egress, where all that is outside can never be in and to hell with it, damn it, for here inside are the bright lights, the purples and the gold, the servants and the servings, the musicians and the music, the dancers and the dance, the Masked Christmas Ball.

Without nothing –

Through the beauty and the beautiful, the security and the secure, the fat and the fat, we are led to our seats, Joan's arm tightening inside my own, our masks in place, through the high double doors into the dim velvet sea and the palatial splendour of the Dining Room, her Gothic windows of stained glass, the thrown shadows of her lamps and candles, her ornaments and tapestries ceiling to floor, all heavy with the weight of wealth, the stains of class and brass and the deep blood colour of Christmas reds, of Herod and his kids.

Within dreams –

'Something wicked this way comes,' smiles Clement Smith, the Chief Constable raising his mask with a wink as our wives fall into the comfort of compliments.

I sit down next to him, shaking hands with an MP, a councillor, a millionaire and all their present wives, local Masons and Rotarians the table of them –

'How goes the war?' laughs Clive Birkenshaw, the councillor drunk on a punch as crimson as his face.

'The hunt more like,' says Donald Lees of the Greater Manchester Police Authority.

'What?' I say.

'You've been over in Yorkshire after their Ripper?'

I nod, the laughter and the music too much.

'Most apt,' Lees carries on, leaning across the corpse of his wife. '*Hunter in Ripper Hunt*, said the *Manchester Evening News*.'

'Apt,' comes the echo around the tablecloth.

'Any luck?'

I look down at my hand, shaking my head, and I bring the whiskey up to my lips and let it fall down my throat.

Joan and Clement Smith have changed seats so the wives can chat.

I take another mouthful.

Clement Smith orders more.

I'm exhausted –

The cigars already out, the dance-floor filling, time flying –

And then suddenly across the room I think I see Ronald Angus and Peter Noble on another table by the door but, when I look again, it isn't –

Can't have been and Leeds is just a dream –

A terrible dream –

Like the Ripper, their Ripper.

I sit back in my chair, letting the Velvet Sea wash over me, playing her tricks with the horizon; the wail of violins, the hoarse voice of Clement Smith deep in debate, his wife and mine making their way through the waves, off to powder their noses.

Then I feel a hand on mine –

I look down at a man crouched beside my chair: 'Pardon?'

'I said we have a mutual friend.'

'Who's that?'

'Helen,' he grins, a short thin man with brown stained teeth.

'Helen who?'

But he just winks: 'From her Vice days. Tell her I said hello.'

'What?'

But he's wading away, back into the velvet sea, waving, back into her dance.

I interrupt Clement Smith: 'Who was that?'

'Who?'

'That man, the one who was just at the table? Talking to me?'

Smith's laughing: 'Wearing his mask was he?'

'No, but I can't place him.'

He sits up slightly in his seat: 'I didn't see him. Sorry. Where is he?'

'Doesn't matter, just wondered who he was.'

I pick up a glass and drink some more, lost –

'Peter?'

I look up from the drink: 'Richard. Merry Christmas.'

'If only,' he says.

The man is tall and gaunt, pale as a ghost, the black mask in his hand and a blood-red shirt only accentuating his grim pallor, mumbling.

'What?'

He asks: 'We talk?'

I stand up, nodding, leaving my cigar in the ashtray, and follow Richard Dawson through the tables and out into the Lobby –

Richard Dawson, businessman, Chairman of one of the local Conservative Parties, a friend.

He's shaking, sweating.

'What is it? What's wrong?'

He says: 'Do you know Bob Douglas?'

Ghosts –

Again the ghosts of Christmases past:

Again the Strafford Shootings –

Again the wounded coppers:

Sergeant Robert Craven and PC Bob Douglas.

I nod: 'Used to. Why?'

'Well, I've been using him as a security advisor. Anyway, late last night he calls to tell me that he's heard that I'm the subject of a bloody police investigation; then at lunchtime today my bank in Didsbury calls and says that a couple of detectives have taken away all their financial records pertaining to my accounts with them.'

'What?'

'I'm in bloody shock.'

'You should've called straight away.'

'I didn't want to. I'd seen you were over in Leeds and I don't like to take advantage of the fact that we're friends or anything.'

'Richard! What are friends for?'

He smiles wanly.

'Let's sit down,' I say, walking us over to a pair of crimson and gold lobby chairs.

'Spoiling your evening,' he mumbles again.

'Rubbish. Start from the beginning.'

'That's a good question in itself. I didn't know there was a beginning, didn't know anything had started until last night.'

'What about Bob Douglas? When did he come on the scene?'

'End of October, start of November. I was worried about the house. He came out and had a look, tightened things up. I got to know him, like him.'

'You know about – '

'Yeah, yeah. Told me all about it. Why? What do you know about him?'

'I went over there after the shootings, but he was sedated so I never actually spoke to him. By all accounts he was a good bloke. Good copper. When he left, he went kicking and screaming.'

'That's what he said. Ten years in the police, then out on his arse.'

I nod: 'So after the house, what kind of stuff was he doing for you?'

'Consulting. Insurance work. Nothing heavy.'

'Until last night?'

'Yes. Called about midnight. Said he'd been out and about, you know. And he'd heard from a so-called reliable source that I'd been targeted for investigation.'

'A *reliable source*?'

'A policeman. One of your lot.'

'He say who?'

'Said he couldn't.'

'He say why you were being investigated?'

He looks down at his hands, the carpet: 'Financial irregularities. Supposedly.'

'What kind of financial irregularities?'

'We don't know. That's all he heard.'

'Did he get a name? Of the man in charge?'

'Roger Hook.'

Fuck.

'What about the bank? They give you anything more?'

'No,' he's shaking his head. 'Bloody humiliating though, I can tell you. Your bank manager, your golf partner and friend, calling you at home to tell you that the police have been in asking about you, taking away their records on you.'

'I'm sorry, Richard.'

'You know this Roger Hook?'

'Yes.'

'And?'

'It doesn't make any difference. You've nothing to hide.'

He looks up from the carpet, his hands: 'Who knows what they'll find.'

'What?' I say. 'There's nothing to find, is there?'

His eyes still aren't meeting mine.

'Richard,' I say. 'Tell me there's nothing to find.'

'Who knows?'

'You do, for Chrissakes man.'

'Look – '

'Jesus, Richard.'

'I need your help.'

I look him in the eye, hold him there, tell him: 'There's nothing I can do for you.'

'Pete – '

I stand up, ready to walk.

'There's something else,' he says.

I stop.

'About you,' he says.

'Me? What about me?'

'You asked me why, why I was being targeted?'

I nod.

'Douglas said it's down to you.'

'What is? What are you talking about?'

'This. I've been singled out because I'm friends with you.'

'Rubbish. Utter rubbish.'

He has hold of my arm: 'Peter – '

'Douglas is wrong. You're wrong.'

'To put you in your place, that's what they told him.'

I turn away, freeing myself from his grip.

Him: 'What are you going to do?'

I turn back: 'Nothing.'

'You're just going to leave me up to my neck in all this?'

'There's nothing I can do, Richard. You're under investigation.'

'Because of you, I am.'

I'm walking away again, deaf to him –

But he has the last word, across the lobby and through the Dining Room doors, spinning me round, hissing into my face: 'What are friends for, eh Pete?'

Walking away, walking away through the velvet sea, Joan talking to Linda Dawson, his wife –

The pair of them turning, smiling.

Him: 'What are friends for, eh?'

Me taking her by the arm, through the darkness and the decay, pulling her away, away from the music and the blood –

'What are friends for?'

Within nightmares.

The house is black.

I put the car in the garage and go inside.

Joan's sitting on the settee in the dark, her coat still on.

I switch on the Christmas tree lights and sit down beside her.

'What is it? What happened with Richard?' she says.

'He's under investigation. To do with his business.'

'You're joking?'

'No. But he thinks it's something to do with his friendship with me, with us.'

'What?'

'Someone told him that's why he's under investigation.'

'Who told him that?'

'An ex-copper. You don't know him.'

'And is it right? Is that why he's under investigation?'

'No. Of course not.'

'What am I going to say to Linda?'

'I don't know but, until all this is cleared up, we're going to have to be careful.'

She is nodding.

'I'm sorry, love.'

She keeps nodding.

I can't think of anything else to say, anything to make any of it any better.

I lean forward and pick the *Evening News* off the coffee table.

It doesn't help:

Laureen's Mum in Ripper Plea.

Dirty Protests.

Under the newspaper are some forms and a pamphlet –

Application forms to adopt.

'What are these?' I ask, picking them up.

Joan tries to take them from me: 'Not now, love,' she says. 'Talk about it another time.'

'A Vietnamese baby?' I say, looking down at the cover of the pamphlet.

'Not now, Peter,' she says again, taking the papers from me as she goes upstairs.

Later in bed, I hug her and we try to have sex but I can't –
And after, I say: 'I think it's a good idea.'
She doesn't say anything –
And after that we lie in the double bed, staring up at the ceiling, apart –
On the dark stair –
She turns away on her side and I get up and put the radio on.
I get back into bed and lie there –
Awake, sweating and afraid –
Eyes wide –
On the dark stair –

The North after the bomb, machines the only survivors –
There were people on the TV singing hymns –
People on the TV singing hymns with no face –
People on the TV singing hymns with no face, no features –
And at my feet, they had her down on the floor at my feet, her hands behind her back, stripped and beaten, three of them raping her, sodomising her, taking their turns with a bottle and a chair, cutting her hair, pissing and shitting on her, making her suck them, making her suck me, ugly gulls circling overhead, screaming –
'Sti rip sll iwl lik Hunter!'

'What is it? What's wrong?'
Joan's holding me, my heart beating, breaking.
'What on earth were you dreaming about?'
I can feel come in my pyjamas.
'Nothing,' I say, thinking –
No more sleep, no more sleep, no more sleep.

cash all this and heaven too missing the news from nowhere what e was once alive e still am dead a complete wreck of a human being wearing a light green three quarter length coat with an imitation fur collar a turquoise blue jumper with a bright yellow tank top over it dark brown trousers and brown suede calf length boots found friday the twenty first of november nineteen seventy five one laceration to the back of her head caused by a hammer and extensive injuries to her head face body and legs caused by violent kicking and stamping on her left breast were bite marks which indicated a gap in the upper front teeth of the attacker there were no stab wounds in a deserted garage in preston in a row of six narrow garages each splattered with white graffiti the doors showing remnants of green paint they lie off church street the garages forming a passage to the multi storey car park at the other end number six has become a home of sorts for the homeless destitute alcoholics drug addicted prostitutes of the area small about twelve feet square and entered through either of the double doors at the front there are packing cases for tables piles of wood and other rubbish a fierce fire has been burning in a makeshift grate and the ashes disclose the remains of clothing on the wall opposite the door is written the fishermans widow in wet red paint in every other space are bottles sherry bottles bottles of spirits beer bottles bottles of chemicals all empty a mans pilot coat doubles as a curtain over the window the only one looking out on nothing and e saw the floor was wet with anguished tears the damned silent and weeping and walking at a litany pace the way processions push along in our world and without a word he handed her a five pound note and she unclipped her shiny black plastic handbag placed it on the floor of the garage and bending down she removed one of her boots lowered her trousers and stepped out of the legs and repeated the process with her panties she braced her back against the garage wall and she was ready a moment later he had entered her lifting her brassiere to play with her breasts he discovered a second brassiere he lifted it up and began to kiss and suck the left breast moving his mouth a few inches above the breast he bit deeply and climaxed turning her around he attempted to bugger her and again he had an orgasm he was still inside her body half leaning away from him when he smashed her on the back of the head and she fell forward onto the floor he zipped up his trousers and began to kick her on the face on the head on the breasts on the body on the legs he kicked her and went on kicking her he dragged her body a few yards further away from the door put her legs back into her trousers and pulled them up leaving the second brassiere above the breasts he pulled down the first one stuffed one boot tightly between her thighs he removed her overcoat and placed it over her body and over her face he picked up the shiny black plastic handbag left the garage and hid the handbag in a refuse tip four hundred yards from the garage the purse he tucked under a bush in avenham park he kept her three rings and lighter swabs from the vagina and anus indicated semen had been deposited by a secretor of the rare blood group B the blood group of the man at the hostel who had had sexual intercourse with the dead woman the previous day was discovered to be group A her shiny black plastic handbag and purse missing a diary thought to be in her bag could hold the clue to the womans killer and e am anxious about anyone who has been missing from preston since last thursday up to four now they say three but remember preston nineteen seventy five come my load up that one

Chapter 4

In the War Room I switch on the cassette recorder:

And when we die
And float away
Into the night
The Milky Way
You'll hear me call
As we ascend
I'll say your name
Then once again
Thank you for being a friend.

I put the thirteenth photograph on the wall, the smell of earth and damp in the twelve photos, in the map, in the files, the smell of earth and damp in the floor and in the walls, and I sit back down in the earth and damp, eyes closed.

No more sleep, no more dreams, no more blood on the sheets –

Just on the floor and on the walls –

On the walls, all over the walls.

I lock the shed door behind me and go back inside.

I wash, dress, and don't wake her.

I drive back into the centre of Manchester, the radio playing:

Afghanistan, Poland, Iran, Northern Ireland, the world –

This whole empty forgotten world at war.

And the lies –

The murder and the lies, the cries and the whispers, the screams of the wires and the signals, of the voices and the numbers:

13% pay demand, 10,000 hunger strike march, 150 of 701 words, 20,000 steel jobs to go, Leeds 1, Forest 0, Ripper 13, Police 0, 13-nil, 13-nil, 13-nil, 13-nil . . .

In the car park at Manchester Police Headquarters there's a car in my space, the reserved space that says:

Peter Hunter – Assistant Chief Constable

There are a lot of empty spaces but I still park next to the other car.

There are two men sat in the car.

I don't recognise either of the men, though the driver's staring at me –

He smiles.

I get out of my car, lock it, and go inside.

I sign in and ask the Sergeant on the desk to go and have a word with the two men in the car outside.

I go upstairs to my office –

It's locked.

I take out my keys and open it.

It's just as I'd left it.

I sit down behind my desk and begin to make the necessary calls:

But no-one's answering at Richard Dawson's house –

Roger Hook is unavailable –

And the Chief Constable's at chapel until twelve, half past at the latest.

I look at my watch:

It's nine o'clock –

Sunday 14 December 1980.

The phone rings: 'Yes?'

'Sir. It's the desk downstairs. That car, sir? It wasn't there. But your space is free so would you like me to arrange to have your car moved?'

'It's OK. Thank you.'

I hang up.

The phone rings again:

'Sir. It's your wife.'

I press the button, the flashing orange button: 'Joan?'

'Peter?'

'What is it?'

'It's the Dawsons, love. Linda's been on the phone, hysterical. Their house was raided first thing . . .'

'Raided?'

'Police. Manchester Police. Turned the place upside down.'

'When?'

'This morning, five o'clock. Taken away all their papers, photos.'

Shit.

'OK,' I say. 'I'll make some calls.'

'I'm sorry, after what you said last night, but Linda's in pieces . . .'

'It's OK. Where's Richard?'

'He was at Linda's parents I think, but . . .'

'OK,' I say again. 'I'll make some calls, try and find out what's going on.'

'What shall I tell her?'

'Tell her not to worry, that I'm dealing with it.'

'Thank you. I'm sorry.'

'Don't be. I'd better go.'

'Bye,' she says.

'Bye.'

I hang up and reach straight for the phone book –

I find Bob Douglas's home number –

I dial –

It rings –

He answers –

I say: 'Is Deirdre there?'

'What?'

'It's Mike. Can I speak to Deirdre?'

'You got the wrong number, mate,' says Bob Douglas and hangs up.

I dial two numbers again:

No answer at the Dawsons –

None from Cook.

I go through my address book:

Mark Gilman at the *Manchester Evening News* is off –

Neil Hanley in Cheshire heard Cook was looking into some dodgy finances –

John Jeffreys heard something about heads rolling –

Big Heads, that's all.

I pick up my coat and go back down to the car, parked in the wrong space.

Bob Douglas lives in a detached house in the nice part of Levenshulme, the part on the way out to Stockport.

I walk up the drive and ring the doorbell.

Douglas opens the front door –

He's put on weight and lost some hair and his clothes give him the look of a short and guilty man on his way to court.

'Morning,' I say.

'Mr Hunter,' he smiles.

'We need to talk.'

'I thought you might say that.'

'You going to invite me in then?'

Bob Douglas holds open the door and sees me through to the lounge.

I sit down on a big settee, the smell of a roast in the house.

'Drink?'

'Cup of tea'd be nice.'

'I'll just be a minute then. Wife's not in,' he says and leaves me alone in his lounge with its unframed Degas print, the Christmas cards and tree, the photos of his wife and daughter.

He brings in the teas and hands me mine: 'Sugar?'

'No, thanks.'

He sits down in one of the matching chairs.

'Nice looking lass,' I say, nodding at a school portrait.

'Aye. Keeps me young.'

'How old is she?'

'Be seven in February.'

'You're a lucky man.'

Bob Douglas smiles: 'Is that what you came to tell me?'

'No,' I shake my head. 'No, it's not.'

'Go on then.'

I tell him: 'I saw Richard Dawson last night.'

'At the Midland Ball?'

'Yes. Although he wasn't exactly having one.'

'Upset was he?'

'Yeah, but I reckon he's feeling even more upset right this minute.'

'You heard then?'

'His wife called mine first thing. He call you?'

'No, but I reckoned it'd be this morning.'

I take a sip of my tea and wait to see if he's going to say any more –

He takes a sip of his and says nothing.

I say: 'What's going on, Bob?'

'What did he tell you?'

I put my tea down on one of his coasters, one of an etching of a famous golf course, and I say: 'Sod what he told me. I'm asking you.'

He's sat forward now, his hands on his knees, looking nervous.

'Spit it out,' I say.

'All I know is Roger Hook, he's heading up some operation into Richard Dawson. Been on the cards a while like, but someone . . .'

'What kind of operation?'

'He's bent isn't he? Everyone knows that.'

'I didn't.'

'Well, that's it, isn't it? It was just going to be taxman, but then they heard Brass might be in for it, so Smith stuck Hooky on it. Dead hush-hush. Get it sorted out.'

'They heard? Heard from who?'

The front door opens –

Child's feet, a woman's voice following –

The lounge door bursts open –

I stand up.

The girl freezes, thin and skinny as a tiny toy rake.

'Hello, love,' I say.

The girl looks at her Daddy –

Her Dad smiles: 'Come say hello, Karen.'

But the girl goes back behind the chair.

Bob Douglas's wife comes in, rain in her hair, and then stops dead.

Her husband says: 'Sharon love, this is Peter Hunter. The Assistant Chief Constable.'

'Yeah?' she says, shaking my hand but looking at him.

'We'll be finished in a minute,' says Douglas as casually as he can.

I nod and smile.

His wife takes the girl by the hand, her face anxious. 'Come on, Karen. Let's get the dinner on,' she says, closing the door on us.

I sit back down.

Douglas is white.

'Who?' I smile.

'I don't know.'

'Fuck off,' I hiss. 'You do.'

'I don't.'

'Another copper?'

He's looking down at the carpet, the big flowers and birds, shaking his head: 'I don't know.'

'But they're saying it's me. I'm dirty.'

He looks up and nods.

'Saying this started because of me?'

'Someone tipped them . . .'

'Who tipped them?'

'I don't know.'

'But you'd tell me if you did, right Bob?'

He smiles –

I don't –

I say: 'OK, so who the fuck was it told *you* all this?'

'Ronnie Allen,' he whispers, glancing at the door.

'There's a fucking surprise.'

Douglas shrugs.

'And you're sure Ronnie didn't give you any other names?'

'I swear.'

'He never said who told him?'

'No.'

'Never said who tipped them?'

'No.'

'Not the Ronnie Allen I know.'

Douglas shrugs again.

'OK,' I say. 'So, according to Ronnie fucking Allen, how is it that I'm supposed to be dirty?'

He's back looking down at the carpet.

'Mr Douglas?'

'No specifics,' he says. 'Just business.'

'Just business?'

He doesn't look up.

'And this is just me and Dawson?'

He nods.

'To put me in my place?'

'That's what Ronnie said.'

'Why? Who?'

'I don't know.'

'Who hates me that much, Bob?'

'I don't know. Honestly, I don't.'

'You?'

He looks up: 'Me? I don't know you.'

'Right. So don't be talking about people you don't know.'

He looks right at me, but says nothing.

I stand up. 'I'll be on my way, Mr Douglas.'

He's still sitting in his chair.

I walk over to the lounge door and then I stop and I say: 'And if I was you Mr Douglas, I'd be careful.'

'How's that then?'

'You don't want to be going about giving folk the impression you know more than you do.'

He stands up: 'Is that a threat, Mr Hunter?'

'Just a bit of advice, that's all,' I say and open the door.

His wife and daughter are in the hall, sitting on the bottom step of the stairs, her holding the tiny little lass tight around her waist.

No-one says anything.

I open the front door and step outside, turning to say goodbye –

But Douglas strides out into the hall and slams the front door.

I stand in their drive, the rain and their door in my face, everything bad, everything sad, everything dead –

Raised voices inside.

I drive back into the centre of Manchester, the place empty and deserted on a wet and bloody Sunday before Christmas, the lights out.

I turn into the car park at Headquarters and that car's back, there in my space –

Two men inside.

I pull in next to it, get out and tap on the glass.

The driver winds down his window –

I tell him: 'This space is reserved.'

'Sorry,' he says and winds the window back up –

I start to knock on the glass again, saying: 'Can I ask you . . .'

But the car reverses and pulls away –

I take down the licence plate:
PHD 666K.

Upstairs, I dial the Chief Constable –
He's back home:
'What the bloody hell happened to you last night,' he's saying. 'One minute you were there, next minute . . .'
'I'm sorry to disturb you, but I need to speak to you.'
'Is this bloody work?'
'Yes.'
'Can't it wait till tomorrow?'
'I won't be here, I have to go back to Leeds.'
'You're at the office now?'
'Yes.'
'OK. Talk.'
'Not on the phone, sir.'
A pause, then: 'What's this about?'
'I think you know.'
He's angry: 'No I don't or I wouldn't ask you.'
'I'm sorry,' I say. 'It's about Roger Hook's investigation into Richard Dawson.'
Silence, then: 'I'll be there in an hour.'
'Thank you, sir.'
I hang up and look at my watch:
It's gone noon, but already night outside.

At one-thirty Chief Constable Clement Smith telephones and asks me to step across the hall to his office.
I knock once and am told to come.
Clement Smith is behind his desk in a sports jacket, writing; Roger Hook across from him with his back to the door, waiting.
'Afternoon,' I say.
Roger turns and smiles: 'Afternoon, Pete.'
I sit down in the chair next to him, facing Smith –
Smith doesn't say anything, doesn't even look up, continuing to write –
Roger Hook sat there, just waiting –
Until, after two minutes of this, Smith looks up and says: 'Go on then.'
I swallow, angry: 'I'd like to ask you some questions about

an investigation that would seem to be involving me on a personal level.'

'So go on.'

I glance at Detective Chief Inspector Hook and back to Smith: 'Now?'

'That's why you dragged us all the way in, wasn't it?'

I say: 'I would prefer to have the conversation in private.'

'Stuff what you'd prefer Pete; it's Sunday bloody afternoon.'

Hook stands up.

'Sit down,' says Smith.

'Sir, I don't mind . . .' says Hook.

Smith has his hand raised: 'I mind.'

Hook stops and sits back down.

Smith is staring at me, eyes black and waiting –

'OK,' I say. 'A friend of mine, Richard Dawson, who I believe we all know?'

Smith and Hook nod.

'Well last night, at the Midland Hotel, he tells me that yesterday morning police officers visited his bank and took away records relating to him. He said that a former Yorkshire police officer, Bob Douglas?'

Smith and Hook nod again.

'He said that Douglas had told him that the reason for this investigation was because of his friendship with me. To put me in my place. Richard Dawson then asked me for help and I declined to assist him, as he was under investigation. This morning, however, I learnt that his house had been raided and, following a meeting I've just had with Bob Douglas, I would very much appreciate being told to what extent this investigation is concerned in any way with my friendship with Richard Dawson, or with me personally.'

I pause, then add: 'I realise this is irregular and against procedure and I would like to stress that I'm not asking for, nor do I expect, any information about the investigation into Richard Dawson, other than whether or not it relates to me.'

Then I stop, waiting –

Smith sighs and turns his gaze to Hook, nodding –

Hook shrugs and says: 'It doesn't.'

Smith turns back to me, eyes black and twinkling.

'That's it?' I say.

'Dawson is under investigation,' continues Hook. 'But, for the moment, it doesn't have anything to do with you or any other police officer.'

'So why the secrecy?'

'Well, that said, Richard Dawson is known socially by a number of senior police officers, as well as a number of other prominent local persons. So we're treading carefully.'

'As should you,' says Clement Smith, those black eyes on me –

I sigh, sitting back in my chair.

Smith continues: 'There could be a lot of fallout – especially if the press start jumping to the same bloody conclusions as one of my own Assistant Chief Constables.'

'Sorry,' I say. 'Thought of being stuck over in Yorkshire, hearing all these stories . . .'

'Two days and cursed bloody place is making you paranoid.'

'No more than usual,' I smile.

'Now you know how you make other folks feel then,' laughs Hook.

'Was that the point?' I say, not smiling.

'No,' says Detective Chief Inspector Hook.

'Then you better tell Ronnie to keep it shut – he's the one been telling Douglas bollocks about secret squads and putting me in my place.'

'Sorry,' he says, fucked off. 'He's got a big mouth and talks bollocks.'

Smith's staring at Hook now, the black eyes on him –

'I'll take care of it,' says Hook.

Smith stands up and says: 'Can I go home now?'

Back down in the car park and there's a man standing by my car.

Familiar, he looks familiar –

Me: 'Can I help you?'

He raises a hand and shakes his head, walking over to another car –

A white one.

'Wrong motor,' he says, smiling.

I get in my car –

The black one.

*

And then somewhere over the Moors, I remember it's a Sunday and almost Christmas and I suddenly hate myself, wondering what the fuck I thought I was doing, what the fuck I thought I was going to do, the bad dreams not leaving, just staying bad, like the headaches and the backache, the murder and the lies, like the cries and the whispers, the screams of the wires and the signals, like the voices and the numbers:

Thirteen.

5:00 p.m.

Sunday 14 December 1980:

Millgarth, Leeds.

Dark outside, darker in:

A ritual –

A séance:

Round the table, hands and knees touching, between the cardboard boxes and the gorged files –

Mike Hillman is calling up the dead, passing out photographs, saying:

'Theresa Campbell, murdered 26 June 1975. 26-year-old mother of three and convicted prostitute. Partially clothed, bloodstained body was discovered on Prince Philip Playing Fields, Scott Hall, by Eric Davies, a milkman.'

Peel –

'Post-mortem revealed multiple stab wounds to abdomen, chest, and throat inflicted by a blade 4 inches in length, ³/₄ of an inch in width, one edge sharper than the other; severe lacerations to the skull and fractures to the crown, possibly inflicted by an axe. A white purse with *Mummy* on the front, containing approximately £5 in cash, was also noted to be missing from the deceased's handbag. Neither murder weapons or purse have ever been found.'

He stops to let the pictures speak –

They all look up from the six by fours, all but DS Marshall –

Are there tears in her eyes?

'Those are the facts,' he says, repeating: 'The facts. The rest is hearsay; but here goes –

'Campbell had spent the evening at the Room at the Top nightclub in Sheepscar. She was last seen attempting to stop

motorists at the junction of Sheepscar Street South and Roundhay Road, Leeds at 1:00 a.m.

'According to the witnesses you have listed before you, it is
believed that an articulated lorry with a dark-coloured cab and
a tarpaulin-sheeted load stopped at the junction of Roundhay
Road and Sheepscar Street South alongside Campbell and it is
believed she had a conversation with the driver.

'This location is the main route from the A1 Wetherby Round-
about to the Leeds Inner Ring Road which services HGVs
travelling on the M62, either east or west.'

Hillman pauses; we all glance up, all but Marshall –

A tune in my head, a song from somewhere:

I only have eyes for you –

The dream still here, here in my mouth, hanging in the room,
the taste in my mouth –

The taste of blood, the smell:

'They call it the Box,' says Hillman.

There's a soft knock at the door and a young constable hands
Bob Craven a note –

He glances at it, looks up at me, and passes it forward –

I open it:

Call Richard Dawson.

I put it in my pocket.

'And that's the last anyone saw of her till the milkman,'
Hillman's saying.

'Thank you,' I say. 'If there are no questions, let's move onto
the structure of the investigation. Mike?'

'Fish and chip job as it was seen then, they still put Chief
Superintendent Jobson on it, plus a couple of other names that'll
keep coming up: Detective Superintendents Alderman and Prentice, DIs as they were back in 75.'

There are nods.

'Good team,' I say, watching Craven –

His face blank but for a slight light in those dark eyes, a
slight smile –

And then he suddenly says: 'Best men we've got.'

'Anyway,' continues Hillman. 'Those were the big guns and
the same team used for Joan Richards and everything up to
Marie Watts. After that Oldman and Noble take the reins and
Jobson's given the early bath.'

'What about Alderman and Prentice? What happened to them?' asks McDonald.

'Still here. A complete list of every copper involved is in the copies I've given you, alphabetically by rank.'

I'm still watching Craven, knowing he was there –

Knowing his name is in there, here –

'Right,' I say. 'Thank you, Mike. We'll be going over the cases in more detail later as we see how they relate. OK?'

Silence –

'Next?'

'Richards or Strachan?' asks Marshall.

'Do it chronologically.'

'Right,' says Mike Hillman, nodding at Helen Marshall. 'Me again:

'OK. Whether you accept Strachan as a Ripper job or not,' says Hillman. 'She died like this:

'A convicted prostitute and registered alcoholic, Clare Strachan was taken to some disused garages on Frenchwood Street, a well-known Preston red-light area. She had sex and was then hit on the head by a blunt instrument, kicked in the face, head, breasts, legs and body. Then the attacker jumped up and down on her chest, causing a rib to puncture a lung and kill her. She had bite marks on her breasts and had been penetrated by a variety of objects and twice sodomised, once post-mortem. She was found the next morning by a woman walking her dog.'

Silence, dark silence –

Mike coughs and then goes on: 'Alf Hill was in charge, Frank Fields his number two, again top men on it. Initially, no link was established with Theresa Campbell. Following the murder of Joan Richards, two detectives went over to Preston and again no evidence was found to connect the killings. Right, Bob?'

Bob Craven nods, saying nothing.

'You went over, right?'

'Yeah.'

Mike Hillman shakes his head and smiles: 'Thanks a lot, Bob. OK, the link with the Ripper was made following the letters received after the murder of Marie Watts in 1977. As you know, the letters made reference to the murder of Clare Strachan and tests conducted revealed that the killer of Strachan and Watts and the letter writer were all blood type . . .'

'B,' says Craven.

'Thanks, Bob,' says Mike. 'Again all the names and dates have been listed on the sheet before you.'

'Bob?' John Murphy says turning to Craven.

'Yeah?'

'They send anyone over from Preston?'

'What?'

'You went over after you got Joan Richards, how about them? Had they sent anyone over after Clare Strachan?'

'Frank Fields.'

Murphy nods: 'And Frank didn't make any link?'

'No.'

I say: 'Right, as Mike's just said, this is the one that the letters and the tape specifically refer to, the letters and tape that have largely been included on the strength of this murder.'

'And the blood group,' adds Craven.

'Thank you,' I say. 'But let's get this straight, initially, didn't you and . . .'

'John Rudkin.'

'Right, didn't you and Rudkin report that this murder shouldn't be considered the work of the same man who killed Campbell and Richards?'

'Yeah,' he nods. 'That was until we got the sample off Watts and the tests on the envelope.'

'So, initially, why did you think otherwise?'

Craven smiles: 'Feel like I'm in bloody court.'

'Relax, Bob. You're among friends,' I say.

'Is that right?'

'Yeah,' says Murphy.

He's still smiling: 'Look, initially, the only real link between Campbell and Strachan, Richards and Strachan was that they were all slags. Strachan had been raped, had a milk bottle up her, had it up the arse, then been kicked to death. Indoors. Completely different.'

'Until the letters and the tape?'

'Until the letters and the tape.'

'And then she was in,' I say.

'You better believe it.'

I ask him: 'Do you want to add anything else?'

'Two kids in Glasgow.'

'Husband?'

'Drowned at sea.'

'Anything else?'

Craven smiling to himself: 'Not about her, no.'

'You want to talk us through Joan Richards?'

'No.'

'Go on. You were in on this one right from the get go, yeah?'

'Just about.'

'Please, it'd help us out a lot.'

'Not treading on anyone's toes, am I?' he asks, looking at Helen Marshall –

There are tears in her eyes –

Fuck –

'No,' I say, trying to catch her eye –

The tears in her eyes.

Craven sighs, shrugs his shoulders and says almost automatically: 'Joan Richards was found on February 6 1976 in an alleyway on the Manor Street Industrial Estate, off Roundhay Road, Leeds. She had severe head injuries caused by a hammer and a total of fifty-two stab wounds to the neck, chest, stomach, and back. Her bra had been pulled up over her tits and a piece of wood placed over her fanny. There were boot prints on her legs. Wellies. Farley, the pathologist, immediately linked it with Theresa Campbell. The Owl, Maurice – he was still in charge, Dick Alderman and Jim Prentice with him. Me and Rudkin were brought in after Farley linked it with Campbell. Sent us over to Preston, the rest you know.'

Marshall is staring at him –

Tears in her eyes.

I say: 'Background?'

'She was new to it. Husband knew what she was up to. Pimped her. Sometimes used his van, but not this time. There was a load of bollocks in papers that didn't help. Stuff about the killer taking her van and shit like that.'

'This when the Ripper stuff started?' asks Hillman.

'No, that was after Marie Watts,'

I say: 'Jack Whitehead, wasn't it?'

'Probably.'

Silence, the room getting smaller, darker –

The cabinets taller.

A knock on the door –
'Mr Hunter?'
'Yes?'
'Telephone. Emergency.'
I stand up.
Craven says: 'Take it next door. It's dead.'
I nod and push past them and out –
The Ripper Room, dead –
Just their photos staring down from their walls, dead.
'Peter Hunter speaking?'
'It's Richard.'
'What is it?'
'*What is it*? What do you mean, *what is it*? You know what happened this morning? Five o'bloody clock this morning?'
'Joan told me.'
'And?'
'And what?'
'And fucking what? They . . .'
'Richard, I can't do anything. My hands are tied.'
'Your hands are tied? Fucking hell, Peter. Talk about . . .'
'I'm sorry,' I say and hang up.
I go back to the small room next door, heart pounding, angry –
No one speaking –
Going up to seven –
'Sod it. Let's call it a night,' I say, the ghosts scattering, scuttling back –
They all stand up at once.
'John,' I say to Murphy. 'Have a word?'
He nods and follows me back next door.
We sit down at a desk in the Ripper Room –
Their Ripper Room.
'Something's going down back home. Pick your brains?'
'Course. Fire away.'
'Bob Douglas? Remember him?'
'Craven's mate from the Strafford, oh aye,' laughs Murphy. 'Moved over our way, didn't he?'
'Yep, Levenshulme. Heard anything of him recently?'
'Into some kind of security work, I think.'
'Well, you know Richard Dawson? He's been using Douglas

for this and that and now Dawson's being investigated for some
kind of financial irregularities or something. Anyway, Douglas
told him that this investigation, it's down to his friendship with
me. That's why he's being investigated; to put me in my place.'

'Bollocks.'

'What I thought. But this morning I went to see Douglas.'

'Yeah?' says Murphy, quietly. 'Was that wise?'

'I just wanted to get it straightened out. Joan's good friends
with Linda Dawson, you know. And I need to be thinking about
this here, not Bob bloody Douglas.'

'And?'

'Douglas said he'd got it from Ronnie Allen.'

'Verbals himself.'

'Yep.'

'He's a bloody knob, isn't he? Ronnie?'

'Gets worse. Hooky's in charge.'

'Fuck.'

'Yeah. And they raided Dawson's house first thing this
morning.'

'Fuck, fuck.'

'Yeah.'

'You want me to put the feelers out?'

'Well I spoke to both Hooky and Clement Smith and they
reckon it's nothing sinister. Finances. Said I'm paranoid.'

'Peter Hunter paranoid?' laughs Murphy, but his eyes are
dead.

'Reckon I am.'

'But him knowing you? That's not paranoia.'

'But it's not only me. Smith's mates as well.'

'I know him too. Might be next?'

I smile: 'Lot of folk.'

'See, don't worry about it,' he says. 'That what the Chief
said?'

'You know Smith; he just said to keep my distance for now.
But . . .'

'But if I do happen to hear anything, or ask someone,
then . . .'

I smile again: 'Thank you.'

'I'll get back to you,' he nods.

'About what?' says Craven suddenly, there in the Ripper Room –

His room –

His Ripper.

'Nothing to worry you about, Bob.'

'I'll see you at breakfast, then?' smiles Murphy.

'Yep,' I say. 'And I'll bid you two gents a goodnight.'

'Not having a swift one?' says Craven.

'Not tonight, Bob,' I say, patting him on the shoulder as I go out.

He winks: 'Got a date, have you?'

Headingley –

It's been four nights now, everything still dead –

Forever dead.

I pull into the Kentucky Fried Chicken car park, once again positioning the car so I face the main road, and then I go inside.

Again, I'm the only customer.

I order the same chicken and chips, the cup of coffee, and wait under the same white lights for another ten minutes while the same Asian staff prepare the order, staring at the light reflected in the coffee.

I take the food back out to the car and sit in another night, the window down, picking at the pale stringy meat again, watching the street –

No-one.

I drink down the cold coffee.

I get out of the car and walk across the road to the bus stop.

It's 9:53, the Number 13 coming up Headingley Lane –

Like clockwork.

And again, it doesn't stop.

I cross back and turn right onto Alma Road –

Alma Road, with its police tape and one dark car waiting.

Again I walk down the dim tree-lined street, crossing to avoid the cordon, past the officers in the police car.

And at the end of the road, by the school, I stop at the gates again and stare back down Alma Road –

Again, Alma Road –

The ordinary street in the ordinary suburb where a man took

a hammer and a knife to another man's daughter, to another man's sister, to another man's fiancée –

The ordinary street in the ordinary suburb where a man took a hammer and a knife to Laureen Bell, an ordinary girl, and shattered her skull and stabbed this ordinary girl fifty-seven times in her abdomen, in her womb, and once in her eye –

And in this ordinary street, in this ordinary suburb, in this ordinary world, I listen to the silence and the song it sings:

And when we die
And float away
Into the night
The Milky Way
You'll hear me call
As we ascend
I'll say your name
Then once again
Thank you for being a friend.

This ordinary world –
This whole, empty, forgotten, ordinary world at war.

dirty cow e know this face from somewhere e am sure transmission two the body of joan richards forty five years found in a derelict building of the industrial estate on manor street leeds seven at five past eight today friday the sixth of february nineteen seventy six it is known that the woman has recently been an active prostitute in the chapeltown area of leeds when found she was wearing blue green and red checked overcoat blue and white horizontal striped dress white sling back shoes fawn handbag black knickers brown tights it is known that between the times six ten PM and ten thirty PM thursday the fifth of february nineteen seventy six she was in possession of a white commer van with ladders on the roof motive appears to be hatred of prostitutes the man we are looking for is the type who could kill again assailant may be heavily bloodstained and is believed to be wearing heavy ribbed rubber boots or heavy wellington boots registration number JRD six six six K vehicle has been found on a car park belonging to the gaiety hotel roundhay road leeds approximately half a mile from the scene of the crime and any sightings of the woman or the vehicle should be notified to this office the deceased suffered severe injuries to the skull consisting of lacerations and a number of small skull fractures believed caused by a hammer and fifty two stab wounds to the lower throat and neck upper chest lower abdomen and back possibly caused by an instrument similar to a philips screwdriver cross pattern type that bordered on the maniacal on one of her thighs the impression of a heavy ribbed rubber boot or wellington boot was found though there had been no sexual interference to the vagina the brassiere was removed to a position above the breasts and dress and there are several indications that the person responsible for this crime may also have been responsible for the death of the prostitute theresa campbell at leeds on sixth of june nineteen seventy five he is a sadistic killer and may well be a sexual pervert particular attention should be paid to persons coming into custody for the footwear described who may also have a vehicle containing tools of the type described and will perhaps be a workmans van a search of records for persons convicted of serious attacks upon prostitutes would be appreciated and here the tears we first wept in the black snow knot and cluster and fill the hollow parts around the eyes lord break these hard veils the pain that swells our hearts here in a place in hell called leeds e saw her outside the gaiety in that place and e picked her up and drove her to derelict land at the centre of this evil plain this the place in which we found ourselves parked away from the lights her overwhelming smell of cheap perfume making me feel nauseated and so e had to get her outside so e got her to hold a torch while e raised the bonnet of the car to examine the engine then e took a couple of steps back and aimed two blows at her head with the hammer then e took her into the shadows and pushed her sweater cardigan and brassiere up to expose her breasts and e stabbed her fifty two times in the breasts neck back and low abdomen with a cross ply philips screwdriver and e took a piece of wood and thrust it between her legs to show her as disgusting as she was in possession of a white commer van with ladders on the roof motive appears to be hatred of prostitutes the man we are looking for is type who could kill again assailant may be heavily bloodstained and wearing heavy ribbed rubber boots e drove to my mother in laws with a feeling of justification and satisfaction and next day it was my mothers birthday and e made sure e delivered her card the snowflakes are dancing on the radio a broken

Chapter 5

6:00 a.m. –
Monday 15 December 1980:
Millgarth Police Station, Leeds.
The room next to the Ripper –
The door open, the light on –
'Helen?' I say.
DS Marshall looks up from the file on the desk, a hand on her heart –
'Peter.'
'I'm sorry, I didn't mean to frighten you.'
'No, I was miles away.'
'How long have you been here?'
'Don't know,' she says, looking at her watch.
'Couldn't sleep?'
She nods.
'Me too,' I say, sitting down. 'Who let you in?'
'It wasn't locked.'
'Bloody hell.'
'Sorry.'
'It's not your fault, don't worry.'
She sits back in her chair, pushing the file away.
'What are you looking at?' I ask.
'Well I got lucky, yeah? 1976.'
'A quiet one. Favouritism from the Boss.'
'People will talk.'
I'm blushing: 'Yeah?'
'Yeah, they'll say you're sexist. Specially if you don't even let me precis them.'
'Me sexist? One murder, one attack; Joan Richards and that Chinese girl? I don't think so.'
She's smiling.
'And,' I say, 'I'm sorry about last night. But Bob Craven was . . .'
She stops smiling: 'You know she's dead?'
'Who?'
'That *Chinese girl.*'

'Sue Peng? No, when?'
'77. Suicide.'
Ghosts, more ghosts –
Chinese ghosts.
'What?' Helen Marshall is staring straight through me.
'Said I didn't know that.'
'As good as murdered.'
We sit in silence –
Helen rubbing her eyes, me with that taste in my mouth –
I ask: 'Have you had any breakfast?'
'No.'
'Want some?'

In the canteen we set down our trays on a table, the morning
papers abandoned by the last shift –
Headlines hurting:
£100,000 Ripper Reward.
Victim's Mother in Ripper Plea.
Women Arm Against Ripper.
Ripper Telephone Threat Studied.
That playground taunt, haunting:
Ripper, Ripper –
Hunt, hunt,
Ripper, Ripper –
Cunt, cunt.
'Well, well, well. What have we here?' says Murphy, joining
us.
'Sorry, John.'
'Just stand me up, why don't you?' he says, winking at
Marshall: 'Watch him, love. He'll make you all these promises;
breakfast at Millgarth, dinner at the Ritz. Then not a dicky-
bird.'
Helen Marshall is looking down at her plate, not smiling.
'Good night?' I ask him.
'A quiet one with your mate Sergeant Bob.'
'Yeah?'
'Yeah,' he sighs.
'As bad as it sounds?'
'He's an odd bloke, isn't he?'

'Don't know. Last time I met him he was in Pinderfields Hospital, wires sticking out of him.'

'Well they managed to rebuild him; just think they forgot a few bits.'

'Like?'

'Oh, I don't know. Just strikes me as odd.'

'Learn anything?'

'Well, he certainly isn't modest, our Bob. Thinks he should have been put in command.'

'So I take it he doesn't think much to what's been going on?'

'Thinks they've wasted a lot of time. Thinks like us, they've probably had Ripper in and let him go.'

'Any names?'

'Not saying if he has; but he has his theories all right.'

'Share them with you?'

'No but I reckon he's got his finger in a few pies, our Bob. Wouldn't be surprised if he wasn't on his way out; thinking of taking his theories with him, take them to the papers,' he says, tapping the *Yorkshire Post*.

'Spying?'

'Oh aye. Course he is.'

'Who for?'

'That's the question,' says Murphy, quietly. 'That's the question.'

Helen Marshall looks up, nodding at the queue for the food –

Detective Superintendent Robert Craven is asking for extra sausage.

The three of us look at each other, eyes meeting, grins broad, laughing for a moment before we get up to go.

I stand at the door to the Ripper Room, catching the tail end of the morning briefing, the backs of a hundred heads before those walls, those walls with their alien landscapes of wastelands and buildings, tires and tools, of wounds –

The shallows and the hollows, the indentations –

The same shallows and hollows, the same indentations from the walls of my room –

My War Room.

Temporary Assistant Chief Constable Noble is telling the packed room: 'So that'll be press conference.'

There's no cheer.

'OK. Get to it.'

The room disperses, half of them pushing through the door past me, the others slumped back over their desks, back behind the piles and piles of paper that rise and tower from each one.

I wait until it's clear and then go over to Noble, huddled with Alderman and Prentice and a couple of his other top men.

They all step back as they see me come, the conversation dead –

'Morning gentlemen,' I say.

Nods are all I get.

'Can I have a word when you're finished?' I ask Noble.

'I was coming next door anyway,' he says.

'Yeah?' I say.

'Yeah. Going up to Alma Road, if you want another look? Daylight?'

Another look? Daylight?

I let it go, face blank –

'Thanks,' I smile. 'Appreciate it.'

'Just room for you, mind.'

'Fine.'

'Meet you out front in ten minutes?'

'Right.'

'I don't envy you,' Noble is saying, as the driver pulls off the Ring Road and onto Woodhouse Lane.

'I never imagined you did,' I say.

We're sat in the back, Dickie Alderman up front with the driver.

'But,' I add. 'Can't say I envy you much either.'

Noble laughs: 'You wait. You will.'

'How's that?' I smile, glancing at the concrete outside, the grey concrete stained black by the rain.

'When I catch the bastard.'

'Feeling lucky are you?'

'Always. Give me a month.'

'You should tell the papers,' I laugh.

'Piss off,' he smiles.

The car slips into silence as Woodhouse Lane becomes Headingley.

As we come up to Alma Road, Noble suddenly asks: 'How you getting on with Bob Craven?'

'Fine,' I say. 'Why?'

'Just asking,' smiles Noble. 'Just asking.'

That's the question.

The car turns right onto Alma Road and pulls up in front of a parked Panda.

It's raining heavily again.

We get out.

There's tape around the shrubbery, the bushes.

We walk towards it.

Noble is stood next to me, squinting back down the road through the rain –

'She got off the bus at nine-twenty,' he's saying –

Saying to himself: 'Crossed the road and walked down here.'

He looks back to the other end of Alma Road –

'Flat's just up there,' he says.

We stand in the rain before the bushes, Noble, Alderman, and me –

'He come up behind her,' says Alderman. 'Hit her on the head and took her behind the bushes.'

No one says anything.

Alderman's words just hanging there until –

Until Noble turns and we follow him back to the car, the driver stood under a black umbrella smoking.

Inside the car, I say: 'Been fifteen months, yeah? Since the last one?'

Noble nods, Alderman turning around in the front seat.

I continue: 'Makes you wonder what he's been doing?'

'We're already running prison checks,' says Alderman.

'He's not done time,' I say.

Noble looks away from the window: 'What makes you so certain?'

'You'd have had him if he had.'

Alderman says: 'What about the Services? Ireland?'

'Maybe, but I doubt it.'

Noble agrees: 'Someone would have said something.'

'What then?' asks Alderman.

'You got a hobby?' I ask him.

'What?'

'What's your hobby?' I say again.
'Shooting. Hunting. Why?'
'Where do you go?'
'All over.'
'Where?'
'Eccup, that way.'
'How often do you go?'
'Not as often as I'd like.'
'Why's that?'
'Work.'
'Work?'
'Aye, work. Because of bleeding Ripper for a start. Why?'
'But before, before all this, you got out fairly regular?'
'Yeah, except when kids were right young, yeah.'
'How about before kids were born?'
'Oh aye. Every day off I had.'
I nod: 'That's my point.'
'What? What's your point?'
I say: 'He's the same.'
'Who?'
'The Ripper.'
Alderman's grinning: 'What? He's into shooting and all?'
Noble's shaking his head: 'He means he's got the same bol-
locks in his life we all have. That's what you're saying, isn't it?'
I nod: 'When we get him, you'll see the same patterns we all
have, same pressures, rhythms: work, the wife, kids, holidays.'
Alderman: 'You reckon Ripper's married with kids? Fuck
off.'
'He's married, I bet you.'
'How much?'
'Whatever you can afford.'
'That the Ripper's married with kids?'
'Married,' I say. 'No kids.'
'A hundred quid says you're wrong,' says Alderman, hand
out.
We shake on it: 'Hundred quid it is.'
Noble interrupts: 'Why you so sure?'
'You're the bloke that got Raymond Morris,' I say. 'It'll be
the same, Pete.'
Stafford, 1965–67.

Noble looks away, the rain in sheets down the car windows.

'What do you mean?' says Dickie Alderman.

Noble, watching the water come down, whispers: 'Raymond Morris had alibis from his wife.'

Three little girls, raped, suffocated, dumped.

His window has misted over, the car stuffed.

Alderman is shaking his head: 'No-one would cover for this cunt.'

'She doesn't think she is doing; doesn't see him for what he is,' I say, then: 'But neither do we.'

'Fuck off.'

'No, half that Ripper Room are looking for a hunchbacked Geordie with hairy bloodstained hands, flesh between his teeth and a hammer in his pocket.'

Noble, a face full of fear and sneer: 'Yeah? So who should we be looking for, Pete?'

I tell him what he already knows – knows in his heart, knows in his head: 'He's mobile, has his own vehicle. It must have come up numerous times in the sweeps, so he has to have a reason to be where he shouldn't be – taxi driver, lorry driver, sales rep . . .'

Noble: 'Copper?'

'Copper . . .'

'Fuck off,' snorts Alderman.

I shrug: 'He'll have a good local knowledge as a result of his work and because he's from round here – lives and works round here.'

Alderman: 'You can't say that? If he's a lorry driver, he could be living any-bloody-where?'

'No,' I say quietly, shaking my head and wiping the side-window clean. 'He's from round here because he hates it, hates it enough to kill it – so he has to have been around here long enough to hate it, to want to kill it.'

Noble: 'Go on.'

'He'll have a record, however minor.'

Alderman: 'Why?'

'Because when he was younger, he couldn't control the hate like he can now. He'll have made mistakes . . .'

'We'd know,' says Alderman.

'Not if you're not looking.'

'We're fucking looking,' spits Alderman, almost over the seat and at me.

Me, hands up: 'But for what? An unmarried hunchbacked Geordie with hairy bloodstained hands, flesh between his teeth and a hammer in his pocket?'

'Fuck off, Pete,' says Noble.

'No,' I tell him. 'You should go back over every statement where the bloke's been covered by his wife.'

'Fuck off,' says Alderman.

'Start with your top ten.'

'Impossible,' says Noble.

'You've had him, you know you have.'

'Fuck off.'

'But somehow you've let him go.'

Silence –

Just the rain on the roof.

Noble leans forward and taps on the driver's window –

The driver opens the door, shakes the rain from his umbrella and gets in, the smell of cigarettes and damp with him.

'Millgarth,' says Noble.

As the car pulls into the underground car park, I turn to Temporary Assistant Chief Constable Peter Noble and ask: 'How did you catch Morris?'

'Luck,' he says. 'Bloody luck.'

'Bollocks, Pete,' I say. 'Bollocks.'

Alderman looks around in the front seat again, but Noble's gone.

Back in our room, the one next to theirs, next to his, I close the door behind me.

They're all there, plus Bob Craven, looking up from their work, waiting, expectant:

'I should have said this before, but when you're taking down all these names, can you denote the married ones.'

John Murphy smiles: 'We have been.'

'Thank you,' I smile back, nodding: 'Then let's move on.'

Another Millgarth afternoon –

Dark outside, darker still in:

Another séance –

Same ritual –

Round the table, hands and knees touching, more calls to the dead –

John Murphy this time, sheet-white with black-rings, calling them:

'What a fucking year it was, 1977:

'First up, Marie Watts, formerly Owens, thirty-two years of age, found dead Sunday 29 May on Soldiers Field, Roundhay; extensive head injuries, stab wounds to the abdomen, and a cut throat. Watts was a known prostitute and the connection with Campbell and Richards was obvious, leading to the formation of what was then known as the Prostitute Murder Squad. This was headed up by ACC Oldman, with Pete Noble the effective day-to-day gaffer.'

Murphy pauses, looking at Bob Craven, then continues:

'As Bob said yesterday, it was the Watts murder where the press coined the Yorkshire Ripper moniker. Also when the first letter arrived. Plus the B type blood grouping taken from semen stains off Watts' coat – it was them stains that linked in Clare Strachan in Preston and the letters, using saliva tests and the content of the letters and later the tape.'

Long pause, a deep, deep sigh, then.

'The names, the numbers, the descriptions, the whole bloody lot, it's all there and, to be honest if it hadn't have been for what came next, who knows if we'd be sitting here today.'

Here she comes, here she comes, here she comes again:

'Skipping over, for now, the Linda Clark attack in Bradford, one week on from Marie Watts and the body of sixteen-year-old Rachel Johnson was found in the Reginald Street adventure playground on the morning of Wednesday 8 June, morning after the Jubilee. She had suffered appalling head injuries, though had probably died some time after the initial attack had taken place. She was not a prostitute, a 'good-time girl', or anything other than a sixteen-year-old Leeds shop assistant on her way home from a first bloody date.'

We're all looking at the floor or the walls or the ceiling, our nails or our pens or our papers, anywhere other than Murphy and his files and photographs of her.

'I'm sure,' he says. 'Like me, you remember her.'

All of you, I'm thinking –
I remember all of you.

'Break,' I say and stand up and walk out of the room, into the light of the corridor, through the phones and the typewriters, into the toilets and into a cubicle and throw up.

I am walking down the stairs, heading for a paper and some air, when there's a hand at my elbow –

Bob Craven: 'Mr Hunter?'

'Yes?'

'I wanted to ask you something?'

'Go on.'

'That business about noting down the married blokes, you're saying you think he's married?'

I look at Detective Superintendent Craven, the black beard and tick, the eyes to match –

I say: 'You got time for a coffee, Bob?'

'Have you?'

'A quick one,' I nod and we walk back upstairs to the canteen.

I bring over the coffees and sit down across the plastic table from him –

'You take all this very seriously,' I say.

'Is there any other way?'

'I'm sorry, I didn't mean it like that; what I mean is, you're in deep.'

'That a crime?'

'No.'

He stops stirring his coffee and looks up: 'I'll be honest with you, it eats me up; same for a lot of the lads.'

'Been a long time?'

'Too long.'

'You got any theories?'

He smiles: 'Oh aye.'

'Going to share them?'

'With you?'

'Why not?'

'Because that's not why you're here, is it Mr Hunter? Not really?'

'What do you mean?'

The beard and eyes shining under the canteen lights: 'It's not just about Ripper, is it? It's about seeing how many of us you can take down with him.'

'Why would I want to do that?'

'It's in your nature.'

I push the cup away and stand up: 'I am here for one purpose, and one purpose only: to catch the Yorkshire Ripper.'

He's staring up at me, almost smiling, smirking.

I should walk away, should leave him to it, but I don't, I stay and I say: 'There is a paranoia in this force, a paranoia that makes it dumb as well as blind.'

He's smiling, laughing now, a white slash of teeth in the black beard.

I can't walk away, can't stop myself: 'Unless that is, you have all got something to bloody hide.'

'Like what?' he's staring up at me: 'Like what?'

'Fuck knows. Your stupidity?' I say and regret it and know I always will.

'Mr Hunter, I'll tell you this: we're going to catch our Ripper, not you.'

'Then you'd better get a fucking move on,' I say and turn and walk away.

Nowhere to run, nowhere to hide –

'Janice Ryan,' says Murphy, and then stops, dead –

We all look up, the room cold and dark –

No way to kill this pain inside –

'I don't know where to begin,' he says, eyes fixed on Bob Craven coming in late, sitting down next to me.

No escape from your heart –

'Bradford prostitute, moved to Leeds, but wound up dead under a sofa on waste ground off White Abbey, back in Bradford. Time of death has never been conclusively proven, but must have occurred sometime in the seven days preceding the discovery of the body on Sunday 12 June, 1977.'

No escape from your lips –

'Furthermore, following the initial discovery, Ryan was not immediately connected to the Ripper. Reasons for this would appear to have been two-fold: scene of crime being Bradford not Leeds, despite the inclusion of Clare Strachan in Preston only the week previously.'

No escape from you baby, from your fingertips –

'The second reason was the type of injuries; so while Ryan suffered head injuries, she had actually died from internal abdominal injuries caused by someone jumping up and down on her, which again linked her only to Strachan.'

No escape from you darling, all night and day –

'Ryan got herself included thanks to the letter that arrived at the *Telegraph & Argus* on Monday 13 June, a letter from a man claiming to be the Yorkshire Ripper and stating that there was a surprise in Bradford.'

No escape from you baby, no place to stay –

John Murphy looks up: 'So, to my mind, that means one of two things: either it was the Ripper or it wasn't. But if it wasn't, then neither was Clare Strachan. And that would mean one thing and one thing only: we'd have got ourselves two Jacks, not one.'

No escape, no escape at all.

At ten-thirty we're sitting in their over-lit canteen, spread over two tables and six plates of uneaten food, the brightness boring into tired eyes.

There is little talk, DCI McDonald and DS Marshall still poring over their notebooks, the rest of us ordering, indexing and referencing; rationalising the things we've read.

'We should call it a night,' I say.

There are nods and yawns, Hillman stretching, some talk of a nightcap.

I walk downstairs with Murphy, neither of us saying much.

At the desk, I say: 'I'm going to walk.'

'Not fancy a quick one?'

'Not tonight, John. Thanks.'

'See you at breakfast then?' he smiles.

'If I don't get a better offer,' I laugh and say goodnight.

Outside it's raining and black, the streets empty.

And as I wait to cross at the traffic lights, I watch the cars, the white faces behind the wheels, wondering, making deals, idle threats –

Beneath the Christmas lights on Boar Lane, I walk without direction, suddenly overwhelmed by immense regret and pain, the terrible and familiar sensation of more to come and the impotence that goes with it.

At the door to the Griffin, I have tears in my eyes, on my cheeks, terrible, cold tears.

I take my key from the desk and am walking across the lobby when he rises from his seat –

'Mr Hunter?' asks a tall emaciated man with long thin grey hair and features.

I nod.

'My name is Martin Laws and I'd like to talk with you if you could spare me five minutes?'

The man is wearing black, carrying a hat and a bag –

'Are you a priest, Mr Laws?' I ask him.

'Yes,' he nods.

'OK,' I say, glancing at my watch and pointing at the nearest pair of high-backed lobby seats.

'Thank you,' he says.

We sit down opposite each other, him with his hat between his fingers.

'What can I do for you, Father?'

'I'm actually here on behalf of Elizabeth Hall.'

'Yes?' I say, looking at the black bag at his feet.

'Eric Hall's wife? Libby Hall?'

I nod.

'Mrs Hall saw you on the news, at the press conference. She's very anxious to talk to you.'

'About what?'

'The murder of her husband.'

I sit back in the chair: 'Father, with all due respect, I think that falls somewhat outside the perimeters of this present investigation. If Mrs Hall has information about her husband's death, I'm sure the – '

Mr Laws has his hand raised –

I stop talking.

'Mr Hunter,' he says softly, handing me an envelope from his pocket. 'From what Libby has confided to me, the murder of her husband falls very much inside the perimeters of your investigation.'

I look at the envelope in my hands, reluctant.

'Please?' says Laws.

'I . . .'

'Mr Hunter – '

I open the envelope, take out the letter, and read:

> *Dear Mr Hunter,*
> *I was heartened to learn that you have been asked to assist in the Ripper Inquiry. I have information that you will find very useful, information concerning the murder of my husband Detective Inspector Eric Hall and his involvement with the so-called Yorkshire Ripper. It is my belief that he was killed because of his acquaintance with Janice Ryan, the sixth victim, and his knowledge of a police cover-up.*
> *I can prove this.*
> *Yours Sincerely,*
> *Elizabeth Hall*

I fold up the letter and put it back in the envelope –

No escape, no escape at all –

'How is she?' I ask Laws.

'Not well, but she is very determined to see you.'

'I can send round one of my team?'

'She is insistent on speaking to you. Only you.'

Bloody hell –

'Tomorrow morning?'

Mr Laws nods but says: 'Now? She's outside in my car.'

Fuck –

'It would mean a lot,' he adds.

I sigh and stand up: 'OK. Let's go.'

I follow Martin Laws out of the Griffin and back into the night and the rain, follow him round the back of the hotel, past the Scarborough Public House, down the dark arches and under the railway tracks until we come to an old green Viva parked in the gloom.

Mr Laws taps gently on the passenger window and a frightened white face suddenly springs from the black to the glass –

I jump back, my heart racing.

He unlocks the door.

'You can talk inside,' he says. 'I'll wait over here till you're done.'

He opens the door for me and I lean down inside, swallowing my heart –

'Mrs Hall?'

The woman nods, her teeth biting into her lower lip, a hand pulling at the skin of her neck.

I push forward the front seat and get in beside her, shutting the door.

'Lock the door please,' she whispers.

I press it down and wait –

She sits here in the dark of the back seat beside me, underneath the arches, rubbing her hands round her neck and up and down her shins –

'They don't believe me,' she says. 'I know that. You won't either.'

'I – '

'No, they'll tell you what they did to me. You probably already know. They'll say that's why she's like that, says the things she does. Then they'll pause and shake their heads and say she'd have been better off dead, the things they did.'

I'm staring ahead, staring between the backs of the front seats.

'Do you know what they did to me?'

'I know a bit – '

'Well, I'll tell you shall I? Get it out of the way.'

'There's really no need, Mrs Hall.'

'But you see there's every need, Mr Hunter.'

She turns to face me in the dark, a hand on my arm:

'It was Sunday 19 June 1977. I'd been to church, evensong. I came home, opened the door, and they grabbed me, dragged me by my hair into the dining room and Eric, sitting there in front of the TV with his throat cut. Then they tied my hands behind my back and left me on the floor at his feet, in his blood, while they went into the kitchen, making sandwiches from our fridge, drinking his beer and my wine, until they came back and decided to have their fun with me, there on the floor in front of Eric. They stripped me and beat me and put it in me, in my vagina, in my bottom, in my mouth, their penises, bottles, chair legs, anything. They urinated in my face, cut chunks of my hair off, forced me to suck them, lick them, kiss them, drink their urine, eat their excrement. Then they took me to the

bathroom and tried to drown me, leaving me unconscious on
the floor for my son to find.'

Silence, darkest silence –

'A robbery, revenge; that's what they said it was, the police.'

She looks at me and I nod: 'The same gang who'd been
responsible for a number of post office robberies and murders,
that's what I heard.'

She's smiling: 'The *Nigger* Gang?'

'They weren't black?'

'Oh, they were black all right, Mr Hunter. As the ace of
spades.'

'Well, I – '

'You don't see my point, do you?'

I turn to face her again: 'It's not that, Mrs Hall. Not that at
all. I just want to say I'm sorry, but it doesn't seem enough. But
I am; I'm really sorry this happened to you.'

She swallows and takes my hand in hers: 'Mr Hunter, before
he was murdered, Eric was suspended. He kept talking about
you, how you were going to be coming over, that he'd done
some bad things and you'd find out and he'd be finished.'

I've got my eyes closed, wanting her to stop.

'And then you never came and he ended up dead and I – '

Summer Seventy Seven –

A10 on a roll:

The Porn Squad, the Dirty Squad –

Drury, Moody & Virago:

*'The architects of this conspiracy of corruption; monumentally evil
men who lived among the sewerage of society.'*

*West Yorkshire next, Bradford Vice, then someone called the dogs
off –*

Eric Hall dead.

'He hated you, Mr Hunter. They all do. But they hate you
because they know you find things out, find them out, that
you're a good man. Even Eric, he called you Saint – '

'Saint?'

'Saint Cunt.'

I smile, but then it's gone and I'm back there:

Summer Seventy Seven –

The last miscarriage.

Baby dead.

I look up –

She says: 'So I think you can help me.'

'How?'

'Eric knew Janice Ryan. Knew her very well. When she turned up under that sofa, he was a suspect and so was another policeman: a Detective Sergeant Fraser at Millgarth. You remember him?'

'Killed himself on the Moors?'

'Yes he did; two days before Eric was murdered. Did you know he'd been involved in the Ripper Hunt?'

'No but, to be honest, today was only our third day.'

'Well, Eric was sure this Sergeant Fraser had killed Ryan. She was pregnant with his child and, as I say, they had him in – '

'Who?'

'This man Fraser. They had him in for it, but then another letter came, supposed to be from Ripper, and that was that. He was out, scot-free, and she was Number 6.'

'And you don't believe she was killed by the Ripper?'

'No.'

'You think Fraser killed her?'

'Or someone else.'

'Someone else?'

'Well, Eric didn't keep his mouth shut did he? He said it was Fraser, especially after the bloke topped himself. That Saturday, the day before, he kept on and on about it. Calling people up, the papers. That journalist Jack Whitehead, he'd been up at the house that same week. Eric was calling anybody, anybody who'd listen. So someone put them onto Eric. To shut him up.'

'Someone put this gang onto Eric? Because he thought Fraser killed Janice Ryan?'

'Because he knew it wasn't the Ripper.'

I'm staring between the seats, the sound of the clock filling the car, watching the lights at the other end of the arches.

'You said you had proof?'

She is nodding: 'Eric wrote a lot of stuff down. He kept copies, tapes. He knew he'd need them someday.'

'Who have you told?'

'Me? Anyone who'd listen.'

'What about the copies, the tapes? You told anyone about them?'

'George Oldman.'

'What did he say?'

'He said I should turn everything over to the man in charge of the investigation into Eric's death.'

'Who was?'

'*Is*, Mr Hunter. It's still open. No-one's been arrested.'

'I'm sorry. Who is – '

'Maurice Jobson.'

The Owl.

'And did you?'

'What?'

'Give him Eric's notes?'

'Yes.'

'When?'

'When it happened; three years ago.'

'And what did Maurice Jobson say?'

'Said he'd get back to me.'

'And did he?'

'What do you think?'

'So you've no idea what he did with Eric's stuff?'

'No.'

'So he might have handed it all over to George Oldman? To the Ripper Squad?'

'He might have, yes. And you might sprout wings and fly home.'

I smile: 'So I take it no-one's ever contacted you about the stuff since?'

'No.'

'Can you remember what was in these notes?'

'Mr Hunter, I made copies.'

'Who knows that?'

'Only you now.'

I nod outside: 'Mr Laws?'

'Only you.'

'I see.'

'He did bad things, Eric. I know that. He was no saint – '

'Not like me.'

'No, not like you. But he didn't deserve what happened to him, not that.'
Not like me –
Saint Cunt.

I take the lift up to my room –
It's stifling, the radiator on full.
I open a window on the unpleasant night and her ugly rain, the haunted station and the silence.
I sit on the edge of the bed, hating Leeds, hating Yorkshire.
I shut the window, draw the dusty curtains.
I close my eyes and let the radio eat the silence thinking –
It's always the way, out this way.

In the middle of the night I'm awake again, sweating and afraid –
Hymns on the radio, that dream of TVs and faces with no face, that taste in my mouth –
Awake, the pains in my back, reaching for Joan, fighting back the tears, reaching for someone –
No-one there.

transmission october nineteen seventy six white abbey bradford ka su peng found in a telephone box by police with two holes in her head in need of fifty eight stitches from a black and crinkly bearded man who picked her up outside the perseverance on lumb lane in my dark car with my tired eyes and crinkly beard we drove to the playing fields and e said how much and she said a fiver and e said ok but you must get out of the car and take off your clothes and lie on the grass and she did not want to e could see it in her eyes where snowflakes were dancing but she said e have to urinate and she was squatting down like a real lady urinating in the grass when e dropped my hammer she said e hope that was not a knife and e said no it was my wallet just strip and she had almost finished her urinating that was when e hit her on the head with the hammer and e hit her on the head with the hammer again and she lay in the grass with her hand to her head the hand all covered in blood lay on the grass and e just stood and watched her looking at her hand the hand all covered in blood the snowflakes dancing and e masturbated and then e threw the tissues at her and put a fiver in her bloody hand and said please do not call the police or e will come and kill you again next time snowflakes are dancing and he stood there looking down at me moving his hand up and down the snowflakes dancing and he said please do not call the police or e will have to kill you and he put a five pound note in my hands and he went away and e managed to half walk half crawl to the telephone box and call an ambulance and they came and took me away and put fifty eight stitches in my head and back and e was in hospital for seven weeks and they said you are lucky to be alive but all e could remember was dialing nine nine nine lying on the floor of the telephone box waiting the snowflakes dancing and a man in a dark car kept driving past and he seemed to be staring and looking for me and it was the man who hurt me you are lucky to be alive they told me but psychic phenomena activated by epileptic discharge arising in the temporal lobe may occur as complex visual or auditory or combined auditory visual halluci-nations or illusions or memory flashbacks erroneous interpretations of the present in terms of the past as an inappropriate feeling of either familiarity or strangeness déjà vu jamais vu phenomena or as emotions commonly fear these phenomena are called experiential as they assume a vivid immediacy for the effected patient which they liken to actual events yet the patients are also aware that these phenomena occur incongruously and out of context as if they were superimposed upon the ongoing stream of consciousness with the exception of fear which is often interpreted as fear of impending events or attack or snowflakes dancing but you are lucky to be alive lucky to be alive to be alive but e am not now for e live in the place where the leaves are black and the branches are twisted and entangled and bloom poisoned thorns and around me echo wails of grief that over and over cry you are lucky to be alive lucky to be alive to be alive but cut this wood and the blood turns dark around the wound and from the splintered trunk pours a mixture of words and blood so eat my leaves in this mournful forest where my body torn away from itself hangs forever among the thorns of my own alien shade my home a hanging place where my many wounds breathe grieving sermons in blood and the mutilations that have separated me from all my leaves gather them round the foot of this sad bush the snowflakes dancing alive in the grass with a fiver in my bloody hand transmission three received

Chapter 6

Leeds –
  Millgarth:
  The canteen –
  Under the hum of the lights, the machines and their numbers: two, one, four, six, eight –
  Tuesday 16 December 1980:
  Almost eight, eight, eight, eight, eight, eight, eight, eight:
  I wait until Murphy's finished eating his breakfast and then say: 'Something else came up last night.'
  He looks up from his dirty plate, a mouthful of toast.
  I say: 'Go for walk?'
  Murphy raises his eyebrows slightly, shrugs, and then follows me down the stairs and out into the Market –
  It's gloomy but dry, no sun, only thick grey sheets of cloud.
  We walk up George Street until we find a small café.
  A couple of sweet teas in front of us, Murphy sits waiting –
  I say: 'You remember we were talking about Eric Hall?'
  He nods.
  'His widow came to the hotel last night.'
  'You're joking?'
  I shake my head: 'With a priest.'
  'What did she want?'
  'Reckons Eric was up to his neck in the Ripper.'
  'Yeah so? Bradford Vice wasn't he? Bound to be.'
  'Yeah, but above and beyond the call of duty.'
  'Ah, fuck.'
  'He was involved somehow with Janice Ryan.'
  'Fucking never-ending this shit,' he sighs: 'Go on.'
  'Says her Eric was even a suspect at one point.'
  'I didn't know that.'
  'So was another copper, one from Millgarth; the one that killed himself?'
  'Bob Fraser?'
  'Yep.'
  Murphy lights a cigarette: 'Load of old bollocks though, yeah?'

I nod: 'Perhaps.'

'And that was it? That was all she said?'

'She spelt it out; says that Eric Hall was killed because he knew it wasn't the Ripper who did Ryan.'

Murphy's smiling: 'I might agree with her that there's a fair chance the Ripper didn't do Ryan, but she can piss right off about Eric. He was as bent as a two-bob fucking note. We were bleeding going to nick him.'

'Yep,' I say, nodding.

Murphy leans forward: 'I thought he was supposed to be into something with a gang of blacks who were knocking off post offices. Remember that?'

I keep nodding.

'It went belly up, so they took it out on Eric. And his wife. That's what we heard, yeah?'

'Yeah.'

'I feel sorry for her, the poor cow. But I still reckon Eric brought it all on himself.'

'And her.'

'And her.'

'Maurice Jobson was in charge; *is* in charge of it.'

'They never got anyone then?'

'Doesn't that strike you as odd?'

'What? That Yorkshire never got anyone? Get away, these blokes haven't nicked anyone since Michael bloody Myshkin.'

'No, no – odd Maurice heading up the investigation?'

'Why?'

'Well he's what? Wakefield?'

'Yeah.'

'And where was Eric Hall done?'

'His house?'

'Yeah, which is Denholme. Bradford.'

'But Eric was out of Jacob's Well. They're hardly going to hand it over to his own mob are they?'

I shrug: 'Suppose not. But why Maurice?'

'Fuck knows and, to be honest, who the fuck cares.'

'Something does bother me, John – but I can't put my finger on it.'

'I can: the same old Yorkshire horse-shit we get every time we come over here,' he yawns. 'But if you want me to add this to the list, after your mate Tricky Dicky Dawson, then I'll ask around.'

I can't tell if he's pissed off with me, or trying to piss me off –

I push away the cold tea: 'She said Eric had notes, copies of stuff, some tapes. She gave them to Maurice Jobson, but never heard anything back. She reckons they prove that the Ripper didn't kill Ryan, and back up a lot of other stuff too.'

Murphy upright, interested: 'Yeah?'

'Yeah. I was thinking, you're doing Janice Ryan right?'

'Yeah.'

'Eric Hall's name is bound to be in there somewhere, bound to come up. And Bob Fraser.'

He's nodding.

'So why don't you ask Craven to let you see the file on Eric and the one on Fraser? See if Eric's tapes and stuff is in there.'

'What stuff?'

'Eric's notes. Anything?'

'Right. And if it's not?'

'She's got copies.'

'Yeah, suppose so,' he says, staring away over my shoulder and out the window.

'You OK?'

'Ah, you know,' he says, standing up. 'It's fucking Liz McQueen next, isn't it?'

The room upstairs –

Smaller and darker than ever –

Another call for the dead, reverse charges:

I say: 'Elizabeth McQueen?'

The Spaghetti Lady –

'This is me,' says Murphy. 'And I'll keep it brief.'

The room is hushed, Craven a notepad out for the first time, waiting for John to begin:

'On Monday 28 November 1977, the naked body of a woman was found in Southern Cemetery, Manchester. She was later identified as Elizabeth McQueen, born on October 31 1946 in Edinburgh. McQueen was married with two children and had two cautions for soliciting. Death had resulted from brain damage caused by several blows to the head from either a hammer or an axe. The lower body had a number of lacerations, which had been inflicted after death by a sharp instrument. An attempt had also been made to sever her head. No weapons have ever been recovered.

'McQueen had been last seen on Saturday 19 November 1977 when she'd left her home in Kippax Street, Rusholme. It has always been the belief that she met her death shortly afterwards.

'When she left her home she was carrying a handbag which was initially not recovered. A workman found the bag on December 5. Hidden in the lining of the bag was a brand new five-pound note.

'I was in charge of this Inquiry.'

Murphy pauses, stops dead, then says: 'And I fucked it up.'

Silence –

It's always the way –

'As I say, our initial search of the crime scene failed to recover the missing handbag. We lost time and we never got it back.'

Another pause, another stop, another silence –

'Before the bag turned up, I'd come over to Wakefield and met with George Oldman. We'd decided that while there were similarities, there were also several dissimilarities.'

On the dark stair, we miss our step –

I'm staring down at George's press release before me:

'*We have no reason to believe at this stage that there is any connection between the murder in Manchester and the ones I am investigating.*'

'Then we found the bag and the fiver, and the rest you know.'

Another release, John's:

'*We have a line of enquiry which is directly connected with the murder of a woman in Manchester and we are following that line of enquiry in the West Yorkshire Metropolitan Police area. There is a team of detectives from Greater Manchester who are working with detectives from West Yorkshire. We will be visiting factories in the Bingley, Shipley and Bradford areas and are interviewing all male employees. As to any links with the unsolved murders in West Yorkshire, it is far too early to draw any conclusion and Mr Oldman and myself are keeping an open mind.*'

Murphy staring at the tabletop, silent –

An open mind –

I say: 'Any questions?'

Silence –

'Break then.'

On the bright stair, John Murphy his head in his hands –
I put a hand on his shoulder –
He looks up, eyes red.
I say: 'I'm going to head over to Wakefield for the press conference; try and get a word with Maurice as well.'
He nods.
'You OK to hold the fort here?'
He nods again.
'I reckon this is a good place to pause, take stock. Also we could do with a recap on the ones that got away: Jobson, Bird, Peng, Clark, and Kelly, yeah?'
'Right.'
I look at my watch:
Eleven –
I say: 'I'll meet you back at the Griffin about sixish?'
'Fine.'
I stand up.
He looks back down at the stair again.
'John?' I say.
He looks up.
'You're too hard on yourself.'
'No, I'm not,' he says. 'That's just it.'

The Road to Wakey Fear –
Rain, rain, and a bucket load of pain:
The Four Horsemen riding on the radio waves, the Ripper laughing at their heels, whip in hand:
2,133,000 record jobless, Helen Smith, the Yorkshire Ripper; all hostages alive and well.
Abba and the football, winter:
The wet lanes, the dark tires, the wet trees, the dark skies, and here she comes again, here she comes again, here she comes again, here she comes again, banging on my head with a piece of rock –
The Wakey turning, braking hard:
Never let her slip away –
And then it was Nineteen Seventy Five again, war across the UK:
Wood Street –

Wakefield, January 1975:
Me and Clarkie sat across from Maurice Jobson –
Detective Chief Superintendent Maurice Jobson, legend:
The Owl.
The Strafford, always the bloody Strafford.
Four dead:
Derek Box.
Paul Booker.
William 'Billy' Bell.
And the barmaid, Grace Morrison.
Box, Bell, and Morrison: D.O.A. Christmas Eve 1974.
Booker never going to make it, dead on Christmas Day.
Craven and Douglas: 'hero cops on the mend' with a visit and a handshake from the Home Secretary.
January 1975 –
Maurice Jobson, legend, said: 'Some bloody Christmas that was, eh?'
'Anything new?'
'No.'
'What about Sergeant Craven and PC Douglas?'
'Doing OK, like the papers say.'
'Anything more from them?'
'No. Dougie still can't remember a thing. Bob, nothing new.'
'But he's . . .'
'The ranting's stopped, aye.'
I opened up my notebook and said: 'So there's not a lot more than shots fired at the Strafford, they respond, up the stairs, bodies, smoke, four blokes in hoods with shotguns, more shots, beaten, left for dead. That's it?'
'That's your lot,' nodded Maurice.
'I'd still like to speak to them.'
Maurice all smiles: 'And you will, Pete. You will.'
But I didn't.
Two hours later the call from home –
On the dark stair, we miss our step –
There are corridors and passages, some lit and some not, there were doors and there were locks, some will open, some would not.
And that was that, until now –
1980 –
On the dark stair:

I knock twice.

'Pete,' he says, on his feet, hand out.

'This a bad time?'

'Not at all. Good to see you, Pete.'

'Thank you,' I say and sit down across from Maurice Jobson –
Detective Chief Superintendent Maurice Jobson, legend:
The Owl.

'You're looking well,' he says.

'Really? Thank you,' I smile. 'You know why I'm here?'

'The short straw?'

I laugh: 'You could say that.'

'So how's it going?'

'Slowly,' I say.

Maurice nods, a sympathetic smile: 'That's war for you.'

I say: 'Anyway, I'd like to go over the initial investigations
with you; the ones you were in charge of?'

'Right.'

'And I've also got a couple of questions about Clare Strachan
and Janice Ryan as well.'

A nod.

'Is that OK?'

'Fire away, Pete. Fire away.'

'All right, you headed up Theresa Campbell and Joan
Richards; so I was wondering, aside from the stuff that's in the
files, all the documented stuff, if there was anything you wanted
to add, anything that you felt needed emphasising, points that
need raising, anything at all basically.'

Maurice Jobson leans forward in his chair and smiles: 'What
you want to know is why they took me off them, yeah?'

'Crossed my mind, yep.'

'Well, I'll tell you shall I? The minute I clapped eyes on the
body of Theresa Campbell, I knew that the man who killed her
would kill again and continue to kill until we stopped him. He's
got the urge Pete, and that kind of urge doesn't go away. Nine
months later, less than two miles from where I'd stood and
looked down at Theresa Campbell, I stood in the dirty snow of
a dismal alley and looked down at what he'd left of Joan
Richards. He'd stabbed her fifty-two times, Pete. Fifty-two
bloody times. I told the Brass, told George, the lads, the press –
anyone who'd bloody listen, told them all that he'd kill and kill

again and keep on killing. But Theresa and Joan, they were slags Pete. Whores, as they say over here. And no-one mourns a whore, except her kids, her husband, her mates, and the bloody coppers that have to look at her dead fucking body in the snow. So no-one was right bothered, except me and my lads, but then we got a stroke of luck. A little stroke Pete, and that's all it takes right?'

I nod.

'Another whore comes forward and says she saw Joan's last customer, saw his face and saw his motor.'

Maurice leans back in his chair, eyes closed, a mantra:

'Thirty years old, short and fat, mouse-coloured hair, full beard with sideburns, round nose and hooded eyes. His left hand was deformed, with a scar as if it had been burned and which extended from the knuckles on the back of the hand up the wrist. He was also wearing a plain gold, square-topped ring on the third finger of his left hand and also a plain gold ring on the second finger of the same hand. He was wearing a dark blue working jacket over dark blue overall-type trousers and black boots or Wellingtons with a thick sole pattern. His clothing was covered in dust. He was driving a dark green Land Rover with a hard top, which was darker than the rest of the body. The passenger door was patched up with silver or grey paint. There was a small aerial on the front nearside wing near the windscreen.'

Maurice pauses, opens his eyes and leans forward, keen:

'When we released this information, other girls came to us and said they also recognised this bloke as a regular punter, thought he was Irish, maybe called Sean. We also got tire marks to match the Land Rover near where we found Joan. A little stroke Pete, and this was the way we went.'

Maurice pauses again for a moment, staring at me.

'Do you think we were wrong, Pete?'

I shrug, unsure what to tell him.

'Anyway, that was the way we went,' he sighs. 'Mind, not that anyone really gave a toss. Still, didn't stop us and we just kept on going, wading through the cars and the tires, knowing we'd come to him, knowing we'd find him. But then it gets to end of 76 and he's not killed again has he, so they start to wind us down, send me back over here and that was that. Six months later Marie Watts comes along, George takes it himself, a couple of weeks later the letters start and we get the Johnson lassie and so then, by time you get to the bloody tape, that really was fucking that.'

'And you think that was a mistake? The tape?'

'Pete,' he says. 'I'm saying nowt, except you wouldn't catch me panting along behind that banner.'

I ask him: 'What about Clare Strachan? You think . . .'

'Same. All tied up with them bloody letters and that fucking tape.'

'75, you sent Bob Craven and John Rudkin over, yeah?'

'Yeah. Be about first thing Bob did when he got back.'

'And, back then, neither them nor you made a link with Theresa Campbell?'

'There was none to make.'

'And now?'

Palms out, open, he says: 'Who can say, Pete? Who can say?'

I say nothing, the pair of us just sat there, just sat there in the silence –

After a bit I say: 'Whatever happened to John Rudkin?'

Maurice Jobson rolls his eyes: 'Not a happy chapter for us, any of us.'

I sit there, more silence, waiting –

He says: 'You were going to ask me about Janice Ryan, weren't you?'

I nod.

'Well,' he says. 'I'll save you some bother. Ryan was involved with two coppers; Eric Hall, who I believe you were all set to come and have a pop at?'

'Yep.'

'Well you probably know then that he was, apparently, pimping Janice Ryan. Janice Ryan who, it turns out, was also fucking one of our lads, Bob Fraser. Heard of him?'

'Yep.'

'Thought you might have. Well, when Ryan turned up dead under a sofa in Bradford, it turned out she was pregnant and Bob Fraser was the father.'

I keep it shut now, letting him go on –

'This is the same Bob Fraser who was married to Louise Molloy. Heard that name?'

'No.'

'Bill Molloy?'

I sit forward: 'Badger Bill?'

Detective Chief Superintendent Maurice Jobson, one half of that same legend, nods –

The Badger and the Owl, boyhood heroes from an Eagle world, a Dan Dare world, a different world –

I say: 'He was your partner wasn't he?'

'Yes. And Bob Fraser was married to his daughter, Louise.'

'Bloody hell,' I say.

'It gets worse, Pete. Much worse.'

I'm nodding, just nodding, my mind turning, spinning.

He says: 'When we found out the Ryan slag had been pregnant, we had Hall and Fraser straight in, Hall saying Fraser had done her, Fraser saying it was Hall, a right bloody mess – George doing all he could to keep it out of papers. Middle of all this, Bill dies; been on the cards, cancer. Next news, a letter turns up from bloody Ripper saying it was him, Ripper who did Ryan, so that was that again. We let Fraser go, but then Fraser only goes and finds out that his Louise has also been having an affair with John fucking Rudkin, his senior officer, and that Rudkin is father of his lad. Tips Fraser over edge this does, gasses himself up on Moors, as you know.'

I nod.

'Couple of days later, Eric Hall gets his throat cut and his wife raped.'

'And you got that?'

'For my sins, aye. Didn't want Bradford on it, didn't want you either,' he laughs. 'I was off Ripper, so it was me. Like I had nowt better to do.'

'Never got anyone?'

'No, and we never will.'

'But?'

'But he was up to his fucking neck in shit, was their Eric. I mean, you were going to do him anyway?'

I nod again.

'Some reckon he was running a string of whores and maybe, just maybe, he was into it with a gang of nig-nogs who were knocking over sub post-offices. You remember that?'

Nodding again, saying: 'You get anywhere with that?'

'You heard of the Spencer Boys?'

'No.'

'Spend time over here and you will. Five of them: two brothers, Steve and Clive Barton, a Kenny somethingorother, a Keith Lee and a Joseph Rose. Thinking was that it were them that did the post offices, but Robbery couldn't pin it on them. Anyway, pain in the fucking arse it was, – but what goes around comes around, as they say: Clive got banged up for GBH or something, Kenny and Keith got fitted up by Drug Squad, all in Armley doing big stretches. No parole. Steve did a runner and then the burned body of a nigger turned up on Hunslet Carr and we've always reckoned that was Joe Rose, who no-one's seen hide nor hair of since 77.'

'And you think they did Eric Hall?'

'Don't think it Pete, I know it.'

'How?'

'Two schools of thought here, but what we know for sure is Eric and these boys had a mutual acquaintance in Janice Ryan. Either Eric was in with them from the start or he wasn't and Ryan told him about the Spencer Boys and their hobby and then Eric tried to blackmail them. Either way, they had to shut him up.'

'Which way you lean?'

'Me? The third way; I like to think best of people Pete, so I'd like to think he was building a case or something and they found out.'

I smile: 'That's what his wife says.'

'You've spoken to her?'

'She came to see me. Said she had information about Janice Ryan. Said Eric was killed because he knew too much, that he had files and stuff, that she gave them to you.'

'Poor cow,' he says, shaking his head. 'The things they did to her. She gave me them files but, between you and me, it's just his bloody ramblings. But like I say, it's a better way to remember a copper.'

I nod and we fall back into the silence, rain outside the window, the room cold –

Then I cough and ask: 'What's this journalist Jack Whitehead got to do with all this?'

'Jack? Well, your Widow Hall claims Jack found out Eric was connected to Janice Ryan and tried to blackmail him.'

'You're joking?'

'No. Tell you Pete, 1977 was one hell of a summer, as they say.'

'Did you question him?'

'Jack? Hardly.'

'What you mean?'

'Well, our Jack's been a bit quiet lately.'

'What? He's dead?'

'Good as. He's in Stanley Royd, isn't he?'

'Stanley Royd?'

'The Bin, Loony Bin, Nut House, Funny Farm? Just up road from here.'

'What happened to him?'

'Only went and tried to hammer a twelve inch bloody nail into his own fucking head, didn't he?'

Say again: 'You're joking?'

'Wish I were Pete, wish I bloody were.'

'Bloody hell.'

Maurice Jobson looks at his watch and says: 'You're going to be late.'

I look at my watch:

Shit, the press conference –

I stand up, shaking hands with him, saying: 'Thank you, Maurice.'

'Anytime, Pete. Anytime.'

Then at the door: 'Christ, Maurice, I almost forgot . . .'

'What?'

'You never said . . .'

'Never said what?'

'What happened to Rudkin, he in the Bin too?'

'As good as,' he smiles. 'Emigrated to Australia.'

'With the Badger's daughter?'

'And the little lad,' he says and hands me a photo from his wallet:

A woman and a boy on a beach with a ball –

'You got kids haven't you?' says Maurice Jobson.

Summer Seventy Seven –

The last miscarriage –

The baby dead –
One hell of a summer –
One hell:
'No,' I say. 'No, I haven't.'

In dark winter the hounds of hate, the steam upon their tongues and
backs, they await –
Out of breath, I take my place at another showdown:
The Training College gymnasium –
'No-one,' Temporary Assistant Chief Constable Peter Noble
is saying, 'no-one wants to stop this man more than me and my
men.'
Ropes dangling from ceilings, hanging –
'Furthermore, all attacks in the last fourteen months are
being, as we speak, rechecked.'
As we speak –
'Have you gained any further insights into the mind of the
Ripper?'
'I would not have thought he is very clever. He has had a
great deal of luck on his side. I am sure if the public are vigilant
and report things early, probably the next time his luck may run
out.'
The next time –
'You're saying that he's not very clever, but your predecessor,
Assistant Chief Constable Oldman, he is on record as saying he
thought the Ripper was very intelligent, crafty even, and that it
would be a mistake to underestimate his intelligence.'
'I am not underestimating him, I'm merely saying that he
has had a lot of luck.'
'Is it not true to say that to some extent the Police have gifted
him certain pieces of luck; I'm thinking of the Manchester Fiver,
of the mess in reporting Laureen Bell's handbag and so on?'
'I would dispute that and the insinuation, but these are obviously matters for due review.'
'Did Mrs Bell's appeal generate any fresh leads?'
'It was a very brave thing to do and we got a lot of genuine
responses, but some are sheer nonsense and they do slow . . .'
'Would Mr Noble care to comment on *The Ripper is a Coward*
posters?'
'I have no comment to make other than to repeat that me

and my men share the public's frustration and, once again, to assure members of the public and particularly the women out there that we are doing all we can to catch this man.'

The women out there –

'What about the reward of £100,000 offered by . . .'

'I have nothing to add to what the Chief Constable said earlier.'

'What about reports that morale in the West Yorkshire force is . . .'

'Again, the Chief Constable has already answered that question.'

'Have you got any feelings about the proposed film?'

'Again, I have nothing to say except to add that I personally share the distaste voiced by some members of the community and press about such an idea.'

Share the distaste –

And then they turn to me:

'Would Mr Hunter care to comment on the progress of the so-called *brains trust* review?'

'It's early days yet and, as you know, we are looking at the whole inquiry and when the entire review is complete I will be more than happy to answer any questions you might have.'

Mark Gilman from the *Manchester Evening News*: 'Would the Assistant Chief Constable care to comment on the arrest this morning of the Manchester businessman Richard Dawson?'

On the dark stair, we miss our step.

No beer and sandwiches today –

Me at a payphone in the corner: 'Joan? It's me. I've just heard they've arrested Richard. You heard anything, heard from Linda or anyone?'

'No, nothing. When did they arrest him?'

'This morning.'

'Who told you?'

'Mark Gilman from the *Evening News*?'

'No, there's been nothing here, nothing on the radio.'

'There will be. I'll call again later.'

'Bye-bye.'

'Bye.'

*

The Stanley Royd Mental Hospital is up behind the Training College, five minutes down the road from Pinderfields Hospital –

Just off Memory bloody Lane:

Pinderfields Hospital, January 1975 –

The only time I'd ever met Jack Whitehead:

I was sitting in the waiting room outside intensive care, Clarkie out getting fish and chips, still waiting to speak to Craven and Douglas, staring at a Yorkshire Post, *thinking about Joan, when there was a hand on my shoulder.*

'Mr Hunter?'

'Yep?' I said, looking up from the paper.

'Whitehead, Jack Whitehead from the Evening Post. *Have a word?'*

'What about?'

'Well,' said the thin-faced man in the Macintosh, sitting down beside me, 'just have a chat about the shooting, the lads.'

'The lads?'

'Bob and Dougie.'

'You know them, Mr Whitehead?'

'Know them? Course I bloody do. Local heroes they are. They're the lads that nicked Michael Myshkin. You heard of him, I take it?'

I nodded.

'George told me you're over here helping out.'

'That's one way of putting it I suppose.'

Jack Whitehead touched my arm and said: 'And what would be another?'

And then I could hear my name over the tannoy: 'Mr Peter Hunter. Telephone for a Mr Peter Hunter.'

And Jack Whitehead, he let go of my arm and winked: 'Let's hope it's good news.'

But it wasn't:

It was Joan and another dead baby –

Another dead dream.

Five years on, five minutes down the road; no respite:

Stanley Royd, a huge old house squatting back from the road amongst the bare trees and empty nests, its modern wings extending out into the shadows.

Burned-black stone and the picked-grey bone of an Auschwitz, a Belsen –

I drive through the gateway and up the long, tree-lined drive.

Were they ash or were they oak?

I park on the gravel and walk through the drizzle up a couple of steps and open the front door.

A wave of warmth and the smell of sickness hits me, the smell of faeces.

I show my warrant card at reception and ask to see Jack Whitehead.

The woman in white behind the desk picks up the black telephone.

I turn around to wait, watching a television hidden in the corner amongst the second-hand furniture, the large wardrobes, the dressers and the chairs, the heavy carpets and the curtains.

I glance at my watch:

Three.

Thin skin and bones shuffle past in their striped pyjamas and their spotted nightgowns, the whisper of their slippers and their vespers, the scratchings and the mumblings of the day room.

'Mr Hunter? Leonard will take you up,' says the woman in white.

A big skinhead in blue denim overalls leads me up the stairs and down corridor walls painted half green and half cream, across the landing and out of the main building, over a cold walkway and into one of the more recent extensions, locking and unlocking doors as we go.

I say: 'How long has he been here?'

'Jack? Best part of three years.'

'And yourself?'

'Worst part of five,' smiles Leonard, proud of his progress.

'You've known him a while then?'

The orderly nods.

'True they found him with a nail in his head?'

'That's what they say.'

'You didn't see it though?'

'He was next door for months.'

'Pinderfields?'

The orderly nods again.

'Get many visitors does he?'

'A vicar and some of your lot. Not that there's much point.'

'Doesn't say much I heard.'

'Oh no, he talks all right. Not that he makes any sense.'

'He's drugged up, I take it?'

The orderly nods one last time and turns another key, opening the door onto a long corridor of locked cells –

'This the secure wing, is it?' I ask.

'Yes.'

'And this is where you keep Jack?'

'He's got his own room,' says the orderly, pointing at the last door.

He unlocks the door and opens it.

'I'll wait outside,' he volunteers.

'You sure that's all right?'

'He's wearing restraints, but they're to protect him not you.'

'Protect him?'

'From himself.'

'Thank you,' I say and step inside, closing the door behind me –

The room is darker and warmer than the corridor, bare but for a bog and his bed, a single chair and a patch of light from a high window.

I sit down next to the metal bed with the high barred sides.

Jack Whitehead is lying on his back in a pair of grey striped pyjamas, his hands chained to the sides of the cot, his eyes open and fixed on the light above, his face bleak and unshaven except for his scalp back in the shadows.

'Mr Whitehead,' I begin. 'My name is Peter Hunter. I'm a policeman from Manchester. You probably won't remember, but we met a long time ago.'

'I remember,' he says, his voice dry and cracked. 'Hexed, I remember everything.'

The toilet is dripping –

'I'd like to ask you some questions if I might; questions about some things that happened in 1977. About a policeman called Eric Hall?'

Dripping, dripping –

Jack Whitehead sighs, his eyes watering, a tear slipping down towards his ear.

'I'm sorry,' I say, softly.

'Don't be,' he says. 'You haven't done anything.'

'Is . . .'

Dripping, dripping, dripping –

'Go on. Don't be afraid.'

'I'm not afraid, Mr Whitehead.'

Dripping, dripping, dripping, dripping –

'Really?'

'Yes, really.'

Dripping, dripping, dripping, dripping, dripping –

With a deep breath, I ask: 'Is it true that you met Eric Hall? True that you knew him?'

'I know Eric, yes.'

'You know he's dead?'

Jack Whitehead blinks, his damp eyes still fixed upon the ceiling –

Dripping –

'Why did you meet him?'

'Information,' says Jack Whitehead, slowly.

'About what?'

'About the dead.'

'The dead?'

Dripping, dripping –

'You're surprised?' he smiles. 'What did you think it'd be about? The living?'

'Mr Whitehead?' I say, gripping the sides of my chair. 'Did you try and blackmail Eric Hall?'

Dripping, dripping, dripping –

'Yes, I did.'

'How?'

Dripping, dripping, dripping, dripping –

'Information.'

'You had information on him or you wanted information from him? Which was it?'

Dripping, dripping, dripping, dripping, dripping –

'Two pieces of a broken heart; but do they fit? That's the question, isn't it?'

'Mr Whitehead?' I say, leaning forward. 'Was this about Janice Ryan?'

Suddenly, a blink and he's changed:

In gargoyle pose he's crouched upright on his feet, hands still chained and clipped to the sides of the bed, his face turned up to where the sky would be –

I stand, knocking over the chair –

'Two doors, always open. Who makes the witches? Who casts the spells? They send me shapes, they show me ways, but they never close the doors. Futures and pasts, futures past, rats teeth into my belly both. The dead not dead, lorry loads of meat rotting in containers, the salt lost. Big black dogs, choking at said containers, the salt gone. The dead not dead, voices prophesizing war, endless war. Why won't you let them sleep? Why won't you let them be? They send me shapes, they show me ways, but they never close the door. Never tonnes undone, loose again, loose again, the dead not dead.'

Silent, his head back, eyes white –

I step towards him and then straight back as he spits and foams through teeth gritted and bleeding:

'Hunter! Hunter! Jbd ias hta edy rot caf sti rip sll iwl lik!'

'What?'

'Hunter! Hunter! Hta edy rot caf sti rip sll iwl lik!'

'What?'

Dripping, dripping, dripping, dripping, dripping, dripping –

Dripping, dripping, dripping, dripping, dripping, dripping –

Dripping, dripping, dripping, dripping, dripping, dripping –

'Hunter! Hunter! Sti rip sll iwl lik!'

'What?'

'Sti rip sll iwl lik Hunter!'

'What are you fucking saying? Tell me!'

Silence, his body empty, his face on his chest –

Dripping –

I step forward from the door and right the chair.

Dripping –

Drawn to his skull, I cannot look away.

Dripping –

Out of the shadows, in the patch from the window, I look down on the top of his scalp and the hole he'd made.

Dripping –

I want to touch, to put a finger in that hole, but I dare not.

Dripping –

Instead, I walk backwards to the door and open it.

I step out into the corridor, looking for Leonard –

I see him coming down the corridor towards me.

I glance back into the room –

Jack Whitehead unbound and upon his knees, gazing to the ceiling in suppliant pose, hands clasped in prayer.

He turns, a torrent of tears upon his cheeks –

Dripping, dripping, dripping, dripping, dripping, dripping –

'Close the door,' he says. 'Please close the door.'

'He's loose,' I shout at the approaching orderly –

'Jesus,' says Leonard, going in to his charge. 'Not again.'

I am standing in a red phonebox somewhere in the dark on the way back into Leeds –

I say: 'Would it be possible to meet?'

'Of course.'

'About seven? In the Griffin?'

'Fine.'

'Thank you,' I say and hang up.

I knock on the door of her hotel room.

Helen Marshall opens the door, hair matted and eyes red again, the top button of her blouse undone.

'Sorry,' I say. 'Where's everyone else?'

'They called it a day.'

'Are you busy? You doing anything now?'

'No.'

'I want you to meet someone. Do you mind?'

'No,' she smiles. 'I don't mind.'

From the high-backed chair, the Reverend Martin Laws rises.

'Reverend Laws, this is Detective Sergeant Helen Marshall.' They shake hands.

'DS Marshall is part of my team,' I say. 'And, to be honest, I'd prefer our conversations from now on to be conducted in the presence of DS Marshall or another member of my team.'

Laws is nodding, smiling: 'I'm not under arrest, am I?'

'No,' I say, without a smile.

We all sit down.

The lounge is empty but for an old woman and a child reading a comic.

'Reverend Laws,' I say. 'Do you mind telling us how you came to meet Mrs Hall and when that would have been?'

'About two years ago. She'd heard of my work.'

'Your work?'

The man leans forward in his chair, his hat on his lap, his bag between his boots, and he says: 'I stop suffering.'

'How had she heard of you?'

'The word gets around, Mr Hunter.'

'So she just rang you up out of the blue?'

'I wouldn't say it was the blue, Mr Hunter. But yes, she just rang me up.'

'And what did she want?'

'What everyone wants.'

'Which is?'

'For the suffering to stop.'

'And that's what you did?'

'I can see you're not a believer Mr Hunter, but that's what I try and do.'

'Stop suffering?'

'Yes.'

'How?' asks Helen Marshall, suddenly.

Martin Laws turns his head slightly and stares at Helen Marshall, silent, just staring –

'How?' she says again, looking down at her own hands.

'I make it go away,' he smiles.

'But how?'

'Magick,' he laughs.

Tired, I say: 'Mr Laws, would you mind calling Mrs Hall and asking when it might be convenient to see her?'

'You wouldn't prefer to do it yourself?'

'I'd like us all to be there.'

Mr Laws stands up and walks over to the telephone on the front desk.

'Are you OK?' I ask DS Marshall.

'I'm sorry, I think I'm just tired.'

'Do you want to go up?'

'No, I'll be OK.'

'Are you sure?'

'Yes,' she snaps.

Mr Laws comes back over.

'Do you want to take my car?'

'We'll follow,' I say.

*

In the car, the drive to Denholme –

In the dark, Helen Marshall beside me.

'You know what happened to her?'

'I hate this place,' she nods, staring out at the black Yorkshire night.

In the car, the drive to Denholme –

In the dark.

We pull up behind the old green Viva in front of a lonely house, its back to the endless night of a golf course.

It's Sunday 19 June 1977 –

'You'd think she would have moved,' says Helen Marshall.

Back from church, evensong –

We walk up the drive, towards Mrs Hall and the Reverend Martin Laws.

I come home, open the door, and they grab me, drag me by hair into the dining room and Eric, sitting there in front of the TV with his throat cut –

She's pulling at the skin around her neck.

'Evening, Mrs Hall,' I say.

'Good evening, Mr Hunter.'

'This is Detective Sergeant Marshall. I hope you don't mind her coming along?'

'Not at all,' says Mrs Hall, shaking her head. 'Please come in.'

Then they tie my hands behind my back and leave me on the floor at his feet, in his blood, while they go into the kitchen, making sandwiches from our fridge, drinking his beer and my wine, until they come back and decide to have their fun with me, there on the floor in front of Eric –

Here in the front room, in front of the TV, we sit down on the big golden sofa, displays of coins and medals in ornate cases.

They strip me and beat me and put it in my vagina, in my bottom, in my mouth, their penises, bottles, chair legs, anything –

Mrs Hall is in the kitchen, making tea, the Reverend Laws watching the road through the bay windows.

They urinate in my face, cut chunks of my hair off, force me to suck them, lick them, kiss them, drink their urine, eat their excrement –

She comes back with a pot of tea and four cups on a tray.

We drink the milky weak brew in silence.

I put down my cup and say: 'Did Eric have a study or anything?'

She stands up: 'It's this way.'

Leaving Helen Marshall with Laws, I follow Mrs Hall out of the front room and into the back of the house.

She opens a door and leads me into a cold room with French windows staring out at the golf course.

Mrs Hall puts on a light, our thin deformed bodies frozen in the cold, cold room, reflected in the black glass –

Among the coins and medals, more coins and medals –

I say: 'I'd like to take a look at Eric's files, if that's OK?'

'Wait here,' she says and leaves me.

I walk over to the windows and strain to see into the night – There is nothing to see.

Mrs Hall comes back with a large cardboard supermarket box and puts it down on the desk.

I ask her: 'These are the copies of all the stuff you gave Maurice Jobson?'

'Yes,' she says. 'Help yourself.'

I open the flaps and pull out envelopes and folders.

'There's quite a bit,' I say. 'I'll need to take it with me?'

She doesn't speak, just looks at the box on the desk.

'You'll get it all back, I promise.'

'I'm not sure I want it back,' she says, quietly.

I close the flaps: 'Thank you.'

'I just hope it helps,' she says, staring at me.

I cough and ask her: 'How did you meet Mr Laws?'

'I was given his name?'

'May I ask who by?'

'Jack Whitehead.'

Then they take me to the bathroom and try to drown me, leaving me unconscious on the floor for my son to find –

'But Jack's in hospital. In Stanley Royd?'

'And where do you think I've been for the last three years, Mr Hunter?'

I close my eyes, saying: 'I'm sorry, I didn't mean to . . .'

'Don't worry,' she smiles and turns off the light.

I pick up the box.

Back in the front room, Helen is still sat on the sofa, the cup balanced on her knees, Laws still watching the road.

'We best be getting back,' I say.

Helen Marshall stands up, her eyes red raw from tears.

'Are you all right, dear?' asks Mrs Hall.

'I'm sorry,' says Helen, looking at me. 'I'm not sleeping well.'

Mrs Hall is shaking her head: 'Isn't that just the worst kind of hell?'

'I'll be OK. Thank you,' says Helen at the door.

'Thank you for the tea,' I say. 'Goodnight Mr Laws.'

'Goodnight,' he replies, not turning from the window.

'I'll be in touch,' I say to them both and follow Helen Marshall back down the drive.

At the car she stops, staring back up at the house, Laws staring back down at her.

I put the box in the boot –

'What did he say to you?'

'Nothing,' she says. 'Nothing at all.'

'Your wife's been calling,' says the man behind the desk at the Griffin.

'Thank you,' I say, taking my key.

'I'm going to go up,' says Helen Marshall.

'Sure you're all right?' I ask.

'Yeah, yeah. I'm fine.'

'Don't fancy a quick drink?'

'Not particularly,' she says, nodding towards the bar –

I look over and see Alec McDonald, Mike Hillman, and some of the Yorkshire lads, all the worse for wear –

'I better go over,' I say.

She nods and says: 'Don't forget to phone your wife.'

'I won't. Goodnight.'

'Goodnight.'

I walk over to the bar just as Bob Craven gets another round in.

'You having one, chief?' he says.

'Go on then,' I say. 'A quick one.'

'Looks like you had one of them already,' says one of the Yorkshire blokes, watching Marshall getting into the lift.

'Steady on,' says Alec McDonald, leaning across the table, drunk. 'That's out of order, that is.'

'Looks fine to me,' laughs Craven.

I take the Scotch from him: 'Thank you, Bob.'

'Mention it,' he smiles.

'Where's John?' I ask Alec.

'Murphy? Fuck knows, sorry.'

'You get much done?'

'Aye,' he slurs. 'Fair bit.'

'Bird, Jobson, that Ka Su Peng girl, Linda Clark,' nods Hillman.

'Kathy Kelly?'

'First thing tomorrow.'

'See we got another roasting,' spits Craven, chucking an *Evening Post* at me:

Clueless –

'Not very nice that, is it,' says Alec McDonald, trying to hit the top of the table.

I put the paper back down on the bar and ask him: 'You heard anything over here about Dawson?'

'Just that they're charging him.'

'Thought he were dead?' says Craven, over my shoulder.

Me: 'Who?'

'John Dawson?'

'John? No, this is Richard.'

'Right, right,' says Craven. 'His brother.'

Fuck –

I say: 'You knew John Dawson?'

'Who fucking didn't.'

Fuck –

'Who fucking didn't,' he says again.

Upstairs in my room, almost midnight, I dial home: 'Joan? It's me.'

'Oh, Peter. Thank god . . .'

'What is it? What's wrong?'

'Come home, please.'

'Why? What's wrong?'

'I've got such a terrible feeling, Peter.'

'What do you mean?'

'An awful feeling that something bad's going to happen.'
'Like what?'
'I don't know Peter, just come home please.'
'I can't, love. You know that.'
Silence –
'Joan?'
'Oh, I don't know what's wrong with me.'
'What is it, love?'
'Just this feeling.'
'When did it start?'
'This afternoon. I'd had a nap and I had this nightmare . . .'
'What happened?'
'I can't really remember. There was a girl in a bath and . . .'
'What?'
'Oh, I don't know.'
'A baby?'
'No. Look, I don't want to talk about it.'
'I'm sorry, love.'
'It's OK.'
I say: 'I'll ring you in the morning, first thing.'
'OK.'
'You go to bed.'
'OK.'
'I love you.'
'Me too. Night-night.'
'Night-night,' and I hang up thinking –

Close my eyes for ten minutes then I'll start on Eric's files, then remembering they're still back in the boot of my car, thinking I'll get them soon, my eyes too tired, my eyes too bloody tired.

Yrotcaf htaed, *in blood above the door.*

The moon was shining through the skylight and I was gazing at her lying in the bath. Thin and pathetic, in a shroud-like garment, lips crooked into a faint and dreadful smile, her hands pressed tightly over her heart. And all around us, people were singing hymns, people with no face, no features, machines. Then she suddenly sat upright, hands still across her heart, and she shrieked with the gulls:

'*Sti rip sll iwl lik Hunter!*'

at six fifteen AM today sunday the twenty ninth of may nineteen seventy seven the body of a woman was found at the rear of sports changing rooms on soldiers field roundhay road near to west avenue leeds with severe head injuries a cut throat and stab wounds to the abdomen description twenty to thirty years five feet seven inches long dark hair medium build wearing a blue and white checked blouse brown cardigan zip up front with yellow two piece cotton suit fawn three quarter length suede coat with fur down the front brown calf length boots she was wearing tights and two pairs of panties one pair of panties had been removed her right leg was out of her tights and the panties that had been taken off had been stuffed down her tights she was struck three times on the head with a ball pein hammer with such severity that a piece of skull penetrated the brain he then stabbed her in the throat and in the abdomen with an equal severity such that her intestines spilled out the three quarter length suede coat was draped over her buttocks and thighs her brown calf length boots were draped neatly over her thighs her handbag was nearby and there was no indication that anything had been stolen from it unlike the previous bodies her brassiere had not been removed tests indicated that she had had sexual intercourse some time in the twenty four hours before her time of death was thought to be around midnight this woman has been living in the leeds area since october nineteen seventy six when she came up from london where it is believed she worked in hotels she was reported missing by her husband from blackpool in november nineteen seventy five love me e walk into the red room the numbers upside down you cannot speak no do not do that there is no need for that we have met before stretching back black nail varnish on your toes the meat no need for that we have met before stretching back black nail varnish on your toes the meat between your teeth e know this face love me the men at upstairs windows without smiles underneath her the dew and the grass this spring day on a sports field in leeds the damp dew and the flattened grass the boots to come and the boots that have been tall trees watching multiple fractures of the skull displaced clothing and mutilation of the lower abdomen and breasts with a knife or screwdriver a clear badge of identity a signature the brown cardigan blue and white checked blouse yellow jacket and skirt did not quite match what is the matter the jogger asked the woman on the ground at the rear of the sports pavilion when they removed my suede coat they saw the massive fracture of my skull from the three blows to my head with the hammer they saw me lying face down with my hands under my stomach and my head turned to the left with my brown hair of which e was always so proud my brown hair washed in my own blood my bra still in position but my skirt had been pulled up and e was wearing tights and two pairs of panties one pair of panties had been removed and my right leg was out of my tights and the panties that had been taken off had been stuffed down my tights for e had been menstruating menstruating for the last time and the coat e had been wearing was draped over my buttocks and legs in such a way as only my feet were showing and when they picked it up they saw my brown calf length boots had been taken off my feet and placed upon my thighs and then they turned me over rolled me over in the grass and they saw e had been stabbed in the neck and throat and had three stab wounds in the stomach all savage downward strokes so severe that my insides were outside the numbers upside down the rooms all red

Chapter 7

In the night, the call –

Clement Smith, Chief Constable: 'I need you back here. Vaughan Industrial Estate, off Pottery Lane.'

'What is it?'

'A bad one.'

'You going to tell me anything more?'

'Roger Hook asked for you. That's all I know.'

'Now?'

'Now.'

'I'll see you there then.'

'See you there.'

Another black drive through another black night –

Over the Moors –

The murder and the lies –

The cries and the whispers –

Of children.

Here always their cries, always their whispers

Always murder and always lies –

Always the Moors –

Always night and always black.

Down through Prestwich, through Cheetham Hill and Collyhurst, to Ardwick and the wrong side of bloody tracks:

The Vaughan Industrial Estate, Ashburys –

Low dark buildings in the cold rain and the blue lights, police the black wraiths against the white light, their cloaks wings about a factory:

DEATH –

All the gods of the North are dead now, moribund –

I park between the vans and the cars, in a crater filled with dead water and a bird, a sparrow.

I turn up the collar of my coat against the rain and stumble –

The young policeman at the gate lifts his hood to check my card and point me towards an open mouth:

DEATH –

A figure walks behind me, dreadful –

In the doorway stand Clement Smith and Roger Hook, white faces staring at the floor, silent eyes raised my way, stung red with the cold and the rain, the tears –

Tongues moving but without words, a cigarette, hands shaking but not shaken –

I walk through them, into:

DEATH –

This is the place, the swans loose –

Heavy workbenches, oil and chains, tools; the stink of machines, oil and chains, tools; the sound of dirty water, oil and chains, tools; dripping, dripping, dripping, dripping, dripping, tools.

High skylights, rain against the pane –

Strapped down upon a workbench, trapped in chains, wrapped in:

DEATH –

Wings nailed to the ash, pornography –

I step towards the bench, closer –

Skinned naked and blistered, closer –

Blooded blackened and beaten, closer –

Skinned and naked, blistered and blooded, blackened and beaten, closer –

Face and hair burnt, twisted towards his left –

In his mouth, a cassette –

Bob Douglas:

DEAD –

All this and heathen too –

To his left, a door ajar, its upper half glazed.

I walk across the wet and bloody concrete floor, walk to the door and with my boot I push it open –

Push and see a muddy bath affixed to the wall, its head towards the light from a skylight, push and see:

DEATH –

On the dark stair, we miss our step –

I step towards the bath, closer –

Into the light from the pane, closer –

Towards her laying there in the bath, closer –

Into the pain from the dark, closer –

A thin and pathetic smile on her face, a black hole in a still heart –

In her hand, a teddy bear –

Karen Douglas:

DEAD –

Never let her slip –

I step backwards, back towards the child's father –

Back towards Smith and Hook in the doorway, towards the hands and the tongues, the cigarettes, the cold and the rain, the tears –

Stepping back from, turning back from, running from:

DEATH –

Always the way.

Two hours later, damp skin and bones sat around the eleventh floor of Manchester Police Headquarters, phones ringing and boots running, this way and that –

Always this way and that.

I count twelve men –

Waiting:

Wednesday 17 December 1980 –

Nine o'clock.

Ten minutes later, another knock at the door –

The cassette in a plastic bag, the science done.

Roger Hook plugs in a tape recorder and Clement Smith takes the cassette from the bag:

'Prints?'

A scientist nods.

'Who?'

The scientist shakes his head: 'They're checking.'

Smith holds it up, turning it in his fingers, the black felt-tip pen scrawled across the clear plastic:

'*All this and Heathen too,*' he reads, looking at me –

'*Ripper Tape,*' I say. 'That was done over a copy of a cassette called *All this and Heaven too* by a singer called Andrew Gold.'

Twelve open mouths and twelve curses: 'Fucking hell fire.'

'This him?' says someone –

'Doesn't make any sense, why . . .'

'A bloke and his kid . . .'

'An ex-copper . . .'

'Poor bastard . . .'

'Unless Douglas fucking knew . . .'

Clement Smith stands up, signalling to Roger Hook: 'Gentlemen, shall we listen to the tape first?'

Twelve men nodding, silent.

Hook presses play:

HISS –

Piano –

Drums –

Bass –

'How can this be love, if it makes us cry?'

STOP.

HISS –

Cries –

Whispers –

Hell:

'How can the world be as sad as it seems?'

STOP.

HISS –

Cries –

Whispers –

More hell:

'How much do you love me?'

STOP.

HISS –

Cries –

Cries –

Cries:

'Sti rip sll iwl lik Hunter!'

STOP.

Silence –

Nothing:

Wednesday 17 December 1980 –

Nine thirty.

Nothing but –

Twelve pale faces, some flabby and some gaunt, twelve faces and twenty-four eyes staring at me –

I stand up –

'Can I speak to you for a moment, sir?' I ask Clement Smith. 'In private.'

He stands and says to Roger Hook: 'My office.'
Hook and I walk towards the door, twenty-four eyes on me.
'And bring that,' says Smith, pointing at the tape recorder.
We follow him down the corridor.
In his office, Hook plugs in the recorder –
'Can we hear it again?' says Hook.
Smith nods –
Hook presses play:
HISS –
Piano –
Drums –
Bass –
'How can this be love, if it makes us cry?'
STOP.
HISS –
Cries –
Whispers –
Hell:
'How can the world be as sad as it seems?'
STOP.
HISS –
Cries –
Whispers –
More hell:
'How much do you love me?'
STOP.
HISS –
Cries –
Cries –
Cries:
'Sti rip sll iwl lik Hunter!'
STOP.
Silence, again silence –
Just the rain black upon the window, running –
The city grey below, swimming –
Drowning.
Roger Hook says: 'What's that last line?'
'That's my name,' I say, looking at the Chief.
Smith swallows, says nothing.

'Those words,' I say. 'Whatever they are, I've heard them before.'

Smith: 'Where?'

'Yesterday I went to see a man called Jack Whitehead. He was a journalist on the *Yorkshire Post*, – until he had some sort of breakdown and hammered a nail into his skull.'

'Fucking hell,' says Hook.

'He's in Stanley Royd Hospital in Wakefield,' I continue. 'Anyway I went to see him because he was involved with Eric Hall. Eric Hall was Bradford Vice and was supposed to be pimping Janice Ryan who, as you know, was Ripper victim number six.'

Smith and Hook are staring at me, blank.

'Ryan was also the girlfriend of a Sergeant Robert Fraser, who was Ripper Squad.'

'He was the one who gassed himself?' asks Hook.

'Yes,' I nod. 'Anyway, there seems to be a school of thought in the West Yorkshire force that some of these murders aren't actually Ripper jobs at all. Ryan being one of them.'

'Really?' sneers Hook. 'They can actually think?'

'Go on,' hisses Smith, impatient.

'I went to see Whitehead in connection with Eric Hall and Janice Ryan. He's under sedation in their secure wing at Stanley Royd, but he was lucid for most of the interview up until the very end when I swear he said words, or words very like the words on the end of this tape.'

'Do you want to listen to it again?' asks Hook.

'No,' says Smith.

The telephone rings –

Smith picks it up: 'What is it?'

He listens, face unchanging, eyes on me, and then he hangs up.

Hook is saying: 'It must be a foreign language or something?'

'I've no idea,' I say, looking at Smith.

'Should send it up to the University?' suggests Hook, no one listening.

Clement Smith leans forward and presses the eject, taking out the cassette –

'This writing,' he says. '*All this and Heathen too*, you said it's a reference to the *Ripper Tape*?'

'Yes,' I say. 'And the music at the start, that's from a song on the same cassette as the song on the *Ripper Tape* – same album: *All this and Heaven too.*'

'Fucking hell,' says Hook. 'It's got Ripper all over it, this.'

'Or that's what someone wants us to think,' I say.

'Or you?' says Clement Smith.

Me: 'Pardon?'

'You're all over this too.'

'I know,' I say.

'You'd been to see Douglas; Douglas was working for Richard Dawson; Richard Dawson is a friend of yours.'

'I know.'

'And he's under arrest.'

'I know.'

Eyes on me, fixed, locked –

The telephone rings again –

Smith picks it up: 'What is it?'

He listens, says: 'Bring it up.'

He hangs up, eyes on me.

'What is it?' asks Hook.

'Another bloody message.'

'What?'

'They've pulled a piece of paper, a note – from the little girl's throat.'

'Fucking hell.'

Me: 'What does it say?'

'Find out, shall we?'

Back with the rest of them, the lost twelve.

Another scientist: 'Preliminary post-mortem on the girl Karen Douglas revealed she died of a single stab wound to the heart.'

Did her Daddy see her die, hear her, – or did she see her Daddy die, hear him?

The pathologist holds up a clear plastic bag containing a grey piece of notepaper:

'We also extracted this from the back of her mouth.'

Twelve-plus large men lean forward, straining, half-standing, shouting –

The pathologist raises a hand to the noise:

'It says: *5 LUV.*'

Twelve open mouths, twelve fresh curses: 'Fucking hell fire.'
The pathologist sits back down, nothing more to say.
Twenty-four eyes on Clement Smith, Chief Constable.
Out of the corner of your eye, a dark figure forms –
'Enough of this fucking bollocks,' spits Clement Smith,
clawing at the table. 'Detective Chief Inspector Hook will break
down the teams with SOCO: door to door, known associates,
witnesses, etc. Bring them in, write it down, the usual.'
The usual –
'Assistant Chief Constable Hunter, come with me.'

The Chief Constable's office, the two of us alone –
'Pete,' he's saying, shaking his head. 'You've got to be com-
pletely honest with me here . . .'
'Of course. I always am.'
'Please, let me finish,' he says, looking up from his desk.
'You can see how this looks, can't you? It's not good: ex-copper
and his daughter murdered, horribly murdered, sadistically,
links to prominent businessmen, top policemen, the Yorkshire
bloody Ripper. A right fucking mess.'
Silence, the two of us looking at each other until –
Until I tell him: 'I don't know what you want me to say. You
seem to be blaming me?'
'That's paranoia, Pete. But I wish to Christ you'd kept out of
this whole Richard Dawson thing.'
'Here, here,' I say. 'But nobody told me there was a *Dawson
thing* to keep out of, did they?'
'But common sense would have told you not to talk to
Douglas.'
'Common sense? So you're saying that was a mistake on my
part?'
'Of course I bloody am. And it's bound to come out.'
'So what do I do?'
'I don't know,' he says, pulling through his beard with his
fingers. 'I don't bloody know.'
Silence, the two of us not looking at each other until –
Until the telephone rings –
Smith picks it up: 'Yes?'
He listens, closes his eyes and says: 'I'll be down.'
He hangs up, eyes still shut.

I say: 'His wife?'

He nods.

'She was there on Sunday, when I went round.'

He doesn't move.

'I've met her. Do you want me there?'

He opens his eyes and picks up the phone: 'Detective Chief Inspector Hook please.'

He waits, eyes still avoiding mine –

'Roger,' he says. 'Mrs Douglas is here. Meet us downstairs will you?'

He listens to Hook on the other end, then looks up at me as he tells him: 'Let him stew. We'll get to Richard bloody Dawson in due course.'

Then, just before he hangs up, he says: 'And Roger? Don't tell Dawson about Douglas. And make bloody sure he doesn't find out.'

He slams the phone down –

It rings again –

'What is it?'

He looks across at me and says: 'Tell him Mr Hunter is unavailable.'

He hangs up again.

I say: 'Who was it?'

'Chief Constable Angus,' he says, standing up.

The telephone starts to ring again –

'Fucking hell,' shouts Smith, sending the phone flying off the hook and across the desk, storming out of the room.

We knock once, softly, Smith, Hook, and I –

The policewoman opens the door –

Mrs Douglas, puffed and bloated with tea and sympathy, looks up: 'He said he was just going into town, do some Christmas shopping. She said she wanted to come. I could tell he didn't want her with him, because of the crowds I thought. But she cried and he gave in. Like he always does. Too bloody soft with her, he is.'

Silence –

Mrs Douglas, about to be gutted by questions and grief, looking at me.

Silence until –

Until Clement Smith begins, extending our official condolences and the like.

'I don't understand,' Mrs Douglas says.

'We're all very, very sorry,' says the Chief Constable.

Mrs Douglas looks across at me: 'Can I see them?'

I shake my head: 'No.'

'Please?'

'They're not here.'

'Where are they?'

'Somewhere else,' I say.

'They're not at home?'

'No,' I say. 'They're not at home.'

'Yes, I thought it was strange they weren't at home,' she says, blinking, – looking from me to Smith, from Smith to Hook, from Hook to me, to the policewoman and back to me.

'I don't understand,' she says again, sucking in her lips, – squeezing her hands together, whispering to herself, – pinching herself, wide awake and dying –

'I just don't understand.'

I push away the sandwich and stand up.

'I'm going to ring Joan,' I say.

Clement Smith nods.

'What time do you want to do Dawson?' Hook asks him.

Smith looks at his watch and then up at me: 'Three?'

'Fine,' I say and leave them under the bright, bright lights.

'Where are you?' she says.

'Here. Manchester.'

You could cut it with a knife, the silence –

'What's going on?'

'A man who worked for Richard, he's been murdered. And his daughter.'

I'd been to sleep and I had this nightmare –

'His daughter?'

'Yes.'

There was a girl in a bath –

'How old was she?'

'Six.'

You could cut it with a knife, the silence –

'What's going to happen?'

'I don't know.'

I'd been to sleep and I had this nightmare –

'I love you, Peter,' she says. 'I love you so much.'

'Me too,' Then: 'Thanks, love. I'll see you later.'

There was a girl in a bath.

Outside the interview suite I say: 'Do you think this is a good idea?'

Smith hisses: 'I think we're past good and bad ideas, don't you?'

Roger Hook comes out of the room: 'He's happy to talk to us without a lawyer if Pete's there.'

'Well that's his decision,' says Smith. 'If it was me, I'd want all the bloody lawyers present I could afford.'

'Do you want me to advise him to get his lawyer here?'

'No. Let's just do it.'

Smith opens the door and we follow him in –

Richard Dawson stands up behind the table, worried.

'Mr Dawson,' says Smith, cutting him off. 'I think you know everyone?'

Dawson is looking at me, nodding his head up and down.

A young uniform closes the door and sits down behind us.

We pull up chairs around the table, facing Dawson.

Hook puts a cassette into the tape recorder on the table and presses record:

'Wednesday 17 December 1980. Three-fifteen p.m. Preliminary interview with Mr Richard Dawson in room one at the interview suite at Manchester Police Headquarters. Present Chief Constable Smith, Assistant Chief Constable Hunter, myself, Chief Inspector Hook, and Detective Constable Stainthorpe.'

Clement Smith lowers his head towards the tape recorder and says: 'Mr Dawson, you've been advised that you may have your lawyer present, correct?'

'Yes.'

'But at this stage you have chosen to proceed without legal representation?'

'Yes. I am not being charged, am I?'

'No, and you are aware that you can request a lawyer at anytime during the course of this interview?'

'That's fine. Thank you.'

'OK. You've been asked here to discuss matters pertaining to allegations of financial irregularities in your company accounts. Specifically regarding tax and insurance payments, expenses.'

Richard Dawson is still looking at me, nodding his head up and down.

'However,' says Smith. 'I'd like to begin by asking you some questions about a Robert Douglas, who I believe you recently hired as a security advisor?'

'Yes,' says Dawson, puzzled, still looking at me.

'Would you mind telling us how you came to meet Mr Douglas and in what capacity he is employed by you?'

'I was introduced to Bob Douglas at a local charity event organised for my son's school. Mr Douglas's daughter attends the same school and my wife and his wife are both on the PTA.'

'And which school would this be?'

'St Bernard's in Burnage.'

'Catholic?'

'My wife is.'

'OK. So . . .'

'So I've known of Bob Douglas for a while and spoken to him on a number of occasions at school functions. My wife said he was a former police officer and I remember being vaguely aware that he had been involved in catching that Michael Myshkin and then he'd had to retire after being shot during some kind of robbery in Wakefield. Anyway, couple of months back there was a spate of burglaries in the Didsbury area and I decided it was as good a time as any to tighten up the security at home. I called Bob Douglas and he came out and did a very thorough but reasonably priced job for us. During the course of this we got on very well and since then he's done other bits of work for me.'

'Like?'

Still nodding, Richard Dawson says: 'Security at the office, insurance estimates.'

'Do you pay him a wage, Mr Dawson?'

'A retainer, plus a fee for specific work.'

'When did you last see or speak to him?'

'To be honest, I can't remember when I last saw him without looking at my diary. I have spoken to him though. Last Friday night he called to tell me he'd heard I was under investigation,' he says, waving a hand at the assembled company.

'And you've had no contact with Mr Douglas since then?'

'None.'

A knock at the door.

Ronnie Allen comes in and hands a slip of paper to Roger Hook –

Hook glances at it and hands it to Smith –

Smith pulls his chair back from the table and reads the note –

He turns to Ronnie Allen: 'Get everyone together. Eleventh floor, thirty minutes.'

Allen nods and leaves, careful to avoid my gaze.

Smith reads the paper again, then folds it up and puts it in his pocket –

He looks at Richard Dawson –

'Mr Dawson,' says Clement Smith, sitting forward in his chair. 'I'm sorry to have to tell you that a security guard found Bob Douglas and his daughter murdered in a warehouse in Ashburys early this morning.'

Richard Dawson pales, swallows, shaking his head from side to side –

Looking into my face, searching –

Desperately lost, pleading –

Mouth opening and closing, choking –

'Mr Dawson?' says Smith.

Richard Dawson, blank –

Smith: 'Do you have anything to say?'

Silence, a long dark silence –

Then Dawson whispers: 'Nothing, but I'd like to see my lawyer now.'

'Fine,' says Smith and stands up. 'Chief Inspector Hook will make the necessary arrangements and set up a time.'

Hook nods and says into the tape recorder: 'Interview suspended at three thirty-five p.m. December 17 1980.'

He presses stop, eject, and takes out the tape and writes on the cassette:

Dawson int/1/171280.

Richard Dawson is still looking at me –

We all stand up, all except Dawson.
I'm following Smith and Hook out when –
'Pete,' says Richard Dawson.
I turn around –
'Thanks for being a friend,' he spits.
'What?'
'You heard.'

Catch-up:
Hook looking at me, Smith holding out the piece of paper –
I take it, read:
Prints on cassette, Jack Whitehead.
Hook staring, Smith waiting –
I say: 'Jesus.'
Hook nodding, Smith waiting –
I say: 'Someone called Stanley Royd?'
Hook nodding: 'Never left his bed.'
Me: 'Fuck.'
Smith: 'First thing tomorrow. The pair of you.'

The room upstairs –
Twelve black suits and twelve blank faces.
'What are we going to tell the press?' asks someone.
'Nothing,' says Smith.
I stand up –
'Where are you going?' says someone.
'Ashburys.'
'Now?'
'We've missed something. I know we have.'
Twelve dark suits and twelve darker faces –
Their patience gone, my time up:
Exit.

On the way back to Ashburys, a prayer:
O Blessed Lord, the Father of mercies, and the God of all comforts;
I beseech thee, look down in pity and compassion upon this thy
afflicted servant.
Thou writest bitter things against me, and makest me to possess
my former iniquities;
Thy wrath lieth hard upon me, and my soul is full of trouble:

But, o merciful God, who hast written thy holy Word for our learning, that we, through patience and comfort of thy holy Scriptures, might have hope;

Give me a right understanding of myself, and of thy threats and promises;

That I may neither cast away my confidence in thee, nor place it anywhere but in thee.

Give me strength against all my temptations and heal all my distempers.

Break not the bruised reed, nor quench the smoking flax.

Shut not up thy tender mercies in displeasure;

But make me to hear of joy and gladness, that the bones which thou hast broken may rejoice.

Deliver me from fear of the enemy, and lift up the light of thy countenance upon me, and give me peace, through the merits and mediation of Jesus Christ our Lord.

Amen.

A prayer, on the way back to Ashburys.

Ashburys, cursed and godless:

Wednesday 17 December 1980 –

Five o'clock.

Seven days before Christmas –

In hell.

I get out of the car and walk towards the factory –

Sun gone, only night and looming buildings dark and towering with their dead eyes, their empty rooms –

Pitch-black and deathlike, silent but for the screams of passing freight –

The ring of wraiths around a yellow drum of fire, breaking to let me pass –

In the bleak midwinter, make a friend of death –

At the door, the tape in my head:

HISS –

Piano –

Drums –

Bass –

'How can this be love, if it makes us cry?'

STOP.

HISS –

Cries –
Whispers –
Hell:
'How can the world be as sad as it seems?'
STOP.
HISS –
Cries –
Whispers –
More hell:
'How much do you love me?'
STOP.
HISS –
Cries –
Cries –
Cries:
'Sti rip sll iwl lik Hunter!'
STOP.
At the door, thinking of the prints on the tape:
Jack Whitehead.
At the door, the note in her mouth:
5 LUV.
At the door, messages –
Messages –
Messages and signs –
Messages, signs and symbols –
Of death.
Everywhere the distractions, everywhere but here –
Here, symbols –
Here, signs –
Here messages:
In the bleak midwinter, make a friend of death –
Here death –
Only death –
No distractions –
Only messages –
Messages –
Messages and signs –
Messages, signs and symbols –
Of death –
Only death, a friend:

In the bleak midwinter, make a friend of death –
I step inside –
Inside:
Silence, deathlike.
Heavy workbenches, oil and chains, tools; the stink of machines, oil and chains, tools; the sound of dirty water, oil and chains, tools; dripping, dripping, dripping, dripping, tools:
Jack Whitehead.
High skylights, night and rain against the pane –
The workbench bare, the body gone:
Bob Douglas.
I walk across the wet and bloody concrete floor, walk to the door and with my boot I push it open –
Push and see a muddy bath affixed to the wall, its head towards the night from the skylight, bare:
Karen Douglas.
Head bowed, I stand before the empty bath –
Silence, deathlike:
Missed something –
Know we have –
Know –

I walk down the side of the garage to the shed at the back.
I take the key from my pocket and unlock the door.
I am cold, freezing.
I go inside, lock the door behind me and put on the light.
My room –
The War Room.
I sit down at the desk and stare at the wall above *Anabasis*:
One map, thirteen photographs –
Each photograph a face, each face a letter and a date, a number on each forehead.
I turn from one of the grey metal filing cabinets to the other –
From the one marked *Ripper* –
To the one marked *Yorkshire.*
I lean over to the grey metal filing cabinet marked *Yorkshire* and I take out a file – one from the front:
Douglas, Robert –
To an old newspaper dated:
Tuesday 24 December 1974 –

To the Front Page and the headline:
3 Dead in Wakefield Xmas Shoot-out –
To the sub-heading:
Hero Cops Foil Pub Robbery.
Then I lean over to the grey metal filing cabinet marked
Yorkshire and again I take out a file – one from the back:
Whitehead, Jack –
To an old newspaper dated:
Monday 27 January 1975 –
To the Front Page and the headline:
Man Kills Wife in Exorcism –
To the sub-heading:
Local Priest Arrested.
Finally I open up a thick blank notebook.
Inside, I write one word in big black felt tip pen:
Exegesis –
Then I switch on the cassette and I begin:

And when we die
And float away
Into the night
The Milky Way
You'll hear me call
As we ascend
I'll say your name
Then once again
Thank you for being a friend.

I push open the bedroom door.
Joan is in bed, pretending to be asleep.
I go over to her and I kiss her forehead.
She opens her eyes: 'Where've you been?'
'The shed,' I say.
'All this time? It's almost dawn.'
'Yes,' I say. 'It's almost dawn.'
She closes her eyes again.
I undress and put on my pyjamas.
I switch off the light and get in beside her.
'I love you,' she says, snuggling up to me, closer –
'Me too,' I say, holding her in the cold bed and staring up at

the ceiling, the smell of her hair, listening to the cars on the road and the rise and fall of her breathing.

They were here again, back –
  People on the TV singing hymns with no face –
  People on the TV singing hymns with no face, no features –
  And at my feet, they had her down on the floor at my feet, her hands behind her back, stripped and beaten, three of them raping her, sodomising her, taking their turns with a bottle and a chair, cutting her hair, pissing and shitting on her, making her suck them, making her suck me, ugly gulls circling overhead, screaming –
  Helen Marshall sucking me, Helen Marshall screaming:
  'Sti rip sll iwl lik Hunter!'

Awake, sweating and afraid, staring up at the ceiling, no cars on the roads –
  Afraid again –
  No more sleep, no more sleep, no more sleep –
  Out of the grey morning, Joan reaching for me: 'What's wrong, love? What is it?'
  Heart racing, beating, breaking –
  I can feel come in my pyjamas again.
  'Nothing,' I say, thinking –
  Nothing –

Part 2
Nothing short of a total war

wearing tights and two pairs of panties one pair of panties removed my right leg out left leg in again the news from nowhere this from bradford saturday the fourth of june nineteen seventy seven linda clark in a green jacket and a long black velvet dress in the shadow of the sikh temple on bowling back lane fresh from the mecca now tiffanys then the bali hai discotheque drunk and dancing he leads me into mystery where sighs cries and shrieks of lamentation echo throughout the starless summer air angry cadences shrill outcries the raucous groans and chants of a football crowd joined with the sounds of their hands him raising a whirling storm that turns itself forever through the starless summer air the day fading and the darkening air releasing all the creatures of the earth from their daily tasks drunk and dancing my plan was to walk until e saw a taxi rather than wait at the rank with the rest of them and as e was walking up pulled a white or yellow ford cortina mark two with a black satan look roof which stopped on the wakefield road the door opens and he leans across and offers me a lift and in e get the man is thirty five years old and maybe just six feet and of a large build with light brown shoulder length hair thick eyebrows puffy cheeks a big nose and big hands here this is the way but e am drunk from dancing and e keep nodding off and we are bumping up and down across some wasteland and e know what he wants but e am too drunk from dancing to care and e hate my husband who is a spoilsport does not like my drinking and dancing not that he has ever bothered to watch me dance and e ask the driver if he fancies me and he says he does so e tell him to drive to wasteland over yonder behind where pakis go nodding off bumping up and down across some wasteland e know what she wants and she says stop here because e have to have a pee and she gets out and is squatting down in the dark the sound of her urine on the wasteland under the starless endless black summer air of this here hell e hit her with the hammer and e rip her black velvet dress to the waist and e stab her repeatedly in the chest in the stomach and in the back but then e see lights going on in gypsy caravan an alsatian dog barking and e think she is dead so e drive away at high speed bumping up and down across wasteland and it is morning and e am not drinking or dancing e am cold freezing cold and crying people coming and looking at me lying on the wasteland my girdle pants and tights pulled down a blow to the back of the head stabbed four times in my chest in my stomach and in my back one a slashing stab wound that stretches from my breasts to below my belly button the surgeons they give me one of them life saving operations and e do not die e cannot die so e live with a hole in my head and scars across my belly where the sighs cries and shrieks of lamentation echo throughout the starless endless black night of this here hell wherein there is no hope of death alone in this starless endless night alone and banished from the disco mountain to never hear the songs that made me dance where he showed me the way where he won again no hope of death alone in this starless night alone among the junk and the rubbish where the dogs the ponies the cats the little gypsy children play with the old fridges and cookers the bicycles and prams and was it not here that one of them gypsy kids they hid in an old fridge and nobody found her and did she not die alone in that old fridge nobody looking for her among the broken sinks and meters the bits and pieces from the old council houses that have all been boarded up while them gypsy folk live in their caravans with their horses their dogs and drink in the farmyard while their

Chapter 8

Lit match, gone –
   Dark Jack.
   Lit match, gone –
   Like dark Jack, out –
   Seeing through his eyes:
   Winter, collapse –
   Dark Jack.
   Winter, collapse –
   Like dark Jack, out –
   Seeing through his eyes:
   1980 –
   Out, out, out.

Thursday 18 December 1980.
   Stanley Royd Hospital, Wakefield.
   I'm sitting in the car park, my back on fire –
   In flames, waiting for Hook, striking matches –
   The hum of pop tunes, Northern songs –
   Listening to the news:
   Civil Service strikes, air strikes, Ripper strikes,
   Maggie, Maggie, Maggie –
   Out, out, out.
   No mention of Douglas and his daughter –
   No mention of the war –
   The murder and the lies, the lies and the murder.
   Black and white, the sky and the snow –
   Black and white, the photographs and news.
   A tap on the window –
   'Morning,' mouths Hook through the window.
   I get out of the car –
   It's freezing –
   The air grey, the trees black –
   The nests still empty.
   'Nice place,' says Hook, a black doctor's bag in one hand.
   'Lovely,' I smile and lead the way up the steps to the inside
   Again, the warm and sickly sweet smell of shit.

The woman in white puts down the black telephone and says: 'Can I help you?'

Warrant cards out, Hook says: 'We're here to see Jack Whitehead.'

She nods.

I add: 'Is Leonard about?'

She shakes her head: 'He's gone.'

'Gone?'

'Quit.'

'Bit sudden, wasn't it? He was here on Tuesday.'

'Called up yesterday, said he'd had enough.'

'We'll need an address,' says Hook.

'And a surname,' I say.

She looks from Hook to me and back again –

'Marsh,' she frowns. 'Lived up Netherton way, I'll have to look out the address.'

'If you would,' smiles Hook.

There's a pause –

'Can you take us up?' I ask.

She shakes her head: 'I'll have to call Mr Papps, he's in charge. He can take you up.'

She picks up the phone and asks for Mr Papps.

'He'll be with you in five minutes,' says the woman in white.

We wait, standing amongst the furniture, watching the skin and bones shuffling past, watch them coming to a stop, standing, watching us watch them, waiting.

'He'll be with you in five minutes,' says the woman in white again.

I turn away from their stares, reading the etched tracts in the lower green half of the wall:

Here house hex'd.

'What do you think?' asks Hook.

'About?'

'This Leonard Marsh bloke?'

'I don't know,' I shrug. 'He was hardly a bloke. Twenty at most. I thought he was a trustee or something. Didn't realise he was staff.'

'He had access to Whitehead?'

'Yep,' I nod.

'Gentlemen?'

We turn back from the green and cream wall –

'Mr Papps?' says Hook.

The small chubby man in the blue blazer with the gold buttons nods: 'Sorry to have kept you waiting.'

'No problem,' says Hook. 'This is Peter Hunter, Assistant Chief Constable of Greater Manchester and I'm Chief Inspector Roger Hook, also of Manchester.'

Mr Papps keeps on nodding, shaking our hands: 'Yes, the call was a bit vague. I'm not sure really how I can . . .'

I tell him: 'Unfortunately, at this stage, it's difficult to be anything other than vague. So I'm afraid you'll have to bear with us, if you don't mind.'

He's still nodding: 'You were on the telly the other day, weren't you?'

'Yes,' I say. 'I came here on Tuesday. I believe I spoke to you on the phone?'

'My assistant,' says Mr Papps. 'Is this about the Yorkshire Ripper then?'

'No,' says Roger Hook. 'It's not.'

I say: 'I spoke to one of your patients, Jack Whitehead.'

Mr Papps, still nodding, thinking too much: putting two and two together and getting four.

'We'd just like to clarify a few things Mr Whitehead said and also get a bit more background on him,' I half-lie.

'Is there anywhere we can talk?' asks Hook.

'This way,' says Mr Papps and he leads us into a big cold room with big cold windows, all big black shadows thanks to the big black trees outside –

We sit shivering in more second-hand furniture.

'What do you want to know?' asks Papps.

'Everything,' says Hook. 'Starters, when was Mr Whitehead admitted?'

'Here?'

We nod.

'Well, he's been here since the September of 77.'

Me: 'He was in Pinderfields before that though?'

'Yes,' says Papps. 'I think it was the June that he was admitted.'

Hook: 'With a nail in his head?'

'Yes,' says Papps, lowering his voice.

'And he did that himself?'

'Yes.'

'Why?'

In this cold and black room Mr Papps is sweating, fiddling with the gold buttons on the blue blazer: 'You don't know about his wife, his ex-wife?'

'No,' says Hook.

Nothing, I say nothing –

Mr Papps, he wipes his brow and he tells Hook: 'In January 1975, a man called Michael Williams believed he was possessed by an evil spirit. A local priest tried to perform an exorcism, however something went wrong and Williams ended up killing his wife and running naked through the streets of Ossett covered in her blood. The woman's name was Carol Williams. She was Jack Whitehead's ex-wife. Williams killed her by hammering a nail into the top of her skull. Worse, Whitehead was there. Saw it all.'

'He was there?'

'Yes, Mr Hook. He was there.'

'Why?'

'I have no idea.'

'And Williams?'

'I believe he's in Broadmoor, but I'm not certain.'

'So in 1977 Whitehead tried to do it to himself?'

'Yes.'

'Where?'

'The top of his skull.'

'No, the place?'

'The Griffin Hotel, Leeds.'

Hook turns to me: 'That's where you lot are staying, isn't it?'

'Yes,' I nod.

'Bloody hell. Did you know?'

'No,' I lie.

He turns back to Papps: 'And so he was brought to Pinderfields, and then here?'

'Yes.'

'You wouldn't think you could survive, would you?'

I'm thinking of hollows and heads, craters and craniums, the pictures on the wall.

'Actually, quite the contrary,' says Mr Papps. 'In the ancient world, a hole in the head was often used as a cure of other trauma or depression. Hippocrates wrote of its merits.'

Me: 'Trepanation?'

Papps is nodding: 'Yes, trepanation. Apparently John Lennon was interested in it. And, as I say, it was quite common in the ancient world.'

'But this is the modern world,' says Hook. 'And John Lennon's dead.'

'Yes,' says Papps. 'The modern world.'

I ask: 'So what progress has he made?'

'You've met him? Not much.'

Hook: 'Is he likely to?'

Papps is shaking his head: 'Hard to say.'

'He's on medication?'

'Yes.'

'Can you write out his prescriptions for us, the names of the drugs?'

Papps nods.

Me: 'Visitors?'

'Not many. I'd have to check.'

'Would you?'

Papps nods again.

I say: 'The lady on the desk, she tells us that Leonard Marsh has left you?'

'Yes,' says Papps.

'Was he in charge of Mr Whitehead?'

'Not in charge, no. But he certainly had helped look after him for quite a time. Since he got here.'

'Whitehead?'

'Yes,' says Papps.

'Why did he leave?'

'Leonard? I'm not sure, just had had enough he said.'

'I see.'

'It's difficult work, Mr Hunter.'

'I don't doubt it.'

Silence –

Then I say: 'Who is his doctor?'

'Jack Whitehead?'

'Yes.'

'Me.'

'It's Dr Papps?'

'Yes,' he smiles. 'Didn't I say?'

'No,' I say, standing up, frozen –

Papps sighs: 'Follow me, gentlemen.'

Up the stairs, down the half-green half-cream corridors and across the landing, out of the main building, over the cold walkway and into the extension, locking and unlocking doors, back to Jack –

The last corridor; long and locked –

In the green paint, another etched tract:

Hex'd, I die.

Down the last corridor, long, to the last door, locked –

Dr Papps, keys out –

Hook, a free hand on the doctor's sleeve: 'Has Whitehead left the hospital in the last twenty-four hours?'

Papps: 'Of course not.'

'In the last week, the last month.'

'Inspector, Mr Whitehead hasn't left his bed, let alone his room, since he got here.'

'He's loose,' I shouted.

'Jesus,' said Leonard. 'Not again.'

Me: 'How can you be certain?'

Papps gives the dangling keys a shake: 'How could he?'

'But . . .' starts Hook, but I give him the wink and he stops –

Papps looks from Hook to me and back again –

I nod at the door –

Papps shrugs, turns the keys, and then the handle –

He pulls back the door –

Silence –

'After you,' gestures Papps and we enter the room.

It's cold this time and lighter, the toilet in the corner still dripping, the chair gone.

I follow Hook's gaze to the bed, to Jack Whitehead –

On his back in a pair of grey striped pyjamas, hands chained to the sides of the cot, eyes open.

Hook is clutching the black bag, searching through the grey light, searching through the shadows, searching Whitehead's scalp, searching for the hole he'd made.

'Mr Whitehead,' I say. 'It's Peter Hunter. I was here the day before last?'

Silence, just the dripping, dripping of the toilet in the corner –

'Mr Whitehead?' I say again. 'I'm here with Inspector Hook.'

More silence –

'Jack?' says Papps.

Dripping, dripping, dripping –

I turn to Dr Papps and tell him: 'We have to ask Mr Whitehead a number of questions. Would you mind waiting down the corridor, sir?'

'He's probably not going to talk.'

'Even so, if you wouldn't mind.'

'Fine,' shrugs Papps, like it's not, and he leaves the room.

Dripping, dripping, dripping, dripping –

I say: 'Mr Whitehead? Jack?'

Dripping, dripping, dripping, dripping, dripping –

Hook coughs and steps forward –

Dripping, dripping, dripping, dripping, dripping, dripping –

'Mr Whitehead,' says Hook. 'Your fingerprints were found on a cassette tape in Manchester yesterday. We've travelled here today to ask you how your fingerprints could have ended up on this cassette tape.'

Silence, complete silence until –

Until Jack sighs, eyes watering, tears slipping down his face, his cheeks, his neck, and onto the pillow –

Dripping –

We both step forward, closer to the bed –

'Mr Whitehead?' asks Hook.

But the tears are streaming now –

Dripping, dripping –

Hook opens the black doctor's bag and takes out a portable cassette recorder.

'Roger,' I say. 'I don't think that's such a good . . .'

He presses play:

HISS –

Piano –

Drums –

Bass –

'*How can this be love, if it makes us cry?*'

STOP.
HISS –
Cries –
Whispers –
Hell:
'How can the world be as sad as it seems?'
STOP.
HISS –
Cries –
Whispers –
More hell:
'How much do you love me?'
STOP.
HISS –
Cries –
Cries –
Cries:
'Sti rip sll iwl lik Hunter!'
STOP.
Silence –
Just tears –
Jack's tears –
Dripping –
Until –
'That's you,' Hook is shouting, over at the bed, shaking Whitehead. 'That's you, isn't it? You knew Bob Douglas, didn't you?'
Then suddenly a shot, a bolt –
Whitehead's chest rises, his body twitches, his teeth gritted and bleeding –
And Hook's turning to me: 'What is it? What's wrong with him?'
Again another shot, another bolt –
Chest risen, body twitching, teeth gritted and bleeding –
'What is it?' Hook is screaming. 'What's happening?'
'Get Papps!'
A last shot, a final bolt –
Chest risen then fallen, a body twitching then still, teeth gritted then mouth open, blood bleeding –

A bloody stream down his face, his cheeks, his neck, and onto the pillow –

Dripping –

Hook is down the corridor shouting for the doctor –

Whitehead still, frozen –

I lean in close to the bed, feeling for the heart –

His mouth opens, bloody bubbles bursting on his lips and gums –

I lean in closer to the mouth, listening –

'What?' I say. 'What is it?'

Closer to the mouth –

'What?'

Listening –

'Futures and pasts,' he whispers. 'Futures past.'

Hook and Papps are tearing back up the corridor –

'What?' I say, but he's gone –

Silence, just their feet down the long, long corridor, then through the door, Papps pushing me to one side, panting, just questions, questions, questions, Papps pushing Hook back down the long, long corridor, for help, help, help, panting, Papps pushing down on Whitehead's chest, breathe, breathe, breathe, panting, pushing open his mouth, kissing him, kiss, kiss, kiss, panting, then pushing me back into the wall, more questions, questions, questions, pushing down on his chest again, thump, thump, thump, panting, more feet down the long, long corridor, doctor, doctor, doctor, panting, Hook to me to Hook to Papps to Hook to me to Papps, questions, questions, questions, panting –

Just questions –

Questions and no answers.

Standing on the gravel in the cold drizzle, the bare trees and empty nests, watching the blue lights take him away, the woman in white from behind the desk handing Papps his blue blazer as he gets in the back of the ambulance with Jack for the short ride next door.

We walk to our cars.

'Inspector!' shouts the woman in white –

We both turn and she comes across the gravel to hand me two pieces of paper:

'Leonard's address,' she says. 'And Dr Papps said you wanted a list of Jack Whitehead's visitors.'

'Thank you,' I say.

'You're welcome,' she smiles, but she doesn't mean it, she can't, why would she.

Lit match, gone –
  Dark Jack.
  Lit match, gone –
  Like dark Jack, out –
  Seeing through her eyes:
  Winter, collapse –
  Dark Jack.
  Winter, collapse –
  Like dark Jack, out –
  Seeing through her eyes:
  1980 –
  Out, out, out.

Millgarth, Leeds –
  Outside the Ripper Room:
  'Inspector Craven? Can I have a word?'

'Certainly Assistant Chief Constable Hunter,' he says, saluting.

I walk over to the top of the stairs, Craven limping behind.

'See much of Bob Douglas, do you?' I ask him.

'Every now and again, why?'

'And how's he doing?'

'Fine. Last I heard.'

'You're not in touch much then?'

'On and off, like I say. Less so now he's over your way.'

'What's he up to?'

'Think it's security work these days.'

'Before that?'

'When he quit he – '

'When was that?'

'75 sometime. He didn't want to, mind – they made him.'

I nod: 'So what did he do?'

'Got a ton of brass, didn't he? Bought a shop.'

'A shop?'

'Yeah, but he was never anything to do with any of this,' he says, waving back over at the Ripper Room. 'Before his time.'

'I know.'

'So why the sudden interest?'

'He's dead, Inspector.'

'What?'

'They found his body and that of his daughter in Manchester yesterday.'

'His body? What are you talking about?' says Craven, pulling at his beard.

'The bodies of Bob Douglas and his daughter.'

'How? How did they die?'

'They were murdered.'

Detective Inspector Robert Craven is swaying back and forth on his heels, shaking his head, eyes back and forth across my face, then over my shoulder –

I turn around and there's John Murphy –

He looks from me to Craven and back again and says: 'You heard then?'

'Yep,' I say, glancing back at Craven. 'I was there.'

'Christ,' says Murphy.

'Yep.'

'His little lass and all?'

I nod.

Craven looks at us both and says: 'Can you give me ten minutes?'

'Forget it, Bob,' I say. 'You've had a shock, go home.'

He shakes his head: 'Ten minutes.'

In the upstairs room again, our room –

The one next to *his* –

With the dead again, always the dead –

Alec McDonald says: 'Tracey Livingston, Preston, Saturday 7 January 1978.'

Eyes upon the table top, upon the notebooks and the files.

'Tracey left the Carlisle Hotel in the centre of town after last orders Saturday night. Her body was discovered in her flat the next day. She was thirty-three years old and had three kids. She was also a convicted prostitute.

'Death was due to four blows to the head with an instrument

that has yet to be recovered. There were also stab wounds to the abdomen and back, though these would not have proved fatal.

'Alf Hill was in charge.'

In the upstairs room, silence –

Then Alec says: 'You want me to go on?'

I nod –

And so he says: 'On the Sunday evening, her friend Bob Jenkins came round for her. They had arranged to go out for a drink. When there was no answer, he was concerned enough to break down the door. He saw blood on the hall floor and followed the trail into the bedroom. Tracey was in bed, apparently sleeping. Jenkins pulled back the blankets to find her dead, covered in blood. His words not mine. The caretaker called the police.

'Alf quickly contacted George Oldman, and Yorkshire sent their boys over. Like with us and Doreen Pickles, it was a combined investigation.'

Alec looks up from his notes: 'You were there yeah, Bob?'

Craven nods, eyes red bloody raw.

Alec: 'Anything you want to say?'

Craven: 'It was full-on.'

'Full-on? How do you mean?'

'Well, it was Alf Hill's show. Had the works; reconstructions, TV, radio, even a bloody séance.'

Murphy: 'A séance?'

'Had us all up there in her flat, this spiritualist trying to make bloody contact.'

'Get anywhere?'

'What do you bloody think?'

'How about this?' asks Alec McDonald and reads:

'It is desired to trace the following man who was involved in an incident with a prostitute in Preston city-centre in November 1975 and a similar described man who was seen to pick up Joan Richards, a prostitute who was murdered in Leeds in 1976. White male 30/40 years, five feet eight inches. Stocky build. Ginger-coloured hair which was untidy and a gingerish-coloured beard which was bushy round the cheeks but trimmed under the chin. Pointed nose and ruddy complexion.

'This man was wearing a well-worn jacket and blue bib and

brace type overalls with a pair of trousers underneath. It is thought he had two rings on fingers of left and possibly one on finger of his right hand. The back of his left hand is scarred. This is described as similar to a burn scar and stretches from the knuckles to the wrist. The back of his right hand is also possibly tattooed. This man has the appearance of a workman and probably spends his time in areas where prostitutes are known to loiter.

'He has the use of a vehicle and it is thought that he had the use of a Land Rover or similar type vehicle from March 1975 to January 1976. It should be borne in mind that the Land Rover could have been in the possession of this man because of his employment and that he might not now have access to this vehicle. Also it could well be that the beard has been shaved off.

'Suggestions to the identity of this man should be passed to the incident room in Preston or the Murder Room in Millgarth.

'Message ends.'

Silence –

Then McDonald says: 'Remind you of anyone we know, Bob?'

'What's that supposed to mean?' spits Craven.

'What do you think it's supposed to mean? Does that description remind you of anyone you know?'

'Fuck off,' he shouts and gets up and leaves the room –

More silence, minutes of it.

Then Hillman: 'What was all that about?'

'He's had a bit of a shock has Bob,' I say, catching Helen Marshall's eye –

The tears in her eyes.

'Roger?' I say into the phone, sat on the edge of the hotel bed –

It's almost eleven.

'Pete,' says Roger Hook, Detective Chief Inspector Roger Hook.

'Pleasant journey back, was it?'

'Delightful.'

'Any news?'

'We've let Dicky Dawson go.'

'Good.'

'He'll be back in on Monday.'

'What time?'

'Ten.'

'Who's his solicitor?'

'Michael Craig.'

'OK,' I sigh. 'You haven't called Pinderfields, have you?'

'Wakefield? No. Did you?'

'No, but I suppose I better.'

'The Chief wasn't right impressed.'

'Didn't think he would be. What did he say?'

'What didn't he say. Apparently that Papps bloke's been raising bloody hell.'

'What did you say?'

'What could I say? We questioned the bloke and he lost consciousness.'

'Sod them,' I say.

'Not like you, Pete,' says Roger.

'Bad day.'

'Bad week?'

'Month.'

'Year?'

'One of the worst,' I laugh.

'You said it.'

'Don't suppose SOCO got anything else from Ashburys?'

'No.'

'The tape?'

'Sent a copy to the University.'

'All right, I'll let you get back to it.'

'Cheers, Pete.'

'Bye.'

'Bye.'

Thirty minutes later the phone goes again –

I pick it up: 'Hello?'

Silence –

'Hello?'

Silence –

'Who is this?'

Silence –

I say nothing –

They hang up.

Thirty minutes later the knock on the door –
    I open it –
    There's no-one there –
    Just an empty corridor, silent –
    I walk to the end –
    But there's no-one there –
    Nothing.

Back in the room, the phone's ringing –
    I pick it up: 'Hello?'
    'Can't sleep?' asks Joan.
    'I've given it up.'
    'What? Sleep?'
    'Yep,' I nod.
    'I just called to say goodnight.'
    'Thanks.'
    'I love you.'
    'Me too,' I say.
    'Bye, then.'
    'Bye,' I say and hang up.

Lit match, gone –
    Dark Jack.
    Lit match, gone –
    Like dark Jack, out –
    Seeing through my eyes:
    Winter, collapse –
    Dark Jack.
    Winter, collapse –
    Like dark Jack, out –
    Seeing through my eyes:
    1980 –
    Out, out, out.

children play among the waste no hope of death alone this night you are the ripper why are you not married who does your washing if you are not married do you like women have you ever been with a whore transmission four at about five forty five AM on wednesday the eighth of june nineteen seventy seven the body of rachel johnson sixteen years of age shop assistant of sixty six saint marys road leeds seven was found in the adventure playground compound between reginald terrace and reginald street chapeltown leeds last seen alive at ten thirty PM tuesday seventh of june nineteen seventy seven in the hofbrauhaus merrion centre leeds she is described as follows five feet four inches with proportionate build shoulder length fair hair and wearing a blue and yellow check gingham skirt a blue jacket dark blue tights and high heeled clog fronted shoes in black and cream with brass studs around the front so far as can be ascertained the deceased had been subjected to violent blows about the head with a blunt instrument and had not been sexually assaulted it would appear that the person responsible may also be responsible for the deaths of theresa campbell at leeds on the sixth of june nineteen seventy five joan richards at leeds between the fifth and sixth of february nineteen seventy six and marie watts at leeds between the twenty eighth and twenty ninth of may nineteen seventy seven details of the injuries to the deceased should not be disclosed to the press there is no evidence that rachel johnson was an active prostitute the body had been dragged a distance of some fifteen to twenty yards from where the initial assault took place her assailants clothing will be heavily bloodstained particularly the front of any shirt or trousers worn by him it is desired to trace the following described man who was involved in an incident at white abbey bradford in november nineteen seventy six and a similar described man who was seen to pick up joan richards a prostitute who was murdered at leeds in february nineteen seventy six white male thirty to forty years five feet eight inches stocky build ginger coloured hair which was untidy and a gingerish coloured beard bushy around the cheeks but trimmed under the chin pointed nose and ruddy complexion this man was wearing a well worn jacket and blue bib and brace type overalls with a pair of trousers underneath it is thought that he had two rings on fingers of left and possibly one on finger of his right hand the back of his left hand is scarred this is described as similar to a burn scar and stretches from the knuckles to the wrist the back of his right hand is tattooed and he has the appearance of a workman and probably spends time in areas where prostitutes are known to loiter he has the use of a vehicle and is thought that he had use of a land rover or a similar type vehicle from june nineteen seventy five to february nineteen seventy six it should be borne in mind that the land rover could have been in the possession of this man because of his employment that he might not now have access to this vehicle also could well be that the beard has been shaved off e had changed my mind and danced with the boy until it was my time to go and eat chips together outside C and A and walk up to saint jimmies and lie together under the big trees and the starless endless black summer air e start walking up past grandways and the gaiety and e was startled by noise her clogs made scraping long ground as e dragged her into an adventure playground to stab her again and again she smelled so sweet so clean when she bent down to kiss me goodbye she was perfect just like a flower almost bursting with optimism and the sheer joy of life

Chapter 9

No more sleep.

No more sleep, just –

Two huge wings that burst through the back, out of my skin, torn, two huge and rotting wings, big black things that weigh me down, heavy, that stop me standing.

No more sleep, just –

Wings, wings that burst through my back, out of the skin, torn, huge and rotting things, big black wings that weigh me down, heavy, that –

And then they're gone –

Just like that.

Just *Exegesis* etched into my chest, my nails bloody, broken –

Et sequentes.

The notes are everywhere, across the floor, the bed, the cheap Griffin furniture, my writing illegible even to me. I rip out and screw up the piece I'm writing, check my watch, turn the radio down, pick the phone up off the bed and get a dialling tone, check my watch against the speaking clock, put the phone back off the hook and leave it on the bed, turn the radio up, and then I start again:

At 3:10 p.m. on Friday 27 January 1978, the naked body of Candy Simon born 6/6/60, a half-caste Jamaican found partially concealed in a timber yard off Great Northern Street, Huddersfield. Severe injuries to the head with blunt instrument and stab wounds to the body. Deceased was an active prostitute, recently moved to Huddersfield from Bradford. Was reported missing from home on 26 January by flat-mate, also an active prostitute. Had last been seen on Tuesday 24 January by flat-mate at 21:00 on Great Northern Street, Huddersfield, getting into a dark blue-coloured saloon car, possibly an Audi 100LS driven by a white male about thirty-five years of age and of smart appearance.

I stop and then writing:

Bradford?

Flat-mate?

Traffic wardens' records?

I move on:

At 8:15 a.m. Saturday 27 May 1978 the body of a female was found on wasteland in Livingston Street at its junction with April Street, Brunswick, Manchester, at the rear of the Royal Infirmary. Deceased identified as Doreen Pickles, born 8/8/40, alias Mary Brown, alias Anne Pickles. Deceased was a convicted prostitute and the area behind the Royal Infirmary known as a place frequented by prostitutes and their clients. Death due to blows to the head with a blunt instrument, a severe abdominal wound, and a stab wound to the neck. Time of death estimated to be between midnight and 3:00 a.m. May 27.

I stop, thinking:

Next murder would be one year later –

Re-check case files on other prostitute murders in North of England, 1970 to 1980, not attributed to YR.

I stare across the floor, the bed, the cheap Griffin furniture. I check my watch, turn the radio down, pick the phone up off the bed and get a dialling tone, check my watch against the speaking clock, put the phone back off the hook, turn the radio back up, and I lie upon the notes, upon the bed –

Et sequentes.

No more sleep.

No more sleep, just –

Two huge wings that burst through the back, out of my skin, torn, two huge and rotting wings, big black things that weigh me down, heavy, that stop me standing.

No more sleep, just –

Wings, wings that burst through my back, out of the skin, torn, huge and rotting things, big black wings that weigh me down, heavy, that –

And then they're gone –

Just like that.

Just *Exegesis* etched into my chest, my nails bloody, broken –

Et sequentes.

No sleep, just –

Dark heart of the night, dark corner of the room:

I check my watch, turn the radio down, pick the phone up off the bed and get a dialling tone, check my watch against the speaking clock, put the phone back off the hook, turn the radio back up, and I walk across the dark room to the dark corner –

Here sits the box from Mrs Hall.

I put the light back on and I open it:

Eric's box –

Files, piles and piles of files, and a couple of cassettes:

A & B.

I take the Memorex cassettes over to the Boots portable cassette machine. I turn the radio off and put the first one in –

I press play –

I sit back down on the bed and I take out the files and begin to read as the cassette plays:

'*He beat the fucking shit out of me. Right there in the fucking car park.*'

'*Eric, Eric . . .*'

'*Don't fucking Eric, Eric me. This cunt's got my fucking car. Broke into my fucking house.*'

'*Eric, Eric . . .*'

'*I want Fraser done and done fucking right.*'

'*Eric, shut up and listen.*'

'*No, you shut up and you listen: I'm telling you he broke into my house, my own bloody house, he's driving around in my fucking car, and he knows everything. Everything. So you tell me what the fuck you're going do about the cunt.*'

'*Eric, I mean it. Listen: it's done.*'

'*Done? What is?*'

'*Don't worry about it. It's finished.*'

'*Finished? What about the car? Where the fuck's my car?*'

'*One of the lads'll bring it round.*'

'*So what happened?*'

'*Eric, another time. Not now.*'

'*I want to know?*'

'*No, you don't Eric.*'

Eject, flip, press play –

'*I've had enough. I can't take anymore of this shit. First Fraser and now fucking Hunter.*'

I stop reading –

'*Eric, you worry much too much.*'

Same voices:

'*Peter Hunter's coming and you're telling me I worry too much.*'

I'm already fucked up thanks to that fucking Fraser twat and now I've got to fucking talk to Hunter the Cunt.'

'Don't say a bloody word, Eric.'

'It's alright for you, isn't it? Not Leeds or Manchester, is it? Has to be sodding Bradford.'

'Eric, for fuckssake.'

'Look what happened to Porn Squad, – Moody and Virago.'

'Eric, I know Peter Hunter and he's not a problem.'

'That's what you say.'

'Yeah, that's what I say and you'll fucking do what I say.'

'Or what?'

'Eric, don't fucking start.'

'No. I want to know what you'll do if I'm not a good boy, if I don't do what I'm told.'

'Eric, we're the only friends you've got. So stop fucking around.'

'Or what?'

'Or we'll start fucking around with you.'

A pause, silence –

'I'm sorry, I'm just upset.'

'I know you are. We all are.'

'I'm going to have to take a fall, aren't I?'

'No, you're not.'

'I can't do fucking time, Richard. I can't.'

'It won't come to that.'

'What do you mean?'

'We'll look after you.'

Stop.

My heart's beating fast, mouth dry –

I'm thinking:

June 1977.

I'm wondering:

Richard?

I'm writing:

Leeds? Manchester?

I say out aloud, say alone:

'Saint Cunt.'

I take out cassette A and replace it with B:

'She's dead.'

'What do you want me to say?'

A different voice, familiar –

'I want to know who fucking did it?'

'Eric, she's dead. Just leave it.'

'Was it Fraser?'

'Eric, you've got to fucking get it together mate. Fraser's saying it was you. They're going to come and have a word.'

'I can't do this.'

'You've got to.'

'Was it him?'

'Fuck knows. Doesn't matter.'

'Course it fucking matters.'

'No, it doesn't. What matters is you keeping it together and getting through this.'

Stop.

Eject, flip, press play:

'He had the fucking mag, didn't he?'

'What did he want?'

'Money. Brass, what else.'

'How much?'

'Five grand.'

'Pay him.'

'But he's a fucking journalist, he'll just keep coming back.'

'No he won't.'

'You sure?'

'Trust your Uncle Bob.'

Stop.

My heart's beating fast, mouth dry –

Wondering:

June 1977.

Thinking:

Uncle Bob?

Writing:

Detective Inspector Robert Craven?

At the bottom of the box, a magazine –

A porno mag:

Spunk.

Issue 13, March 1976.

65p.

Inside –

SPUNK is published by MJM Publishing Ltd, printed and distributed by MJM Printing Ltd, 270 Oldham Street, Manchester.

I turn the pages, the bodies and the hair, the faces and that stare –

Page 7:

A dark-haired girl with her legs spread, mouth open and eyes closed, a cock in her face and come on her lips –

Saying out loud, alone:

'Janice Ryan.'

No more sleep.

No more sleep, just –

Two huge wings that burst through the back, out of my skin, torn, two huge and rotting wings, big black things that weigh me down, heavy, that stop me standing.

No more sleep, just –

Wings, wings that burst through my back, out of the skin, torn, huge and rotting things, big black wings that weigh me down, heavy, that –

And then they're gone.

Just like that –

Just *Exegesis* etched into my chest, my nails bloody, broken –

Et sequentes.

embedded in her chest a broken bottle of pop the screw top still on the cuts that will not stop bleeding the bruises that will never heal thoughts lost and thoughts found transmission twelve noon sunday the twelfth of june nineteen seventy seven the body of janice ryan a twenty two year old known prostitute found secreted under an old settee on waste ground off white abbey road bradford death due to massive head injuries caused by a blunt instrument or boulder or rock and is thought that death occurred some seven days before due to partial decomposition of the body the killer had jumped on her chest causing broken ribs which ruptured the liver there were no stab wounds and is thought from the pattern of the injuries that this death is not connected with the other circulated prostitute murders publicly referred to as ripper murders the cuts that will not stop bleeding the bruises that will never heal occult dreams psychic themes war crimes to map out the demon spheres with webs and wires that bind the days together man in amongst the golems dwells and scars them with his thoughts lost and thoughts found such terror can his hammer do her brassiere had been pulled above her breasts her panties pulled down to the pubic region her skirt which had been removed was found under her body she was killed in some other place and had then been dragged by her collar to the settee her handbag not found when her body was discovered her left arm was tangled in the springs of the settee indicating that the killer had placed it on her body after rigor mortis had set in a period of at least four hours after death some days after death the body had been moved and a yorkshire post dated saturday the eleventh of june nineteen seventy seven headline victims of a burning hate placed underneath it could not have blown there it had been deliberately placed there the body then moved on top of the cuts that will not stop bleeding the bruises that will never heal occult dreams psychic themes war crimes to map out the demon spheres with webs and wires that bind the days together man in amongst the golems dwells and scars them with his thoughts lost and thoughts found such terror can his hammer do six six six times a killer more victims as murder hunt police say there is no copy cat dear george from hell e am sorry e cannot give my name for obvious reasons e am the ripper e have been dubbed a maniac by the press but not by you you call me clever because you know e am you and your boys have not a clue that photo in the paper gave me fits and that bit about killing myself no chance e have got things to do my purpose is to rid streets of them sluts my one regret is that young lassie johnson did not know cause changed routine that nite but warned you and jack at the post up to five now you say but there is a surprise in bradford get about you know warn whores to keep off streets cause e feel it coming on again sorry about young lassie yours respectfully jack the ripper might write again later e not sure last one really deserved it whores getting younger each time old slut next time hope initially the corpse had been well concealed soil rubble turf had been piled on top of it then the abandoned sofa placed on top of the heap apparently some time after rigor mortis had set in because the arm was well entangled in the sofa springs horse hair from the sofa had been stuffed into her mouth and the autopsy revealed she was also pregnant and told a friend e was going to earn some money and he was cruising along slowly when he had to brake suddenly because of the car in front e recognised the car and e tapped on the window and got in and he said where did you spring from so sud-

Chapter 10

Oldham Street, Manchester –

Saturday 20 December 1980.

In the car, the radio on:

Provisionals to end Dirty Protest as forty men take food.

More London policemen suspended as a result of Operation Countryman.

Hunt to find sadistic gangland killers of ex-policeman and daughter.

Funeral of Ripper victim Laureen Bell.

I switch the radio off and get out of the car and cross the road.

It's raining, a cold and dirty Manchester rain –

A funeral rain.

270 Oldham Street, black and from before the war, six or seven storeys high without a light.

Just inside the doors are the nameplates, various textile and clothing firms.

No MJM Publishing or Printing Ltd –

Fuck.

I look around, the ground floor offices silent.

There are stone stairs to the left, a lift to the right –

I take the stairs.

On the first floor, lights and the slight hum of machinery.

I tap on the old glass door that says *Manchester Divan* and open it –

It's a big room, desks and cabinets by the door, machines and other equipment at the back. There are a lot of brightly dressed Indian or Pakistani women working the machinery. The windows are grey and give no light and the room smells of sweat.

An old Indian or Pakistani man with a beard and a hat looks up from his desk and says: 'Yes?'

'My name is Peter Hunter and I'm a police officer,' I say and show him my identification.

'Yes?' he says again, nervously.

'I'm looking for a company called MJM Publishing or MJM Printing Limited? I believe they had offices in this building?'

The man is nodding: 'Yes, they were on the third floor.'

'Can you remember when they left?'

'About two or three years ago.'

'You don't know what happened, do you? They move, go under?'

He's shaking his head: 'No, I'm sorry.'

'Who owns the building?'

'Asquith and Dawson are the agents.'

'Dawson?'

Richard Dawson, businessman, Chairman of one of the local Conservative Parties –

A friend.

'Yes, Asquith and Dawson by the library.'

'Thank you,' I say, an echo –

'I can't do time, Richard. I can't.'

On the third floor landing the window is broken and there is dust and rubbish in the corners, in front of a door that still says *MJM Publishing & Printing Ltd.*

Across the landing is a second office: *Linton & Sons.*

There are no lights on and no-one's answering the door.

I squat down and pick through the rubbish outside MJM's door –

Nothing, just rubbish.

I try the door and it rattles but I think better of it.

Nearly 10:30 –

Manchester Police Headquarters –

The eleventh floor –

The Assistant Chief Constable's office –

My office –

Just as I'd left it, but for the mountains of post in the tray.

I walk across the corridor and knock on the Chief Constable's door.

'Come.'

I open the door –

Chief Constable Smith behind his desk, Christmas carols playing.

'Good morning,' I say.

'Thought you were in Leeds,' he says, not looking up.

'Yeah, I should be but something's come up I thought you'd want to know about.'

He looks up: 'What now?'

'MJM Publishing and Printing?'

He's shaking his head: 'Never heard of them.'

'They used to have premises on Oldham Street. Publish pornography.'

'Really? Pornographers?' he asks, eyes lighting –

Pet hates.

'Yeah, under-the-counter type stuff,' I say, reeling him in.

'Is that right? Oldham Street?' he says. 'You'd better sit down then, hadn't you.'

I nod.

'Go on,' he says.

'Janice Ryan was in one of MJM's magazines.'

'And?'

'I found the magazine among Eric Hall's papers. This morning I went to check out the address and found out that MJM have either gone under or moved. But guess who owns the lease on the building?'

'On Oldham Street? Who?'

'Asquith and Dawson.'

'Richard Dawson's firm?'

'Yep.'

'That doesn't mean anything,' he shrugs. 'Asquith and Dawson must own half the bloody buildings in Piccadilly. They own lease on the Arndale, don't they?'

'But there's a clear link here, yeah? With the Ripper?'

'On Wednesday you were saying chances were Ryan wasn't a Ripper job?'

'I don't know, but I'm sure this is the link between Dawson, Douglas, and Whitehead and the words on that tape; the link we were looking for.'

'We? You, more like.'

'OK, the link I think we should be looking into: Dawson, Douglas, Whitehead, Hall, Ryan, and now back to Dawson.'

'And you Pete, don't forget yourself.'

On the dark stair –

'Right,' I say. 'And me.'

Chief Constable Clement Smith sniffs up: 'Roger says you didn't get right far with Mr Whitehead.'

'No.'

He sighs, sits back in his chair, then says: 'We've got Dawson coming back in on Monday morning. Are you going to be here?'

'Don't think so, no. Not in the morning.'

'Well, have a word with Roger and see if he can follow up this MJM stuff and put a question in on Monday.'

'OK,' I say and stand up.

'Pete?'

I stop at the door: 'Yes sir?'

'You look shattered,' he says, looking back down at the work on his desk. 'You want to cut out all this back and forthing between here and there.'

'I know,' I nod.

'Too much for you, you just say the word.'

'No, it's OK.'

He looks up again: 'You spoken to Philip Evans recently?'

'No.'

'You ought to. You should tell him about all this.'

'Yes, I will.'

'Best he hears it from you first.'

I nod and close the door behind me.

'Small bloody world, isn't it,' says Roger Hook, shaking his head –

We're sitting in his office, drinking coffee with lumps of artificial milk swimming on the surface.

I say: 'You see that's just it; I don't think it is.'

'What?'

'A small world.'

'So let me get this straight: you're telling me that your mate Tricky Dicky rents out a building to some pornographers who use Janice Ryan as a model, the same Janice Ryan who's knocking off Robert Fraser and Eric Hall, the same woman who gets done in by the Ripper, so then Jack Whitehead tries to blackmail Eric Hall, and three years later his prints turn up on a cassette tape that also has your name on it, turns up in the mouth of an ex-Yorkshire copper, a dead ex-Yorkshire copper who was working for, wait for it, wait for it – working for

Richard Dawson, Tricky Dicky himself. Your mate. But it's not a small world, eh Pete?'

'No.'

'So what is it then?'

'It's a big black bloody world full of a million black and bloody hells, and when those hells collide it's time for us to sit up and take fucking notice.'

Silence –

Roger Hook uncomfortable, he takes a mouthful of cold coffee before he says: 'So what now?'

'I'll go round to Asquith and Dawson, see what happened to MJM Publishing Limited.'

'You don't have to do that. Send Ronnie.'

I roll my eyes and stand up.

'Not Ronnie then. Anyone, it's just bloody legwork.'

'I like legwork.'

'Please yourself,' he says. 'Usually do anyway.'

I stop at the door, turn around and say: 'Reminds me. Did anyone talk to that orderly at Stanley Royd, Leonard Marsh?'

'Shit, sorry.'

'Don't worry,' I say. 'I'll do it when I'm back over there.'

'Lucky you like legwork,' Hook smiles.

'Isn't it.'

Asquith and Dawson, big fat offices on the corner of Mosley Street and Princess Street.

At reception, I ask the young girl in the roll-neck sweater: 'Is Mr Dawson in?'

'No,' she says. 'It's Saturday.'

'I'm from the police, love,' I say. 'And I know it's Saturday.'

'But he's not in,' she says, her eyes filling with tears.

'OK, then I need you to help me get some information.'

'I don't think I can do that.'

'Why not?'

'I'm new.'

'Is there anyone old here?'

'No, it's Saturday. Sorry, I mean no.'

I sigh: 'You're on your own then?'

'Everyone else is out,' she nods.

'When will they be back?'

'I don't know.'

'OK,' I say, taking out my ID. 'I'd like you to find the records on one of your properties on Oldham Street. Number 270.'

'But I don't know how.'

'I'm just after a forwarding address.'

'A forwarding address?'

'Yes, the people have moved and we need to get in touch with them. It's very important police business.'

'But I don't know where they keep that kind of information.'

'Well, where are the records?'

'Upstairs, on top floor I think.'

'Can you show me?'

'Mr Asquith says I'm not to leave the desk.'

'OK, I don't want to get you into trouble. I'll just nip up and have a look and be back in a sec.'

'I'm not sure that's OK.'

'Is it open?'

'Yes, it's open but . . .'

'OK, then. You can hang on to this,' I say, handing her my ID. 'Any questions you have you call the Manchester Police Headquarters. I'll be back in five minutes.'

I leave her holding the wallet and start up the stairs –

'Top floor?' I call back.

She nods, staring at the ID.

I take the stairs two at a time, past the empty offices with their big yellow computers and their potted black plants, their posters of foreign lands and pastel wallpapers –

At the top of the stairs, there's a set of double doors –

I open them and –

Fuck:

I stare at rows and rows of filing cabinets –

I walk down the rows and rows, peering in drawers as I go, properties listed by obscure references –

I turn and walk down another row, again opening drawers as I go –

Bingo:

Client records.

Down the row I go, heading for the *Ms* –

I pull open the drawer marked *Mi – Mo* –

I flick through, I flick through, I flick through –

Yes:
MJM Publishing & Printing Limited.
It's a thick file, bound in manila card.
I want copies, but I've no chance.
I flick through, I flick through. I flick through –
Flicking through for a forwarding address –
Yes:
MJM Publishing Ltd, c/o 230 Bradford Road, Batley, West Yorks.
I take it and am away –
Down the stairs –
The young girl at the desk is still holding my wallet, staring at it.
'Thank you,' I say.
She hands me my ID.
'What's your name?' I ask her.
'Helen.'
'That's a nice name,' I say. 'My favourite.'
'Thanks,' she smiles.
'Bye,' I say.
'Bye.'

Back in the office, I call Philip Evans:
'Hello, this is Peter Hunter. Could I speak to Mr Evans please?'
'I'm afraid Mr Evans is not at work today.'
'OK. I'll call back on Monday then.'
'I'm sorry, but we're not expecting Mr Evans back until after Christmas.'
'Really? OK. Thank you.'
'Goodbye.'
'Bye.'
I put the phone back and stare at the back of the door, thinking back. I flick through my address book, looking for Evans' home number –
It's not there.
I pick up the phone and call his office again but the line's engaged.
After a few minutes I try again but it's still engaged, so I go back to the cards and the letters in my tray.

*

At about three, I call Leeds:

'Can you put me through to Chief Superintendent Murphy, please?'

'Who's calling?'

'Assistant Chief Constable Hunter, from Manchester.'

'Hang on.'

I hang on –

'Chief Superintendent Murphy's not here.'

'Thank you.'

I put the phone back and stare at the back of the door, thinking back.

I pick up the phone and call Philip Evans' office again:

No-one's answering.

I go back to the cards and letters in my tray.

At about half-four, I call Wakefield:

'Can you put me through to the Chief Constable, please?'

'Who's calling, please?'

'Assistant Chief Constable Hunter, from Manchester.'

'Just a moment, sir.'

'Thank you.'

I wait –

'This is Chief Constable Angus speaking.'

'Sorry to bother you, sir. This is Peter Hunter.'

'What can I do for you Mr Hunter?'

'I'd like to arrange to have some time with a couple of your senior detectives, ones who've been involved in the inquiry.'

'I see.'

'Is that going to be a problem?'

'I shouldn't think so, provided we can spare them.'

'Of course.'

'Who are we talking about?'

'Dick Alderman and Jim Prentice.'

'OK. When?'

'Tomorrow?'

'Tomorrow? Tomorrow's Sunday.'

'I know, but we're going to be into Christmas soon. It won't take long.'

'I'll give Pete Noble a call and see what we can do.'

'Thank you, sir.'

'I'll have him call you. You at Millgarth?'

'No, sir. I'm in Manchester.'

'Manchester? Any progress with Bob Douglas?'

'No, sir.'

A pause, then: 'I see, so when will you next be deigning us with your presence over here?'

'Tomorrow morning.'

'OK, then I'll either have the lads waiting for you or a message.'

'I can call back later?'

'No, you get off home Mr Hunter.'

'Thank you,' I'm saying, but the line's already dead.

I put the phone back and stare at the back of the door, listening to the radio:

The football scores coming in:

Thirteen-nil.

After a few minutes I get up, take my coat from the back of the door, switch out the light and leave, locking the door behind me –

Back a minute later to check, then gone again.

The Vaughan Industrial Estate, Ashburys –

The scene of the crime:

It's dark as I park on the empty wasteland, just a police car sitting in the gloom, here to watch:

DEATH –

All the gods of the North are dead now, moribund –

Trains pass, a dog barks, a man screams words I can't catch.

I stumble across craters still filled with dead water, torch in hand, nodding at the officers in the car –

Before me, the building looms – dark and towering, eyes dead, here to stare:

DEATH –

A figure walks, dreadful –

Trains pass, a dog screams, a man barks words I can't catch –

I turn, but there's no-one.

In the doorway I switch off the tapes in my head, here to listen:

DEATH –

This is the place, the swans loose –

I step inside –

The workbenches, the chains and the tools; the machines silent.

I step forward, listening:

DEATH –

Wings nailed to the ash, pornography –

I run my hand across the heavy bench, across the dark stains, across the etchings and the carvings, the messages, the signs and the symbols –

The cry of the wind through the pane –

The torchlight across the chains, a searchlight:

DEATH –

All this and heathen too –

The beam falls upon the door, ajar –

I walk across the floor to the door and push it open, a third time –

The muddy bath, the dirty water, the light from up above, from:

DEATH –

On the dark stair, we miss our step –

I bend down and run my hand over the dark sides, over the heavy water, across the scratchings and the markings, the messages, the signs and the symbols –

In my hand, black and bloody water –

I turn the torch upon my own hands, looking:

DEATH –

Never let her slip –

I turn and walk back out towards the door, following the light from the torch, ceiling to floor, wall to wall, and back to the floor –

Above the door, in the beams above the door –

Swastikas, huge white swastikas and two words:

HTAED –

Yrotcaf htaed.

I'm sat in the car in the drive outside my house.

The Christmas tree lights are on inside.

I switch off the radio and go in –

Joan's watching the TV.

'Hello,' I say.

'I wasn't expecting you back tonight,' she says, getting up, kissing me on the cheek. 'You're cold, freezing.'

'Had some stuff to take care of at the office.'

'Should have said,' she says, going into the kitchen. 'Are you hungry?'

'No,' I say.

'Sandwich?'

'No, I'm fine.'

She comes back in with a cup of tea: 'There you go.'

'What are you watching?' I ask.

'*Christmas at Robin's Nest*,' she laughs, sitting down beside me on the settee.

'Funny?'

'Mm, suppose,' she shrugs.

I lean forward and pick up the pamphlet on adoption from the coffee table –

'A Vietnamese baby?' I ask.

She nods: 'What do you think?'

'I told you, I think it's a good idea.'

'Really?'

'Yes, really,' I say. 'What do we have to do?'

She hands me an application form and says: 'We both have to complete one of these, send it off, and then they'll call us for an interview.'

'Sounds straightforward enough,' I say. 'Better pass me a pen then hadn't you.'

'You're sure then?' she asks.

'Positive, love.'

'Thank you,' she smiles. 'Thank you.'

I catch him, stop him murdering mothers, orphaning children, then you give us one, just one.

In the middle of the film, the telephone:

'Peter Hunter speaking?'

'Peter? This is Richard.'

Fuck –

'What can I do for you, Richard?'

'You were at the office today?'

'Yes.'

'What the bloody hell were you doing there?'

'Looking for you.'

'Me? Why? What now?'

'Look, calm down.'

'Fuck off, this has got completely out of hand.'

'Richard, look: I just wanted to ask you about some property you rented to a company. That was all.'

'Company? Which company?'

'Not on the phone, Richard. We'll talk about it on Monday.'

'No we bloody won't. We'll talk about it now.'

'That's not a good idea.'

'Well neither was gaining entry to my office without a warrant.'

Fuck, fuck –

'Richard – '

'Which company?'

Fuck, fuck, fuck –

'MJM Publishing.'

A pause, silence, then: 'What about them?'

'Look Richard, we'll go into it on Monday.'

'Fuck off, Peter. What about them?'

'Look, it's probably nothing to do with you.'

'Probably nothing to do with me? What then?'

'OK, look: their name came up in connection with something to do with the Ripper Inquiry.'

'The Ripper? The Leeds Ripper?'

'Yes.'

'So?'

'So when we did a check it turned out the building they'd been renting was one of yours.'

Another pause, silence, then: 'And that's it?'

'You tell me?'

A longer pause, silence, finally: 'There's nothing to tell; Colin dealt with them anyway.'

'Fine. Don't worry about it then.'

'I won't.'

'Goodbye Richard.'

'See you on Monday,' he says and hangs up –

Fuck.

In the War Room, in the night –

The photographs and maps –
The computer and cassettes –
The papers and pornography –
The words and the notes, the *Exegesis* –
The bodies and the faces, *Spunk* –
Page 7 –
A dark-haired girl with her legs spread, mouth open and eyes closed, a cock in her face and come on her lips –
In the War Room, in the night, on my knees –
Before the photos and the maps –
The computer and the cassettes –
The papers and pornography –
The words and the body, the notes and her face –
Exegesis and *Spunk* –
Page 7 –
A dark-haired girl with her legs spread, mouth open and eyes closed, a cock in her face and come.

Early June, 1977 –
We were sitting in the A10 suite at Manchester Police HQ –
On the blackboard I had written two words:
Bradford Vice.
'Any idea on where the tip came from?' asked Mike Hillman.
I shook my head: 'Obviously someone inside, but the deal was no names.'
'It's bound to come out,' Murphy shrugged.
I nodded: 'Not much we can do about that.'
'Be nice for whoever it is when it does,' smiled Murphy.
'So who we got?' asked Hillman.
'The statement implies a number of senior officers . . .'
'Fuck,' tutted Murphy.
'But,' I continued. 'Only one officer is actually named, this Detective Inspector.'
I stood up and wrote two more words on the board:
Eric Hall.

I wake in the War Room, in the night, on my knees
I put the stuff away and switch off the computer, the cassette recorder, the heater and the light.
I go back inside and upstairs –

Joan is asleep.

I switch on the radio and undress and get into bed next to
her –

I stare up at the ceiling, listening to the country music, trying
to stay awake, but –

Yrotcaf Htaed, *in blood and above the door.*

*The moon was shining through the skylight, and I was gazing at
the little girl lying in the bath. Thin and pathetic, in a shroud-like
garment, lips crooked into a faint and dreadful smile, her hands pressed
tightly over her heart. And all around us, people were singing hymns,
people with no face, no features, machines –*

Yrotcaf Htaed, *in blood and swastikas above the door.*

*And I turned and walked away and everything outside was white
and also without feature, without feature except for the parked police
car, except for the police car and the white gulls and the black ravens,
the white gulls and black ravens circling overhead screaming, circling
overhead screaming –*

Helen Marshall and the girl screaming:

'Sti rip sll iwl lik Hunter!'

– and then there was a shot.

denly and e said just good timing you can put it down to fate and off we set transmission five from the office of the dead found on monday the twenty eighth of november nineteen seventy seven in southern cemetery manchester elizabeth mcqueen dead a week or more from brain damage caused by blows to the head from a hammer or an axe with a number of postmortem lacerations being in total eighteen stab wounds to the breasts and chest the stomach and vagina stomach ripped open intestines pulled out knife wounds from her left shoulder to her right knee and there were six further wounds to her right side some of the gashes were eight inches deep an unsuccessful attempt had been made to sever her head body was then attacked by the vermin of the field alas a handbag was not recovered vinyl leather look believed to be dark brown nine inches long seven inches high three inches wide with two carrying handles and one shoulder made of the same material zip fastener and wrap over strap which fastens with a clasp on the side of the bag on which there are two external pockets it contained approximately fifteen pounds in bank of england notes items of cosmetics and a few pieces of yellow tissue paper alas the children in bed missing mummy the children wake missing mummy the children eat cornflakes for breakfast missing mummy the children get dressed missing mummy the children go to school missing mummy the children play with their friends in the cold missing mummy the children eat spam for lunch missing mummy the children listen to the teacher read a story about a spider missing mummy the children buy a texan on their way home from school missing mummy the children eat beans for tea missing mummy the children have a bath missing mummy the children watch starsky and hutch missing mummy the children fight missing mummy the children cry missing mummy the children sleep missing mummy the children dream missing mummy the children dream terrible dreams of missing mummy with no head moving along no differently from all the rest mummy holds her severed head up by its hair swinging it in one hand just like a lantern and it looks at them and says alas from the office of the dead out of the terrible depths have e cried unto thee lord hear my voice o lord let thine ears be attentive to the voice of my supplications if thou lord should mark iniquities o lord who should stand but there is forgiveness with thee and e have stood by thee according to thy law my soul has waited on thy word my soul has hoped in thee o lord from the morning watch unto the evening there is hope in the lord for with the lord there is mercy and with him is redemption and he shall redeem me from all my iniquities give me eternal rest o lord and let perpetual light shine upon me lord our father have mercy christ have mercy on e who was known in the reno and the nile as mad lizzie but am now known only as the spaghetti lady two kerbies waiting but e had to go and choose him did e not with his nice smile and clean clothes that would not frighten anybody we drove up to the southern cemetery because it is dead quiet here e laughed and he smiled and said e bet it is and e lead him into the darkness where he hit me with the hammer and e fell to the ground and e was moaning and he hit me again and again eleven times then he left me alone until one week later he comes again drags me out of the bushes strips me of everything e am wearing even my boots stabs me in my breasts and chest and with a knife he cuts me open from my knee to shoulder with a piece of broken pane

Chapter 11

Half past seven –

Sunday 21 December 1980:

Bradford Road, Batley, halfway between Leeds and Bradford.

I park by a woollen factory that has *219* as an address and cross the road –

I walk past an estate agents, cross another smaller road leading up to the Batley Grammar School, and there it is, between the *Chop Suey* and a chemist –

Number 230, Bradford Road, Batley, West Yorks:

RD News.

I walk past the newsagents, cross the road by the red bus shelter with no glass left, and stand on the other side of the road, taking a good look:

One door, big window full of Christmas adverts and gas heaters downstairs –

One window, curtains drawn upstairs.

I cross back over and go inside the shop –

There's a tall Indian or Pakistani putting the papers out in front of the counter.

He turns and he nods when he hears me come in –

I look at the piles of Sunday papers, the shelves of sweets and boxes of chocolates, the gas canisters and heaters, the cans of pet food and processed meat, the birthday and the Christmas cards, the beer and the spirits, the cigarettes behind the counter covered with more sweets.

I go through the top shelf –

Penthouse, Playboy, Escort, Razzle, Fiesta etc.

'You got *Spunk*?' I ask.

'You what?' says the Indian or Pakistani.

'Magazine called *Spunk*?'

'Never heard of it mate,' he says.

'Mucky mag, it is.'

'Never heard of it,' he says again, but he's stopped what he's doing and is moving back behind the counter.

I pick up a *Sunday Mirror* that promises photographs from Laureen Bell's funeral –

I hand him the right money and ask him: 'You own this place do you?'

'You what?' he says, putting the coins in the till.

'Just asking if this is yours?' I say, looking round.

'Why?'

'Just asking that's all.'

'We rent it actually, if you must know.'

'And the upstairs, you rent that as well?'

He's pissed off is the Indian or Pakistani and he lets me know: 'What's it to you?'

I take out my warrant card.

'Why didn't you just say?' he asks me.

'You got a licence for that lot?' I ask him, nodding at the booze.

'Yeah.'

'There's no sign.'

'Sorry. We're getting one.'

'That's all right then.' I shrug.

He stands there behind the till, looking nervous.

I ask him again: 'So what about upstairs?'

'You what?'

'That yours?'

'I told you, we just rent it.'

Again: 'The upstairs?'

'No.'

'Who's upstairs then?'

'Don't know do I.'

'You don't know who lives upstairs? Come on.'

'I don't.'

'Who does?'

'Landlord, I suppose.'

'Who is?'

'Mr Douglas.'

Fuck –

'And where's he?'

'Other side of Moors somewhere.'

'You don't have the address, do you?'

'Not on me, no.'

'So how do you pay him?'

'He comes round once a month, doesn't he.'

'His first name Bob, is it?'

'Yeah, it is. He was a copper and all – you probably know him.'

'Probably do,' I say. 'Small world.'

I take the Bradford Road through Batley and into Dewsbury, then the Wakefield Road up through Ossett and into Wakefield, the radio talking about the Laureen Bell funeral:

'A packed village church listened in tears and silence to Laureen's favourite record, Simon and Garfunkel's Bridge Over Troubled Water, *before which the vicar had read from St John.'*

In the centre of Wakefield I park off the Bullring, staring up at the first floor of the Strafford –

The first floor of the Strafford still boarded up after all these years –

After all these years back again, back in this big black bloody world –

This big black bloody world full of a million black and bloody hells –

A million black and bloody hells in this big black bloody shrinking world –

Where hells collide:

Wakey Fear –

January 1975, that second week:

Black snow blowing across the Bullring, blue tape keeping the pavement and the entrance clear.

Clarkie and I climbed over the tape, Clarkie saying: 'So half one, just as they're about to knock off, Craven and Douglas get the call – shots fired at the Strafford and, while Wood Street are scratching around for the Specials, Craven and Douglas park right out front and head straight up here.'

'Call logged 1:28 a.m., anonymous?'

'Yep,' said Clarkie. 'Anonymous.'

We started to climb the stairs to the left of the entrance to the ground floor pub, me saying: 'And they're aware that shots have been fired and that the SPG are being deployed, yet still they charge right up here?'

'Hero cops, remember?'

'Dumb bastards, morelike.'

At the top of the stairs, I pushed open the door –

Two weeks on and the room still stank of smoke, still stank of the bad things that had gone on here, still stank of death –

The mirror and the optics behind the bar, shattered; the jukebox in the corner, in pieces; the carpets and the furniture in sticks, stained.

Clarkie said: 'So in they come and see bodies and men in hoods and it's bang! Douglas gets a bullet in the shoulder and thwack! Craven gets a butt to the skull and then the gunmen exit, just minutes before the Specials arrive.'

I was nodding, taking out the SPG report, reading out loud: '1:45 a.m., Tuesday 24 December 1974, officers deployed to the Strafford Public House in Wakefield in response to reports of shots fired. On arrival at the scene, officers found the downstairs empty and proceeded up the stairs. On entering the first floor bar, officers found three people dead at the scene and three seriously injured, two with gunshot wounds. There was no sign of the people responsible and calls were made to immediately set up roadblocks. Ambulances were called and arrived at 1:48 a.m.'

I stopped reading –

Clarkie was squatting down, eyes closed.

'What you thinking?' I asked him.

He looked up: 'OK, let's back up a bit?'

I nodded.

'We've got to sort out what happened before Craven and Douglas, before the Specials.'

Me: 'Go on.'

'Well, looking at the sketches and the photographs,' he said, doing just that. 'We've got the barmaid Grace Morrison, dead behind here,' and he walked behind the bar, putting the photograph down next to the till –

'Then we've got the three men: Bell dead here,' and Clarkie put a photo down on the sofa that ran along the window –

'Box there,' he pointed, handing me a photo to put down on the floor in front of the bar. 'And Booker, bleeding to death next to him.'

Four photographs –

Four black and white photographs –

Stood there in the centre of the wreckage, Clarkie and me staring at the four black and white photographs laid out across the room.

'Order?' he asked me.

'Well,' I said. 'We've got three guns: a shotgun, a Webley, and an L39 rifle.'

'An L39? That's the new police rifle,' said Clarkie.

'Yep. Popular weapon these days.'

'So who got what?'

'Box, Booker, and Douglas get the shotgun; Bell the L39 and the barmaid the pistol, the Webley.'

'Well, Craven reckoned on a four-man team. We got three guns.'

'Still can't get the order clear, can you?' I said.

'This is what I reckon,' said Clarkie, back over by the door. 'Night before Christmas Eve, everywhere quiet waiting for the big night tomorrow; gone one, the downstairs closed. Strafford a well-known afterhours, bit of brass. Car pulls up outside, they hit the stairs running, burst in, shouting for the till – but there's buttons, it's a fuck up. They turn on the public – except this public is Derek fucking Box, professional villain and hardman, and his mate Paul. And they're fucked if they're going to hand over their big posh new watches to some crew of out of town nonces.'

'Out of town?'

'No-one local's going to do the Strafford, Pete.'

'Kids?'

'Come on, an L39? This is some heavy bloody ordnance they've got here.'

I stared over at the sofa, at the hole in the back of the chair, the hole that went through into the wall –

The hole where Ol' Billy Bell had been sitting, his broken glass still on the floor.

Clarkie was saying: 'So Derek and Paul are giving them bollocks and one of them let's Derek have it, then Paul, and then it's in for a penny in for a pound, bye-bye Billy, bye-bye Gracie – who's been screaming her fucking tits off anyway.'

I was nodding along, glancing at the photo on the bar.

'Then they're doing the till and their pockets, when in come our hero cops, and it's thwack, bang, thank you Wakefield.'

Me: 'Thanks for nothing.'

'Four dead, two wounded coppers – and all for the change in their pockets.'

'Can't see it,' I said. 'Can't see it.'

'You will,' said George Oldman, in through the back door with Maurice Jobson. 'You will.'

Millgarth, Leeds –

Sunday 21 December 1980:
Murphy, McDonald, Hillman, Marshall.
'Where's Bob Craven?' I ask –
Everyone shrugs their shoulders.
'Well,' I say. 'This one's me.'
Eyes down –
Silence in the dark room for the ritual of the dead –
Thinking, *is this how the dead live*:

'At 6:30 a.m. on Saturday 19 May last year the body of
Joanne Clare Thornton, a 19-year-old bank clerk, was found in
Lewisham Park, Morley. She was not a prostitute nor was her
moral character questionable. She was last seen alive when she
left her aunt's house at 11:55 p.m. on Friday 18 May to walk to
her own home, a distance of just over one mile. Death was
estimated to have occurred between 12:15 a.m. and 12:30 a.m.
on Saturday 19 May 1979.

'That death came from two blows to the back of the head as
she walked through the park and was instantaneous, her skull
fractured from ear to ear. Her killer then dragged her onto the
grass, repositioned her clothes and stabbed her twenty-one times
in the abdominal area, six times in the right leg, and three
times on and in the vagina. When he had finished he placed
one shoe between her thighs and her own raincoat over her.

'Joanne lay like that until 6:30 when she was initially spotted
by a bus driver who believed it was a bundle of rags and
reported it as such when he returned to his depot. By that time,
however, a local woman on her way to work had already
realised what exactly that pile of rags was and reported it to the
police.

'George Oldman issued the following statement:
'*If this is connected with the previous Ripper killings, then he has
made a terrible mistake. As with Rachel Johnson, the dead girl is
perfectly respectable. It appears he has changed his method of attack
and this is concerning me; now in a non-red light area and attacking
innocents. All women are at risk, even in areas not recognised as
Ripper Country.*'

'There was a big response,' I continue, glancing at Helen
Marshall. 'And witnesses came forward providing us with one
solid description plus three motors –

'At about nine on the Friday night, a man had attempted to

pick up a Jamaican woman as she walked along Fountain Street in the centre of Morley. He was driving a dark-coloured Ford Escort and was described as being about thirty years of age with dirty blond collar-length hair, which was greasy and worn over his ears. He had what was described as a Jason King moustache which ended halfway between the corners of his mouth and chin, with a square face and jaw and was generally described as being of a scruffy appearance. He was wearing a brown-brushed cotton shirt with a tartan check, open at the neck, under a tartan lumber jacket with a beige or white fur collar.

'The same man was spotted at about midnight parked in the same Ford Escort outside a café on the Middleton Road, across from Lewisham Park. The witness described the Escort as being made between 1968 and 1975, which would make it something between a G and N redg.

'A photofit of this man was shown to Linda Clark, who was the woman who'd been attacked in Bradford in June 1977, and has to date provided us with the best description of the Ripper.'

'Assuming she was attacked by Ripper, that is,' says Murphy.

'Yep,' I sigh. 'Assuming she was attacked by the Ripper.'

'Sorry,' says Murphy, palms up –

'No John, you're right; we can't assume anything. However,' I continue: 'When she was shown the photofit of the Morley man, Linda Clark said: "That's him, Dave. The man who attacked me." According to Oldman.'

'Dave?' says Helen Marshall.

'That's the name the man who picked her up had given her.'

'Sorry,' she says. 'I didn't know that.'

'That car was a Cortina, yeah?' asks Murphy.

'Mark II, white or yellow,' adds Hillman.

'Anyway,' I say. 'Other Morley motors that have yet to be eliminated are a dark-coloured Datsun saloon, parked by the park with its lights off, and a tan or orange-coloured Rover 2.5 or 2.6 litre that was also seen passing the park on two occasions just before midnight. Neither of the drivers of these two vehicles have ever come forward.'

They're taking notes, getting ready to check their files, their lists –

Hillman looks up: 'Going back a bit, the positioning of the shoe, that's similar to Clare Strachan and the boot.'

'Good point,' I say. 'And that's obviously another thing keeping Strachan in the frame.'

Marshall: 'It's also similar to the piece of wood found on Joan Richards.'

'Yes,' I nod, then: 'One other odd thing.'

They stop writing and look up.

'A woman of Joanne's age and description was seen walking close to the park in the direction of her home with a man described as being in his early twenties, five foot eight, with mousy-coloured greasy hair brushed right to left and a little wavy. He had stubble and prominent cheekbones, sunken cheeks, and was wearing a three-quarter-length dark-coloured coat and jeans.

'If this wasn't Joanne and the Ripper, then this couple have yet to come forward. If it was Ripper and victim, then the description is at odds with previous ones.'

'Unless there were two of them,' whispers Marshall.

'That's what I said,' winks Murphy.

'No, not two separate Rippers. Two of them together – doing the killings together.'

'What? A bloody tag-team?'

'Yes,' she says. 'A *bloody* tag-team.'

No-one speaks, eyes moving from her to me and back again until –

Until there's a knock on the door and a uniform says: 'Mr Hunter, Detectives Prentice and Alderman are here.'

'Thank you,' I say, looking at my watch. 'One last thing – they pulled a size eight boot print from the park very similar to the ones also found on Joan Richards and on Tracey Livingston.'

Taking notes, getting ready to check their files, their lists –

Finished, I close my notebook and stand up.

'John,' I say to Murphy. 'I'm going to have a chat with Jim Prentice and Dickie Alderman; would you mind sitting in?'

'Not at all,' he says, getting up.

'OK, I'll see the rest of you back at the hotel tonight, if not before. Tomorrow we'll do Dawn Williams after the morning briefing and I'll also update you on Laureen Bell.'

'If there's anything to update,' says Hillman.

'Yeah, if there is anything.'

*

Dick Alderman and Jim Prentice are waiting for us downstairs.

Dick doesn't even say hello –

Jim says: 'Where do you want to do this?'

'It's your Nick,' I say –

'But it's your show,' he says.

'Interview room?' offers Murphy –

'The fucking Belly?' laughs Alderman.

'Lead on,' I say.

Alderman's grinning as we follow him and Prentice down the stairs to their interview rooms; to the Belly –

Alderman opens a heavy door and we step inside one of their well-scrubbed bright rooms –

'Just get another chair,' says Prentice and goes next door.

We sit around the empty table, me and John Murphy on one side, Alderman on the other, Prentice sitting down beside him when he comes back in –

We've got our notebooks out, me and Murphy.

'All right if we smoke?' asks Prentice.

'Go ahead,' I say, declining the open pack.

Murphy takes one and the three of them light up.

'Got any sandwiches?' laughs Alderman.

'No,' I say, flicking through my notes. 'No beer either.'

'Just pulling your leg,' he says.

'Right,' I say, finding my place. 'Let's get started.'

'All ears,' winks Alderman.

'First of all, many thanks for making yourselves available. As you know, we've been asked to review all aspects of the Ripper Inquiry and to make any recommendations we might find, based on what we see.'

'And what do you see?' asks Alderman.

'Please,' I smile. 'We aren't at that stage yet; that's why we're grateful that you've agreed to have this talk with us.'

'Like we had a choice?' he sniffs.

I ignore him: 'Both of you have been involved with the inquiry from the off, and are still involved, so obviously you both have a tremendous amount of knowledge about the different investigations, the methods and procedures.'

I pause, glancing their way –

Prentice is stubbing out his cig, eyes on me; Alderman jumpy, not like him.

'Let's start at the beginning: Theresa Campbell.'

'That's not the beginning,' says Alderman. 'What about Joyce Jobson and Anita Bird?'

'Sorry, I didn't realise either of you were involved with those attacks.'

'We weren't,' says Prentice, looking at Alderman.

'Just saying that Campbell wasn't the first, that's all,' says Alderman.

'OK then,' I nod. 'The first murder.'

'That'd be a bit more accurate,' smiles Alderman.

'Both Campbell and Richards were the same team?'

Prentice nods: 'Chief Superintendent Jobson, out of here.'

'And you two were the senior detectives?'

'Yes,' says Alderman. 'Still are.'

'Other detectives involved then were John Rudkin and Bob Craven?'

Jim Prentice nods.

'I spoke with Maurice last Tuesday, he spoke very highly of this set-up.'

Prentice is still nodding, Alderman staring straight at me now –

I say: 'Impression I got was that Maurice thinks that, had this team been kept together, you'd have caught the Ripper by now.'

Silence –

'So,' I continue. 'I'm obviously interested in what you both think, given you've worked under both Maurice and George Oldman, and now Pete Noble?'

'What?' laughs Alderman. 'You're asking us whether we think if Maurice had been kept on, whether we'd have got the Ripper by now?'

'I'm just interested . . .'

'You drag me in here on a Sunday, my first fucking Sunday off in three months, to ask me that? Is that your best fucking question Mr Hunter?' he says, standing up –

'Sit down,' I say. 'And don't fucking try this on me.'

'Try what?'

'You sit down and you hear me out.'

He's staring at me, my heart fucking pounding –

'Superintendent,' I say, nodding at the chair –

He sits down.

'Thank you,' I say. 'Now, I'd like to know about the differences in the styles of the various operations, if you don't mind.'

Prentice coughs and says: 'Everything was different, yeah? I mean, you've got to remember this was five years ago, much smaller inquiry.'

'Who put them together?'

'Campbell and Richards?'

I nod.

'Maurice did, but it was obvious minute we saw her.'

Murphy: 'Richards?'

He nods: 'But we didn't have Preston in. Not Strachan at this stage.'

Me: 'And when was that then?'

'77, after the blood tests and the letters,' says Alderman, smiling: 'Like you don't know.'

'You'd been over there though? In 76?'

'Not us personally, but we'd sent people over and they'd sent some of their lot here.'

'John Rudkin and Bob Craven right?'

Alderman shrugs: 'In 75?'

I nod.

'Sounds right,' he says. 'But we've been back and forth across them sodding Moors so many times, you tell us; you're one with it all written down in front of you.'

Ignoring him: 'So then Rudkin and Bob Fraser went back in 77?'

Prentice nods.

Me: 'But by this time it's George and Pete Noble?'

They're both nodding.

'Prostitute Murder Squad?'

'Yes,' says Prentice.

I ask him: 'So Strachan was in and out for quite some time?'

'Initially, yeah.'

'And that's also been true of a number of the other murders and attacks?'

'Like who?' says Alderman.

'Well, Strachan, Janice Ryan, Liz McQueen, Tracey Livingston?'

Alderman smiles: 'Well you'd have to ask John here about
Liz McQueen.'

'Thanks,' says Murphy.

'No offence, mate,' says Alderman. 'But that was you, not
us.'

'And,' I continue. 'There are a number of other murders and
assaults that at one time or another have been linked to the
inquiry and are now considered separate.'

Alderman: 'Like who?'

I flick forward: 'Vera Megson, Bradford, February 1975;
Rachel Vaughan, Leeds, March 1977; Debbie Evans, Shipley, also
1977?'

'What about Mary Wilkie?' asks Alderman.

'What about her?'

'Prostitute, battered to death by Leeds Cathedral in 1970.'

'April ninth,' I say and look at him, waiting –

'Unsolved,' he says.

'Like all the others,' I say.

Him: 'So what's your point?'

'My point is, what's in and what's not and who decides?'

There's silence again, silence until Prentice sighs and says:
'Any murder or assault of a woman in the North of England
has to go through here. You know that.'

'Yes,' I say. 'I know that.'

'So,' grins Alderman. 'You want me and Jim to go through
every fucking unsolved murder in Yorkshire?'

'A lot are there?' winks Murphy.

Alderman ignores him, but the grin's gone: 'And you want
us to tell you why or why they're not Ripper cases?'

'Not every one,' I say. 'Just one.'

Silence –

Then: 'Just Janice Ryan.'

Bull's eye –

Eye to eye with Alderman across the table –

Hate, naked fucking hate –

You could cut it with a knife, the fucking hate in this room –

The fucking hate across this table down here in the Belly –

Cut big slices, big fucking slices off the bone until –

'So what do you want to know about Janice?' asks Prentice,
playing the Smart Man.

'Well from what we've read, the two of you were put in charge after Bradford passed it to the Ripper Room. But neither of you thought it was the Ripper until that letter turned up at the *Telegraph & Argus.*'

'Sounds like you've got everything,' says Alderman and stands up –

'Sit down,' I say, quietly.

Prentice reaches up and pulls him down into his seat.

I say to them both: 'I want you to tell us why you thought Janice Ryan wasn't murdered by the Yorkshire Ripper.'

Prentice: 'The injuries; there were no stab wounds.'

'Same as Strachan,' I say.

Prentice shrugs.

'Look,' I say. 'You're both senior detectives, good at your jobs some folks reckon. But the way this looks to me, pair of you didn't recognise a Ripper job when you saw one – losing days and days trying to fit up Bob Fraser, another bleeding copper.'

Alderman's on his feet again: 'Fuck off! You can fucking talk, fitting up coppers, you hypocritical fucking cunt . . .'

Bull's eye –

But Prentice is again pulling him back down, again playing the Smart Man: 'Sit down, Dick.'

But I'm leaning across the table, into Dick's face: 'So what were you doing, letting him get away?'

'Fuck you!'

'No, fuck you Dick!' says Murphy, between us. 'We're asking you how come you didn't think it was Ripper. You'd worked on enough . . .'

'Fuck off!'

'Bit of a balls up, all in all,' I smile –

He's red-faced is Alderman –

Red-faced and ready to fucking pop –

'Lucky he fucking wrote that letter,' I say. 'Else you'd never have put it together. She'd have just been another one of those many unsolved . . .'

And he's across the table again, shouting: 'Because it wasn't the fucking Ripper, was it. It was fucking Fraser, everyone knows that. Tell him Jim.'

Bull's eye –

'Shut up, Dick. Shut up,' Prentice is saying, the last of the Smart Men –

Dick Alderman out of his tree and control: 'No, you fuck off. I'm not having this fucking piece of shit stroll into here and tell me I can't . . .'

Murphy: 'Jim? Jim? What's he talking about?'

Prentice: 'He's talking bollocks, course it was Ripper.'

Alderman: 'Fuck off!'

'No, you fuck off Dick!'

I stand up and say: 'I think we'd better leave you gentlemen to it.'

They stop arguing, staring up at me –

'We'll come back another time,' I say. 'When you've got your stories straight.'

I'm sat in our room, the one next to the Ripper Room –

Hillman and Marshall are cross-checking cars from the Joanne Thornton inquiry.

The door opens, no knock –

It's Peter Noble, a face of bloody black thunder.

'Pete?' I say.

'Can I see you in my office?'

'Sure,' I say. 'Give us a minute, will you?'

He nods and slams the door –

Hillman and Marshall are looking at me.

'What's all that about?' asks Hillman.

'Can't imagine,' I smile and stand up.

I knock on Noble's door –

'Come,' he says and I do.

'Pete,' I say. 'What can I do for you?'

'You spoke with Dick Alderman and Jim Prentice, right?'

'That's right.'

'What happened?'

'What do you mean, *what happened*?'

'What I say I mean, *what happened*?'

'Nothing,' I shrug.

'Nothing?'

'Look, no offence, but I'm not obliged to report to you on interviews conducted for a Home Office review.'

Bad move –

He's furious, absolutely seething, fucking livid: 'No, but you are obliged to disclose information you might have that would assist in an on-going investigation.'

'And who told you that?'

'The Chief Constable, just after he'd got off the phone with Philip Evans, the man who drew up the parameters of your review.'

'Well firstly, I'd have to check that myself with Mr Evans and, secondly, it's an academic argument anyway seeing as we don't have any information that is not already available to your inquiry.'

'Bollocks,' he shouts.

'There's no need for that,' I say.

'No need for that,' he laughs. 'What about this?'

And he tosses a copy of *Spunk* across the table, *Issue 13*.

I ask him: 'Where did you get this?'

'Manchester, who tell me you've had it at least two bloody days.'

'So what? You've had it best part of three bloody years.'

'What?'

'Ask George and Maurice.'

'Ask George and Maurice what?'

'Copies were given to them by Eric Hall's widow.'

He's shaking his head: 'You should have said something.'

'I thought you knew.'

He lights a cigarette: 'This still doesn't mean you can come in here and intimidate my officers.'

'Intimidate your officers?' I say. 'Like who?'

'Prentice and Alderman.'

'Intimidate Dick Alderman? Now that is bollocks, Pete.'

'No it's bloody not,' says Noble, gathering steam again. 'I've had Dick in here threatening to resign, saying you insulted him, insulted his reputation.'

'Look,' I say. 'Dick lost his temper. He said things I'm sure he regrets and we will need to speak to him again. But that's as far as it went.'

'Not according to Dick and Jim.'

'What did they say?'

'Said you made insinuations about their handling of the Janice Ryan inquiry.'

'Yep, I did. And Dick Alderman refuted those *insinuations*, saying he didn't believe Janice Ryan was in fact killed by the same man responsible for the other Ripper murders.'

'Come on Peter, that's rubbish.'

'Is it?'

'In my opinion, absolute rubbish.'

I shrug: 'What do you want me to say?'

'Nothing,' he says, furious again.

'OK,' I nod.

'Nothing until we speak to the Chief Constable tomorrow.'

'Fine,' I say and leave him to it.

The Griffin, the bar downstairs –

It's late and everyone else has gone to bed, everyone but me and Helen Marshall and the bloke behind the bar who wishes we would:

'I'd have liked to have seen the look on his face,' she's laughing –

'Priceless,' I'm saying, miles away – no idea who or what we're talking about.

She's drunk I think, saying: 'They don't like us, do they?'

'Listen,' I say. 'It's late. You should go up.'

'What about you?'

'I've got some things to do.'

'What?' she laughs, looking at her watch.

'Just going for a drive, that's all.'

'Can I come?' she says, not looking so drunk anymore.

'If you want,' I say and stand up, my hand out.

It's gone midnight –

We walk through the deserted city centre, freezing.

'Horrible place,' she says, looking up at the ugly black buildings, then down at the dirty pavement.

I nod and lead the way through the Kirkgate Market, grateful for the cold and the night.

Minutes later, we pull out of the Millgarth car park and are away.

'Where are we going?' she asks as I switch on Radio 2.

'Batley,' I say.

'Batley?'

'Yeah,' I say and then I tell her about Janice Ryan and Eric Hall, about Eric Hall and Jack Whitehead, about Jack Whitehead and Bob Douglas, about Bob Douglas and Richard Dawson, about Richard Dawson and MJM Limited, about MJM Limited and Richard Dawson and Bob Douglas and Jack Whitehead and Eric Hall and Janice Ryan –

About murder and lies, lies and murder –

War.

And after all that she just sits and stares out of the window until she says again: 'Horrible place.'

Parked on the Bradford Road, the light on in the car, I show her the magazine –

'Page 7,' I say –

And she flicks through the pages until she comes to Janice Ryan.

Helen Marshall, ex-Vice Squad, glances at the photo and nods and hands it back.

'You heard of it?' I ask –

'No,' she says.

'Wait here,' I say and get out of the car, hard.

I've not put on the torch yet as I stumble around in the alley behind RD News –

There are cardboard boxes and piles of rubbish heaped up in front of the back-gate to the shop –

And it's locked, the gate –

I jump up and hoist myself far enough over to slip the bolt at the top of the gate –

And I jump back down, but the gate still won't open –

So I jump back up and hoist myself over and down the other side and into the tiny yard –

I go to the back door and knock –

There's a dog barking somewhere down the alley, but no lights go on.

I'm frozen, but I've got my gloves on now –

I take out my key-kit and break the lock and more laws than I can think of, but fuck 'em all – locks and laws.

I turn the handle and open the door –

The hallway is cluttered, full of boxes and gas canisters, stairs going up on the right –

And I've got the torch on now, heading up the stairs –

At the top, there's a wooden door, solid –

I knock, wait, and then I take out the kit again –

And it's a fucker this one, especially with the light on the floor and these gloves, but it gives in the end, – like they all do.

I turn the handle and open the door –

Another hall, the air stale, dead –

I walk down the hall to the front of the flat, the place deserted, no carpet –

In the front room, I pull back a curtain and can see the car and Helen Marshall parked down the road –

The light from the street, the torch, they show me what I already know:

No-one lives here –

Just scraps of furniture, – a sofa, two chairs, a table, a telephone –

I shine the torch on the dial, but there's no number –

I pick up the phone and get a dialling tone that tells me what I already suspect:

Someone comes here.

I put the receiver down, but leave it off the hook –

I walk back down the hall, an empty kitchen to the right, a bathroom and toilet next to it, a bedroom to the left –

I step into the bedroom –

I take a chance and switch on the light:

A big bedroom, a big bed with a stained orange-patterned mattress, a pair of black curtains –

Fitted cupboards down the side of the bed –

I take out *Spunk* –

I turn to page 7:

Under the spread legs, below her cunt, an orange-patterned mattress –

Back behind her open mouth and closed eyes, above that cock, black curtains –

I drop the magazine on the bed and open the cupboards –

Lights, cameras, the action:

In piles –

*Spunk*s, the whole bloody lot –

And I want photos, all the photos I can get –

I race through the piles, taking out all the different ones I can find –

They're in order, the piles, and in the end I've ten copies; only issues 3, 9, and 13 missing –

But I've already got 13, the last one.

I close the cupboard door and gather the magazines –

I turn off the light with my elbow and walk back down the hall –

I kick open the door and close it with my back –

It won't lock and they'll know I've been –

But that's OK:

I WANT THEM TO KNOW I'VE BEEN HERE.

I go back downstairs and leave the back door open and kick off the lock on the gate:

JUST SO THEY'LL KNOW ABOUT IT SOON.

I walk down the alley and back round to the car –

Helen Marshall sees me coming and gets out –

'What's all that?'

'*Spunk*,' I say –

She opens the driver's door and I get in –

She comes back round and sits down beside me in the passenger seat –

I've got the *Spunk*s in a pile on my knee –

She takes them from me, silently skimming the covers, the spreads –

'What we going to do?' she asks.

'Go through these, keep an eye on that place, and see what happens.'

'I see,' she says.

'You tired?' I ask her.

'No,' she says, defensive.

'Good,' I smile. 'Because we're going to have to do this in shifts.'

'What?'

'We're going to need to watch this place twenty-four hours.'

'What about the others?'

I shake my head: 'Maybe later, but for now I want it to be just you and me.'

'Me, you mean.'
'If you don't want to do it, just say.'
'No, it's fine,' she says, like it's not.
'Thank you,' I say –
'Mention it,' she says.

I'm drifting –
Pornographic dreams of empty rooms, black curtains and orange-patterned mattresses –
Empty TV sets, black birds and –
'What?'
I open my eyes –
The car – the air dirty, the dawn grey.
'What did you say?' Helen Marshall is asking me –
'Nothing,' I say. 'Think I must have nodded off.'
'You said my name, that's all.'
'Sorry, must have been dreaming.'
She laughs: 'Should I be flattered?'
'No, it was a nightmare,' I say.
'Charming first thing, aren't you?'
'Sorry,' I smile. 'I better go.'
'Taxi?'
'Have to be,' I say and get out of the car.
'What about these?' she asks, pointing at the pile of *Spunk*s on the back seat.
'Best pass them here,' I say.
'You got a bag for them?'
'In the boot,' I say and go and get it –
After we've done that, I lean back into the car and say: 'Take care and thank you.'
'Mention it,' she says again, an echo.
'Call Millgarth or the Griffin if you see anyone.'
'Yeah, yeah, yeah,' she's saying.
'And get the plates,' I say, handing her the keys and closing the door, – her sliding into the driver's seat.
And then I turn away and walk off towards Batley Bus Station and as I go she presses the horn once and I turn back and wave – but I can't actually see her, and in the Bus Station I use the phone and call Joan and then I get a taxi back to the Griffin, eleven issues of a pornographic magazine on my lap

but, as I count them there in the back of the taxi, there's only ten and for a sudden moment my blood runs cold thinking I left *Issue 13* on the bed above RD News, but it's here, so I think I must have miscounted and I'm another issue short, but they'll turn up, the missing ones, they always do, – eventually.

from a greenhouse and e smell bad lying there for over a week and he vomits and tries to cut off my head with a hacksaw because he wants to make a big mystery of me but alas this is still nineteen seventy seven and it is december now and e am cold down garthorne terrace hoping to do a bit of business outside the gaiety before e go home and now e am on gipton avenue a dark coloured car driving slowly along looking for love the car parked by the kerb the driver waving to someone in a house bye now see you later take care and he is all right about thirty years old stocky around five feet six inches tall with dark wavy hair and beard wearing a yellow shirt and a dark anorak with a zip and a pair of blue jeans he turns to me he says are you doing business e say yes and he says five pounds e say yes and e get in his car he says he knows a right quiet place on spare ground off scott hall street and e know it is about a mile and a half away and he is very chatty and friendly and says his name is david but he prefers dave e say very well dave it is and he says what is yours e say carol but my name is really kathy kathy kelly e ask him what he was doing back on frankland place he says he was saying goodnight to his girlfriend who is sick and he has his needs you know e say yes e know do not we all and he has them come to bed eyes and it might sound daft now but e quite fancy him a bit of a good looking and he knows it type and he would not frighten anybody because he knows a lot of the girls he is a regular punter and he is talking away about hilary and gloria and is not hilary the one with jamaican boyfriend so e am thinking that he cannot be leeds ripper can he we get to spare ground off scott hall street and dave says we should have sexual intercourse in the back of the car e say ok but you must pay me first and he says he will pay me after e say you can fuck right off e know your plan my knickers off with your muck up me and fuck all else as you drive off with your bloody fiver and e get out but wait he says there is no need for that he has his wallet out so e try the back passenger door but it is locked and he says he will come round and open it and as he passes behind me e feel a searing sickening blow on top of my head and e am screaming loudly holding my head e am falling to the floor trying to grab hold of his blue denim jeans and e can feel more blows coming until there is only darkness blackness dirty prostitute bitch you whore you bitch you dirty stinking prostitute bitch e can hear a dog barking and him walking back to his car the slam of the door the back wheels skidding with a lot of spin as he drives off e just lie there on the spare ground the terrible pain in my head the dog barking no one coming no siren so e try to stand walk across the rough ground on to road try and get to a telephone e see this lad and lass and they see my head and face all covered in blood and she starts screaming he runs off to phone an ambulance and e am sitting there in street with this girl who is hysterical and one of girls e know comes up asks me what has happened here e tell her and she says you have come in your hair with the blood e say it was the ripper then that is rippers come she says you are luckiest woman in england and e sit there in road with blood and come in my hair my head with a hole young lass screaming freezing to death and e say e do not feel lucky she says you will mark my words you lucky cow with a depressed fracture behind my ear on the left side of my head measuring one and a half inches by one inch and the seven lacerations each about two inches long plus a four inch scar on my left hand where bruises were and police said it was definitely him ripper because they found

Chapter 12

The Ripper Room –
  Millgarth, Leeds –
  Monday 22 December 1980:
  Standing room only –
  Smoke, sweat, and no smiles on 150 sad bloody faces.
  Chief Constable Angus and Temporary Assistant Chief Constable Noble down the front –
  Me at the back, by the door –
  No Alderman or Prentice.
  'It was a long weekend,' Noble is saying. 'I know a lot of us were at the funeral, Saturday.'
  Shit, I'm thinking.
  'And I know like me, for all of us who were there it's only strengthened our resolve to catch this bastard. But now we've got this – '
  Noble picks up a piece of paper off the table and reads aloud:
  'Sunday 21 December, 9 p.m., Manchester offices of the *Daily Mirror* received a telephone call delivered by a man with an accent strongly resembling the one on the so-called *Ripper Tape*. No recording was made, but the content was as follows:
  'I'm Jack and I warned you I'd strike again and I'll kill again on Tuesday, this time student so warn them to keep off streets.'
  Noble stops reading, looking up at the room –
  The Ripper Room:
  Smoke, sweat, and 150 bloody curses.
  'Jim Prentice and Dick Alderman are in Manchester now talking to the people at the *Mirror*, but whether it's him or not,' Noble continues over the rising din, 'it's already on radio and it'll be on every front page tonight and tomorrow.'
  150 more bloody curses, louder and louder until –
  Until Chief Constable Angus stands up: 'All right, I know this is the last thing we need but, once again, I have no choice but to cancel all leave for the next forty-eight hours. We're already stretched thin thanks to all these bloody protests at the cinemas, but I have spoken with a number of the local councils to try and get some sort of ban on some of these films.'

Nods all round.

'Luckily most of the students have already gone home but,' says the Chief Constable. 'Tonight and tomorrow night we have to put on a show of strength. Assistant Chief Constable Noble's drawn up the rota for you lot here and will hand it out at the end of this briefing. But I just want to add that, as the Assistant Chief Constable said, I know a lot of you were in Hartlepool for the funeral and I know you want to keep at it and that this kind of thing is the last thing you want. But we'll nail the bastard, so let's all just keep our wits about us. Thank you.'

Noble steps forward again: 'OK, better news; we have now eliminated all vehicles sighted by witnesses on Alma Road last Wednesday night, Thursday morning. Bar one: the old dark-coloured car seen reversing the wrong way down the street. Officers have once again sat with the witness to try and get a more detailed description of the car in question. But officers should pay particular attention to old and dark-coloured vehicles as you crosscheck old statements and take any further statements.

'Later today we also hope to have the new photofit complete and available for distribution. As some of you know, this description of a man seen in the vicinity of Alma Road last Wednesday night very much resembles those descriptions given by Linda Clark and statements taken in Morley, following the murder of Joanne Thornton.

'Finally, surveillance will continue on the five individuals at the top of our lists and, obviously, we will step up these efforts over the next forty-eight hours in light of the Manchester call. Thank you,' he says and nods at an assistant who begins to hand out sheets of paper.

I'm the first out the door, heading back next door, when there's an arm on mine –

Bob Craven: 'The Chief Constable asked me to have you meet him in Assistant Chief Constable Noble's office after the briefing.'

'Thank you very much, Inspector,' I say.

'Don't mention it,' he mutters, walking off.

'What?' I say –

He turns: 'Pardon?'

'I said what did you say?'

'Don't mention it,' he smiles –

'Don't mention it?'

'Yes,' he says, walking away. 'Don't mention it.'

I knock on the door –

'Come.'

I open the door and step inside Noble's office –

'Good morning, gentlemen,' I say.

Angus is sat in Noble's chair, Pete on the other side of the desk.

The Chief Constable gestures for me to sit down next to Noble –

I take my seat and wait.

'You were at the briefing then?' asks Angus, eventually.

'Yes,' I say.

'Last thing we bloody need,' says Noble, to my right.

'Can imagine,' I agree.

There's a bit of silence now, pens tapping, paper shuffling –

A bit of this, then Angus says: 'Look, I hear there were some words exchanged yesterday. Some confusion?'

'Confusion?'

'Well, from what I gather,' says Angus, glancing at Noble. 'Your interview with Detective Superintendents Alderman and Prentice ended badly and then there was some question mark about disclosure of information pertinent to the on-going investigation.'

'I'm sorry,' I say. 'I don't know what you mean.'

Angus frowning, picks up a copy of *Spunk* and says: 'Well, for a start, what about this?'

'As I told Pete yesterday, I'd been led to believe that this magazine had been given to George Oldman by Maurice Jobson, or vice versa, courtesy of Eric Hall's widow.'

'That's true,' Angus nods.

'Right,' I say. 'So I presumed George had passed it to the Ripper Squad, as he was in charge at that time.'

'Well, you'd have to ask Assistant Chief Constable Oldman about that.'

'I'd like that very much,' I say.

Angus is smiling, hands up: 'Now just a minute. In case you weren't aware, George Oldman is on sick leave.'

'Sick leave? No I wasn't aware of that.'

'So, unfortunately, any interview would be out of the question at this time.'

'I see. Is it serious?'

'He has a heart condition.'

'I'm sorry to hear that.'

'I would like to know from you however,' he goes on, 'as to the progress you're making and if there's any other information you'd like to share with us?'

'I'm sorry, sir,' I say. 'But I think it would be improper of me to speak with you before I'd spoken with either Mr Evans or Sir John Reed.'

'Of course, but I did speak with Mr Evans myself yesterday and he wanted me to emphasise to you the unique circumstances here, this being an on-going investigation and the possibility of you discovering or being in possession of information that might lead to the conclusion of this investigation.'

'Sir, I assure you, had I information that I felt would lead to the arrest of a suspect – I would waste no time in sharing it with the Assistant Chief Constable here.'

'I hope so.'

'You have my word.'

'Then that's that then.'

I nod.

Silence –

Silence until I say: 'Is that all?'

'One other thing,' says Noble, turning in his chair. 'There's been a request for a press interview with you.'

'Who from?'

'*Sunday Times*, I think.'

I look at Chief Constable Angus; he's frowning: 'Do you want to do it?'

'Not bothered, unless it helps publicity-wise?'

Noble sighs: 'We've got more than enough of that.'

'Would have to be with our Press Officer,' says Angus.

I nod: 'Let's see what they have to say. Any problems, I'll talk to you and Philip Evans.'

Angus shrugs his shoulders: 'Fine.'

Noble says: 'I'll have the Press Office set it up. This afternoon?'

I nod again.

'Thank you,' says Angus –

I take my cue and stand and leave.

I press play:

'I'm Jack. I see you are still having no luck catching me. I have the greatest respect for you George, but Lord! You are no nearer catching me now than four years ago when I started. I reckon your boys are letting you down, George. They can't be much good can they?

'The only time they came near catching me was a few months back in Chapeltown when I was disturbed. Even then it was a uniformed copper not a detective.

'I warned you in March that I'd strike again. Sorry it wasn't Bradford. I did promise you that but I couldn't get there. I'm not quite sure when I'll strike again but it will be definitely some time this year, maybe September, October, even sooner if I get the chance. I am not sure where, maybe Manchester, I like it there, there's plenty of them knocking about. They never learn do they George? I bet you've warned them, but they never listen.'

Pause –

Thirteen seconds, count them:

One two three four five six seven eight nine ten eleven twelve thirteen seconds of hiss, then –

'Take her in Preston, and I did, didn't I George? Dirty cow. Come my load up that.

'At the rate I'm going I should be in the book of records. I think it's eleven up to now isn't it? Well, I'll keep on going for quite a while yet. I can't see myself being nicked just yet. Even if you do get near I'll probably top myself first. Well it's been nice chatting to you George. Yours, Jack the Ripper.

'No good looking for fingerprints. You should know by now it's as clean as a whistle. See you soon. Bye.

'Hope you like the catchy tune at the end. Ha. Ha.'

And then –

'I'll say your name

Then once again

Thank you for being a friend.'

Stop.

Silence –

Seconds, minutes of silence in the dark room –

Minutes of silence until –

Until I say: 'This was received June 20, last year. I'm sure you're all probably as sick to death of the sound of that voice as I am, – but I want to spend some time on this today because it has had such a bloody bearing on the investigation, both in what came next and what it meant for all that had gone before.'

Murphy, McDonald and Hillman, the three of them nodding along –

Craven in the corner –

No Marshall.

'Right, as you know, they'd had the letters; four in all: the first three were all in June 77, two addressed to the *Yorkshire Post* journalist Jack Whitehead,' I say, eyes on Craven –

No reaction.

'The third one was to George Oldman, but sent to the *Telegraph and Argus* offices in Bradford. And the last one was sent in March 1978, again addressed to Oldman, but this time to the *Daily Mirror* in Manchester.'

Murphy: 'That's where they got the call last night?'

I nod: 'Right, but that call aside for now, the tape and all four letters are without any real doubt the work of the same man. All five items share the same handwriting, blood groupings from saliva tests, and the same traces of oil and minerals. The first three letters and the tape make specific reference to the murder of Clare Strachan in Preston, while the fourth letter talks about the murder of Doreen Pickles in Manchester.'

'May I?' interrupts Hillman.

'Go on.'

'That fourth letter was also postmarked Preston.'

I nod: 'And that is?'

'Scene of the Strachan and Livingston murders.'

'Good point, Mike,' I say. 'So the amount of publicity the recording, the letters generated, the sheer number of leads as you've all seen – it's staggering.'

'Overwhelming,' says Alec McDonald.

'But let's remember,' says Murphy. 'It was a bloody leak that got them into this.'

'That's right,' I say, again with a glance at Craven. 'They'd made no decision on whether to go public with the tape. In fact, word is George was dead against it, especially since he'd always claimed the June 77 letter to the *Argus* had been a hoax. But then there was the leak, again to the *Argus*, and they had no choice.'

'Bad time for them,' Murphy continues. 'They were leaking like a bloody sieve, all them stories about faked overtime, dubious expenses, it was all coming out.'

Craven in the corner has his eyes closed, head forward.

'And three months later,' I say, quietly. 'It got even worse.'

I open the notebook and read:

'On the morning of Sunday 9 September last year, the body of Dawn Williams was found hidden in a pile of rubbish behind an empty terrace house in Ash Lane, behind the Bradford University at which the deceased was a student.

'She had been killed by a single blow to the back of her skull. Her clothing had then once again been repositioned and she had been stabbed nine times in the trunk, mostly in the abdominal area.'

I stop and hand them the copies I've made of the lists of witnesses, the lists of police officers, the lists of vehicles, lists of the possible tyre widths and so on –

Twenty-three pages of lists.

I continue: 'It was after this murder that Oldman issued the following information and instructions to all police forces in the North of England –

'Taken from the introduction to the revised and updated *Murders and Assaults upon Women in the North of England* it said:

"It is significant that although most of the early victims are prostitutes or women of loose moral character, in the majority of cases no obvious sexual interference has taken place, and the motive for each time is a pathological hatred of women. In the most recent cases, innocent women have been attacked. In the majority of these offences, vicious hammer blows to the back of the head have occurred, and it is generally thought that this precedes the stabbing of the victim. In some cases the clothing of the victim is moved to expose the breasts and lower abdomen, prior to stab wounds being inflicted. No stabbing has occurred through clothing.

"The three common factors in all the crimes are:

a) The use of two weapons: a sharp instrument and a 1¹/₄ pound ball-pein hammer.

b) The absence of sexual interference, except in one instance.

c) *The clothing moved to expose breasts and pubic region.*

"Through evidence gathered, the following five-point list should be used for the purposes of elimination:

1. The man was born before 1924 or after 1959.
2. The man is an obvious coloured person.
3. The man is a size nine shoe or above.
4. The man has a blood group other than type B.
5. The man does not have a Geordie or North Eastern accent.

"It should be remembered that it may be that the man responsible has come to police attention in the past for assaults on prostitutes and women which did not result in serious injury, and suggestions regarding the identity of the person responsible, or any other information about similar assaults, not necessarily fatal, would be appreciated." '

I stop.

Silence.

I say: 'And that brings us to here and Laureen Bell.'

I close the folder and look at my watch:

Noon –

Fuck –

I need another car, need to get back over to Batley, to Marshall –

Murphy, McDonald, and Hillman looking at me –

Craven's fucking asleep in the corner –

'OK,' I say. 'We need to now start compiling the crosschecks, completing various lists, speaking to the officers involved. We'll start now and then meet tomorrow morning, first thing, see how far we've got.'

'Wake him, shall I?' grins Hillman, nodding at Craven –

I put my finger to my lips: 'Better let him sleep.'

I'm at the desk downstairs, trying to get a car, when there's a word in my ear:

'Press are here, sir.'

I turn round –

It's one of the Yorkshire Press Office, Evans I think –

'*Sunday Times*?' he says.

'Shit,' I say, looking at my watch again.

'Problem, sir?'

'No. Where are they?'

'The Assistant Chief Constable's office. Mr Noble said we could use that.'

'Fine,' I say and follow him back upstairs.

There are two journalists waiting for us:

'Anthony McNeil,' says a tall man in glasses.

I shake his hand.

'Andy Driscoll,' says the other man as I take his hand.

'I've never been interviewed by two people at the same time,' I say, smiling at Evans as he sits down at the back of the room.

'Well,' says McNeil. 'Andy's just along for the ride.'

I sit down at Noble's desk: 'Is that right?'

'No, he's only joking sir.'

'Well, OK. Shall we make a start?' I ask.

'Do you mind?' asks Driscoll, putting a small pocket cassette recorder on Noble's desk.

'Should get one myself,' I smile, switching on the one in my pocket.

'OK,' says McNeil. 'You were brought in here as part of the *Brains Trust* and – '

'Your words not mine,' I interrupt.

McNeil smiles: 'Right, fair enough. So I wonder if you could tell us what progress you and the other members of this *Super Squad* have made so far?'

I smile: '*Super Squad* is it now?'

'Well, it is supposed to be the top detectives from across the country.'

'I'm flattered.'

'But,' he says, sitting back in his chair. 'Is it deserved?'

'Pardon?'

'Progress; that's what people want to hear about,' he says. 'What progress you have or haven't made.'

I say: 'Is that a question?'

He closes his eyes for a moment and then opens them and says: 'Yes, that's a question.'

'Mr McNeil,' I say as quietly and calmly as I can. 'Our job is to look at the operation and to advise and to make appropriate recommendations.'

McNeil smiles and gives me a bloody wink: 'Is that an answer?'

'That's putting it a touch mildly, is it not?' interrupts Driscoll.

I try and smile: 'I thought you were along for the ride?'

'I'm not – but can the same be said of you and this so-called *Super Squad*?' laughs Driscoll.

Before I can respond, McNeil's already telling me: 'What I mean to say is, this team were brought in for what was described as, and I quote: "*a complete and thorough review of past and present police strategy in the hunt for the Ripper.*" Was that or was that not the brief?'

'That is the brief and that's what we are in the process of doing.'

'Thank you,' snorts McNeil. 'So would you mind telling us then how much progress you've made in the course of this review.'

'It's on-going, Mr McNeil.'

'Obviously.'

'Well, *obviously*, if it's on-going it is therefore not complete and so I can't comment,' I say, my voice rising, looking at my watch, thinking about Helen Marshall. 'What more do you want me to say?'

But then he pounces: 'Something to give hope to the thousands of students fleeing the cities of the North tonight; something to give hope to the millions of women who aren't lucky enough to be able to flee from the cities of the North, who must spend another Christmas, their sixth, trapped inside their homes, dependent on lifts from fathers and brothers, husbands and sons, any one of whom might be the Yorkshire Ripper himself; something to say to these mothers and sisters, these wives and daughters, not to mention something for Mrs Bell and the twelve other mothers who have no daughters and the nineteen children who have no mothers, all thanks to him; him and your inaction.'

Silence; silence but for the noises of the station around us –

The station where somewhere men's voices can be heard singing an obscene version of *Jingle Bells* –

The man at the back from the Press Office or Community Affairs or whatever they call it, he gets up and leaves the room –

I look up at McNeil who's shaking his head, his eyes on me –

Outside the singing stops, leaving just the silence until Evans returns and takes his seat at the back again.

McNeil sighs and says: 'If you've nothing to say in response to that, then I wonder if I might ask you for comment on a number of fundamental criticisms that have been levelled in the direction of West Yorkshire and the inquiry in general?'

I've got my hands up, but to no avail –

'Firstly,' he presses on. 'There's the issue of Miss Bell's missing bag and it turning up covered in blood and marked as lost property a good twenty-four hours after her body was discovered, despite being handed in to police officers prior to the discovery of her body, not to mention the statements given by her flatmates insisting that officers look for Miss Bell when she failed to return home on time.'

'The Chief Constable has already publicly addressed those criticisms, as you are fully aware.'

'So you've nothing to add?'

'Nothing.'

'OK then, how about the fact that Candy Simon and Tracey Livingston were also both reported missing to police officers prior to the discovery of their bodies and, in Candy's case, her bloodstained underwear was also found.'

'I've nothing to say about that either.'

'OK, something closer to home then. Have you managed to get any explanation for the fact that it took Manchester police a whole week to locate Elizabeth McQueen's handbag, despite the fact that it was less than 100 yards from where her body had been discovered.'

'Mr McNeil,' I say, fists up. 'All these issues that you raise are obviously matters of concern to us and are part and parcel of the review that we've undertaken but, honestly and I hope for the last time, let me say that it would be unprofessional of me to pass comment on these matters at this time.'

'Unprofessional?'

'Yes.'

Driscoll hands McNeil a piece of paper from his briefcase and McNeil says: 'May I read you something?'

'Feel free,' I sigh.

McNeil reads: '*So much about the Ripper is ifs and buts – one cannot be 100% certain, for instance, that all the murders are linked. What we are saying is that they are all similar and are the ones we are most interested in. For reasons obvious to all officers there is a certain amount of information that has to be kept back for the vital confrontation with the man responsible for the killings.*

'*On the balance of probability the man who sent the tape and wrote the letters is the Ripper but there can always be a question mark and it would be wrong for officers to eliminate suspects because they had not got a Geordie accent. We give certain guidelines but in the end, I feel, it will be some officer's intuition that leads us to the killer. Hopefully, some officer will be in the right place at the right time and give us the break we need. So let's make that break and nail him.*'

McNeil stops reading.

Silence once again –

Until Driscoll says: 'You've never heard that before, have you Mr Hunter?'

I shake my head: 'No, that's the first time. Who said it?'

'Assistant Chief Constable Noble in this month's issue of the *West Yorkshireman*.'

I glance over at Evans, who says: 'It's the West Yorkshire Police newspaper.'

'Right,' I nod.

'Do you have any comment to make about that?' asks McNeil.

'It's good advice.'

'What about him saying that all the murders might not be linked, that the tape might be a hoax?'

'He didn't actually say that. But what he did say was good advice.'

'What about the murders not all being linked, what about that?'

'He's right, you can't be 100% certain.'

'Janice Ryan? What about her? Always been a big question mark over her.'

'Like I just said, you can't be 100%.'

'So you're not at present investigating any connection between the murders of Janice Ryan and a Bradford Vice detective called Eric Hall?'

Evans is on his feet, trying to interrupt –

I'm shaking my head: 'No we aren't.'

'That's not what his widow is saying.'

Me: 'You've spoken to Mrs Hall?'

McNeil and Driscoll both nod –

'She's mistaken then,' I say.

'And so there's no truth in reports that the murders of Hall and Ryan are being linked in any way to raids earlier today on premises in Greater Manchester, which are in turn being connected to the murders there of Robert Douglas and his six-year-old daughter Karen last week?'

'I don't know anything about any raids.'

Driscoll: 'Well we've received information that the offices of Asquith and Dawson and various city centre premises belonging to them were raided at dawn today.'

I'm looking at Evans, who's still stood up and looking at me, our eyes and hands all over the place –

'I wasn't aware of that,' I say, eventually.

McNeil: 'Are you aware that there are rumours circulating to the effect that you are to be removed from this so-called *Brains Trust*, this *Super Squad*, due to your personal connections to Richard Dawson, the man targeted in today's raids?'

'That's it,' says Evans. 'I've heard enough of this.'

They both stand up, McNeil and Driscoll, their hands raised in apology –

Mouthing and whispering this and that about getting off on the wrong foot –

Foot in their mouths, no offence intended –

But I'm just sat there, reeling –

When Anthony McNeil leans across the desk, hand out: 'Thank you for your time.'

I put my own hand out automatically, unable to speak –

And then he tightens his grip on my hand and whispers: 'You think the tape's a hoax, don't you?'

Evans: 'Mr McNeil – '

'Yes or no?'

Evans: 'He's not going to be drawn into – '

'Yes or no?'

Silence again, fucking silence –

McNeil, Driscoll, and Evans, all staring at me –

Staring at me sat there behind Noble's desk –

In Noble's chair –

'Yes or no Mr Hunter?'

'No.'

*

Searching for a phone and a car, upstairs and down, Millgarth giving me the bloody run around, the finger –

At last, long bloody last, into a phone in a corner of the Ripper Room: 'Roger?'

'Pete? Thank Christ for that.'

Me: 'What the fucking hell's going on?'

'Smith's only had Vice raid Dawson's office and that place you went on Oldham Street.'

'Shit.'

'And he's told the press of possible links to the Douglas murders.'

'Fuck!'

'Gets worse, mate.'

'What?'

'Dawson never showed up this morning.'

'Where was he?'

'Fuck knows. His solicitor knows nothing, sat there waiting like us, couldn't get in touch with him.'

'You called his wife?'

'Not a clue. Hysterical.'

'Shit, she'll have been onto Joan.'

'He called you has he?'

'No.'

'You heard about the raids?'

'From the *Sunday* bloody *Times*.'

'Fucking hell.'

'Yeah, told me I was going to be removed from the Ripper because of it.'

'Because of Dawson?'

'Yep.'

'Bollocks. You coming back over?'

'Can't,' I say, looking at my watch again –

Fuck:

Gone two.

'Pete?'

'Sorry, what did you say?'

'Said, keep in touch mate.'

'OK.'

I hang up and sprint downstairs, then *shit* –

Back up to our room again for the bag of *Spunk*s –

Nods at Murphy and McDonald, weird looks from the pair of them –

Then back downstairs again, underground.

Snow –

At least they've given me a Saab –

I push out of Leeds, radio on:

'Some shops are closing early today to allow staff to go home in daylight, this following a telephone threat to the Daily Mirror from a man claiming to be the Yorkshire Ripper, saying he would kill again today or tomorrow.'

Black snow –

The car freezing –

So this is Christmas?

Roads dead, coming down through Morley, thinking of Joanne Thornton, heading down into Batley, thinking of Helen Marshall –

And what have we done?

On to the Bradford Road, out of Batley itself and I can see the car up ahead, parked in the same spot –

I pull up a little way behind and lock the car and jog down the road, the snow now just a dirty cold grey rain, the long night coming down.

I tap on the driver's door and look in –

No-one.

Fuck.

I try the door –

Locked.

I look up the road, down the road, across at RD News –

Deserted, the whole place, but for a steady stream of lorries in the rain.

Fuck, fuck.

And then I see her, coming out of the phonebox further up, her jacket over her head, running back towards the car in the lorry lights and sleet –

She sees me, jumps –

'I was just calling you,' she says, opening the car door, glancing back over at the newsagents.

'Why? Something happened?'

'No, no,' she says, getting in and opening the other side for me –

We close the doors and sit there, the car cold and stale, her looking old and rough.

'I just wanted to know when you'd be coming back,' she says, embarrassed.

'Sorry,' I say. 'It's been a bloody rotten day.'

'Laugh a minute here,' she smiles.

'Quiet?'

'As the grave.'

'You eaten anything?'

'A pair of driving gloves and a map book.'

'Sorry, should have brought something.'

'I can last,' she says.

I say: 'You get off now.'

'What about you?'

'I'll stay.'

'What time shall I come back?'

'You've done enough.'

'No, I want to.'

'You sure?'

'I wouldn't say if I wasn't.'

'Thank you,' I say.

'Is there anything else you want me to do?'

'No, you better get something to eat, get some sleep.'

'Think I've gone past sleep.'

'Actually there is one thing,' I say, taking out my notebook.

She's smiling: 'Thought there might be.'

'Could you just ring Mrs Hall? Seemed to get on, didn't you?'

'Yeah. Why?'

'Just see how she is.'

'That it?' she laughs. 'See how she is?'

'I don't know,' I say, shaking my head. 'I had this interview with a right pair from the *Sunday Times*. They said they'd been talking to her. You could just ask her about them?'

'Ask her what about them?'

'What they'd asked her, what she said.'

'OK. The subtle approach?'

I tear out the page with Mrs Hall's number on it –

'It's the top one,' I say.

'Who's the other one?'

'The Reverend Laws.'

'I was just thinking about him,' she says.

'How awful for you.'

'You don't like him, do you?' she asks.

'No.'

'Fair enough,' she says.

I open the passenger door –

'What time do you want me back?' she asks.

I look at my watch and say: 'Eleven, eleven thirty?'

She nods and starts the car: 'See you then.'

'Take care.'

'Don't do anything I wouldn't do,' she laughs as I close the door.

'No,' I say, and she pulls away, – gone.

Back in the Saab, I drive up the road for a bit until I'm opposite the park where I reverse into the drive of a house with an unlit Christmas tree in the window and then head back down past RDNews, parking near enough to be able to watch the upstairs window in the rearview mirror and the back of the alley in the wing, winding down the window a crack to stop the car steaming up and then I sit there, radio on, – listening, watching, waiting.

same half worn india autoway cross ply tyres that were on front wheels at the scene of my mate marie watts so e truly am luckiest woman in yorkshire a lady well known in the preston area short black leather jacket blue jeans blue shirt carrying a blue denim handbag slim dark haired and attractive with a full sensual mouth stare into her you still breathing looking at the dead see if you find suffering equal to transmission six tracey livingston thirty one found in her flat on ash lane preston saturday the seventh of january nineteen seventy eight death due to four blows to the head with an instrument which has not been recovered stab wounds to the abdomen and possibly to the back which would not have proved fatal the wounds were such that the assailants clothing will be heavily bloodstained stare into her misery and she looks at you and with both hands she opens her chest and says see how you tear me see the monstrous punishment you still breathing looking at the dead see if you find suffering equal to a lumpy bundle covered in blankets she had initially been attacked as she stepped through her door and had received four massive blows to the head her killer had then removed her coat before lifting her onto the bed her faded denim jeans and pants had been dragged down together but her jeans had been partially pulled back up her bra had been hoisted above her breasts which were exposed she had been stabbed six times in the stomach and there were further signs of stabbing attempts to her back although her skin was not broken and some slash marks along the left side of her body caused by a knife or chisel approximately half an inch wide a blood sample showed that tracey had consumed twenty measures of spirits and had died at midnight a vaginal swab revealed the presence of semen but this was thought to be as a result of sexual activity some time before a size seven boot print from a dunlop warwick wellington boot the same as that found on joan richards thigh found on the bottom bed sheet in the silence of a flat after death just the clock and the drip of the tap the blood in pools in the hall the lumpy bundle covered in blankets on the bed just the clock and the drip of the tap the thick dark hair matted with the thick dark blood the repeated knocking on the door the silence of a flat after death on her thigh a bloody hand print on her bed sheet a bloody boot print she was banging on the roof of a car obviously the worse for drink and using the sort of foul language no decent woman would have been using and when e stopped she jumped in beside me without any coaxing and we drove to her flat and e took my claw hammer from under the seat and stuffed it inside my coat and hung my coat up inside her flat and then e waited until she was sitting on the bed with her back to me before e struck with four blows that knocked her to the floor and then e hoisted her up and back onto the bed and exposed her breasts and the lower part of her body and then e hit her with one end of the hammer and clawed at her with the other watching the marks appear in her flesh and e stuck a knife into her stomach and because we were inside the blood looked red for the first time and not the black colour it always looked in the dark and e threw the sheets over her and left her alone in her bedroom making horrible gurgling sounds though e knew she would not be in any state to tell anyone what had happened for e knew it would be a long time before they would come and e knew they would look away e knew they could not stare into her misery her looking at them with both hands opening her

Chapter 13

A shot –

Awake, sweating and afraid in the car in the night – the car dirty, the night black.

I look at the clock:

Midnight –

Shit.

I switch on the overhead light and check my own watch.

I switch off the light again:

Sat in the dark, thinking –

Where is she?

I get out of the car –

I walk up the road in the sleeting rain to the phonebox –

I open the door and –

BANG!

I'm flat on my back on the pavement, glass raining down –

There are bells ringing and there are screams, feet running –

People tearing out of the *Chop Suey* –

And I'm trying to stand up when –

BANG!

More glass raining down, more bells ringing, more screams, more feet running and I'm up –

Up and across the road, a car braking and swerving to avoid me –

There is smoke billowing out of RD News, the whole front gaping open –

'Gas!' someone's shouting. 'Gas!'

I sprint past the chemist, its glass all gone, alarm deafening –

Chinese waiters running here and there, the restaurant emptying –

Women customers tripping in long dresses and high heels, men with blood in their hair, on their faces, their hands –

Round the back and into the alley, people in their dressing gowns and coats coming out, dogs barking –

And I get to the back gate and it's open and I go into the yard and there are sirens now –

And I reach for the back door and I open it and –

BAAAAAAAAAAAAANG!

I'm flat on my arse again –

Face burnt back by the intense heat, the smoke and the flames –

And there are people in the yard pulling me away, talking in different tongues –

Back out in the alleyway, an old woman saying: 'You all right, love? Told them about all them gas canisters, I have.'

I push her away and go back down the alley but the fire engines are already here, an ambulance pulling up –

And the flames are licking out the windows, touching up the walls –

I turn and see two uniforms at the other end of the alley, so I jog back the other way –

Back round on to the Bradford Road, melting into the crowd that's forming back down the road, all muttering and chuntering on about gas –

Scanning the faces –

Then I ease myself away, back to the car –

And I get in and am gone.

Foot down, heading up through Hanging Heaton, making my way back through Morley and into Leeds.

I park under the arches near the station and switch on the light:

I've got cuts across my face, blood in my ears, blood in my hair, blood on my hands.

I switch off the light and take the bag of *Spunks* from the back seat and get out, locking the door, tearing back up to the Griffin.

'Helen?' I shout, banging on her door –

I keep knocking: 'Helen?'

A door opens down the corridor:

It's Hillman, a pair of blue pyjamas –

Shit.

'What's wrong?' he's saying, coming down the corridor. 'What's happened?'

'Nothing,' I say, stood there covered in blood and clutching a bag of porn.

'What happened to you?'

'There was a fire. It's nothing serious. Where's Helen?'

'A fire? Where?' he's asking, saying: 'You look terrible, you should go to hospital.'

'Mike,' I say, grabbing him. 'Where's Helen?'

He's shaking his head: 'She was in the bar earlier.'

'When?' I say, looking at my watch.

'I don't know. What time is it now?'

'Almost two,' I say. 'Where is she?'

'I don't know,' he keeps saying. 'I think she was going to meet someone.'

'Who?'

'I don't know,' he says again. 'She was acting a bit odd.'

'Odd?'

'Like she had something on her mind.'

'What time?'

'About eight, nine maybe.'

'She say anything to John or Alec?'

'Doubt it; I was sat with Mac and no-one's seen Murphy since this afternoon.'

'Where is he?'

'Murphy? No idea.' Then he says: 'You're hurting me, sir.'

And I look down at my hands gripping the tops of the arms of his pyjamas and I let him go, bloody marks across him.

'I'm sorry,' I say.

'You need to see someone,' he says, an arm helping me along.

'Who? See who?'

'A doctor I mean.'

I pull away: 'I can't.'

'You look bloody awful.'

'Just cuts and bruises,' I say, taking out my key.

'You need to get them looked at.'

'I'm going to my room, I'll be fine.'

He stands in front of his own door, watching me.

I walk off: 'I'll see you tomorrow.'

'You sure you're all right?'

I nod and raise my hand, a thumb up.

At my door, I turn and look back down the corridor –

But he's gone.

*

I open my eyes –

The telephone's ringing –

I reach across the bed, across the open copies of *Spunk*, the sheets from the *Exegesis*, and I pick up the phone: 'Helen?'

'Peter?'

I say: 'Joan, I'm sorry.'

'Been so worried about you.'

'I'm sorry,' I say, trying to sit up on the bed, grey light coming through the thin hotel curtains.

'Where have you been?'

I look at my watch:

It's seven o'clock –

Tuesday 23 December 1980.

'Peter?'

'Sorry. What did you say?'

'I asked where you've been?'

'Surveillance.'

'Surveillance?'

'There was no phone, I'm sorry.'

'I was just worried, that's all.'

'I'm sorry.'

'You sound terrible.'

'Just tired.'

'Were you asleep?'

'Doesn't matter. Have you heard from Linda?'

'That's why I've been trying to call; Richard hasn't been home since Sunday and she thought he might be with you.'

'With me?'

'She drove over looking for you.'

'Oh no.'

'You don't know where he is then?'

'No; Roger Hook told me he didn't show up for the questioning yesterday morning.'

'Questioning?'

'It was just routine. He knew it was, but then Clement Smith went and had Vice raid his offices.'

'Vice?'

My head's throbbing: 'Yeah, Vice.'

Joan says: 'You think he's all right?'

'I think he might have gone abroad, you know?'

'No, not Richard. Not without telling Linda.'

'He's not been himself, love. Really nervous, paranoid.'

'Where would he go?'

'The house in France.'

'No? You really think so?'

'Where else would he go?'

'Should I say anything to Linda?'

'If she calls again, you could mention it,' I say. 'I can't remember if it had a phone, can you?'

'It didn't.'

'You sure?'

'You said that was the best thing about the place.'

I'm sat on the bed, on one of the magazines, holding the phone, nodding –

My head splitting: 'You're right.'

Joan says: 'When you coming home, love?'

'I'm not sure.'

'It's Christmas Eve tomorrow.'

'I know. I'll be definitely back tomorrow night. Maybe before.'

'Hope so.'

'I love you.'

'Me too,' she says.

'Bye-bye.'

'Bye-bye.'

She hangs up and I sit on the bed, on one of the magazines, the phone dead in my hand, staring into the hotel mirror.

After a few minutes, I stand up and go into the bathroom and change my clothes and wash the blood from my face and my hair, off my hands, rinsing the sink clean after I'm done, clean of the brown water.

'Helen?' I say, banging on her door –

I keep knocking: 'Helen?'

I try the door –

Locked –

Fuck.

Downstairs in the lobby of the Griffin, I ring the bell

'Can you tell me if Miss Marshall is in?' I ask the receptionist.

He looks down his list and turns to the keys hanging on the pegs behind him and then looks back at me and shakes his head: 'She's out.'

I'm about to go but then ask him: 'Any messages?'

'Mr Hunter?'

I nod.

'I believe your wife called a number of times last night.'

'That all?'

'Yes,' he says.

'You sure?'

'Yes,' he says. 'I'm sure.'

It takes the best part of an hour to Levenshulme, the rain sleet then snow then sleet then rain, the roads empty, the landscape dead.

At ten o'clock, local radio tells me the news:

'An explosion last night destroyed a newsagents and badly damaged adjoining premises on the Bradford Road, Batley. Nine people were taken to hospital to be treated for shock and cuts caused by flying glass. One person had to be kept in for further treatment. Fire officers are investigating claims that the explosion was caused by gas canisters sold at the newsagents.

'Many shops will again close early tonight as police continue to investigate a call made to the Daily Mirror *from a man claiming to be the Yorkshire Ripper and threatening to kill again today. Meanwhile police released a new description and photofit of the man seen in the Alma Road vicinity of Headingley at the time police estimate Laureen Bell was brutally murdered.*

'The man is described as . . .'

I switch off the radio –

I know what he looks like.

I park on their road in the nice part of Levenshulme, the part on the way out to Stockport, the *Exegesis* on my lap, listening to the tapes in my head:

Robert Charles Douglas: October 12, 1946 – born Mirfield, West Yorks; April 1964 – joins Bradford police; August 1973 – marries Sharon Pearson; February 1974 – daughter Karen born; December 17, 1974 – arrests Michael Myshkin; December 24, 1974 – shot and

*wounded Strafford Arms, Wakefield; October 13, 1975 – forced to
retire from West Yorkshire Police. Moves to Manchester.*

Stop –

Rewind:

Bradford police –

Eric Hall, Detective Inspector Eric Hall –

Bradford Vice.

Rewind:

'Trust your Uncle Bob.'

Thinking –

Uncle Bob?

Wondering –

Detective Inspector Robert Craven –

Or former policeman Robert Douglas –

Stop.

I take a couple of painkillers for my back –

Then I put a couple of copies of *Spunk* in a carrier bag and I
get out, lock the door, and walk up their road through the slight
rain to their detached house.

There are no lights on, no car in the drive.

I walk up to the front door and ring the bell and wait –

A woman's voice from behind the patterned glass says: 'Yes?'

'Mrs Douglas?'

'Yes?'

'Police, love.'

I hear the chain go on and then the door opens –

Sharon Douglas peers through the gap and over the chain:
'Police?'

'Yes,' I nod, showing her my identification.

'This about Bob and Karen?'

'Yep, in a way. Can I come in?'

She takes the chain off and opens the door –

I step inside the dark detached house.

'Go through,' she says, nodding at the lounge door to the
right –

I go into the lounge with it's unframed Degas print, the
Christmas cards and the tree, the photos of their daughter,
the TV on, the sound off.

'Sit down,' she says –

I sit down on the big settee.

She sits down in one of the matching chairs next to an electric fire with artificial glowing coal –

Mrs Douglas is still red and black around her eyes, but no longer bloated with tea and sympathy; good-looking, she's got short blond hair, like Lady Diana Spencer, purple trousers and a black sweater.

I say: 'There was a fire in Batley last night at the newsagents your husband owns.'

'They called in the night,' she nods.

'Who did, love?'

'The police,' she nods again, fighting back the tears: 'I wanted to go over there, to the shop, but I've no car have I?'

'Family, friends, give you a lift?'

'Not local, no.'

'Where you from?'

'Bradford.'

'Manchester born and bred me,' I say. 'Live out at Alderley Edge.'

She smiles: 'Nice.'

'We like it,' I say. 'Miss it, do you? Being a Yorkshire lass, stuck over here with us pagans?'

She nods again.

I say: 'Will you go back?'

She shakes her head, biting her lip.

'You shouldn't be on your own.'

'It's too soon to go,' she says. 'All her things are here, her toys, all his stuff.'

I ask: 'Why did you move over this way?'

'Bob,' she says. 'Wanted to get away.'

'From Yorkshire?' I smile. 'Can't say I blame him.'

She smiles politely, eyes dead and blank.

I ask: 'Were you married long?'

'Seven years.'

'So he was a copper when you met him, Bob?'

Nodding: 'Yeah, did you know him well?'

'No,' I say. 'Not well.'

'He didn't want to leave, you know?'

'So I hear.'

'We did all right though.'

'He never worked at this shop in Batley then?'

'No. Wasn't him, was it. He rents it to some Pakis.'

'So what did he do?'

'He's got his business interests.'

'His *business interests*?'

'Don't ask me,' she shrugs.

'Fair enough,' I say.

'Sorry, look at me forgetting my manners,' she says, standing up suddenly. 'Have a cup of tea, will you?'

'Go on then. If you're making one.'

She crosses the room and then stops in the doorway: 'I'm sorry, I didn't catch your name?'

'Peter Hunter,' I smile.

'Sharon,' she smiles back. 'Sharon Douglas . . .' and then she stops –

Stops and turns right round –

I'm still smiling at her.

'Peter Hunter, did you say?'

I nod, smiling.

'You were here on Sunday, that was you. You're the bloke that investigates all the police, aren't you?'

I try to keep smiling: 'And we met at Headquarters – '

'And you were over in Wakefield after Bob got shot, I remember you now. They were always – '

'They were always what, love?'

But she looks right at me, shaking her head: 'I think you'd better leave.'

I stay put, right where I am: 'They were always what, Sharon?'

'I want you to leave.'

I stand up and take a *Spunk* out: 'I need to talk to you about these.'

'Get out!' she shouts, not even a glance at the magazine.

'These his *business interests*, are they love?'

'Get out!'

'Look at it, Sharon.'

'Get out!'

I walk towards her: 'This how you two met, was it?'

'Fuck off!' she shouts, heading for the door –

I follow her out into the hall: 'Don't worry, love. I've got them all. Every bleeding issue.'

She opens the door and grabs my arm, pulling and then pushing me out into the drive –

'Bastard!' she screams. 'My daughter's dead, you fucking bastard!'

'Which issue were you – '

'Fucking bastard!' she spits and slams the door.

I hold the magazine open up to the glass, saying: 'Have to make some copies for your neighbours.'

'I'm calling the police,' comes the voice from the other side of the door –

'Good idea,' I say, walking off. 'We love a bit of smut.'

And then somewhere over the Moors again, I remember it's almost Christmas and I hate myself afresh, wondering what the fuck I thought I was doing, what the fuck I thought I was going to do, the bad dreams not leaving, just staying bad, like the headaches and the backache, the murder and the lies, the cries and the whispers, the screams of the wires and the signals, like the voices and the numbers:

666.

Parked by a church on the way into Denholme, the *Exegesis* on my lap, listening to the tapes in my head again –

Listening and revising, filling in the blanks –

Fleshing out the bones –

Convinced:

Robert Charles Douglas was born in Mirfield, West Yorkshire on October 12, 1946, sharing a birthday with the cultist and black magician Aleister Crowley. Attended Mirfield Grammar School, briefly enrolling at a technical college before leaving to join the Bradford police when he was eighteen. Age of twenty-seven, Douglas married Sharon Pearson, a glamour model ten years his junior. February 1974, daughter Karen born. 1974, as a Detective Constable, Douglas became nationally known as one of the two policemen responsible for the arrest of Michael Myshkin, the man later convicted of the murders of Jeanette Garland, Susan Ridyard, and Clare Kemplay. Only weeks later Douglas was again in the headlines, this time as the victim of a serious gunshot wound received as he attempted to foil a robbery at the Strafford Arms public house in the centre of Wakefield. Forced to retire from the police on disability grounds on October 13, 1975, the day after his twenty-ninth birthday. It was a decision he'd appealed three times. With the substantial compensation for the injuries and his forced retirement, Douglas bought a new house in Levenshulme in Manchester and a newsagents in Batley. He later sublet the newsagents in order to concentrate on other business interests with a Bradford Vice detective named Eric Hall and a Manchester businessman called Richard Dawson. They started publishing a pornographic contact magazine – Spunk. His life however began to deteriorate from October 13, 1975. Always a heavy drinker – even as a serving policeman Douglas was considered to be 'unstable' and 'a weak link' by some of his colleagues – from 1975 on, Douglas was involved in a number of minor incidents all of which, however, highlighted a growing dependency on alcohol. Throughout 1977, Douglas was frequently reported missing by his wife and, on his intermittent returns to their Manchester home, police were called by neighbours reporting insulting and threatening behaviour and physical assaults upon his wife. In June 1977 both Eric Hall and his girlfriend, a sometime Spunk model called Janice Ryan, were murdered. Douglas was not mentioned in either investigation. During the summer of 1979, Douglas was actually listed as a missing person by local police who were unable to locate him. He eventually turned up at his brother's flat in Glasgow in September 1979. He returned to his wife later the same month, apparently having given up drinking. He remained in Manchester until late November 1980 when he once again began disappearing for days at a time. Bob Douglas was scared, running – sometime between Tuesday 16 and Wednesday 17 December 1980, Bob Douglas and his daughter were murdered.

Douglas, Dawson, and Hall –
Convinced:
Obsessed, possessed, convinced.

I pull up once more in front of that lonely house with its back to the Denholme golf course and I walk up the drive and I ring the bell –

Another voice from behind another door: 'Hello?'

'Mrs Hall? It's Peter Hunter.'

I listen to a chain being dropped and two locks sliding back –

The door opens:

'Good afternoon, Mr Hunter,' smiles Libby Hall –

'Is it?' I say, looking round at the looming night and the

constant rain into sleet into snow into rain into sleet into snow
that seems to be haunting me, plaguing me, cursing me.

'Come in,' she says. 'I seem to be quite the flavour of the
month.'

'Thank you,' I say and walk through into the front room.

'Do sit down,' she says.

'Thank you,' I say again and sit down on the big golden sofa.

'What happened to your face?'

'It's nothing.'

'Really,' she smiles. 'Will you have a cup of tea?'

'No, thanks,' I say. 'I've just had one.'

'If you're sure I can't tempt you?' she laughs, sitting down
beside me on the sofa.

'You said you'd been having a lot of visitors?'

'It seems so,' she smiles. 'First you and DS Marshall, then
the Reverend called by again, not that that was such a surprise,
then Helen Marshall came back last night, and now you again,
not to mention my son; he's forever popping in and out,
checking up on me no doubt.'

'You saw DS Marshall yesterday then, did you?'

'Yes, she rang and asked if it would be OK. Because it was
a bit late.'

'What time was it when she got here?'

'About nine thirty, I think,' she says, puzzled.

'Did she stay long?'

'No, why? Is anything the matter?'

'No.'

'Nothing's happened to her, has it?'

'No, why should it have done?'

She's tugging at her necklace, at the skin beneath: 'Well, you
know? The Ripper promising to kill again?'

'Mrs Hall, I assure you there's nothing wrong. I was up this
way and I thought seeing as I'm in the area, I'd pop in and say
hello. But I know DS Marshall was planning to have a chat with
you, just our paths haven't crossed today. That's all.'

'I'm sorry, Mr Hunter. But it's just she didn't look so well
either.'

'I think she's just tired, what with the Ripper Inquiry and
all.'

'That's what she said. I thought you were going to say she'd been in some kind of accident or something.'

'No, not at all.'

'That's all right then,' she smiles.

'She didn't ask you about these two fellers from the *Sunday Times*, did she?'

'Yes, yes. That's a queer business, that is.'

'Why's that?'

'Well I never spoke to anyone from the *Sunday Times*, did I?'

'You speak to any journalists recently?'

'Mr Hunter, would that I had,' she sighed. 'I've tried, but no-one wants to know.'

'Talk to anyone recently? Other policemen? Anyone?'

She's shaking her head: 'That's what Helen Marshall asked and I'll tell you the same as I told her: No – unfortunately.'

'Did DS Marshall ask you anything else?'

'Bit about the Reverend, bit about Mr Whitehead.'

'Right,' I nod.

'Hear Mr Whitehead isn't so well?'

'That's right, yes.'

'Had some kind of seizure?'

'Yes, I believe that's what it was.'

'But he's out of the woods apparently?'

'Is that what DS Marshall said?'

'Helen? No, it was the Reverend Laws told me.'

'So what time did she leave?'

'Oh, about ten, ten thirty maybe? She didn't stay more than an hour, if that.'

I glance at my watch.

'You're sure nothing's happened? Not trying to spare me something, are you Mr Hunter?'

I say: 'She's fine. But do you mind if I just ask you a couple more questions?'

'Not at all.'

'I've been going through Eric's things, the stuff you gave me, and I came across a magazine; a pornographic magazine.'

'Yes,' she says, not missing a beat, a blink: '*Spunk*.'

I nod and say: 'You know anything about it?'

'Only that Janice Ryan was in it.'

'You never heard Eric mention it?'

'No.'

'How about a company called MJM Limited?'

'Does sound familiar actually.'

I sit forward: 'Yes?'

'They make films, don't they?'

'Maybe. What do you know about them?'

'They have that lion at the start? Them yeah?'

I sit back in my chair and smile: 'That'd be MGM, Mrs Hall.'

'Sorry, who did you say?'

'MJM.'

'No, I don't think so then.'

'What about a man called Richard Dawson?'

She's shaking her head: 'No.'

'Your husband know anyone at all called Richard?'

She pauses, then says slowly: 'No; not that I can think of.'

'No-one? Not one single person?'

'Well, there's our son Richard of course.'

I say: 'How about a Bob Douglas? Did he ever mention a policeman called Bob Douglas?'

'Yes,' she says, sitting up. 'Dougie? Yes. His wife Sharon and the little girl – '

'Karen,' I say.

'Yes, Karen.'

'You friends with them, were you?'

'Friends? Suppose we are – were anyway.'

'Been over to their house, have you?'

'Me, no. Manchester?'

'Levenshulme.'

'That's right. I know Eric went there a couple of times and Dougie used to come over here and play a round or two with Eric every now and again.'

'Golf?'

'Yes,' she smiles. 'Though Dougie, Bob that is – he apparently thought he was a lot better than he actually was. They did come to dinner once as well.'

'Bob Douglas and his wife?'

'Yes, just the once. She's a lot younger than I am, so I suppose you couldn't expect them to, you know, be coming down all the time.'

'When did you last see them?'

'Not since . . .'

'Right,' I say, quickly.

'Same with a lot of folk.'

Moving fast now: 'How did they meet?'

'Bradford, when Dougie first started.'

'Of course,' I nod.

'Wasn't there long before he was transferred,' she's saying, staring off into the heavy gold curtains. 'But then when he got shot and there was all that business and then they got the house over there, well I think they just had less chance to see each other.'

'But they got on well?'

She frowns: 'He wasn't right was Dougie – not after the shooting.'

'So I hear.'

'But would you listen to me?' she says, suddenly. 'I'm as bad as them that talk about me, aren't I?'

'No,' I say. 'No you're not.'

'Better off dead, kicking him out like that – that's what they say about him; what Eric said. Better off dead – just like they say about me.'

'It's not the same.'

'Better off dead, that's what they say.'

I say: 'Mrs Hall, I'm afraid Bob is dead.'

She tugs at the skin of her neck and says: 'When?'

'Last week. I thought you would have heard.'

She shakes her head: 'No.'

'He was murdered.'

Tugging at the skin of her neck, shaking her head: 'No.'

'I'm sorry,' I say, looking out at the road and the looming night and the constant rain into sleet into snow into rain into sleet into snow that seems to be haunting me, plaguing me, cursing me –

'It was Eric's worst nightmare that, you know?' says Mrs Hall suddenly.

'What was?'

'Being kicked out like Dougie was. That and having to do time.'

'Bob Douglas was hardly kicked out. Got a load of brass.'

'Eric always said he'd kill himself rather than lose his job or go inside.'

'That's not an uncommon sentiment,' I say.

'Suppose that's why they hate you so much. Call you what they do.'

Thinking, *Saint Cunt* –

Saying: 'I suppose it is.'

'Why Eric hated you.'

I can't think of anything else to say, so I say: 'It mightn't have come to that.'

She smiles: 'That's not true, Mr Hunter. But thank you.'

I look at my watch –

When I look up, Mrs Hall says again: 'What would you do?'

'Pardon?'

'If they threw you out?'

'I don't know.'

'What about prison? Could you do that?'

'I've never thought about it.'

'Would you think about killing yourself? Suicide?'

'No.'

Then she says quietly: 'He was all right was Dougie. Caught that Myshkin bloke, didn't he?'

'He did,' I say and stand up –

'You're going?'

'I better had.'

She stands up.

I walk over to the door –

She comes up behind me and opens it.

I say: 'She didn't say where she was going I suppose, did she?'

'Helen? No.'

'Well, thank you for your time again,' I say, then add: 'And you're absolutely certain no-one else's been to see you or called you in connection with Eric and Janice Ryan?'

'I'm certain.'

'Looks like I'll have to be giving the *Sunday Times* a call,' I say, eyes on the night.

'Does sound like someone's been telling you lies.'

'It wouldn't be the first time,' I sigh. 'Wouldn't be the first time.'

'Doubt it'll be the last either,' she smiles.

I take the A644 down into Brighouse and then make my way through Kirklees and back into Batley, stopping for a look at the black shell of RD News, still smouldering in the white flurries of snow, car lights picking out the flakes as they pass, Pakistanis and Chinamen coming and going, in and out, the windows of the *Chop Suey* and the chemists all boarded over.

On the M1 again, outskirts of Leeds –
  The radio on, when:
  'Police have still been unable to identify the body of a man discovered this afternoon in the burnt-out flat above a newsagents on the Bradford Road, Batley, which was destroyed by fire late last night. Police and fire investigators were not initially treating the blaze as suspicious, however police confirmed tonight that they were appealing for witnesses to come forward. A police spokesman refused to speculate on the cause of both the fire and the man's death but did confirm that arson had not been ruled out.'
  I'm on the hard shoulder, hazard lights on, screaming into the Yorkshire night:
  Fuuuuuuuuuuuuuuck!

Millgarth, Leeds:
  Looking for Marshall –
  Looking for Murphy –
  Looking for anyone, upstairs and down.
  Ripper Room half empty; forty eyes on me in the door and then back down into their books and their papers, the files and the photographs, Christmas streamers strung from corner to corner across the ceiling.
  I swipe a paper off an empty desk and head next door –
  Dead:
  The fuck were they?
  The *Evening Post* headline:
  Batley Blaze Body Found.
  I skim it:
  Firemen investigating the cause of last night's fire at a Batley newsagents on the Bradford Road made a grim discovery late this morning when the body of an unidentified man was found in the first

floor flat above the shop where the fire was thought to have started. The body was removed to Pinderfields Hospital for a post-mortem and identification.

Both the newsagents and flat were badly damaged in the fire which also caused extensive damage to adjoining properties and left nine people needing hospital treatment. Neighbours told the Evening Post that they heard three loud explosions at the time and believe the fire may have been caused by gas canisters which were stored on the premises. There was a shock among local people at the fatality and surprise that the flat had been occupied.

I reach for a phone and try to get through to Pinderfields, find out who's doing the post-mortem, but they've all gone home or they're lying.

I look at my watch:

Nine going on ten.

I stand up, I sit down, I stand up again –

Going down the corridor, looking for Angus or Noble, about to turn the corner when I hear two voices round the bend –

Two voices that stop me dead:

Craven: 'I'm not going to be the fucking goat, no fucking way that's going to happen and you can tell him that from me.'

Alderman: 'It won't come to that.'

Craven: 'Better fucking hadn't. Because there's none of that all for one and one for all bollocks if it does. It's Bob for Bob.'

Alderman: 'Is that a threat? Is that what you want me to tell him?'

Craven: 'It's out of hand, that's all I'm saying.'

Alderman: 'We've seen worse, we both have. You know we have.'

Craven: 'Yeah, and that's what I'm telling you: there's always been a goat and it isn't going to be me.'

I walk backwards a few paces and then head forward, loud as I can, round the corner –

They both freeze, Alderman and Craven.

'Gentlemen?' I say.

'Fuck off,' spits Alderman and pushes past me down the corridor –

I ask: 'What's wrong with him?'

'Bad day,' says Craven.

'Aren't they all,' I nod and hand him the Evening Post –

He looks down at the headline and the photograph of the burnt-out newsagents on the Bradford Road, looks at it and says: 'I saw it.'

'So who is it?'

'Who is what?'

'The body?'

'Fuck knows,' shrugs Craven, handing me back the paper.

'You know who owned the place?'

'Couldn't give a shit,' he says and walks off the way Alderman went.

I stand there, paper in my hand in the corridor, their corridor.

After a few moments, I knock on Noble's door –

There's no answer –

No-one home.

I park the Saab under the dark arches and walk back up to the Griffin, the carrier bag full of *Spunks* in my hand.

I walk straight into the bar, but there's no-one there, no-one I know.

I go upstairs and I knock on Helen Marshall's door –

Then Murphy's –

Mac's –

Mike Hillman's –

Fuck.

Furious, I go back downstairs and have one whiskey in the bar and decide to head back to RDNews because I've got nowhere else to go and I can't sleep until I get the post-mortem on the body, my back killing me anyway, although I'm fucked if I know how I'm going to get the post-mortem, and I'm heading out the front door of the Griffin when the smug little man from behind the desk says:

'Mr Hunter?'

And I stop and I say: 'Yep?'

'Message for you.'

'Thank you,' I say and he hands me a crumpled old manila-brown envelope and I open it and –

chest saying see how you tear me see the monstrous punishment you still breathing looking at the dead see if you find suffering equal to this lumpy bundle covered in blankets on the bed in the silence of a flat after death the repeated knocking on the door transmission seven received at three ten PM on friday the twenty seventh of january nineteen seventy eight in a world where people do not care cast aside by those so cruel and treated like a mule unloved is to miss the love that all parents should give yet they cast you aside put you out of their minds they put you in care there is no love there yet the staff really care or they would not be there yet why was it me lord why me lonely and unloved in a timber yard off great northern street huddersfield why me last seen alive on tuesday the twenty fourth of january nineteen seventy eight where loneliness is to go outside and get into a white corsair for a quick five pounds to go outside to the lumber yard on great northern street in the black and dirty snow the viaduct overhead the liverpool leeds hull trains passing by lonely and unloved the taxi rank the black bricks the black wood the black damp the tip damp the derelict school damp the tripe works and abandoned houses damp the canal and the cattle market bloody and damp where the snow will not settle where people do not care the public toilets a countryside of pain and ugly anguish where you fall down in despair falling to your knees in prayer asking god to rescue you from this cruel snare but no one comes no one comes but him in his white corsair with his five pounds for a quick one amongst the wood the timber and the lumber in a world where people do not care e was lured into the deepest hole and e undid my trousers and wait he said he had to urinate and got out of the car and when he came back he asked me to get out and get into the back so we could have sexual intercourse and it was then he hit me and at first e thought it was with his hand and e said there is no need for that you do not even need to pay but he hit me again and it was not his hand but a hammer and he hit me again then e dragged me by my hair into a far corner of the yard and e was not moaning but e was not dead and e could not take my eyes off of him he said do not make any noise and you will be all right then he took off my panties and had intercourse with me and e lay there with him on top of me unloved and when he had finished intercourse he took out a knife and he stabbed me six times in my heart and chest stripped me threw all my clothes and things about and put my body into a narrow space between a stack of wood and a disused garage and covered me with a sheet of asbestos then he went home the next morning a driver found my black bloodstained panties and he hung them on the door to give the lads a bit of a laugh they also saw the bloodstains in the mud and on the polythene but they thought nothing of it because all sorts of things went on at night in the wood yard and they left me between the stack of wood and the disused garage in this countryside of pain and ugly anguish and still e wait for them to come and find me on friday e was a missing person so they gave the alsatian police dog my black bloodstained panties to sniff and within ten minutes the alsatian had found me between the stack of wood and the disused garage found me with my sweater and my bra pushed up and just a pair of socks left on it was three ten PM on friday the twenty seventh of january nineteen seventy eight and they say there is no greater pain than to remember in our present grief past happiness but e will tell you the greatest pain is to remember in our present grief past grief and only grief

Chapter 14

Five hours later and half the Manchester Police force are round my house but I'm still sat in Noble's bloody office waiting for Chief Constable Ronald Angus to show his face, standing up and sitting down, on and off the phone to Joan, standing up and sitting down, Noble and Prentice and the rest of them in and out.

'Sit down, Peter,' says Angus as he comes in, patting me on the back.

Noble gets up from behind his desk to make way for Big Chief Ron.

'Let's have a look,' he says, sitting down.

Noble hands him the sheet of paper encased in the plastic bag, the envelope in another –

Angus holds up the envelope: 'Mr Peter Hunter,' he reads. 'The Griffin, eh?'

I nod.

'Saturday?' he says, squinting at the postmark –

'Manchester,' I say.

He puts down the envelope on the desk and picks up the letter:

Dear Officer,
Sorry I haven't written before, but heed this early warning: will kill wife and kids.
Jack the Ripper.

Ronald Angus puts down the letter and looks up at me and then across the room at Peter Noble –

'Handwriting's same,' says Noble.

Angus nods: 'Or at least a very good likeness.'

'We were waiting for you, but we've got the lab at Wetherby standing by.'

Angus ignores him and asks me: 'Have you been in touch with Mrs Hunter?'

'Yes.'

'You told her?'

'Yes.'

'You don't have any kids, do you?'

'No,' I say.

'That's lucky.'

I look at my watch:

It's three in the morning –

Christmas Eve, 1980.

I look up and say: 'I want to go home, sir.'

Chief Constable Ronald Angus looks at Temporary Assistant Chief Constable Peter Noble and shrugs: 'Fair enough.'

I stand up and turn to Noble: 'Thanks, Pete.'

He nods and says: 'We'll be in touch.'

I turn to go as the phone starts ringing –

'Drive carefully,' says Angus as Noble picks up the phone.

I nod and open the door.

'Mr Hunter,' says Noble, one hand over the mouthpiece, gesturing for me to wait.

Me: 'What is it?'

Angus, looking at Noble: 'What?'

Noble nodding, into the phone: 'Fucking hell.'

Me, at his side: 'What?'

'Right,' says Noble and slams down the phone –

'What?' say Angus and me at the same time.

'Eric Hall's wife.'

Me: 'What?'

'She's dead.'

Me: 'What?'

'Son found her hanging in the kitchen thirty minutes ago.'

The drive back out to Denholme:

Prentice, Noble, and me –

The snow blowing about but not settling, the car silent but for Christmas carols on the radio.

Prentice, Noble, and me –

There are tears in my eyes.

We park behind a blue and white at the bottom of the drive, a Ford outside the garage.

Noble leads the way up to the door, Prentice hanging back, and knocks –

A uniform opens the door, introduces himself, mutters a few

words and we go through into the front room where a young man is sat on the gold sofa staring into what looks like a glass of whiskey.

Noble says: 'Mr Hall? My name is Peter Noble, I'm the Assistant Chief Constable.'

The young man nods.

'This is Peter Hunter, a policeman from Manchester who knew your mother.'

He nods again, glancing up at us.

The house is silent, just policemen walking about, here and there, as quietly as they can.

'It's Richard, isn't it?' asks Noble.

The young man says: 'Yes.'

'Well Richard, in a bit, someone will take you down to the hospital.'

'The hospital?' he asks.

'I'm afraid someone has to formally identify the body.'

'I see.'

'Yes,' says Noble. 'And I'm afraid we're also going to have to go over a few things with you.'

'Now?'

'If you can. It's best to get everything out of the way, saves having to keep going over things.'

He nods again and takes a sip from the glass.

Noble glances at me and we both sit down, me taking out my notebook.

Noble: 'Do you want to tell us what happened then?'

'I came back about twoish. I'd been out and I came in and the house was dark and I thought she must have gone to bed and I put on the light in here and there was a piece of paper on the floor and I picked it up and saw it was a letter so I just put it down here,' he says, tapping the coffee table.

'And then, as I was putting it down, I saw her out of the corner of my eye, through there in the kitchen. She was kneeling and I thought, "Now what you up to?" I went over to her, about to say something. Her head was bowed, her hands on top of the washing machine. I just stared at her, she was so still. Then I saw the rope, I hadn't noticed it. The rope from the clothes rack was around her neck. I ran through into the hall and picked up the phone but then I went back into kitchen because I wasn't sure, you know. But then I saw her face, all the saliva dangling from her mouth and so I went back and called 999.'

He stops and there's just the sound of a clock ticking –

Then Noble asks: 'What did you do then?'

'I tried to cut her down but I couldn't find a knife sharp enough.'

Noble nods.

'Then police and the ambulance came,' says Richard Hall, looking at his watch. 'Think it was the police first.'

'Was she expecting you?' I ask. 'Expecting you tonight?'

'No.'

'Is this the letter?' asks Noble, picking up an envelope –

He nods.

Noble opens the envelope and reads the letter and then hands it to me:

> *Dear Richard,*
> *I'm so very sorry to do this to you after everything you've had to deal with, but I just can't keep going on like this. I hope now you'll be able to make a clean break and get on with your life.*
> *I love you and I'm sorry.*
> *Please forgive me.*
> *Mum.*

I fold up the piece of paper and put it back inside the envelope and pass it over to Noble. He hands it to a uniform who bags it and takes it away –

Richard Hall looks round, confused.

'You'll get it back Richard. Don't worry,' says Noble.

He takes a big swig from the glass, swallows and says: 'This bloody house.'

I nod, thinking the same, thinking about Joan.

'Have you got anywhere you can go?' asks Noble. 'Anyone we should call?'

'I'll be right,' says Richard Hall.

'Let's take you down the hospital, get everything out of the way.'

We all stand up and turn to the door –

Helen Marshall is stood in the doorway.

She moves to one side as Noble and a uniform take Richard

Hall outside, Noble turning and asking me: 'You going to be
OK to get back?'

I nod.

'See you later then,' he says, looking at Marshall.

I nod again and walk back into the front room, Marshall following.

I sit back down on the sofa –

She sits down next to me.

The clock's ticking.

'I'm sorry,' she says.

'Where've you been?'

'I had to go home.'

'Why?'

'I don't want to talk about it.'

'I see.'

'I'm sorry.'

'I was worried.'

'I'm sorry,' she says again, swallowing.

'How did you hear about this?'

'Martin Laws.'

'Laws? Reverend Laws?'

She nods.

'He called you at home? At the hotel?'

'At home.'

'What's he got your home number for?'

'Leave it, Peter. Please?'

'And how did he know?'

'Said the son had called him.'

'Fucking hell,' I say, standing up and going into the kitchen.

A uniform is stood in the back door, smoking a cigarette.

I stand there, under the clothes rack, in front of the washing
machine.

She comes up behind me and puts a hand on my arm: 'I'm
sorry.'

'What a mess,' I say. 'What a fucking mess.'

She drives me back through the night, through the dark towns
and villages, the snow then sleet then rain, down the deserted
streets and roads, the empty hills and fields, the rain then sleet

then snow, everywhere dead, everyone dead, everything dead, and I'm wondering how long it's been like this:

Night –

Dark, deserted, and empty night –

Everywhere dead.

Thinking about October 1965 and Brady and Hindley and all that came after, me a Detective Sergeant back then, twenty-five and freshly wed, that dark, deserted, and empty night David Smith called Hyde Police Station –

Everyone dead.

Digging ever since –

Everything dead.

Thinking, *how much longer?*

'Joan?' I say into the phone, sat on the edge of the hotel bed, the bed all covered with pages from the *Exegesis*, photographs from *Spunk*.

'Peter? What's happening?'

'Nothing. Someone's there with you?'

'There's a car outside, yes.'

'Anyone call?'

'Clement Smith.'

'Did he?'

'Yes, just to see everything was all right. Asked if you were there.'

'Good of him to call.'

'You know Roger Hook stopped by as well?'

'I didn't, no.'

'Just after the first car came.'

'That's nice.'

'Yes, just to check everything was OK.'

I say: 'Are you OK?'

'I'm fine,' she says. 'Wish you were here though.'

'I'll be back soon,' I tell her, looking at my watch:

Fuck, almost noon:

Wednesday 24 December 1980.

There's a knock at the door –

'I'd better go,' I say. 'There's someone at the door.'

'Drive carefully,' she says.

'I will,' I say. 'See you later.'

'Bye-bye.'

'Bye,' I say and hang up and go to the door –

It's John Murphy.

'You all right?' he asks.

'All things considered,' I smile.

'What a night, eh?' he sighs.

'Yeah.'

'You coming down, going over to Millgarth, what you doing?'

'I don't know. Got a million things to get sorted before tonight. What about you lot?'

'We've gone about as far as we can, for now.'

'Right,' I say.

'When we going to be back over here?'

'Monday.'

'They'll be happy about that,' he nods.

'Tell you what,' I say. 'Let's all meet at Millgarth at two. Tell you lot what's been going on, then we can all head home.'

'That'd be nice,' says Murphy.

'I'm sorry, John,' I say. 'I did try and get hold of you.'

'I know,' he shrugs. 'Just kept missing each other.'

'Didn't mean to keep you out of the loop or anything like that.'

'I know.'

'See you over there at two then?'

'Two it is.'

I sit back down on the edge of the hotel bed and pick up the phone and dial directory inquiries and get the number of the *Sunday Times*:

'The Editor, please?'

'I'm afraid he's not in today,' a woman's voice says.

'OK. My name is Peter Hunter and I'm the Assistant Chief Constable for Greater Manchester.'

'Good afternoon, Mr Hunter. How can I help you?' she asks.

'Good afternoon. I was wondering if you could put me through to Anthony McNeil or Andrew Driscoll?'

There's a pause, then the woman says: 'I'm sorry, sir. Can you just hold on a minute?'

'Sure,' I say and hold on –

Moments later, the woman says: 'I thought so, we don't have an Anthony McNeil working for us and we did have a Mr Driscoll, but he retired quite a while ago.'

'Retired? How old was he?'

'Sixty something. He'd be seventy now – if he's still alive.'

'I see.'

'Was there anything else?'

'No. Thank you.'

'Bye then.'

'Bye,' I say and hang up and then dial Wakefield:

'Community Affairs. Inspector Evans please?'

'Who's calling?'

'Assistant Chief Constable Hunter.'

'One moment, sir.'

Then: 'Community Affairs. Detective Inspector Evans speaking.'

'Inspector? This is Peter Hunter.'

'Good afternoon, Mr Hunter. What can I do you for?'

'McNeil and Driscoll? *Sunday Times*?'

'Right.'

'Wrong. I just called the *Sunday Times* and they've never heard of any Anthony McNeil and the only Driscoll they know is retired and seventy years old if he's not already dead.'

'Shit.'

'Yep.'

'They had press cards.'

'That's nice. You didn't call and check though?'

'No.'

'Well done, Inspector.'

'Shit,' he says again. 'So who were they?'

'Who were they? You're asking me who they were? You're bloody Community Affairs, Inspector. I suggest you start bloody finding out.'

'Yes, sir.'

I hang up.

Millgarth, Leeds:

Murphy, McDonald, Hillman, and Helen Marshall –

Craven in the corner.

I sit down at the table, the table full of piles, piles full of files, files full of lists, lists full of names, names full of death and paranoia.

I tell them what they already know: 'Eric Hall's wife killed herself last night.'

John Murphy's nodding, writing in one of the files: 'Better off.'

'Shut up,' says Helen Marshall.

'Things they did to her, I'd have topped myself years ago.'

'Leave it, John,' I hiss.

Murphy, palms up: 'Sorry.'

'I'd been going through Eric Hall's files,' I say. 'And it turns out Janice Ryan had done some work for a porn mag called *Spunk*. This was published by a company called MJM, but it turns out they've gone under.'

'Bust,' winks Craven. 'Get it?'

'Yeah thanks,' I say. 'Their forwarding address was a flat above a paper shop owned by Bob here's partner, the late Bob Douglas.'

'Ex-partner,' says Craven, no more jokes.

'Ex-shop as well,' I say. 'It was burnt down night before last. One fatality.'

Marshall's about to say something, but stops.

'Any news on the body, Bob?' I ask Craven –

He sniffs up and says: 'Looks like murder and arson.'

I count to five, then say: 'You're joking?'

'Unless the bloke had no hands or teeth when he moved in, no.'

'What?'

'Whoever it is, they'd cut off his hands and smashed in his teeth.'

Jesus, Jesus, Jesus, I'm thinking, counting to five.

'What a fucking place,' says Hillman for all of us.

Me: 'So they can't get a name?'

Craven's shaking his head.

'You any ideas?' I ask him.

'Me? Why would I know who it is?'

'You were his bloody partner, Bob?'

'For all of six months.'

'Who's handling it?' I ask.

'Alderman.'

Fuck, fuck, fuck, I'm thinking, counting to ten.

Then I look back across the room at Craven and I say: 'Six years today, Bob?'

Craven: 'Who's counting?'

I am, I think –

I fucking am.

Hillman: 'Can I ask something?'

I nod.

'This letter you got? Any word on that?'

'Pete Noble sent it over to Wetherby. Still waiting for word from them.'

Murphy: 'Everything all right?'

'How do you mean, John?'

'On the home front?'

Joan, Joan, Joan, I'm thinking, counting to fifteen.

'She's fine,' I say. 'Thank you.'

Murphy: 'How about Bob Douglas? Any word from Roger and the lads on that?'

'No, John,' I say, shaking my head and thinking:

Never fucking ending –

Death and paranoia –

Murder and lies, lies and murder –

A total war.

We're all downstairs at the Griffin, bags packed –

John Murphy getting us all a round in –

A Christmas drink.

He brings over the beers and the shorts, Mac singing along to the piped electronic versions of Christmas carols, but I've had a belly full of Christmas music:

Ray Conniff and *We Wish You a Happy Christmas* –

The Little Drummer Boy.

And I'm already on my third drink, the room suddenly hot, Hillman asking me if I ever met Mr Ray and I'm saying I can't say I ever did but Mac is saying I must have done – big bearded man who kept pigeons.

'Pigeon fancier, was he?' laughs Murphy. 'Knew a bloke got five years for that.'

'Another?' shouts Mac, getting up.

'A quick one for the road,' I say, looking across the table at Helen Marshall and smiling –

She smiles back and raises her glass and says: 'Make mine a double, Mac.'

There are blue lights in the rearview mirror, sirens –

And I'm thinking, *fuck, fuck, fuck, fuck, fuck, fuck, fuck, fuck, fuck, fuck, fuck, fuck, fuck* –

I pull over somewhere on the Moors and wait for them.

The tap comes on the glass –

I wind down the window.

'Would you mind stepping out of the car please, sir?'

I nod and open the door –

Get out and stand there, against the car.

'May I see your driver's licence please, sir?' asks the young policeman, about twenty-five –

About the same age I was when they brought me up here –

Up here to dig.

He's looking at the licence with his torch, then he shines it up at me and glances back at the police car.

'Mr Hunter?' he asks.

'Yes,' I say

'Just a minute, sir,' he says and goes back to the police car, its blue lights spinning silently in the night.

And I stand there, against the car, and I stare up at the sky – quiet for once with just the stars twinkling, and then I look back down at the ground, at the Moors all around me, stained with snow –

Digging ever since.

'I'm sorry, sir,' he mumbles, coming back. 'We didn't realise it was you.'

I nod.

'Here you are, sir,' he says and hands me my driver's licence.

'Thank you,' I say.

'Sir?' he says –

I try and focus.

'Would you like us to call you a taxi or something?'

I shake my head.

'You're sure? It's no trouble.'

I raise my hand, swallowing sick, and shake my head.

He looks back at the police car and says: 'You don't look very well, sir?'

I say: 'What's your name, son?'

'Williams,' he says. 'Mark Williams.'

'How old are you Mark Williams?'

'Twenty-four, sir.'

'And do you like being a policeman, Mark Williams?'

'Yes, sir.'

'Well Mark Williams,' I say loudly, taking his hand and shaking it and shaking it. 'You have a merry Christmas.'

'Thank you. And you sir.'

'I will,' I say, getting back in the car. 'I will.'

'Drive carefully,' he says, closing the door for me.

'Merry Christmas Mark Williams,' I say. 'Merry bloody Christmas.'

There's another police car outside the house when I get there.

I nod at the two officers as I pull in and park in the drive.

I wave at them as I get out and struggle to lock the car door.

I nod again as I walk round the house to the back door.

It's locked and I fumble with my keys and then turn and walk down the path to the shed.

I unlock that door and open it, staring in at the maps and the photographs on the wall in the dark, the thirteen faces staring back at me, and I turn to the garden, to the washing hanging on the line in the dark in the snow, a bag of pornography in one hand, sick down my shirt, my fly undone, the carols deafening, thinking:

How much longer?

Part 3
We are all prostitutes

and pain and never happiness to go outside and find no one there but a man who would not frighten anybody sat in a white corsair with a five pound note in his hand and a ball pein hammer under the seat of his car asking are you doing business transmission eight found on saturday the twenty seventh of may nineteen seventy eight sitting on wasteland in a slumped position against the fence of a car park at the rear of manchester royal infirmary identified as doreen pickles and when her reversible coat was removed it could be seen that her stomach had been so badly mutilated that her intestines had spilled out onto the ground where they wallowed like pigs in the mud below a sign around her neck that in cruel words read e am the way into the doleful city e am the way into eternal grief e am the way to a forsaken race before me nothing but eternal things were made and e shall last eternally abandon every hope all ye who enter and she opens her lids to show the white blank eyes of the dead and says who is this one approaching who without death dares walk into the kingdom of the dead by a chain link fence on a rubbish pile in the corner of the car park looking like a doll lying on her right side face down her arms folded beneath her legs straight and her shoes placed neatly on her body and rested against the fence after three operations and with just one lung death came with three hammer blows twelve feet away hit on the head three times help help help and dragged across the gravel to the fence where e raised her dress and underskirt and stabbed her in the stomach repeatedly through the same wound also in the back just below the lower left ribs her right eyelid was also punctured the eye bruised but after this there will be silence and people will think e have gone away that e have found a woman and settled down a woman who is the opposite of a tart who is religious or even the devout member of a religious sect someone e can pamper at whose feet e can worship someone who is in my eyes a paragon of virtue wearing a reversible coat blue and brown town chequered on one side and all blue on the other a short length floral dress blue canvas shoes a pink cardigan white knickers white underslip and a blue and white bra and e opened my lids to show the white blank eyes of the dead and said dear officer sorry e have not written about a year to be exact but e have not been up north for quite a while e was not kidding last time e wrote saying the whore would be older this time and maybe e would strike in manchester for a change and you should have took heed that bit about her being in hospital funny the lady mentioned something about being in hospital before e stopped her whoring ways the lady will not worry about hospitals now will she e bet you have been wondering how come e have not been to work for ages well e would have been if it had not been for your cursed coppers e had the lady just where e wanted her and was about to strike when one of your cursing police cars stopped right outside the lane he must have been a dumb copper cause he did not say anything he did not know how close he was to catching me tell you the truth e thought e was collared the lady said do not worry about the coppers little did she know that bloody copper saved her neck that was last month so e do not know when e will get back on the job but e know it will not be bloody chapeltown too bloody hot there maybe bradford manningham might write again if up north jack the ripper he who thought to walk so boldly through this realm let him retrace his foolish way alone and you who led him here through this dark land you will stay and they slam the heavy gates in

Chapter 15

It was the night before Christmas. There was a house in the middle of the Moor, lights shining in the windows. I was walking across the Moor, light snow underfoot, heading home. On the front doorstep I stamped my boots loose of snow and opened the door. A fire was glowing with artificial coals and the house was filled with the smell of good cooking. Under a lit Christmas tree, there were boxes of beautifully wrapped presents. I took a big box, gift-wrapped in newspaper from under the tree and pulled the red ribbon loose. Carefully I opened the newspaper so I might read it later. I stared at the wooden box on my knee. I closed my eyes and opened the box, the dull thud of my heart filling the house.

'What is it?' said Joan, coming into the room and switching on the TV.

I tried to cover the box with my hands but she took the box from me and looked inside.

The box fell to the floor, the house full of good cooking, the thud of my heart, and her bloody screams.

I watched as the fetus slid out of the box and across the floor, writing spidery messages and swastikas with its bloody cord as it went.

'Get rid of it,' she screamed. 'Get rid of it now!'

But I was staring at the TV, the people on the TV singing hymns, the people on the TV singing hymns with no face, no features – machines, the gulls circling overhead screaming, the wings in my own back, out of the skin, torn, huge and rotting things, and I stared down at the baby on the floor and it sat up, hands across its heart, and smiled a faint and dreadful smile and I looked at the tag on the box, the tag on the box that said:

Love Helen – *the night before Christmas.*

I open my eyes –

The radio's on:

Christmas messages: Carter telling the world that all fifty-two hostages are alive and well; the Pope's message for Poland; Thatcher's for Northern Ireland; nominations for people of the year: Ayatollah

Khomeini; the eight US soldiers who died trying to rescue the hostages; the boat people; JR Ewing; Voyager 1; or John Lennon?

The Yorkshire Ripper?

Radio off –

I close my eyes.

'Merry Christmas,' says Joan –

I open my eyes.

'Merry Christmas,' I say.

'How do you feel?'

'Not so good.'

'What happened to you?'

'A few too many Christmas drinks.'

'Where?'

'Leeds.'

'How did you get back?'

'I drove.'

She sits up in bed: 'Peter!'

'Sorry.'

She gets out of bed and puts on her dressing gown.

'Sorry,' I say again.

She goes downstairs.

My head is killing me, my stomach churning, on the verge of throwing up –

I close my eyes.

Downstairs, she's put on the Christmas tree lights and started making breakfast.

I go into the kitchen.

'Do you want a cup of tea?'

'Please,' I say.

I go back into the lounge and look out of the window at a wet and grey Christmas Day.

'Here you go,' she says and hands me a cup of tea –

'Thanks.'

'You think I should take them something?' she asks, looking at the police car parked at the bottom of the drive.

'They might as well get off,' I say. 'Now I'm here.'

'Doesn't it make you feel secure?' laughs Joan.

'Watched more like.'

I walk down the drive in the drizzle and my dressing gown –

'Merry Christmas,' says Sergeant Corrigan, winding down the car window.

'And to you Bill,' I say, bending down and nodding at another man I don't recognise.

'Thought you were bringing us a bit of turkey, sir?'

'Bit early for that,' I say.

'Aye, hear you had a late one,' he laughs –

'Don't,' I say.

'Not feeling too good, are you?'

I shake my head: 'Listen, you can get off if you want.'

'Yeah?'

'Yep,' I say. 'We'll be doing the rounds of the relatives most of the day anyway.'

'You sure?'

I nod: 'Go on.'

'Right then,' says Corrigan, starting the car. 'You know where we are if you need us.'

'Thanks, Bill.'

'Have a Merry Christmas, sir.'

'Same to you.'

We eat bacon and scrambled eggs on toast at the kitchen table, the TV on in the other room – a church service.

I ask: 'What time they expecting us?'

'Twelve, mum said. Same as always.'

I nod.

'You going to be OK?' she asks.

'I'm fine.'

I get dressed upstairs and come back down, the presents in two big bags by the door.

She comes out of the kitchen, her coat on.

I say: 'Shall we go?'

She smiles and hands me a small and beautifully wrapped box in green Christmas paper with a red ribbon: 'Merry Christmas, love.'

'I'm sorry,' I say. 'I didn't have time.'

She nods: 'I know. Don't worry.'

I say: 'Can I open it?'

'Of course.'

I pull the red ribbon loose and carefully open the paper –

'Can you guess what it is?' she says.

I shake my head and open the box –

'Happy?' she asks, squeezing my arm –

I nod, taking out the digital watch.

'It's a calculator as well,' she says.

I take off my father's old watch and put it on.

'Happy?'

I smile: 'Thank you.'

'Merry Christmas,' she says, kissing me on the cheek.

I say again: 'I'm sorry, I haven't got you anything yet.'

'Don't worry. You can take me to the sales.'

I put my father's watch on the windowsill and look at my new one.

'What time is it?' she laughs.

'Just gone eleven-oh-one and seventeen seconds.'

'Shall we go?'

I nod and open the door.

She points at the tree: 'Going to leave the lights on?'

'Better had,' I say and lock the door behind us.

We drive slowly into Warrington, listening to the local radio as we go, pop songs and carols, not saying very much, and we're early when we get to her parents but they're already back from church, waiting –

We park on the road just as her brother and his family arrive.

Their three kids are out of the car, carrying brand new toys up the drive and stretching to reach the doorbell, but her dad's already there at the door, wearing a paper hat and waving a cracker, wishing us a merry Christmas.

I reach over and take the two bags of presents off the back seat.

'What's in there?' asks Joan, looking at another bag on the back seat.

'Just work,' I say, but taking the bag full of back issues of *Spunk* and locking it in the boot – sure I'd left them in the shed last night.

I say hello and merry Christmas to Joan's brother John and Maureen, his wife, and we all walk up the drive talking about

the miserable weather we're having and how there are never
any white Christmases any more.

Her father is carving the bird, mother in the kitchen, Joan and
Maureen bringing in the vegetables, John and I holding sherries,
moaning about City and the terrible season they're having, his
son and two daughters, the twins, itching to get eating so they
can open the presents from their Nanna and Grandad Roberts
and their Uncle Peter and Aunty Joan and then watch *Top of the
Pops* in peace.

The food smells great and my mouth is wet.

We all sit down and I uncork a bottle of *Asti Spumante* and
pour as Joan's father serves the turkey and sausage and we all
help ourselves to vegetables, bread sauce and gravy, the children
wanting some of this and none of that, their parents laughing
and frowning, telling stories about Carl, Carol and Clare, how
they're growing so fast and there's really no denying they do
seem to grow up quicker these days.

The pudding gone, we're slumped in various chairs watching
Top of the Pops, various new pens and socks, diaries and chocolates to our name, Joan's parents telling us how they really
liked the Beatles all along, Joan and John disputing the fact, the
kids wanting us all to pipe down as after Kelly Marie it's The
Police, Carol insisting we play *Monopoly* later, although Carl's
got a new game about Napoleon he wants to play and his dad
had promised him that Uncle Peter would want to play, which
his dad denies and says Uncle Peter's here for a rest and not to
play with him, but Clare prefers *Cluedo* anyway, although her
mum thinks Uncle Peter's probably also had enough *Cluedo* to
last him a lifetime, but I shake my head and tell her would that
it were so, would that it were so.

There's a round of ham sandwiches and jelly at half-five, just
after it turns out to have been the Reverend Green in the study
with the candlestick, just after *Live and Let Die* and just before
Eric & Ernie's Christmas Special, just before we say we really
must get going as we've still to pop in at Hale on the way home.

With the kisses and the thank yous and all the merry Christmases and happy new years done, we pull away, Joan waving at the seven figures stood in the doorway, the kids racing off back into the house before we're even at the end of the road, and I put the radio on and Joan asks:

'What time is it?'

And I press the button that illuminates my new digital watch and say: 'Six-thirty one and eight seconds.'

'Thought Carl was going to have it off your wrist,' she laughs.

'Took a shine to it, didn't he?'

She's nodding: 'They're lovely, aren't they?'

And I'm thinking the same too, nodding.

We pull in to her Aunty Edith's drive and get out, Joan with another present.

I ring the doorbell and listen to the sound of laughter from the TV as Edith comes to the door of her bungalow –

'Peter!' she says. 'Joan!'

And we hug and we kiss on her doorstep, wishing each other a merry Christmas and then she ushers us in.

And we get another cup of tea and some *After Eight's* and Turkish Delight as Edith opens her present and gives us ours.

Then we sit and admire the tea-towels, the handkerchiefs, and the red and black striped tie, as a war film starts on the TV.

Joan's asleep as we head down the Altrincham Road and on into Alderley Edge and we're about to turn on to the Maccles-field Road when the first fire engine overtakes us and it's then I know, know instantly what's happened –

'Joan,' I'm saying. 'Wake up, love!'

'Are we back?'

'It's the house, love! Look!'

And I pull in to the side of the road and we stare up at the house, another fire engine and another and another –

The house in flames –

Lit match –

Gone.

my face and e shake my fists at the black sky that rains morning noon and night and cry who
are these faceless people who forbid my entrance to the halls of grief has no one before
descended to this sad hollows depths from that place where pain is host and all hope cut off
transmission nine murdered in bradford in november nineteen seventy eight but not received
until nineteen eighty noorjahan davit who was initially reported missing in september nineteen
seventy eight after leaving an acquaintance looking after her two children and failing to get
back in touch which was out of character on leaving home she had stated that she was going
to visit her mother at her leeds address and would return later that day however she never
arrived at her mothers house person in question is a convicted prostitute who left home in
possession of only train fare and stated that she expected her mother to provide her with
money for the children extensive inquiries in the manningham area have failed to trace subject
this woman is on bail and due to appear at bradford magistrates court to answer charges of
soliciting for prostitution at bradford conditions of bail are a curfew between nineteen hundred
hours and seven hundred hours daily it is believed that miss davit intended to attend court and
had made tentative enquiries to arrange for the custody of her children in the event of her
losing her liberty which indicates that she had no intention of absconding also she thereafter
failed to keep an appointment with her defending solicitor she is described as being pakistani
born february second nineteen fifty six five feet five inches tall of slim build wearing black polo
necked jumper yellow trousers green and black wavy striped woollen jacket with wide sleeves
black shoes and carrying a small handbag of the kind that is carried under the arm without
strap or handles missing until her body found secreted under an old wardrobe on waste ground
off arthington street bradford a post-mortem was carried out and death was due to massive
head injuries possibly caused by a heavy blunt instrument it is thought that death occurred
some weeks ago and the body is partially decomposed davit was living with a friend off lumb
lane when she left home saying she was going away for a few days and was reported as
missing from home one week later and in view of the recent spate of prostitute murders a large
scale search was carried out and enquiries made regarding her whereabouts all of which proved
negative and there had been no positive sightings of her from her being reported missing until
the discovery of her body but it is thought from the pattern of the injuries that this death is not
connected with the other prostitute murders publicly referred to as the ripper murders from the
pattern of the injuries this death is connected with the other prostitute murders publicly referred
to as the ripper murders connected with the other prostitute murders the ripper murders other
prostitute murders the ripper in the red room the numbers upside down the tape playing singing
along you are a pal and a confidant and it always will stay this way my hat is off see the biggest
gift would be from me the card attached would say thank you for being a friend and when we
both get older with walking canes and hair of grey have the fear for it is hard to hear so e stand
real close as we walk on across this marsh of shades beaten down by the heavy rain our feet
pressing on their emptiness that looks like human form we make our way through the filthy
mess of muddy shades and slush moving slowly talking a little he says when we die and float
away into the night the milky way you will hear me call as we ascend e will say my name then

Chapter 16

Dawn –

Boxing Day:

Friday 26 December 1980 –

I stand in front of a burnt-out shell, thinking this is the second time in a week I've seen these marks and smelt this smell, tasted this taste, but this time –

This time I'm stood in front of the burnt-out shell of my own house, seeing those marks and smelling that smell, tasting that taste, this time –

This time the marks on my house, the smell of my house, the taste of my house, this time –

Getting tears in my eyes –

Unable to stop the tears, getting the fear –

Unable to stop the fear –

The stench of that fear and all it's claimed stinging the inside of my nose and throat, but I can't move away –

Unable to stop the fear –

And I can only walk through the places where there were doors and windows, where the walls are now black, can only keep walking along the side of the garage until I come to the War Room –

The War Room –

Where the smell is worse still, another door gone, more walls black, the photographs and the map gone, the cassette recorder and the reel to reel, the television and the typewriter, the computer parts melted, *Anabasis* gone – all of it gone, the metal filing cabinets stained black, the boxes of paper, the stacks of magazines and newspapers, charred and gone –

Everything gone –

Everything but the fear –

Thinking they did this to me because of who I am, because of what I am –

Because of who I know, of what I know –

Because of the fear –

To give me the fear –

And I bend down and take a handful of hot black ash –

The Fear here.

'They burnt my house down! My fucking house down!'

'I know, I know,' says Roger Hook, his hands up.

'So where is he? Where the fuck is Smith?'

'He's not here.'

'I can bloody see that.'

'Pete, please?'

'Burnt my house down! Burnt my house down and threatened to kill my wife!'

He's nodding, asking: 'Where is Joan?'

'I'm not fucking telling you. I'm not telling anyone.'

'You want a car? Two cars? They're yours.'

'No,' I say. 'I want to see the Chief fucking Constable because I want to ask him what the fuck he's going to do about all this.'

'Let me go and make some calls; see what I can do.'

I nod, then say: 'Thanks, Roger. Thank you very much.'

He stands up and leaves me sat there, sat there in one of the eleventh floor offices of one of the Assistant Chief Constables of the Greater Manchester Police force –

My office.

And I stare at the Christmas cards and all the unopened post in my tray, the photographs and certificates on the wall, the awards and commendations, sitting there in my eleventh floor office –

But it doesn't feel like my office.

I look at my watch, my new digital watch:

10:09:36 –

And I remember leaving my old watch, my father's watch on the windowsill yesterday morning, remember it like it's someone else's memory, yesterday someone else's yesterday –

And sitting here, here in my office that doesn't feel like my office, I'm unable to stop the tears, getting the fear again –

Unable to stop the fear.

The telephone on the desk is ringing –

The telephone on my desk, my telephone –

I pick it up: 'Hello?'

'Mr Hunter? Mr Lees is on line two.'

'Thank you,' I say, pressing the flashing button, thinking:

Donald Lees, the Clerk to the Greater Manchester Police Authority.

I say: 'This is Peter Hunter speaking.'

'Mr Hunter, allegations have been made against you that indicate a disciplinary offence on your part and these allegations are to be investigated by Mr Ronald Angus, the Chief Constable of West Yorkshire.'

'What?'

'Mr Hunter, you are to be in your office at two this afternoon.'

'What are you talking about?'

'That's all I can tell you, Mr Hunter.'

'Mr Lees, what's going on? What allegations?'

'Mr Angus will give you the necessary details this afternoon. Goodbye.'

'Mr Lees – '

The line dead, the room spinning –

The Christmas cards and the unopened post in the tray, the photographs and certificates on the wall, the awards and commendations, spinning –

My whole office –

But it doesn't feel like my office –

It feels like I'm choking in someone else's office –

And I try to stand –

But I stumble –

I walk to the door –

I open it –

Roger Hook is in the corridor, Roger Hook talking to John Murphy –

I look at them –

They look away.

I'm outside, outside in the car park –

Outside in the car park, looking at my new digital watch:

10:27:09 –

Struggling with the car door –

Slumped behind the wheel:

Fucked.

Struggling, slumped and fucked –

In the reserved space that says:

Peter Hunter – Assistant Chief Constable.

Back upstairs, the corridors dead –

I dial his home number:

He picks up: 'Clement Smith speaking.'

'It's Peter Hunter.'

'Good morning, Mr Hunter.'

'You know we lost the house?'

'Yes,' he says. 'I know.'

'And I suppose you know I've also had a call from Donald Lees?'

'Yes.'

'I want to know what the bloody hell is going on?'

'It would be inappropriate of me to say anything to you at this point.'

'So you do know what these allegations are then?'

'I can't say anything. It would not be appropriate.'

'So you're not going to tell me what this is all about?'

'Mr Angus will give you all the information you're entitled to later on today, I believe.'

'But what about the Ripper Inquiry? It's to do with that, isn't it?'

'Peter,' he says, quietly. 'You must, from now on, worry only about yourself.'

'That's it?'

'Duty dictates I can say no more.'

'What?'

'Goodbye to you Mr Hunter.'

Speechless, I slam down the phone.

The office of one of the Assistant Chief Constables of the Greater Manchester Police force –

My office:

Friday 26 December 1980 –

Boxing day:

13:54:45.

A knock –

Chief Constable Ronald Angus and Detective Chief Superintendent Maurice Jobson are shown in –

Nods and handshakes:

Angus: 'Mr Hunter.'

'Peter,' says Maurice Jobson, *the Owl*.

Angus is looking at my chair behind my desk but I gesture at the two chairs in front of the desk –

We all sit down.

I look across my desk at Mr Ronald Angus, the Chief Constable of West Yorkshire, and I wait –

He says: 'Maurice is here because unfortunately George Oldman, as you know, has not been well and Pete Noble is a bit busy.'

He's smiling, the tables turned.

I say: 'That explains why Maurice is here. But what about you?'

He's not smiling now, not smiling as he tells me: 'I have been invited here today by your own Police Committee to investigate certain matters affecting yourself. This is not a formal interview and I will be taking no notes.'

I hold up my pen: 'I will be.'

'As you wish.'

I say: 'My wish Mr Angus is that I wasn't here at all, that I was with my wife. As you may or may not know, may or may not even care, our house was destroyed in a fire last night, a fire that followed a threatening letter from a man claiming to be the Yorkshire Ripper, a letter that you are aware of. So I would be very grateful if you could tell me what these *certain matters* are that you've been asked to investigate, so that I can clear this whole thing up as quickly as possible.'

'I cannot at this moment tell you what these matters are. They amount only to rumour, innuendo, and gossip about your associations with various people in Manchester.'

'Who?'

'I cannot tell you.'

'Cannot or will not?'

'I am not able to tell you. We have a number of inquiries to make.'

'I have done nothing wrong and I would like you to note that here and now.'

He doesn't –

He says: 'No evidence or written statements have been provided to me, but I'm sure this investigation . . .'

'Investigation?'

'No, that's too strong a word – this inquiry – I'm sure it shouldn't take too long.'

'How long?'

'About a month, I should think.'

'I have to be back in Leeds on Monday.'

He coughs and sits forward slightly in his chair and says: 'I have been authorised by your Police Committee to invite you to take extra leave. You will not be going back to Leeds and you can consider yourself off the Ripper Investigation.'

'For now or forever?'

'Forever.'

'You've spoken to Philip Evans, Sir John Reed?'

'Yes. It's been agreed that Chief Superintendent Murphy will take over the investigation, using your team.'

I say: 'What am I supposed to have done?'

'I cannot say.'

I look at Maurice Jobson –

He's looking at the floor.

Angus says: 'I can tell you that it has absolutely nothing to do with Leeds or the Ripper Investigation.'

'I didn't ask.'

'Well, I'm telling you.'

'Well, let me tell you something: I have no intention of accepting any free leave. If you have the grounds for a suspension, then suspend me. Otherwise, I will continue with my duties as an Assistant Chief Constable.'

Ronald Angus stands up: 'Mr Hunter, it is now my intention to ask you to leave your office and these headquarters right away.'

'What?'

Maurice Jobson stands up next to him.

Me: 'You're joking?'

Angus shakes his head.

Jobson is looking past me, out of the window behind me.

Slowly I stand, looking around the office –

The Christmas cards and the unopened post in the tray, the photographs and certificates on the wall, the awards and commendations, my whole office –

But it doesn't feel like my office –

Because it isn't my office –

I'm choking –
Trying not to sway as I stand there –
Trying to think –
Think, think, think.
I reach for my briefcase and I open it, sweeping the cards
and the unopened post into it –
And I stare at the photographs and the certificates on the
wall, the awards and commendations; their awards, their com-
mendations, thinking:
Fuck 'em – fuck 'em all.
And I walk to the door –
Trying not to stumble, briefcase under my arm –
And I open the door.
Angus says: 'Two o'clock tomorrow.'
'What?'
'Meet us here at two o'clock tomorrow please.'
And I just nod and walk out into the corridor –
And I stand there, in the corridor, until Jobson comes up
behind me.
'This way,' he says and leads me over to the lift.
He presses the button and we wait.
The lift arrives and the door opens –
He says: 'Sorry about your house.'
I look at him –
He looks away.

Outside, outside in the car park –
Outside in the car park, looking at my new digital watch:
14:36:04 –
Struggling with the car door and my briefcase –
Slumped behind the wheel:
Fucked.
Struggling, slumped and fucked –
In the reserved space that still says:
Peter Hunter – Assistant Chief Constable.

Someone's tapping on the glass –
I open my eyes:
Dark, night.
The policeman is saying:

'I'm sorry, you can't park here.'

Fuck.

'It's reserved.'

And I switch on the engine and the headlights in the reserved space that says:

Assistant Chief Constable.

No name –

Only:

Assistant Chief Constable.

I drive out of Manchester, through Wilmslow, and on to Alderley Edge.

I turn on to the Macclesfield Road.

There are no fire engines tonight.

And I pull up on the road and park there, the drive covered in the debris –

The house, what's left of our house in silence –

Our home –

Gone –

Lit match, gone.

I get out of the car and pick my way up the drive through the debris until I'm stood in front of the burnt-out shell of my house, seeing those marks and smelling that smell, tasting that taste, again –

Tears in my eyes –

Unable to stop the tears, the fear –

Unable to stop the fear –

And I walk through the places where there were doors and windows, where the walls are now black, and I keep walking along the side of the garage until I come to the War Room –

The War Room –

Everything gone –

Everything but the fear –

Knowing –

Knowing they're doing this to me because of who I am, because of what I am –

Because of who I know, of what I know –

Because of the fear –

To give me the fear –

And I bend down and take a handful of warm black ash and

I spit in that black ash and rub it between my fingers and my palms and then I take the ash and draw a cross upon my face –
  A cross to keep the fear away –
  A cross to keep the fear –
  A cross to keep –
  A cross to –
  A cross.

once again thank you for being a friend for you have seen my face in the stamp on the envelope of the letter e sent and e will leave this place to meet a friend in the winter that never leaves and says in a yorkshire way e say the weather is letting us down again winter still in the middle of may transmission ten sent may eighteenth nineteen seventy nine in morley joanne clare thornton found dead in lewisham park the following morning struck twice on the head dead instantly clothes repositioned body stabbed twenty five times with a kitchen knife with a four inch blade extensive damage to abdominal area and to vagina one shoe placed between thighs coat thrown over her e parked and ran to catch up with her and e said excuse me and e asked her the time and she squinted at the clock across the way and said it was half past eleven and e said my what good eyes you have and she said thank you and e said where have you been and she said to see her grandmother and e said have you got far to go and she said it was quite a walk and e said have you not thought about learning to drive and she said she preferred to ride horses and e said well you should be careful out here alone in this park at this time of night you cannot trust anybody these days and e stooped to pretend to tie my shoelace and then e took the hammer from my pocket and e hit her twice on the top of the head and dragged her from the path and e sorted out her clothes then e took out the ten inch philips screwdriver which e had sharpened to a point and e took out the kitchen knife and e stabbed her twenty five times and three times e inserted the screwdriver into her vagina and e punctured her uterus winter still the following received june twentieth nineteen seventy nine e am jack e see you are still having no luck catching me e have the greatest respect for you george but lord you are no nearer catching me now than four years ago when e started e reckon your boys are letting you down george they cannot be much good can they the only time they came near catching me was a few months back in chapeltown when e was disturbed even then it was a uniformed copper not a detective e warned you in march that e would strike again sorry it was not bradford e did promise you that but e could not get there e am not quite sure when e will strike again but it will be definitely some time this year maybe september october even sooner if e get the chance e am not sure where maybe manchester e like it there there is plenty of them knocking about they never do learn do they george e bet you have warned them but they never listen take her in preston and e did did e not george dirty cow come my load up that at the rate e am going e should be in the book of records e think it is up to eleven now is it not well e will keep on going for quite a while yet e cannot see myself being nicked just yet even if you do get near e will probably top myself first well it has been nice chatting to you george yours jack the ripper no good looking for fingerprints you should know by now it is as clean as a whistle see you soon bye hope you like the catchy tune at the end ha ha thank you for being a friend traveled down road and back again your heart is true you are a pal and a confidant e am not ashamed to say e hope it always will stay this way my hat is off will you not stand up and take a bow if you threw a party invited everyone you knew you would see biggest gift would be from me and the card attached would say thank you for being a friend if it is a car you lack e would surely buy you a white corsair whatever you need anytime day or night it always will stay this way when we both get older with walking canes and hair of grey have no fear even though it

Chapter 17

Joan's parents' house, sitting in their front room among the Christmas cards, their front room and Christmas cards like the front room that was our front room with its Christmas cards, the front room that was our front room until Thursday night, in front of their tree, their tree like the tree that was our tree until Thursday night, sitting in their front room, Mr and Mrs Roberts trying to leave us alone, give us some time, give us some space, some time and some space like the time and the space that was our time and our space until Thursday night, but they're in and out all the same, me and Joan sitting in their front room on their sofa, the sofa like the sofa that was our sofa until Thursday night, sitting in their front room on their sofa like the teenage couple we never were, me wanting to hold her hand –

Holding her hand –

Holding her hand, holding back my tears, trying to catch hers, trying to stop them, – but all the things we've lost, there's so much, we've lost so very much, too much, the things we've lost, there are so many, we've lost so very many things, too many.

'The application forms,' she's sobbing.

'We can easily get more, that won't be a problem.'

'But we haven't got a house, Peter. They'll never let us . . .'

'We'll get a new one, rebuild the old one. The insurance . . .'

'Not if it was those lights.'

'It wasn't the lights,' I snap. 'And it doesn't make any difference even if it was.'

'But it'll be years.'

'No, it won't.'

'They'll never let us, not now.'

'Of course they bloody will.'

Holding her hand, holding back my tears, trying to catch hers, trying to stop them, – but all the things we've lost, there's so much, we've lost so very much, too much, the things we've lost, there are so many, we've lost so very many things, too many.

Her mother puts her head round the door again: 'Another cup of tea anyone?'

I glance at my new watch, shaking my head and lie: 'I've got to be in the office.'

'At least you've still got a job,' Joan sniffs. 'Least you've still got that.'

I get into the car.

I sit behind the wheel.

I look at my watch again:

10:08:00 –

I turn the key in the ignition and pull out of their drive.

I head into Manchester –

Head into Manchester because I've got nowhere else to go:

Nowhere but here.

Saturday 27 December 1980 –

Two o'clock:

Manchester Police Headquarters –

The eleventh floor:

I knock on the door of the room that was my office, that was my office up until yesterday afternoon.

'Come.'

I open the door.

Ronald Angus is sitting in the chair that was my chair, the chair behind the desk that was my desk, the desk in the office that was my office, that was my office until yesterday afternoon at 14:35:00.

'Sit down,' says Angus, nodding at the empty chair next to Chief Superintendent Jobson –

I sit down.

Angus leans across the desk, the desk that was my desk, and he hands me a piece of paper –

I take it from him and I read:

Information has been received which indicates that during the past six years you have associated with persons in circumstances that are considered undesirable, and by such associations you may have placed yourself under an obligation as a police officer to those persons.

'That's it?' I ask.

'Yes.'

'No names, no times, no dates, no places?'

'It's not an allegation, nor a complaint.'

'So what is it?'

'It is information received that needs to be investigated.'

'So let me help; tell me the names of these people with whom I'm supposed to have associated?'

'I can't.'

'Well then, tell me what kind of obligations I'm supposed to have placed myself under?'

'I cannot.'

I'm smiling –

Despite myself I am smiling –

Smiling at Ronald Angus, the Chief Constable of West Yorkshire, the West Yorkshire force that forty-eight hours before I was investigating, smiling at him sat there in the chair that was my chair, the chair behind the desk that was my desk, the desk in the office that was my office, that was my office until yesterday afternoon.

'Mr Hunter,' he says. 'I know how this looks, so I know what you're thinking. But I can assure you my own reputation for fairness and integrity is as much on the line here as your own.'

I can't help myself: 'Is that supposed to make me feel better or worse, sir?'

Angus has had enough: 'Mr Hunter, to be blunt: I don't care how you feel.'

Silence –

In the office that was my office, that was my office until yesterday afternoon, silence –

Silence until Maurice Jobson says: 'Peter, we're going to have to ask you to provide us with full details of your bank account and any credit cards and savings accounts you might have had in the last six years.'

'Why?'

Jobson shakes his head: 'I can't tell you, you know that.'

'No, I don't know that.'

'OK, well I'm telling you now.'

'OK, Maurice,' I smile. 'I'll tell you something shall I? I am under no legal obligation whatsoever to provide you with that information.'

'No, you're not,' interrupts Angus. 'But if you don't oblige us, I'll just get a judge to make you.'

'Then you'd be wasting even more of your time than you already are.'

'And why would that be?'

'I can't give you it.'

'Can't or won't?' smiles Angus.

'Can't.'

'Why not?' asks Jobson.

'The fire.'

Angus sits back in his chair and sighs: 'Convenient.'

'What?' I say, voice raised: 'You what?'

Jobson's holding onto my arm, pulling me back down into the chair in front of the desk, the chair in front of the desk that was my desk, the desk in the room that was my room, the room that was my office, that was my office until yesterday afternoon, Jobson telling me: 'Take it easy, now. Take it easy.'

'What about your passport?' asks Angus.

'What about it?'

'Lose that as well?'

I tell him: 'We lost everything.'

'That's a pity.'

'Why?' I ask. 'Going to take that as well were you?'

'Yes.'

'Fucking hell,' I say, shaking my head.

Again silence –

Again silence in the office that was my office, that was my office until yesterday afternoon –

Again silence until Angus says: 'Two o'clock. Monday.'

'That's it?' I say.

'Wakefield,' he says.

'What?'

'Two o'clock. Monday. Wakefield.'

'You're joking? You're supposed to come here. It's procedure.'

'Mr Hunter,' sighs Mr Angus. 'We want this thing over and done with as much as you do. But you also know more than most the pressure we're under over there, so if you want us to get a move on with this we'd be grateful if you wouldn't mind coming over to Wakefield on Monday.'

I nod and stand up.

'Good day Mr Hunter,' he says.

'One thing,' I say –

He looks up.

'Disciplinary Regulations demand that information be given to an accused officer in sufficient detail for him to be able to defend himself, and that the full name and address of the person making the complaint must also be provided to him.'

Angus nods and says: 'I know.'

'OK,' I say. 'Then I look forward to receiving that information from you at two o'clock on Monday in Wakefield.'

Angus is looking at me, staring at me, staring at me stood there.

More silence –

More silence in the office that was my office, that was my office until yesterday afternoon –

More silence until the phone starts ringing –

Angus picks it up: 'Chief Constable Angus speaking.'

He's listening, still looking at me.

'Yes he is,' he says into the phone, eyes never leaving mine –

Mine never leaving his.

'Just a moment,' he says and puts his hand over the mouth-piece –

'It's for you,' he says. 'Won't give his name, but says it's an emergency.'

Never leaving his.

Ronald Angus leans forward and hands me the phone, the phone that was my phone until yesterday afternoon –

I take the phone from him and lean across the desk, the desk that was my desk, and I press the flashing red button: 'This is Peter Hunter.'

'Are you alone?' a man's voice asks – young.

'No, I'm not.'

'Well then, I'll make this brief.'

'I'm listening.'

'I've got some information concerning one of the Ripper murders.'

'I'm still listening,' I say, thinking –

ASSUME THIS PHONE IS TAPPED.
Him: 'Be in Preston tomorrow lunchtime.'
'Where?'
'St Mary's? It's a pub on Church Street.'
'What time?'
'One?'
'Fine.'
The line goes dead.
I hand the phone, the phone that was my phone until yes-
terday afternoon, I hand it back to Ronald Angus –
He takes it from me, his eyes black and burning to know
who that was, Jobson the same.
I say nothing and turn and walk to the door, the door that
was my door, the door to the office that was my office, that was
my office until yesterday afternoon.
'Mr Hunter?' says Angus as I open the door. 'One thing for
you.'
I turn around –
'We will be asking you for authorisation to go directly to
your bank and we will also be asking you to turn over official
diaries and expenses, not forgetting all files pertaining to the
Ripper.'
I nod and turn back to the door –
'Is that a yes, Mr Hunter?'
I nod again, my back to him, and I step out into the corridor
and shut the door, shut the door to the office that was my office,
that was my office until yesterday afternoon.

I pull into the drive of Joan's parents' house at almost six o'clock
and I can see Joan watching for me in their front room.
She comes out into the drive as I'm locking the car –
'Why didn't you say something? Why didn't you tell me?'
I can see her parents standing in the hall, her father with his
arms around her mother –
'What?'
'It's all over the papers, the news. It's everywhere.'
'What is?'
'Your suspension,' she says, holding out the evening paper –
'What?'
'You didn't know?'

I take the paper from her and stand in the dark and the rain of her parents' drive straining to read the front page of the *Manchester Evening News* under a headline that's as large as it is a lie:

Suspended.

In big, black, bold type –

With my photograph underneath, one taken of me wrestling a student to the ground during a recent demonstration when Keith Joseph came North on a visit to Manchester Polytechnic.

Manchester Assistant Chief Constable Peter Hunter was today suspended from duty due to what police sources are describing as serious allegations.

In a carefully worded statement, Mr Donald Lees of the Greater Manchester Police Authority told reporters that, 'Information has been received in relation to the conduct of a Senior Police Officer which disclosed the possibility of a disciplinary offence. To maintain public confidence, the Chairman of the Police Committee, Councillor Clive Birkenshaw, has requested the Chief Constable of West Yorkshire, Mr Ronald Angus, to investigate this matter under the appropriate statutory provisions. The Assistant Chief Constable involved is on temporary leave of absence whilst the matter is being investigated.'

Mr Lees repeatedly refused to confirm or deny that the officer was Peter Hunter, but police sources confirmed that Mr Hunter had been suspended from duty. Attempts were made to contact Mr Hunter for comment, but he was unavailable at the time of going to press.

Councillor Birkenshaw meanwhile was quoted as describing the complaint as 'very trivial' and had 'blown up over the last two days'.

However Mr Clement Smith, the Chief Constable of Greater Manchester, told the Evening News *that the allegations were, 'very regrettable indeed and it is my hope that they will be cleared up as quickly as possible.'*

Mr Lees was unable to give details of the allegations involving Mr Hunter but he did deny conflicting newspaper reports that the suspension was a result of a fire two days ago at Mr Hunter's Alderley Edge home or his handling of the inquiry into the Yorkshire Ripper or rumoured links to the recent horrific murder of former Yorkshire policeman Robert Douglas and his young daughter in the Ashburys area of the city.

I stop reading and look up at Joan standing there, standing there in the drive of her parents' house, her own arms around herself.

'You didn't know?' she's asking me –

I shake my head and say: 'Bastards, the fucking bastards.'

And she's crying and so am I, unable to hold back my tears, unable to catch hers, unable to stop them, and all the things we've lost, there's so much, we've lost so very much, too much, the things we've lost, there are so many, we've lost so very many things, too many, and I put my arm around her and lead her back up the drive and into her parents' house, her parents' house like the house that was our house, the house that was our house until Thursday night, her mother and father stood in the hall, his arm round her, her hands to her face, my arms round Joan, her hands to my face, my black ash face, and I look at the three of them and I say –

'I'm sorry.'

is hard to hear e will stand real close and say thank you for being a friend and when we die and float away into the night the milky way you will hear me call as we ascend hear me cry but surely we were meant to win this fight not howl like dogs in the rain transmission eleven received on ash lane bradford on sunday the ninth of september nineteen seventy nine identified as dawn williams a large laceration on the back of her head and seven stab wounds in her trunk three of them round her umbilicus the knife reintroduced into the chest wound on a number of occasions she had numerous bruises and abrasions and had been struck on the head with a hammer and stabbed with a giant three sided screwdriver new suffering in the round of rain eternal a piteous sight confusing me to tears cursed cold and falling heavy unchanging thick hail and dirty water mixed with snow coming down in torrents through the murky air the earth stinking from this soaking rain wherein a ruthless and fantastic beast with all three of his throats howls out doglike above the drowning sinners of this place his eyes red his beard slobbered black his belly swollen he has claws for hands and he rips the spirits flays and mangles her in the shadows of the yard behind number thirteen pulling at her blouse lifting her brassiere pulling down her jeans and panties putting away the hammer taking out the screwdriver the knife stabbing stabbing stabbing stabbing stabbing stabbing stabbing replacing the blouse under a piece of carpet some leaves the rain welcome back to bradford said the sign above the door round the back in an old carpet a dead girl in a distorted jackknife posture in a cheesecloth shirt bra pushed up to expose her breasts and her jeans undone and partly pulled down stabbed seven times in the stomach and the shoulder blade with a four inch blade he is thirty two dark five feet eight inches tall calls himself ronnie or johnnie related to the detective no he is an electrician from durham no he is a former sailor now electrician who loves dancing no e have seen his face in the stamp on the envelope of the letter he sent and e will not leave this place until he is caught no he is a father of two who works at a pumping station and has a dog no he is a lorry driver called peter who drives a cab with a name beginning with the letter C on the side and he lives in bradford in a big grey house elevated above the street behind wrought iron gates with steps leading up to the front door number six in its street peter will have committed crimes before and is connected to the containerbase at stourton and he will kill for the last time in leeds on wednesday the tenth of december nineteen eighty a piteous sight confusing me to tears the onedin line finished this is the bradford police dawn has been reported missing since yesterday evening and we wondered if she had gone home no she has not and this is most unusual right we will keep checking and we will let you know as soon as we have any news this is just not like her perhaps it is a hoax a sick joke there are so many e thought e would ring you and have a chat we have no news yet e have got daughters too and e know what it is like then the doorbell and she is gone and we would like you to come up and identify her we will send a car around the colour of the coward on my face his body one mass of twitching muscle grabbing up fistfuls of mud quiet only with mouthfuls of food then barking thunder on dead souls who wished they were deaf and e say it is not usual for one of us to make the journey e am making now but it happens e was down here once before soon after e had left my flesh in death she sent me through these walls and down as far as the pit of judas

Chapter 18

The breakfast is greasy, the conversation cold, the weather both and the radio on:

'*Accusation and counter-accusation fill many of the Sunday papers this morning concerning the suspension of Peter Hunter, an Assistant Chief Constable with the Greater Manchester Police.*

'*Under the headline,* Hunter: Conspiracy or Coincidence? *an editorial in the* Observer *asks whether Mr Hunter's suspension is in any way linked to an apparently hostile report he was preparing into the management and practices of the West Yorkshire Police in regard to their handling of the on-going Ripper Inquiry. A report that has now been shelved.*

'*However the* Mail on Sunday *carries quotes from unnamed police sources claiming that the suspension is due to Mr Hunter's own associations with a prominent local criminal from whom Mr Hunter had accepted lavish hospitality, photographs of which are 'doing the rounds' in some of the less salubrious Manchester pubs and clubs.*

'*Meanwhile other papers continue to lead with either the hunt for the Yorkshire Ripper or the prospects for the release of the fifty-two hostages being held . . .*'

I swallow my food and get up from the table.

'Where are you going?' her mother asks.

'Preston.'

'Preston?' repeats her father.

'Preston,' I nod.

Joan doesn't even look up from the plate before her, greasy and cold.

Preston –

Sunday 28 December 1980:

11:05:02 –

I'm too early –

Much too early.

I don't need to find St Mary's, so I park in a multi-storey car park near the station and listen to the radio for a bit longer before I decide to sort out the car, stuffed full of half the office – the unopened post and cards; plus the Christmas presents

– the various pens and socks, the diaries and chocolates, the handkerchiefs and tie; then the stuff from the Griffin – the *Exegesis* and the tapes, Hall's notes and mine, the boot full of *Spunk*s.

I open the doors and the boot and start shifting stuff about and when I've got the porn and the important stuff lying in the boot under a sea of socks and diaries, handkerchiefs and the tie, then I close the boot and get back inside, the unopened post and cards in a pile on the passenger seat, and with a mouth full of chocolate liquors I start going through the envelopes, one by one, the cards and the post, one by one, the official and the personal, one by –

One:

Flat and manila, in slanting black felt-tip pen:

Peter Hunter,

Police Chief,

Manchester.

Flat and manila, in slanting black felt-tip pen:

Photos Do Not Bend.

Flat and manila –

I rip it open and take them out –

Photographs, four of them –

Four photographs of two people in a park:

Platt Fields Park, in wintertime.

Photographs, black and white –

Black and white photographs of two people in a park by a pond:

A cold grey pond, a dog.

Four black and white photographs of two people in a park –

Two people in a park:

One of them me.

St Mary's, Church Street, Preston –

12:54:05.

I'm sitting at a sticky-topped table by the door, the rain outside, the cold inside.

I've got a half of bitter in front of me, salt and vinegar crisps spilling here and there, sideways glances from the regulars.

I keep looking at my watch, my new digital watch –

12:56:05.

Sitting at the sticky-topped table by the door, wondering if he's here or if he'll show, wondering if I would if I were him, wondering just who the fuck he is – the fuck I am.

An empty glass in front of me, salt and vinegar stinging my fingers, front-on stares from two men by the dartboard.

I look at my watch –

12:58:03.

Sat there, damp and cold –

Evil eyes –

I look at –

'Peter Hunter?' shouts out the woman behind the bar, waving a telephone about –

And I've got my hand up, crossing the room.

She hands the phone across the bar –

'This is Peter Hunter,' I say into the receiver.

Him, that voice: 'You alone?'

'Of course I am.'

'How do you know?'

I pause, replaying the route, scanning the room – the eyes and the stares – and then I say: 'I am. Are you?'

'Of course.'

'Where are you?'

'Near enough.'

'Where?'

'Step outside, walk up the hill, turn left onto Frenchwood Street.'

'And?'

But the phone is dead.

I walk up Church Street, the top of the multi-storey car park looming over the hill, the rain cold upon my face.

I turn left onto Frenchwood Street, a row of garages on the left side of the road, wasteland to the right, and I walk towards the last garage, the door banging in the wind, in the rain.

I pull back the door and there he is, standing among the bottles and the cans, the rags and the newspapers, leaning against a bench made from crates and boxes.

'Afternoon,' says a young man in a dirty black suit –

Face puffed and beaten, punctured and bruised, a plaster

across a broken nose, one hand bandaged, the other pulling lank and greasy hair out of blue and black eyes.

'Who are you? You got a name?'

'No names.'

I shrug, touching my own cuts: 'What happened to you?'

He's sniffing and touching his nose: 'Occupational hazard. Goes with the places I go.'

I look away, looking around the garage, the bottles and the cans, the rags and the newspapers, the chipboard walls, the rusting cans and the broken bottles, the rotting rags and the soiled papers, the splattered chipboard walls –

The swastikas.

Staring at him in the dark room, I ask him: 'Is that what you wanted to talk about? The places you go? This place?'

'You been here before, have you Mr Hunter?'

I nod: 'Have you?'

'Oh yes,' he says. 'Many times.'

'Were you here the night of Thursday 20 November 1975?'

He pushes his hair back out of his beaten eyes, smiling: 'You should see your fucking face?'

'Yours isn't that good.'

'How's that song go: *if looks could kill they probably will?*'

'I don't know.'

'Well, I do,' he says and hands me a folded piece of paper.

I open it and look at it, then back at him –

He's smiling, smiling that faint and dreadful smile.

I look back down at the piece of paper in my hands –

A piece of black and white Xeroxed paper –

A piece of black and white Xeroxed pornography –

Fat and blonde, legs and cunt –

Clare Strachan.

Across the top of the page, in black felt-tip pen:

Spunk, Issue 3, January 1975.

Across the bottom, in black felt-tip pen:

Murdered by the West Yorkshire Police, November 1975.

Across her face, in black felt-tip pen:

A target, a dartboard.

I look back up at him, standing there among the bottles and the cans, the rags and the newspapers, leaning against a bench made from crates and boxes, face puffed and beaten, punctured and bruised, a plaster across his broken nose, one hand bandaged, the other picking at his scabs, his sores –

Itching and scratching at his scabs and his sores, running –

Running scared.

He smiles and says: 'Here comes a copper to chop off your head.'

'You do this?' I ask.

'What?'

'Any of it?'

He shakes his head: 'No, Mr Hunter. I did not.'

'But you know who did?'

He shrugs.

'Tell me.'

He shakes his head.

'I'll fucking arrest you.'

Shaking his head: 'No, you won't.'

'Yes, I will.'

'For what?'

'Wasting police time. Withholding evidence. Obstruction. Murder?'

He smiles: 'That's what they want.'

'Who?'

Shaking his head: 'You know who.'

'No, I don't.'

'Well then, you've obviously been overestimated.'

'Meaning?'

'Meaning a lot of people seem to have gone to a lot of bother to make sure you're not in Yorkshire and not involved with the Ripper.'

'So why do they want you arrested?'

'Mr Hunter, they want me dead. Arresting me's just a way to get their hands on me.'

'Who?'

He shakes his head, smiling: 'No names.'

'Stop wasting my time,' I hiss and open the door –

He lunges over, slamming the door shut: 'Here, you're not going anywhere.'

We're chest to chest, eye to eye in the dark room, among the bottles and the cans, the rags and the newspapers.

'Start fucking talking then,' I say, the Xerox up between us and in his face –

He pushes the paper away, a hand up: 'Fuck off.'

'You called me? Why?'

'I didn't bloody want to, believe me,' he says, moving back over to the bench of crates and boxes. 'I had serious doubts.'

'So why?'

'I was going to just post the picture, but then I heard about the suspension and I didn't know how long you'd be about.'

'Just this,' I say, holding up the Xerox. 'That was all?'

He nods.

'Why?'

'I just want it to stop. Want them to stop.'

'Who?'

'No fucking names! How many more times?'

In the dark, dark room, there among the bottles and the cans, the rags and the newspapers, the chipboard walls, the rusting cans and the broken bottles, the rotting rags and the soiled papers, the splattered chipboard walls, I look at him –

Look at him and then Clare, and I say: 'So why here? Is this where it all started? With her?'

'Started?' he laughs. 'Fuck no.'

'Where it ended?'

'The beginning of the end, shall we say.'

'For who?'

'You name them?' he whispers. 'Me, you, her – half the fucking coppers you've ever met.'

I look back down at the piece of paper in my hands –

The piece of black and white Xeroxed paper –

The piece of black and white Xeroxed pornography –

Fat and blonde, legs and cunt –

'Why Strachan?' I ask. 'Because of the magazine? Because of *Spunk*?'

'Why they murdered Clare?' he's saying, shaking his head. 'No.'

'Not the porn? Strachan's murder had nothing to do with MJM?'

'No.'

'I want names – '

'I'll give you one name,' he whispers. 'And one name only.'

'Go on?'

'Her name was Morrison.'

'Who?'

'Clare – her maiden name was Morrison.'

'Morrison?'

He's nodding: 'Know any other Morrisons, do you Mr Hunter?'

In the dark room, there among the bottles and the cans, the rags and the newspapers, the chipboard walls, the rusting cans and the broken bottles, the rotting rags and the soiled papers, the splattered chipboard walls, I say –

'Grace Morrison.'

Nodding: 'And?'

The dark room, there among the bottles and the cans, the rags and the newspapers, the chipboard walls, the rusting cans and the broken bottles, the rotting rags and the soiled papers, the splattered chipboard walls, I say –

'The Strafford. She was the barmaid at the Strafford.'

Nodding, smiling: 'And?'

Dark room, there among the bottles and the cans, the rags and the newspapers, the chipboard walls, the rusting cans and the broken bottles, the rotting rags and the soiled papers, the splattered chipboard walls, in this dark room I whisper –

'They were sisters.'

Nodding, smiling, laughing: 'And?'

In the dark, dark room, there among the bottles and the cans, the rags and the newspapers, the chipboard walls, the rusting cans and the broken bottles, the rotting rags and the soiled papers, the splattered chipboard walls, I look down –

I look back down at the piece of paper in my hands –

A piece of black and white Xeroxed paper –

A piece of black and white Xeroxed pornography –

Fat and blonde, legs and cunt –

In the dark room, there among the bottles and the cans, the rags and the newspapers, the chipboard walls, the rusting cans and the broken bottles, the rotting rags and the soiled papers, the splattered chipboard walls, I look up and say again –

'The Strafford.'

He smiles: 'Bullseye.'

In this dark room, I ask: 'How do you know this?'

Not nodding, not smiling, not laughing, he says: 'I was there.'

'Where? You were where?'

'The Strafford,' he says and opens the door –

I lunge over, slamming the door shut: 'You're not going anywhere, pal. Not yet.'

We're chest to chest again, eye to eye in the dark room, here among the bottles and the cans, the rags and the newspapers –

He sniffs up: 'That's your lot, Mr Hunter.'

'Fuck off,' I yell. 'You tell me what happened that night?'

He pulls away: 'Ask someone else.'

'You mean Bob Craven? There isn't anybody else, they're all dead.'

'Exactly.'

'Fuck off,' I say, reaching over and grabbing at his jacket, but –

He pushes me back and leaves me reaching out again in the dark room, there across the bottles and the cans, the rags and the newspapers, the chipboard walls, the rusting cans and the broken bottles, the rotting rags and the soiled papers, the splattered chipboard walls, me reaching out, grabbing him, dancing in the dark room, here among the bottles and the cans, the rags and the newspapers, the chipboard walls, the rusting cans and the broken bottles, the rotting rags and the soiled papers, the splattered chipboard walls, dancing in the dark room, dancing until –

I'm down, his fist in my face, fingers at my throat –

And I reach up from the floor, from the bottles and the cans, the rags and the newspapers, but –

'What the fuck are you doing?' he's shouting, trying to get away.

'Time to stop running,' I'm shouting, but –

He's kicking me, there among the bottles and the cans, the rags and the newspapers, kicking –

'Get fucking off me.'

'What happened?'

Kicking me, the bottles and the cans, the rags and the newspapers –

'I'm saying no more.'

'Tell me!'

But he's free and at the door –

Telling me: 'They haven't finished with you.'

Here among the bottles and the cans, the rags and the news-papers, inside my coat I can feel the photographs –

Four black and white photographs of two people in a park –

Two people in a park:

One of them me.

And from among the bottles and the cans, the rags and the newspapers, I hiss: 'You're dead.'

'Not me,' he laughs. 'I got my insurance. How about you?'

'They'll find you and they'll kill you if you don't come with me.'

'Not me,' he says.

'Go on, run then,' I spit –

'Fuck off,' he says, stepping outside. 'It's you who should be running; you they haven't finished with – you.'

Face puffed and beaten, punctured and bruised in the dark room, there among the bottles and the cans, the rags and the newspapers, the chipboard walls, the rusting cans and the broken bottles, the rotting rags and the soiled papers, the splatt-ered chipboard walls, I shout –

'You're dead.'

In the dark room, there across the bottles and the cans, the rags and the newspapers, the chipboard walls, the rusting cans and the broken bottles, the rotting rags and the soiled papers, the splattered chipboard walls, the garage door banging in the wind, in the rain –

'Dead.'

In the multi-storey car park, I sit in the car and weep –

Fucking weep –

Four black and white photographs –

Four black and white photographs of two people in a park –

Two people in a park:

One of them me.

Four black and white photographs on the seat beside me –

Four black and white photographs and one piece of black and white Xeroxed paper –

One piece of black and white Xeroxed paper –

One piece of black and white Xeroxed pornography –

Fat and blonde, legs and cunt –

Spunk, Issue 3, January 1975.

'Clare Morrison,' I say aloud. 'Clare fucking Morrison.'

In the multi-storey car park, I sit in the car and dry my tears.

I get out and open the boot and when I've got the bag of *Spunks* and got the *Exegesis*, when I've got them from under the sea of socks and diaries, the handkerchiefs and the tie, I get back inside and start looking for *Issue 3*, but it's not there –

One of the missing issues.

I stuff the *Spunks* back, thinking back, playing back the tapes in my head –

And I look back down at the piece of paper on the seat beside me –

The piece of black and white Xeroxed paper –

The piece of black and white Xeroxed pornography –

Fat and blonde, legs and cunt –

Thinking back, playing back the tapes in my head:

'Why Clare Strachan?' I asked. 'Because of the magazine? Because of Spunk?'

'Strachan?' he was saying, shaking his head. 'No.'

'Not the porn? Strachan's murder had nothing to do with MJM?'

Stop –

Rewind:

'Not the porn? Strachan's murder had nothing to do with MJM?'

Stop:

Lying piece of shit –

I start the car, thinking:

'It's you who should be running; you they haven't finished with.'

Richard Dawson lives in West Didsbury in a large, white and detached bungalow which had been designed by the architect John Dawson as a wedding present for his younger brother and his bride Linda –

I park on the road at the bottom of their drive and walk up the gravel to the front door.

Little Cygnet says the sign on the gatepost.

I press the chimes and look out over the garden, across the rain on the pond, trying to remember the last time I was here.

I turn back to press the bell again and there's Linda –

Linda in a blouse and skirt, looking like she hasn't slept in a week.

'Hello, love,' I say. 'How are you?'

But she's already crying and I put my arms round her and lead her back inside, closing the door, back into the cold, quiet house –

We sit down on the cream leather sofa in the gloom of their all-white lounge, *Kelly Monteith* on the TV without the sound.

And when she's stopped shaking in my arms, I stand up and walk over to the mirrored drinks cabinet and I pour two large Scotch and sodas –

I hand her one and she looks up from the sofa, her eyes red raw, and she says: 'What's going on Peter?'

And I shake my head and say: 'I've no idea, love.'

'How's Joan?'

'You heard about the house?'

She nods: 'You staying with her parents?'

'Yep,' I say. 'What about you? Where are the kids?'

'With my parents.'

'What have you told them?'

'That their Daddy's gone away.'

'Linda,' I say. 'You got any idea where he's gone?'

She shakes her head, the tears coming again: 'Something's happened to him, I just know it has.'

'You don't know that,' I say.

'He would have called me, I know he would have.'

'What about the house in France?'

'That's what everyone says, but he wouldn't – not without saying anything.'

'Has anyone been in touch with the local police in France?'

'That Roger Hook, he said they would.'

I sit down and take her hand: 'When did you last see Richard?'

'It's been a week now.'

'Last Sunday?'

She nods.

I squeeze her hand: 'He tell you where he was going?'

'He said he was going to sort things out.'

'Sort things out?'

She nods again: 'I thought he might mean he was going to see you.'

I shake my head: 'He did call me.'

'When?'

'Would have been Saturday night.'

'Did he say anything to you?'

'Said he was worried about Monday, about going back to see Roger Hook.'

She looks up: 'You think he was worried enough to run off?'

'I don't know, love. Do you?'

She looks back down at the drink in her hand and says quietly: 'I don't know anymore.'

'Linda, love,' I say, squeezing her hand. 'How much did he talk to you about work?'

'What do you mean?'

'Did he usually talk to you about his day at the office?'

She nods: 'A bit.'

'Did he mention people's names? Sound off if he was upset?'

'He was upset about Bob Douglas and their little girl Karen.'

'Of course,' I say. 'Who wasn't. But usually?'

'I don't know,' she says and lets go of my hand. 'I don't know what you mean.'

'For example, you knew Bob Douglas and his wife?'

'But that was different, I introduced them.'

'Right, right,' I'm nodding. 'Through the school?'

'Yes,' she says, standing up and beginning to pace.

'I'm sorry, Linda,' I say. 'But can I ask you some names, see if they ring any bells?'

She stops by the window, the big cold front window.

I say: 'Bob Craven?'

She has her back to me and the room, looking out of the window, silent –

'Linda?'

Looking out of the window over the garden, across the rain on the pond.

I ask her again: 'Bob Craven?'

Out of the window, over the garden, across the rain on the pond.

'Linda?'

'No,' she says, standing slightly on tiptoes.

'Eric Hall?'

The window, the garden, the rain, the pond, silent –

I say again: 'Eric Hall?'

Silent, then –

'Peter!'

'What?'

'No,' she says, her hands on the glass, turning to me – turning back: 'No!'

I get up, over to the window –

Linda saying over and over: 'No! God, no!'

Roger Hook and Ronnie Allen are walking up the gravel to the front door.

'No!'

I swallow and walk towards the door.

'Oh no, please no!'

And I open the door and see the looks on their faces –

'No, no, no,' she's screaming, tearing into the back of the house: 'No, no, no, no, no, no, no, no, no, no, no, no, no, no, no, no, no, no.'

The doorbell rings again –

'Where is she?' says Joan.

'In the bedroom.'

'What about the kids?'

'They're not here. With her parents.'

'Do they know?'

I shake my head.

'What happened?' she asks, her face twitching, lip trembling.

'Come in here,' I say and lead her into the lounge –

'You know Roger?' I say. 'And this is Ronnie Allen.'

Roger Hook smiles and Ronnie Allen shakes my wife's hand: 'Nice to meet you, Mrs Hunter.'

We sit down on the cream leather sofa and I say: 'His body was discovered following a fire at a newsagents in Batley, West Yorkshire.'

'Batley? A fire?'

I shake my head: 'He'd been murdered, love.'

'How? I mean what – '

I've got my hand up: 'Listen love, I'm going to tell you the details because Linda will want to know and right now you're the only person she's going to let into that bedroom.'

Joan's twitching, trembling.

'The fire was on the Bradford Road, Batley, at a newsagents

called RD News in the early hours of Tuesday morning, 23 December. His body wasn't discovered until about lunchtime on Tuesday in the flat above the shop. It looks like the fire started in the flat.'

Roger Hook is listening, nodding along.

'He had been stripped, stabbed, and strangled – his hands cut off, his teeth smashed in with a hammer. His body had then been doused in petrol and set alight.'

Joan's trembling.

'They were only able to identify the body because of his feet.'

'His feet?' she says.

'He'd been born without a heel on his left foot,' I'm telling her, when I hear –

'No.'

A faint and dreadful sound from the doorway, and we all look up and there she is –

Her blouse gone, just a bra and skirt, blood dripping from her wrists onto the cream carpet –

'No!' screams Joan. 'No, Peter please – '

And Ronnie's got Linda in his arms, his hands across her wrists, the blood everywhere –

Me holding Joan back –

The blood everywhere –

Roger shouting into the telephone –

The blood –

The blood everywhere.

to bring a spirit out and that place is the lowest and the darkest the farthest from the sphere that circles all and e saw him down there a lorry driver called peter who drives a cab with a name beginning with the letter C on the side and he lives in bradford transmission interrupted on the twentieth of november nineteen seventy nine in batley tessa smith attacked on a path on grassland on the council estate where she lived with her boyfriend and her baby cutting across the grassland from a late opening estate grocery shop she was struck on the head from behind so hard that the hammer went through her skull and as she fell remembers the man with the beard and a moustache and he hit her again on the forehead but she was screaming and he ran away will not somebody help me will not somebody help me will not somebody help me her boyfriend watching from the window is chasing him down the street shouting ripper ripper hunt hunt ripper ripper cunt cunt but e am too fast for them e am away like a thief in the night to leave them standing upon the brink of griefs abysmal valley that collects the thunderings of endless cries so dark and deep and nebulous it is that try as you might you cannot see the shape of anything faces painted with pity there are no wails just the anguished sound of sighs rising and trembling through the timeless air the sounds of sighs of untormented grief cut off from hope to live on in death in a place where no light is her personality changed drastically since the attack she was always quick with a smile but now she seems to flare up at the slightest thing she only seems happy to be in the company of the baby she argues about every little thing in fact e am sad to say she has become a bit of a tyrant it will never be the same for any of us again even now we tell each other when we go out and where we are going we are all very nervous cut off from hope e have a great mistrust of men jimmy and e had planned to get married in the near future and when e came out of the hospital we got back together for a while but it just did not work out e am on edge all of the time and frightened at being alone with him all that mattered was that he was a fellow and e did not feel safe e preferred to be at home with my mother and my sisters e am obsessed with having my back to the wall all the time even when e am surrounded by friends e have tried to stop myself but e simply cannot stand anyone at my back cut off from hope in a place where no light is where the damned keep crowding up in front of me where the notes of anguish play upon my ears where sounds on sounds of weeping pound and pound at me a place where no light shines at all the laments the anguished cries of grief cut off from hope where we live behind wires and alarms alone with five cats and the three inch dents in my head the hair e cut myself in my own world crying in the chapel the curtains pulled in a housecoat with my cats to walk in the middle of the road scared of the shadows and the men behind me that in a yorkshire way they say weather is letting us down again but he is not here is a lorry driver called peter who drives a cab with a name beginning with the letter C on the side and lives in bradford in a big grey house elevated above the street behind wrought iron gates with steps leading up to the front door number six in its street peter will have committed crimes before and is connected to the containerbase at stourton and he will kill for the last time in leeds on wednesday the tenth of december nineteen eighty standing upon the brink of griefs abysmal valley faces painted with pity e beg of you in the name of the god e never knew save me from this evil place and worse and lead me there

Chapter 19

I wake in a dead man's house on his cream sofa in his blood-splattered white front room, his wife in the hospital, my own at her side.

I drink his tea and use his razor, his soap and his towels, listening to his radio play songs about videos, songs about Einstein, songs about spacemen, songs about toys, songs about games – waiting for the news:

'Refusing to comment on various reports in yesterday's papers, Mr Clement Smith, the Chief Constable of Greater Manchester issued the following statement:

' "Unless there are exceptional circumstances in a particular case, and it is thought necessary in the public interest, it is not ordinarily the Chief Constable's policy to comment on any police inquiry or investigation which may be in progress, or to confirm or deny the existence of any such investigation, should it or should it not exist."

'Meanwhile an unemployed man will appear before Rochdale magistrates later this morning in connection with the hoax call made to the Daily Mirror in Manchester last week from a man claiming to be the Yorkshire Ripper. Police managed to trace a second call placed to the Mirror offices on Friday night and arrested Raymond Jones at his parents' home in Rochdale . . .'

I switch off his radio, wash his cup, straighten his kitchen, and check I've left nothing on.

Then I lock his door and leave his cream sofa, his blood-splattered white front room, his house, this dead man's house –

Leave this sofa, this room, this house of the dead –

Leave it for another –

Yorkshire, bloody Yorkshire –

Primitive Yorkshire, Medieval Yorkshire, Industrial Yorkshire –

Three Ages, three Dark Ages –

Local Dark Ages –

Local decay, industrial decay –

Local murder, industrial murder –

Local hell, industrial hell –

Dead hells, dead ages –
Dead moors, dead mills –
Dead cities –
Crows, the rain, and their Ripper –
The Yorkshire Ripper –
Yorkshire bloody Ripper.

Thornton Crematorium is halfway between Denholme and Allerton, on the way back into Bradford.

I know the way, know the place –

On the dark stair, we miss our step.

Raining heavily, it's nearly ten-thirty:

10:25:01 –

Monday 29 December 1980.

I park on the road and stare up the hill towards the dark building with the chimney, black in the weather, past small stones with small names, the dead flowers, cigarette ends and crisp packets, the dead leaves, tyres in the rain the only sound.

Know the place well –

I've been here before:

Sunshine hurting, it's gone ten:

The leather strap of my father's watch, itching in the heat –

Thursday 7 July 1977 –

Parked on the road, staring up the hill towards the pale building with the chimney, white in the bright light, the small stones with the small names, flowers, the white clouds in the blue sky, trees, the birds singing –

I'm taking down number plates, putting faces to names, on my own time and of my own leave –

Compassionate leave:

Another miscarriage, the last –

Joan at her parents' house.

Thursday 7 July 1977 –

Burying him today, almost three weeks on:

Sunday 19 June 1977 –

Detective Inspector Eric Hall, Bradford Vice, murdered –

Wife beaten and raped –

Murdered and raped at their Denholme house by a gang of four men –

Black men –

Described by police as being of West Indian origin.

Parked on the road, staring up the hill, taking down number plates, putting white faces to white names –

Police faces to police names:

Chief Constable Ronald Angus, Assistant Chief Constable George Oldman, Detective Chief Superintendent Maurice Jobson, Detective Chief Superintendent Peter Noble, Detective Superintendent Richard Alderman, Detective Superintendent James Prentice, Detective Inspector Robert Craven, all Leeds –

No family, only coppers –

Not Bradford –

All Leeds.

There's a tap on the window and I jump –

Back:

It's Murphy, jacket over his head.

'Christ,' I say, winding down the window.

'You going up?'

I nod and wind back the window and get out.

'What you doing here?' I ask him. 'Didn't know her did you?'

'Feel like I bloody did,' he says, shaking his head. 'But I knew you'd be here.'

'What?'

'What do you mean *what*?' he laughs, the rain pouring over us. 'We're worried about you?'

'Well, don't be.'

'Come on,' he says, looking up at the black sky above. 'Let's make a run for it.'

And we run up the hill towards the dark building with the chimney, black in the weather, past small stones with small names, the dead flowers, cigarette ends and crisp packets, the dead leaves, our boots in the rain the only sound.

Murphy is there first, panting and holding open the door –

I step inside –

The service, the ritual about to begin.

Mrs Hall is already here, along with a handful of spectators –

Raw and blank –

Her son Richard and a girl in black, some old women, a couple who look like they might live across the road, the odd person at the back, a man who's here to take notes for his paper, the police –

Pete Noble and Jim Prentice, John Murphy and me.

The professionals –

One down the front, kit on –

And the Reverend Laws –

The Reverend Martin Laws shaking Richard's hand, smiling at the girl in black.

I look round at all the folk I don't know and I want their names, wanting to tell Noble to make sure he puts names to faces –

But that's not going to happen –

Not today –

Not ever.

She's gone –

They're just here to make sure.

So we stand there in the pew, behind Noble and Prentice, making double sure.

When she's gone and when they're sure, Noble turns round –

'Pete? How are you?'

'All right,' I say.

'Heard about the fire. I'm sorry.'

'Yeah,' Jim Prentice says. 'Bad news.'

'Thanks,' I say, dropping my eyes to the floor as Richard Hall and the girl in black walk past us to the door.

'Sorry to hear about all this other stuff as well,' he says, glancing at Murphy. 'This stuff with Angus and Maurice?'

I say: 'It'll get sorted out.'

'Be a mountain out of a molehill,' he smiles.

'There's not even a bloody molehill to make a mountain of,' hisses Murphy.

'What I heard,' says Noble, embarrassed.

I put up my hand, stopping us here: 'Thanks, Pete.'

Silence, embarrassed silence –

Just nods and sniffs, the rain on the roof, until –

Until I ask: 'Any news from your end?'

'Nabbed the bloke who called the *Mirror*.'

'So I heard.'

'What'd he do it for?' asks Murphy.

Prentice, shaking his head: 'Got a telephone put in but didn't know anyone to call, so he rings Ripper Line and listens to tape a couple of times, gets bored of that and thinks he'll have a laugh, calls *Mirror*.'

'Daft cunt,' laughs Murphy.

'One down.' I say. 'Two to go.'

'Two?' says Prentice. 'What do you mean two?'

Noble smiles – thinks about saying something, something else, something more – but turns to Prentice and says: 'Head up to the house, shall we?'

'Right,' shrugs Prentice.

They look at us, but we're both shaking our heads.

'See you, then,' says Noble, hand out –

I take it and say: 'By the way, when's the inquest?'

He looks back down the aisle at the place where he last saw Mrs Hall and then at Jim Prentice: 'Week on Friday?'

'Yeah,' says Prentice. 'Couldn't get it in any earlier because of New Year and the weekend.'

'Right,' I say.

'See you later, Pete,' says Noble again, nodding to Murphy –

A handshake here and they're gone too.

'He's all right,' says Murphy, once they're out the door. 'For a Yorkie.'

'A *Yorkie*?' I say, then: 'Listen, can I meet you outside? I just want to have a word with that man down there.'

'The priest?'

'Yes,' I say and walk down the aisle towards the front.

The Reverend Martin Laws is knelt down, hands on the rail of one of the front pews.

'Mr Laws?'

Hands still together, he turns to look up at me: 'Mr Hunter.'

'Nice service.'

'In the circumstances,' he nods.

'Do you mind if I sit down?'

'Be my guest,' he says, sitting back up on the pew – moving his hat to make room for me.

I sit down beside him.

He turns and looks at me, his clothes stinking and smelling of damp: 'You've got a lot of questions Mr Hunter?'

'Hasn't everyone?'

'Not everyone,' he says. 'Not everyone.'

'Well, do you mind if I ask you some of mine?'

'Be my guest,' he says again.

I ask him: 'Are you really a priest, Mr Laws?'

'Yes.'

'Still a priest?'

'Yes.'

'I see,' I nod. 'You told me that Mrs Hall rang you because she'd heard of your work?'

'Yes.'

'She'd heard of it from Jack Whitehead, hadn't she?'

'Yes.'

'You met Mr Whitehead through his ex-wife Carol?'

'Yes.'

'And you were both there the night Carol's second husband murdered her?'

'Yes.'

'His name was Michael Williams?'

'Yes.'

'And he was found to be insane and is now in Broadmoor?'

'Yes.'

'And, at his trial, you were singled out for criticism by the judge, Mr Justice Caulfield, were you not?'

'Yes.'

'And by Dr Eric Treacy, the Bishop of Wakefield?'

'Yes.'

'And didn't Jack Whitehead, didn't he hold you responsible for Carol's death?'

'Yes.'

'And do you think that Jack's grief, the grief over the death of his wife, a death he blames on you, that this grief led to his suicide attempt in 1977?'

'Yes.'

'That's it? That's all you're going to say? Yes, yes, yes?'

'Yes.'

'I see,' I say. 'You still visit Jack? In Stanley Royd?'

'Yes.'

'Mr Laws,' I say. 'On these visits, has Jack ever given you anything?'

Laws pauses and then says: 'No.'

'Never given you any books, letters, or cassettes?'

'No.'

'Have you ever given anything to him?'

'No.'

'Not even a bunch of grapes?'

'It's against the regulations.'

'But people break regulations; that's what they're there for.'

'The people or the regulations, Mr Hunter?'

'Both.'

'You're a policeman. Not everyone else thinks like that.'

'Know a lot about the police, do you Mr Laws?'

'No.'

'Know a lot about Helen Marshall though, don't you?'

'Is that what this is about? Helen?'

'*Helen*? Detective Sergeant Marshall to you.'

'Yes.'

'You've been seeing her, haven't you? Privately?'

'Yes.'

'Why?'

'Mr Hunter, I can't tell you that.'

'She wants your help though?'

'Yes.'

'Why?'

'I can't tell you that.'

I grab the sleeve of his raincoat, cold and wet, grab it and turn him to face me: 'Tell me!'

He's shaking his head, asking me: 'Why?'

'Because you're going to try and fucking exorcise her or whatever it is you fucking do.'

'Sticks and stones, Mr Hunter,' he says. 'But this is my Father's house, so please . . .'

'Fuck off!' I shout, standing up: 'She's not going to end up here like Libby Hall, not going to end up like Carol fucking Whitehead.'

'Please . . .'

'Leave her alone or I'll kill you,' I say, pulling him up by his coat.

'You don't believe in demons, Mr Hunter?' Laws is laughing. 'Don't believe in them, do you?'

'No!'

'After all you've seen, all they've done to you?'

'No!'

'You still don't believe in them?'

'No!'

'All those miscarriages, those . . .'

And I punch him once, hard –

Breaking his nose, dark blood across his pale skin –

My arm back and coming in again when –

When Murphy gets a hold of me, a hold of my arm, pulling me back, pulling me away, pulling me off, dragging me back, dragging me away, dragging me off –

Blood on my knuckles –

Tears on my face –

Tears and rage –

Raw.

Sat in my car, under the dark building with the chimney, black in the weather, under the small stones with the small names, dead flowers, the cigarette ends and the crisp packets, dead leaves, the only sound John Murphy asking me:

'What the fuck was that all about?'

'He's an evil man and he's got inside Marshall's head, I know he has.'

'Long as it's only her head he's inside.'

'Fuck off,' I say.

'Pete, he's just a dirty old priest. Probably a puff.'

'No, he's . . .' I'm shaking my head, saying: 'I don't know what he is.'

'I'll tell you what he could be,' says Murphy. 'He's a priest who could bloody well press charges, and then you'd be fucked – boat you're in.'

I'm nodding: 'I know, I know.'

'Go home,' says Murphy. 'Please – '

'Home?'

'Sorry,' he says. 'Joan's folks or wherever, anywhere but bloody Yorkshire.'

'Got an interview with Angus at two,' I say, looking at my watch:

11:22:12.

'Where?'

'Wakefield.'

Murphy furious: 'You're fucking joking?'

I shake my head.

'Why there?'

'They're too busy to keep coming over to Manchester.'

'It's bollocks, isn't it. The whole bloody thing.'

'What about you?' I ask. 'Shouldn't you all be back at work?'

'Monday week,' he says. 'If they let us.'

'What do you mean?'

'I don't know, there's talk of another force coming in,' he sighs. 'And to be honest with you Pete, I don't bloody care.'

I stare up at the dark building with the chimney, black in the weather, past small stones with small names, the dead flowers, cigarette ends and crisp packets, the dead leaves, only sound the clock in the car, the only sound until –

Until I ask him: 'You heard about Dawson then?'

He nods: 'Alderman's tearing his hair out looking for some fucking rent boy.'

'Rent boy?'

'Yeah, apparently some little puff was renting the flat above the shop.'

'What?'

'The flat above the newsagents. Where they found Dawson.'

'No?'

He nods: 'Alderman reckons your mate Dicky was definitely tricky.'

'Fuck off, John,' I say.

'Just telling you what I heard,' he says, palms up. 'Just telling you what I heard.'

'You hear a name?'

'For who?'

'The rent boy?'

'BJ something. Get it?'

'BJ what?'

He shakes his head, smiling: 'Sorry, can't remember that part.'

I say: 'I think I saw him yesterday.'

'Shit, no?'

I nod.

'Where?'

'Preston.'

'Fucking hell, Pete.'

I nod.

'What did he say? Say anything about Dawson?'

I shake my head: 'But he gave me this.'

Murphy takes the piece of paper from me –

The piece of black and white Xeroxed paper –

The piece of black and white Xeroxed pornography –

Fat and blonde, legs and cunt –

Clare Strachan.

Across the top of the page, in black felt-tip pen:

Spunk, Issue 3, January 1975.

Across the bottom, in black felt-tip pen:

Murdered by the West Yorkshire Police, November 1975.

Across her face, in black felt-tip pen:

A target, a dartboard.

Sat in my car, under the dark building with the chimney, black in the weather, under the small stones with the small names, dead flowers, the cigarette ends and the crisp packets, dead leaves, the only sound the piece of paper in his hand:

The piece of black and white Xeroxed paper –

The piece of black and white Xeroxed pornography –

'A bullseye,' says Murphy, quietly.

I nod.

'He give you names?'

I say: 'Just one.'

'One?'

I nod: 'Morrison.'

'Morrison?'

'Clare Morrison.'

'Clare Morrison? Who's that?'

I tap the piece of paper –

The piece of paper in his hands –

The piece of black and white Xeroxed paper –

The piece of black and white Xeroxed pornography –

Fat and blonde, legs and cunt –

'Thought her name was Strachan?'

'Morrison was Clare Strachan's maiden name.'

'So?'

'You know any other Morrisons?'

John Murphy sits there in my car, under the dark building with the chimney, black in the weather, under small stones with small names, the dead flowers, cigarette ends and crisp packets, the dead leaves, only sound the clock in the car, the only sound until –

Until John Murphy whispers: 'Grace Morrison?'

I nod.

Whispers: 'The Strafford.'

I nod.

'Fuck.'

I nod.

'What you going to do?' says Murphy.

'What do you mean?'

'You going to tell anyone?'

'Like who?'

'Alderman? Smith?'

'Why? What will they do?'

He shakes his head: 'What will you do?'

'You wait and see.'

'What?'

'Wait and see, John.'

'You're going to rip this thing open, aren't you? The whole fucking place?'

'Wait and see,' I smile. 'Wait and see.'

'Fuck, Pete.'

I nod.

'Fuck, fuck, fuck.'

I nod, thinking –

I know the time, I know the way –

I know the place, know the place well.

Wakefield, deserted Wakefield:

Monday 29 December 1980 –

The same ill-feelings and same memories, the same thwarted investigations and same walls of silence, the same black secrets and paranoia, the same hell:

January 1975 –

The same ill-feelings and same memories, the same thwarted investigations and same walls of silence, the same black secrets and paranoia, the same hell:

December 1980 –

The same impotent prayers and the same broken promises, the same blame and the same guilt, reneged and returned:

Monday 29 December 1980 –

Wakefield, barren Wakefield.

Wakefield –

Laburnum Road –

West Yorkshire Police Headquarters –

The Chief Constable's office.

I look at my watch –

13:54:45.

I knock on the door –

'Come.'

I open the door –

Ronald Angus is sat behind a big desk, his own big desk, Maurice Jobson and Dick Alderman sitting before him.

'Gentlemen,' I say –

'Mr Hunter,' says Angus, looking at his watch. 'You're early.'

'Call it a curse,' I smile.

Angus looks at Alderman and says: 'It's OK. Richard was just leaving.'

Dick Alderman stands up, a hand on Maurice's shoulder: 'I'll speak to you both later.'

They both nod.

Detective Superintendent Richard Alderman pushes past me and out –

Not a word.

'Sit down,' says Angus, gesturing to the empty chair next to Jobson.

'You wanted these,' I say before I sit down – tipping every official diary I've ever had, copies of every expense I've ever submitted, every other official form I've ever received – tipping them all over his desk.

'Thank you,' says Maurice Jobson.

'And this,' I say, handing Angus authorisations to examine my bank account, my credit card and my Post Office savings accounts –

Angus looks at it and says: 'Thank you.'

I sit down and I wait –

Mr Angus sifts and shuffles through the mess and the mire on his desk, eventually pulling out a number of pieces of paper from under my stuff, and then he looks up at me and says: 'I'd like to put some names to you and I'd be grateful if you could tell me if you have either heard of these people, know them, or are friends with them at all?'

I nod, waiting –

Jobson picks up a pen and opens a notebook, waiting –

Then Angus says: 'Colin Asquith?'

I nod: 'Local businessman. Partner of Richard Dawson.'

'*Former* partner,' says Angus.

'Yes,' I say. '*Former.*'

'Do you know him?'

'Not personally, no.'

'But you have met him?'

I nod.

Angus: 'Socially?'

I nod: 'Through mutual acquaintances.'

Angus is staring at me –

I stare back.

He says: 'Cyril Barratt?'

I shake my head.

Angus: 'Barry Cameron?'

I nod.

Angus waits –

Me: 'Never met him. Know the name.'

'How?'

'Newspapers. Station talk.'

Angus: 'But you've never met Barry Cameron?'

I shake my head.

'Michael Craig?'

I nod: 'Local solicitor.'

'You know him?'

'Only through work.'

'Richard Dawson?'

I stare at Angus –

Angus stares back.

I say: 'You know I know Richard Dawson.'

'I know you *knew* him,' he says. 'But how would you describe that relationship?'

'We were friends.'

'*Were?*'

'Well, as you emphasised, he's dead.'

'But you were friends right up until his death?'

I swallow and I say: 'Yes, we were friends right up until his death.'

'OK,' nods Angus. 'We'll come back to your relationship with Mr Dawson, the employer of Bob Douglas, the business partner of Colin Asquith, the client of Michael Craig. Come back to him, shall we?'

'So that's what this is about? Richard Dawson? Bob Douglas?'

He shakes his head: 'Not only Mr Dawson and Bob Douglas, no.'

I shrug my shoulders and let it go –

But Angus won't: 'How about Bob Douglas?'

'How about him what?'

Angus: 'You knew him?'

'You bloody know I knew him. I was over here for the Strafford, wasn't I?'

'The Strafford aside?'

'The Strafford aside,' I smile. 'Met him once.'

'When?'

Not smiling, I say: 'The Sunday before he was murdered.'

Angus looks across his desk at Jobson –

Maurice Jobson shakes his head ever so slightly –

Angus looks back down at the notes sitting on the mess and mire of his desk –

Then he looks up and asks: 'Sean Doherty?'

'Pardon?'

'Could you tell me if you have either heard of, know of, or are friends with a Sean Doherty?'

I shake my head.

'David Gallagher?'

I shake my head.

'Marcus Hamilton?'

I nod: 'Local MP for Salford.'

'Former local MP,' says Angus. 'But you know him?'

'Not well, no.'

'But you have met him?'

I nod.

'In what capacity?'

'How do you mean in what capacity? In the capacity of watching a football match at Old Trafford, that was the usual capacity.'

'So you would say you know him socially?'

I nod: 'To say hello to, yes.'

'Has he ever been to your house?'

I shake my head.

'Have you been to his?'

I shake my head again.

'Did you ever suspect he was a homosexual?'

I look at him, head down in his notes, and I say to the top of his grey head: 'I had my hopes.'

Angus looks up from his notes: 'Pardon?'

Smiling, I say: 'A man can dream can't he?'

Jobson is smiling behind his pen, watching the face of his boss.

'Mr Hunter, these are serious questions.'

I shake my head: 'Whether or not Mr Hamilton is a puff is not what I'd describe as a serious question.'

'No-one is asking you to describe the questions, Mr Hunter. Just to answer them.'

I look down at my right knee, crossed and over the left, and I say: 'Go on.'

'Peter McCardell?'

I nod: 'Arrested by Manchester Vice, got ten years for various things under Obscene Publications etc. I think he was also involved with prostitutes and some dubious clubs.'

'You knew him then?'

'Interviewed him once or twice down the years.'

'When was he banged up?'

I shake my head: 'I can't remember off the top of my head; five, maybe six years ago?'

But I do remember, remember now:

'I said we have a mutual friend.'

'Who's that?'

'Helen.'

'Helen who?'

'From her Vice days. Tell her I said hello.'

Jobson is watching me, waiting for something –

I look at Angus and say: 'Pardon?'

'I asked if he was still inside?'

'Who?'

'McCardell.'

'You tell me.'

'OK,' says Angus. 'How about Roger Muir?'

I nod: 'Journalist. Don't know him socially.'

Angus: 'Donald Ryder?'

I shake my head.

'Martin Sharpe?'

I nod: 'Local solicitor. Never met him outside of work.'

'Michael Taylor?'

I shake my head.

'Alan Wright?'

I nod: 'Local businessman. Not socially.'

'What exactly does *not socially* mean to you, Mr Hunter?'

Voice raised, I say: 'It means I didn't know him socially.'

Angus looks across the desk at Jobson and then opens a folder on the desk and takes out four photographs –

And I'm thinking of four other photographs, praying they're not the same –

Four photographs of two people in a park:

Platt Fields Park, in wintertime.

Black and white photographs of two people in a park by a pond:

A cold grey pond, a dog.

Two people in a park –

One of them me.

Jobson is watching me again, waiting for something –

I look at Angus and say: 'Pardon?'

'Will you take a look at these?' he asks and hands me the four photographs –

I sit back in my chair and look at them.

They're not the same –

They're colour, full colour.

'Look pretty social to me,' says Angus.

'Pardon?'

'Every name I've read to you today is present in these photographs. Every name except McCardell, who was in Strangeways.'

'So? What's your point?'

'Look at the photographs, Mr Hunter,' he sighs. 'Every person I've asked you about is sitting round that table with you, glasses raised.'

'It was Richard Dawson's fortieth birthday party,' I say. 'It was held at the Midland Hotel and half of bloody Manchester was there.'

'That's obvious from the photos, Mr Hunter,' he smiles. 'The question is which half? By the looks of these photographs it was strictly convicted criminals, homosexuals, pornographers, and you.'

I start counting, letting him smile – letting that smile get bigger and bigger and bigger, bigger and bigger and bigger – bigger and bigger and bigger until I lean forward and spread the photos across his desk, fingers to the faces, and tell him –

'Actually sir, I don't think it was *strictly* convicted criminals, homosexuals, and pornographers; not unless you're implying that Chief Constable Smith or Chief Inspector Hook fall into any of those categories.'

Silence –

Silence while Chief Constable Ronald Angus decides whether or not to reach forward and take a magnifying glass to the photos, to the faces under my fingers, silence until –

Until he coughs and looks at Jobson and says: 'Well we've obviously been given erroneous information, Mr Hunter.'

I nod, careful not to gloat, waiting.

'And I am grateful to you for shedding light on the nature of these photographs,' says Angus.

'My pleasure,' I tell him, unable to resist.

'However,' continues the Chief Constable. 'I'm afraid we're still going to have to ask you to make yourself available tomorrow afternoon in the hope that you'll be able to shed similar light on your relationship with Richard Dawson and some of his associates.'

Fuck –

'Where?'

Fuck, fuck –

'Here.'

Thinking, *fuck, fuck, fuck* –

Asking: 'Same time?'

He nods.
Silence again, silence until –
Until I stand up –
'Good afternoon,' I say.
They mumble as I see myself out.
I close the door behind me, stop for a moment outside – expecting to hear raised voices inside.
Disappointed, I turn and walk straight into Dick Alderman –
'Letting you go, are they?' he winks.
I smile back: 'Good behaviour.'
'I find that very hard to believe,' he grins, knocking on the Chief Constable's door. 'From what I've heard.'
I smile, thinking –
I know the time, I know the way –
I know the place, know the place well.

Leeds, fucking Leeds:
Medieval Leeds, Victorian Leeds, Concrete Leeds –
Concrete decay, concrete murder, concrete hell –
A concrete city –
Dead city:
Just the crows, the rain, and the Ripper –
The Leeds Ripper –
King Ripper.

Monday Night in the City of the Dead –
I park under the dark arches, dripping and damp, walls running with water and rats –
The driest place in the whole bloody city.
I gather up the *Exegesis* and the various pieces of pornography and blackmail that litter the car and heap them into a Tesco's bag, then I walk up through the arches, past the Scarborough, into the Griffin.
I ring the bell and wait, listening –
Electronic Beethoven.
The receptionist comes out of the back, a faint smile as he recognises me –
'Mr Hunter?'
'Good evening,' I say.
'What can I do for you, Mr Hunter?'

'I'd like a room, please.'

'For how long?'

'I don't know,' I shrug. 'A couple of nights perhaps?'

'Fine,' he says and pushes the paperwork across the desk.

I put down my Tesco bag and pick up a pen from the desk.

The receptionist goes over to the keys hanging behind the desk, takes one from its hook and places it next to the forms I'm filling in.

'I'm sorry,' I say, not looking up. 'I was hoping to have my old room again? 77?'

'That's what I've given you, sir,' he says.

I look at the key lying on the desk next to my hand –

'Thank you,' I say, but he's already gone.

In the room, the dark room –

No sleep.

No more sleep, just –

Two huge wings that burst through the back, out of my skin, torn, two huge and rotting wings, big black things that weigh me down, heavy, that stop me standing –

Solemn and grave.

No more sleep, just –

Wings, wings that burst through my back, out of the skin, torn, huge and rotting things, big black wings that weigh me down, heavy, that stop me standing –

Solemn and grave from birth.

No sleep, just –

Just *Exegesis* etched into my chest, nails bloody, bleeding, broken –

Et sequentes.

Notes everywhere, across the floor, the bed, the Griffin furniture, I check my watch, turn the radio down, pick the phone up off the bed and get a dialling tone, check my watch against the speaking clock and dial, hoping her parents don't answer again:

'Joan?'

'Peter? Where are you?'

'Leeds.'

'Why?'

'They haven't finished with me,' I whisper. 'I have to be back there at two tomorrow.'

'Really?'

'I'm sorry.'

'Oh how I wish you weren't there,' she says, voice splintered. 'I hate that place, those people. Every time you're ever there we've had nothing but bad luck and news.'

'Don't worry,' I say. 'Couldn't get any worse.'

'Don't tempt fate, Peter. Please . . .'

'I won't,' I say, then ask: 'How's Linda?'

'Sedated.'

'What time did you get back?'

'Tenish. But I went over to see her mum and dad, the kids.'

'How are they?'

'How do you think they are?'

'Do the kids realise what's happened?'

'I think the army of reporters outside the house should help.'

'Fuck,' I say. 'I'll call Smith, tell him to get his act together.'

'I already did,' she says.

'You called Clement Smith?'

'Yes.'

'You're joking? What did you say?'

'Told him what I thought of his treatment of the Dawsons and us.'

'What did he say?'

'He told me he was *only acting as duty dictated.*'

'What did you say?'

'Told him he would rot in hell for what he'd done.'

'You didn't? What did he say?'

'I don't know, I hung up.'

'Joan!'

'He's a pompous fool, Peter.'

'But he is only doing his job.'

'So was Herod.'

'Joan, please . . .'

'If that's the job, I honestly hope you won't be doing it for much longer. I really do, Peter.'

Silence, silence as I wonder if anyone else is listening – silence as I wonder if I even am, silence until –

Until I say: 'I'm sorry it's come to this.'

'Stop saying you're sorry,' she sighs.
'But I am.'
'Don't be sorry,' she says. 'Just be careful.'
'I will.'
'I love you.'
'Me too,' I say.
'Night-night.'
'Night, love,' I say and hang up.

No sleep, just –
    Tearing through the bedside drawers –
    Flapping about through the sheets and the blankets –
    Windows open –
    Tipping over the bed –
    Stripping every sheet and curtain –
    Windows closed –
    Tearing and flapping and tipping and stripping the whole
fucking room until –
    Until there it is –
    There behind the radiator –
    Behind the radiator –
    The Holy Bible –
    Lying on the sheets and the blankets –
    Flapping through the pages –
    Job open –
    Skipping this page and that –
    Skimming that one and this –
    Psalms –
    Lying and flapping and skipping and skimming the whole
bloody book until –
    Until I'm sure –
    Sure it's gone –
    Ripped and torn, stripped and shorn –
    Revelation, gone –
    No *Revelation* –
    Not tonight –
    Not tonight the foot upon the dark stair, the knock upon the
door, the key in the lock –
    Turning once and only once –
    Not tonight –

No *Revelation* tonight –
Revelation gone –
The missing pages –
The missing –
Missing –
Missing her.

to the place you spoke about that e might see the gate that another peter guards but they say it is a local incident and we are convinced a local man is involved and all talk that tessa may have been attacked by ripper is only making it more difficult for me to catch her assailant transmission twelve sent from harrogate in august nineteen eighty received new years eve nineteen eighty and identified as prudence banks strangled and severely bludgeoned in the densely wooded grounds of a local magistrates house but again no one is receiving do not feel this is the work of the yorkshire ripper and he may very well have retired or topped himself as it has been more than a year he may even have met a nice girl and settled down got married like a normal bloke or he may have moved abroad or have been nicked over something else but this is not him he has gone away but prudence banks still avoided the short cut that would have taken ten minutes off her journey preferred the brightly lit main roads and she walked quickly along the road with the big empty houses and their long drives but we do not feel this is the work of the yorkshire ripper this is not him he has gone away e do not like the method of strangulation it takes them even longer to die but e did it because the press and the media had attached a stigma to me e had been known for some time as the yorkshire ripper e did not like it was not me did not ring true e had been on my way to leeds to kill a prostitute when e saw prudence banks it was just unfortunate for her that she happened to be walking by stepping out from the shadows hitting her on the head she staggers along the pavement blood gushing screaming again he hits her and again she does not fall so he puts his hands to her throat strangles her dragging her into the driveway of one of the big empty houses into the shrubbery the bushes down the side of a garage prudence dead he tears off her clothes her black gabardine coat her cardigan her purple skirt her brassiere her panties her shoes her tights and handbag the body naked in the shrubbery the bushes down the side of the garage the hammer out again he rains down blows upon her flesh then he takes a pile of leaves and covers the body but e am sleeping less and less every night e wake and watch moon after moon go by before e dream the evil dream which ripped away the veil that was my future and awoke to hear the children sobbing in their sleep missing mummy and if you are not weeping now do you ever weep for from below e heard him driving nails into the dreadful tower door and e stared in silence at my flesh and blood but did not weep but turned to stone inside e held back my tears and bit my hands in anguish and my daughters who thought hunger made me bite my hands were quick to say father you would make us suffer less if you would feed on us for you were the one who gave us this sad flesh you take it from us but we sat in silence behind the wires and the alarms until on the fourth day my first daughter fell prostrate before my feet crying why do you not help us father and she then died and just as you see me here e saw the other twelve fall one by one as the days passed became weeks months years and e who had gone blind groped over their bodies though some were dead five years e called their names until hunger proved more powerful than grief and e attacked again their wretched skulls with teeth as sharp as a dogs and as fit for grinding bones before e then moved to by where the frozen waters wrap in harsh wrinkles across another sinful set their faces not turned down but looking up where here the weeping puts an end to weeping and the grief that finds no outlet from the eyes turns inward

Chapter 20

It was New Year's Eve:

I was walking across a car park, puddles of rain water and motor oil underfoot, heading for a door –

A door to an upstairs room –

A door banging in the wind, in the rain –

I climbed the dark stairs one at a time and stopped before the door –

The door to the upstairs room –

The door banging in the wind, in the rain.

I pulled open the door and stepped inside –

Inside:

Inside there was a man sat upon a low table, a man with a beard and a shotgun in his hands, staring at a TV with the sound turned low, the walls tattooed with shadow and pain –

The pain of the photographs –

Joyce Jobson, Anita Bird, Grace Morrison, Carol Williams, Theresa Campbell, Clare Strachan, Joan Richards, Ka Su Peng, Marie Watts, Linda Clark, Rachel Johnson, Janice Ryan, Elizabeth McQueen, Kathy Kelly, Tracey Livingston, Candy Simon, Doreen Pickles, Joanne Thornton, Dawn Williams, Laureen Bell, Karen Douglas, Libby Hall –

The pain of twenty-two photographs, plus the one on the low table next to him –

The one on the table next to him –

I picked up the photograph –

The one on the table –

It was Helen Marshall.

The man turned from the TV –

From the people on the TV singing hymns, the people on the TV singing hymns with no face, no features, machines –

The people on the TV singing hymns with no face, no features, machines –

People on the TV singing hymns of hate:

'You are a beast with no feelings, a coward, not a man. All people hate you. I think you are the Devil himself.'

On the TV singing hymns of hate:

'You are a very inadequate person, certainly physically and

mentally. You can't make a relationship with a live woman. Possibly your only relationships are with dead women.'

The TV singing hymns of hate:

'Doesn't it bother you to think people hate you for doing this? It is nothing to be proud of, the things you do.'

TV singing hymns of hate:

'You are the worst coward the world has ever known and that should go down in the Guinness Book of Records.'

Singing hymns of hate:

'You are an obscenity on the face of the earth. When they catch you and put you away, they will throw away the key.'

Hymns of hate:

'Look over your shoulder, Ripper. Many people are looking for you. They hate you.'

Of hate –

The man with the beard turned from the TV –

Turned from the TV, from the hate –

Turned and said:

'You don't see them, you don't – but I see them; they are hunting me down – I must move on.'

And he put the gun to his mouth, fingers on the trigger, and –

– a shot.

I'm awake –

Awake in my car on Alma Road, Headingley –

Sweating, afraid –

Birds overhead, screaming.

I look at my watch:

06:03:00 –

Tuesday 30 December 1980:

Alma Road –

The ordinary street in the ordinary suburb, not one hundred yards from a main road.

The ordinary street in the ordinary suburb where a man took a hammer and a knife to another man's daughter, to another man's sister, another man's fiancée.

The ordinary street in the ordinary suburb where the Yorkshire Ripper took his hammer and his knife to Laureen Bell and shattered her skull and stabbed her fifty-seven times in her abdomen, in her womb, and once in her eye –

In this ordinary street in this ordinary suburb, this ordinary
girl –

This ordinary girl, now dead.

'I'm not sure about this,' the woman in white is saying, trying
to take hold of the sleeve of my raincoat. 'I really think you
should speak to Mr Papps.'

But I'm away –

Away through the second-hand furniture, the large wardrobes, the dressers and the chairs, the heavy carpets and the
curtains –

Away through the skin and the bones, their striped pyjamas
and their spotted nightgowns, their slippers and their vespers,
their scratchings and their mumblings –

Away up their stairs, down their corridors –

Half green, half cream –

Fresh green, fresh cream –

Wet paint –

Away –

My wings, away –

The woman in white at my heels, still saying: 'I'm not sure
about this'

My warrant card in her face: 'Open the doors.'

And she starts turning keys, unlocking doors, until –

Until we come to the last door at the end of the last corridor –

Jack's door.

We stand there, panting –

Panting until –

Until I say: 'Open it, please.'

And she turns the key, unlocks the door.

'Thank you,' I say and open the door.

I step inside, closing the door behind me –

Behind me, so it's just me and Jack –

Jack's lying on his back in a pair of grey striped pyjamas, his
hands loose at his sides, eyes open and face blank, his whole
head and face shaven.

'Mr Whitehead,' I say.

'Mr Hunter,' he replies.

'Sounds like someone fixed the toilet?'

He nods: 'And I miss it.'

'The dripping?'
'Yes, the dripping.'
And there is silence –
Just silence –
Just silence until –
Until I ask: 'How was Pinderfields?'
'Blood on the floor.'
'Pardon?'
'There's always blood on the floor over there.'
'Pinderfields?'
And Jack sighs, eyes watering –
Tears slipping down his face –
Down his cheek –
His neck –
Onto his pillow –
The mattress –
Onto the floor in puddles –
Puddles of tears upon the stone floor –
The tips of my wings wet.
'Carol?' I say.
And he looks up at me, the tears streaming, and he nods:
'Two pieces of a broken heart.'
'But do they fit?' I ask.
'That's the question,' he weeps. 'That's the question.'
I look down at the tips of my wings –
The puddles of tears –
The blood on the floor and –
And I lean towards him and I ask him: 'The things you've
seen . . .'
He nods, the tears streaming –
'All the things you've seen,' I say. 'Who did those things?'
The tears streaming –
I lean close, wings across us both –
'Who?'
Tears streaming –
Closer, wings across us –
'Who?'
His tongue against my face –
'Who?'
His lips to my ears –

'Who?'
His words in whispers –
'Who?'
Whispers –
Whispers in the dark –
And I listen:
'What looks like morning – '
Listen to the whispers in the dark:
'It is the beginning of the endless night – '
To the whispers and the tears:
'Hab rachmones.'

Foot down –
    Empty streets, rain –
    Straight onto Laburnum Road –
    West Yorkshire Police Headquarters –
    Voices singing –
    Christmas songs and football songs –
    Rugby songs and Ripper songs –
    At the desk: 'Angus? Chief Constable Angus?'
    A uniform shaking his head, the smell of alcohol upon his breath: 'He's not here, sir.'
    'Pete Noble?'
    'Not here, sir.'
    'Bob Craven?'
    'No-one's here.'
    Me: 'Where are they?'
    'Dewsbury.'
    'Dewsbury?'
    'They've got him, haven't they.'
    Me: 'Who?'
    'Ripper!'
    'What?'
    'The fucking Ripper!'
    Me: 'What about him?'
    'Caught the fucking Ripper, haven't they,' he laughs, bringing up a can of bitter from behind the desk and draining it –
    'The Yorkshire bloody Ripper!'

Dewsbury:

12:03:03 –

Tuesday 30 December 1980 –

The End of the World:

In a car park up the road from the police station, puddles of rain water and motor oil underfoot –

Birds overhead, screaming –

Rain pouring –

The hills black above us, the clouds darker still.

Locking the door, coat up over my head, running –

Running for Dewsbury Police Station –

Dewsbury Police Station –

Modern bricks amongst the black –

Crowds gathering, word spreading –

Off-duty coppers coming in, shifts not going home –

I push on through, card out amongst the many:

'Assistant Chief Constable Hunter to see Chief Constable Angus.'

'Downstairs,' shouts one of the men behind the desk, struggling to keep the pack at bay.

And downstairs I go –

Through the double doors and down the stairs –

Downstairs –

Underground –

Until I come upon them –

A dark room full of dark men:

Ronald Angus, Maurice Jobson, Peter Noble, Alec McDonald, John Murphy –

Plus two faces –

Familiar faces –

Familiar faces, dark faces –

Dark faces in a dark room –

A dark room with one wall half glass –

The glass, a two-way mirror –

Light from behind the glass –

Behind the glass, the stage set –

Three chairs and a table –

The players –

Alderman and Prentice –

Today's special guest:

Peter David Williams of Heaton, Bradford –

34-year-old, married, lorry driver –

Black beard and curly hair, a blue jumper with a white v-neck band –

Behind the glass –

Prentice saying: 'What about Wednesday 10 December?'

Williams: 'I was at home with the wife.'

Alderman: 'Every time you've been seen, you always have same story – at home with the wife.'

'But it's right.'

'I think it's strange.'

'Why?'

'How can you be so sure that's where you were?'

'I'm always at home every night when I'm not on an overnight stay.'

Prentice: 'So how come you were in Sheffield on Sunday?'

'I picked up a couple hitchhikers and they paid us a tenner to take them to Sheffield.'

'Where'd you pick them up, Peter?'

'Bradford.'

'So they paid you a tenner to take them to Sheffield?'

He nods: 'Yes.'

Alderman: 'Bollocks.'

'It's right.'

'Is it fuck; you went to Sheffield to pick up a prostitute.'

'That's not true.'

Prentice: 'So how come your car's been clocked in all these daft bloody places?'

'Daft places?'

'Manchester, for one. Moss Side.'

'Manchester?'

Alderman: 'Been there, have you Pete? Moss Side?'

'No, never.'

'Never?'

'Never.'

'But I got it here: *FHY 400K, Moss Side, Manchester.*'

'I don't know how.'

'I don't know how either; but I tell you this – it's bad bloody news, I know that.'

'Why?'

'Well, car's there but you're not. No-one's going to swallow that in a month of bloody Sundays, are they?'

'But I remember now. I left it outside Bradford Central Library one night after it broke down and then I went back and picked it up next day. Someone must have taken it for a ride over that way and then put it back.'

Alderman, laughing: 'Fuck off.'

'It's true.'

'Someone nicks your motor and – hang on, first someone fixes your motor and then they nick it and drive round red-light areas and then put it right back on same spot where you left it night before?'

'Yes.'

Alderman: 'Fuck off, Pete.'

Silence –

Silence until –

Until Prentice says softly: 'You put the false plates on because you knew you were going to Sheffield, knew you were going to red-light district, and you knew we'd be watching.'

'That's not true.'

'I think it is. I think you know it is.'

'To be honest with you, I've been so depressed that I put plates on because I was thinking of committing a crime with the car.'

Silence –

Silence until –

Until Prentice says: 'When you were arrested Pete, why did you leave your car and go down the side of that house?'

'To urinate.'

Alderman: 'To what?'

'To piss.'

Prentice: 'I think you went for another purpose. Do you understand what I'm saying?'

Williams nods.

Alderman picks up a brown sports bag from under the table and he opens it and takes out four plastic bags and he places them on the table:

Two hammers, a screwdriver, and a knife.

Prentice: 'I think you're in serious trouble.'

Peter Williams: 'I think you've been leading up to it.'

'Leading up to what?'

Silence –

Silence until –

Until Peter D. Williams says: 'The Yorkshire Ripper.'

Silence –

More silence until –

Until Prentice leans forward and says: 'What about the Yorkshire Ripper?'

Silence –

One last silence until –

Until Peter David Williams says: 'Well, it's me.'

And Prentice stands up and then sits down again, Alderman in his chair with a glance back at the glass –

Back at the glass –

The other side of the glass –

Nine hearts pounding –

Pounding, pumping –

Pumping, the adrenaline pumping –

Pumping and turning and smiling and nodding and then there –

There behind me –

Oldman –

George Oldman –

Assistant Chief Constable George Oldman –

And he's smiling and nodding, leaving us –

Going next door –

Noble: 'George, no!'

Leaving us with our hands to the glass, the two-way mirror –

Hands to the glass, the two-way mirror –

'George!'

The glass, the mirror –

On the other side of the glass, the other side of the mirror –

Where Prentice is asking: 'You feel better now Peter, do you?'

And the Yorkshire Ripper –

The Yorkshire Ripper looks up as the door opens –

The door opens and in steps George –

And he walks up to him –

To the Yorkshire Ripper and he says –

Says to the Yorkshire Ripper: 'I'm the one you almost bloody killed as well.'

And the Yorkshire Ripper –

The Yorkshire Ripper, he looks at George and he says: 'They are all in my brain, reminding me of the beast I am.'

Prentice saying: 'You'll feel better now.'

'Just thinking about them all reminds me of what a monster I am.'

And Alderman stands up and takes George by the arm, leading him away, Jim Prentice asking the Yorkshire Ripper –

Asking him: 'You want anything, Peter?'

'I want to tell Monica,' says the Yorkshire Ripper –

Says the Yorkshire Ripper with a glance into the glass –

A glance into the glass –

The glass –

The glass, the mirror –

The other side of the glass, the other side of the mirror –

On the other side of the mirror where Angus –

Chief Constable Angus is saying –

Shouting –

'Get the whiskey out!'

Noble giving the orders: 'Put him in a cell – someone inside and someone outside the door, round the clock.'

Maurice Jobson in his ear, whispering –

Noble nodding along: 'Yeah, and get out a couple of shotguns.'

Maurice, whispering –

Noble, another nod, calling the shots: 'We're taking no chances tonight, so I want the paperwork and the guns out.'

Angus shouting –

'And the bloody whiskey!'

Up the stairs –

Beaming coppers at every turn –

At every turn only too glad to point the way –

To point the way, to shake your hand, to pat your back and crack another can –

Shaking hands, patting backs, cracking cans –

Cans, backs, and hands until –

Until we're all in an upstairs office:

Ronald Angus, George Oldman, Maurice Jobson, Peter

Noble, Dick Alderman, Jim Prentice, Alec McDonald, John Murphy –

No Craven, no Bob –

And twenty faces I don't know –

Twenty faces I don't want to know –

Plus the two faces I do –

The two familiar faces I want to know –

Murphy introducing me: 'This is Sergeant John Chain, he's the one who nicked him.'

'Me and John Skinner,' nods Chain.

'And this is DS Ellis, here at Dewsbury.'

'Call me Mike,' says Mike, hand out.

I take Murphy to one side: 'What the fuck's going on? What happened?'

'Pulled him in Sheffield, didn't they?'

'Sheffield?'

'Yeah,' nods Murphy, a big whiskey in his fist.

'Who?'

'That Sergeant Chain and some PC Skinner.'

'Which station?'

'Hammerton Road, I think.'

'When?'

'Sunday night.'

'How?'

But then there's boots up the stairs, telephones ringing –

Head around the door: 'She's here, sir!'

And everyone's heading out the door –

Back down the stairs –

Me saying: 'Who? The wife?'

This Sergeant Ellis, Mike, he's shaking his head: 'Slag he was with.'

'Luckiest bitch alive,' laughs someone else and then –

Then we're all heading back downstairs –

Beaming coppers at every turn –

At every turn only too glad to point the way –

To point the way, to shake your hand, to pat your back and crack another can –

Shaking hands, patting backs, cracking cans –

Cans, backs, and hands until –

Until we're downstairs –

Underground –

Back underground –

In the dark room with the one wall half glass –

Behind the glass, the two-way mirror –

Light from behind the glass –

The stage set –

Act II:

Three chairs and a table –

The players –

Alderman and Prentice and –

Today's special guest:

Sharon Yardley, a 24-year-old convicted black prostitute and mother of two from some Sheffield shit-hole.

'What's going on?' she's asking.

Prentice, ever the gent: 'Have a seat Miss Yardley.'

'It's a fucking jungle out there,' she's saying –

Alderman smiling, best behaviour: 'Cigarette?'

'Don't mind if I do.'

He leans forward, his back to us, lighter out: 'There you go.'

'Ta very much.'

Alderman: 'We've taken a bit of shine – no offence – taken a bit of a shine to one of your punters.'

'Yeah? Why's that?'

'Bit of a naughty boy this one.'

'Aren't they all.'

'Yeah,' nods Prentice. 'Aren't they all.'

Alderman: 'Tell us about him, this one from Sunday night?'

'What about him?'

'Just tell us what happened?'

She rolls her eyes, stubs out her cig and says: 'About nine I'm sitting with Karen on Wharncliffe Road, junction with Broomhall . . .'

Alderman: 'Karen?'

'Yeah, Karen.'

'Last name?'

'Not a clue, officer,' she smiles. 'Never met her before.'

Prentice: 'Go on.'

'About nine, a brown Rover pulls up, window down, are we doing business? Karen goes across, gives him once over, says no ta.'

'Why she say no?'

'Bit creepy.'

'How?'

'Didn't say.'

'Go on.'

'Ten minutes later, some Paki pulls up and she's off with him.'

Alderman: 'Not that choosy then, this Karen?'

'Listen lover,' she laughs. 'There's nowt wrong with Pakis; shoot their muck and they're gone. All over in ten seconds.'

Prentice: 'Go on, love.'

'So anyway, Rover comes back and I go over and he seems all right.'

'All right?'

'Looked like a good-looking Bee Gee.'

Alderman: 'A good-looking bloody Bee Gee? What the fuck's one of them?'

Prentice: 'Ignore him. Go on, love.'

'So I tell him it's a tenner and he nods and I get in and he asks if I know anywhere and I tell him to head straight up the road and turn left by Trades House.'

Prentice: 'How long that take? Up to the Trades House?'

'Five, ten minutes.'

'He talk?'

'Never bloody shut up, did he?'

Alderman: 'He tell you his name?'

'Dave.'

Prentice: 'What else did he say?'

'About how he didn't usually do this kind of thing, the usual. About his wife and how she nagged him morning, noon, and night and how they'd wanted to have kids and all the miscarriages they'd had and I said he should adopt and he reckoned they were thinking about one of them Vietnamese Boat People, that kind of thing. Usual bloody excuses.'

'Then you came to Trades House?'

She nods: 'Reversed in, didn't he.'

'Odd?'

'Never seen it before.'

'And?'

'And he keeps yapping and after a bit I tell him I want the tenner and he gives it me and I give him rubber.'

'And?'

'And I take my knickers off but he says he wants to do it in back seat but I say it'll be all right here, nothing to worry about, and he unzips it and lies on top of me but he's too nervous, cold as ice he is, and after a couple of minutes of this I tell him we're not going to be able to do it.'

'What did he say? Angry was he?'

'No,' she shrugs. 'Just nodded and said that's what it looked like.'

'Then what happened?'

'Then what happened was you lot bloody turned up, didn't you?'

'What did he do?'

'Froze, then said he'd do all talking and I'm his girlfriend, aren't I? Didn't have heart to tell him, I'd shagged every copper this side of Hallam.'

Alderman, laughing: 'That include Sergeant Chain and PC Skinner?'

'You're a bad man you are, aren't you lover?' she tuts, winking at the glass.

Prentice: 'So what happened then?'

'One of you lot comes over.'

'And?'

'And he taps on glass, and *Dave*, he winds down window and asks if there's a problem and this young copper . . .'

'PC Skinner.'

'Yeah, he asks who we are and what we're doing and *Dave*, now he says he's Peter Logan and I'm his girlfriend but Skinny, he shines his torch on me and says, hello Sharon, thought you were inside and he asks *Pete* or *Dave* or whoever he is, he asks him if it's his car and whatever-his-bloody-name-is tells him it is and then PC Plod says something witty like, don't go anywhere lovebirds, and he walks off back to the Panda.'

'And so you two are alone again?'

'Yeah, dead romantic it was.'

'What was he saying now?'

'Dave? Asks me if we should make a run for it.'

'And what did you say?'

'Said there wasn't much point, seeing as how they knew me anyway.'

'And what did he say?'

'Nothing. Tweedle Dee and Tweedle Dum are back aren't they – taking his keys, tax disk off window, asking who he really is and now he's saying he's Peter Williams and how he doesn't want his wife to know and how he's been done for drunk driving or something and how he's going to lose his job. Usual bloody nonsense.'

'Then what?'

'Well then they get us out of the car and they see that the plates are only held on with bleeding tape and for a split second I honestly thought daft bugger was going to make a run for it, but he's just off for a piss he says and then when he comes back, they take us down to Hammerton Road.'

'He say anything on way down?'

'No,' she laughs. 'Too busy trying not to shit himself, wasn't he?'

Prentice: 'Probably had a lot on his mind.'

And then she stops laughing at her own joke and says: 'Why?'

Prentice: 'Why what?'

'Why all questions? Who is he?'

And Alderman, he picks up the bag off the floor and he tips the two hammers, the screwdriver, and the knife onto the table and says –

Says: 'The Yorkshire Ripper.'

And in her eyes she sees –

In her eyes –

Her own death –

Her own death with these tools –

With these tools –

These two hammers –

This screwdriver –

This knife –

Her own death with these tools –

Her own death –

In her eyes –

In her eyes she sees –

The Yorkshire Ripper –

And she pukes –
Pukes down the side of herself –
Her left leg –
The table leg
In a puddle on the floor, the yellow bile.

Up the stairs –
Beaming coppers at every turn –
At every turn to shake your hand –
To shake your hand, to pat your back and crack another can –
Shaking hands, patting backs, cracking cans –
Cans, backs, and hands until –
Until we're all back in the upstairs office:
Ronald Angus, George Oldman, Maurice Jobson, Peter
Noble, Dick Alderman, Jim Prentice, Alec McDonald, John
Murphy, Mike Ellis and me –
No Bob Craven –
And the twenty faces I don't know –
The twenty faces I don't want to know –
Plus Sergeant John Chain –
Holding court –
The King is dead, long live the King:
The King of all Detectives –
The King of all Detectives telling us how it was:
'I mean, you see a car up the side of the Trades House and
you know what they're up to inside that.'
Me: 'What time?'
'Eleven,' he shrugs. 'No later. Anyway I send Skinny over
with his torch and he's like a ferret down a hole is that one,
thinks he's going to cop some quim and sure enough if it isn't
Sharon Yardley with some punter. So Skinny, he comes trotting
back and we put the plates through . . .'
Thirty people nodding –
Not me, me asking him: 'What were they? The plates?'
'Can't remember can I, but they weren't right ones, tell you
that. So we get the word from Hammerton that whatever they
were, these plates they should've been sitting on a bloody Skoda
not a big brown fucking Rover 3500 and Skinny's seen plates
are only taped on anyway. So we go back over to them and take
keys off him and have a look at his disk and he tells us his real

name is Peter Williams from Bradford and he says he doesn't want his missus to find out, does he. I tell him he'll have to come down station because we reckon plates are nicked and he just nods and we ask them to get in our car and, right, this is when he dashes off behind water-tank and I'm like, hold your horses, where you off to? But he's bursting for a pee, he says and he's back in a couple of minutes. Did cross me mind he was going do a runner, but he comes back and we go down Hammerton Road and all way down he's quiet, not a word.'

Thirty people, all nodding along –

Not me, me: 'What about his car? Did you have a look inside?'

'Yeah, yeah – messy, it was. Tools, rope, bits and pieces, you know – windscreen wipers, a Speedo, carpet, wood.'

'Go on, John,' says someone. 'What happened then?'

'Well then we interview them and we let her go but he tells us he'd taken plates off a car in a scrap yard in some place called Cooper's Bridge near Mirfield. So we're right, where the fuck is Cooper's Bridge? And we call Leeds and Wakey and then find out it's Dewsbury, so we call here and by now it's like gone 5 in morning and they tell us they'll send some lads down when Early Boys get on and so we call his missus in Bradford and tell her that her husband's been nicked for dodgy plates.'

Me: 'What she say?'

'I don't know,' he shrugs again. 'Not much, I heard. Anyway, that was me. I knocked off and it wasn't until yesterday night when I come back on for another bloody graveyard and gaffer tells us that they're still holding punter from Sunday night and Ripper Squad are giving him once over. So that gets me old brain ticking and that's when I go off back up to Trades House . . .'

Thirty people, nodding, in awe –

The King of the Detectives.

Not me, me: 'You call here first?'

'No.'

'You tell anyone what you were up to?'

'No,' he says, shaking his head. 'I didn't really think there'd be anything there, did I. But I just wanted to make double sure.'

'Go on, John. Go on.'

'So I get up there and I remember him saying he needed a slash like, going behind tank. So that's where I go and fuck me if there isn't a hammer and a bloody knife on ground by back wall.'

Me: 'You touch them?'

Him: 'No.'

'What did you do?'

'Ran straight back to car and called station and they're straight on to here and Ripper Room and then word comes back to leave them, *in situ* like, and photographer's on his way and someone, Bob Craven, he's on his way from Leeds.'

Applause –

Thirty beaming coppers –

Shaking his hand all over again –

Shaking his hand, patting his back and cracking him cans –

Cans, backs, and hands until –

Until Noble says –

'It's time.'

Underground –

Back underground –

In the dark room with the one wall half glass –

Behind the glass, the two-way mirror –

Light from behind the glass –

The stage set –

Act III, the Final Act:

Four chairs and a table –

The players –

Noble and Alderman and Prentice –

Today's special guest –

Back by popular demand:

Peter David Williams of Heaton, Bradford –

34-year-old, married, lorry driver –

Black beard and curly hair, a blue jumper with a white v-neck band –

The Yorkshire Ripper –

Behind the glass –

Noble: 'This is going to take some time, Peter?'

The Yorkshire Ripper nods.

Noble: 'Let's just get straight who it is we're talking about, OK?'

The Yorkshire Ripper: 'OK.'

Noble: 'So first would be Joyce Jobson?'
The Yorkshire Ripper: 'Yes.'
Noble: 'Then Anita Bird?'
The Yorkshire Ripper: 'Yes.'
Noble: 'Theresa Campbell?'
The Yorkshire Ripper: 'Yes.'
Noble: 'Clare Strachan?'
The Yorkshire Ripper shakes his head: 'No.'
Noble: 'You sure about that?'
The Yorkshire Ripper: 'Yes.'
Noble: 'Joan Richards?'
The Yorkshire Ripper: 'Yes.'
Noble: 'Ka Su Peng?'
The Yorkshire Ripper: 'Yes.'
Noble: 'Marie Watts?'
The Yorkshire Ripper: 'Yes.'
Noble: 'Linda Clark?'
The Yorkshire Ripper: 'No.'
Noble: 'Rachel Johnson?'
The Yorkshire Ripper pauses, then says: 'I . . .'
Noble repeats himself: 'Rachel Johnson, Peter? Yes or no?'
The Yorkshire Ripper: 'Yes.'
Noble: 'Janice Ryan?'
The Yorkshire Ripper: 'No.'
Noble: 'Elizabeth McQueen?'
The Yorkshire Ripper: 'Yes.'
Noble: 'Kathy Kelly?'
The Yorkshire Ripper: 'Yes.'
Noble: 'Tracey Livingston?'
The Yorkshire Ripper: 'Yes.'
Noble: 'Candy Simon?'
The Yorkshire Ripper: 'Yes.'
Noble: 'Doreen Pickles?'
The Yorkshire Ripper: 'Yes.'
Noble: 'Joanne Thornton?'
The Yorkshire Ripper: 'Yes.'
Noble: 'Dawn Williams?'
The Yorkshire Ripper: 'Yes.'
Noble: 'No relation?'
The Yorkshire Ripper: 'No.'

Noble: 'Laureen Bell?'

The Yorkshire Ripper: 'Yes.'

Noble: 'Missed anyone have we, Peter?'

The Yorkshire Ripper looks directly into the mirror –

The mirror, the glass –

The other side of the glass, the other side of the mirror –

On the other side of the mirror where we're all sitting –

Angus, Oldman, Murphy, McDonald, Ellis, and me –

Looks through the mirror, the Yorkshire Ripper –

And he nods at us –

Noble: 'Who, Peter? Who?'

The Yorkshire Ripper: 'Noorjahan Davit.'

On the other side of the glass, the other side of the mirror –

On the other side of the mirror where Ellis is on his feet –

Where I'm thinking –

Noorjahan Davit, murdered Bradford, November 1978.

Back up on stage Noble says: 'That was you, was it?'

The Yorkshire Ripper: 'Yes.'

Noble: 'Go on.'

The Yorkshire Ripper: 'Tessa Smith.'

On the other side of the glass, the other side of the mirror –

Where I'm thinking –

Tessa Smith, Batley, November 1979.

On stage Noble shaking his head: 'Afraid I don't know that one, Pete?'

Alderman: 'Attacked Batley, November 1979?'

The Yorkshire Ripper: 'Yes.'

Noble: 'Anyone else?'

The Yorkshire Ripper: 'Prudence Banks.'

On the other side of the glass, the other side of the mirror –

Where I'm thinking –

Prudence Banks, murdered Harrogate, August 1980.

Noble: 'Harrogate? This August?'

The Yorkshire Ripper: 'Yes.'

Noble: 'Strangled, wasn't she?'

The Yorkshire Ripper: 'Yes.'

Noble: 'Anyone else?'

The Yorkshire Ripper: 'That's all.'

Noble: '*That's all*? That's a bloody lot of women, Peter?'

The Yorkshire Ripper: 'Yes.'

Noble: 'This is going to take a fair while, Peter.'

And the Yorkshire Ripper –

The Yorkshire Ripper, he nods directly into the mirror –

The mirror, the glass –

The other side of the glass, the other side of the mirror –

On the other side of the mirror where Ellis is going out the door –

Going out the door, shouting –

Shouting at everyone and anyone:

'Davit, Smith, and Banks – get us them files.'

And back behind the mirror –

The mirror, the glass –

The other side of the glass, the other side of the mirror –

On the other side –

On the stage –

On the stage where Noble says: 'All right, Peter. I just want to clear these up, these ones you're saying aren't you?'

The Yorkshire Ripper: 'OK.'

Noble: 'Clare Strachan? This was in Preston in November 1975?'

The Yorkshire Ripper: 'I know.'

Noble: 'But it wasn't you?'

The Yorkshire Ripper: 'No, it was him.'

Noble: 'Who?'

The Yorkshire Ripper: 'Other one.'

Noble: 'Who we talking about Peter?'

The Yorkshire Ripper: 'That headbanger, the one that wrote the letters, that sent that tape.'

Noble: 'So that wasn't you?'

The Yorkshire Ripper: 'No.'

Noble: 'You don't know who it was, do you?'

Silence –

Silence until –

Until the Yorkshire Ripper with a glance into the glass –

A glance into the glass –

The glass –

The glass, the mirror –

The other side of the glass, the other side of the mirror –

On the other side of the mirror where I am standing with my hands and face up to the glass –

Up at the glass, the mirror –

Until –

Until the Yorkshire Ripper says: 'No.'

Noble: 'And Linda Clark?'

The Yorkshire Ripper: 'No.'

Noble: 'It wasn't you?'

The Yorkshire Ripper: 'No.'

Noble: 'You sure you know who we're talking about? When it happened?'

The Yorkshire Ripper: 'Yes.'

Noble: 'June 77. Bradford?'

The Yorkshire Ripper: 'I know.'

Noble: 'Was it you?'

The Yorkshire Ripper: 'No.'

Noble: 'You think that it was this other bloke, this *head-banger*?'

The Yorkshire Ripper shrugs and says: 'I don't know.'

Noble: 'Janice Ryan?'

The Yorkshire Ripper: 'No.'

Noble: 'Also June 77. Also Bradford.'

The Yorkshire Ripper: 'I know.'

Noble: 'Was it you?'

The Yorkshire Ripper: 'No.'

'You sure?'

Silence –

Silence until –

Until the Yorkshire Ripper with a glance into the glass –

A glance into the glass –

The glass –

The glass, the mirror –

The other side of the glass, the other side of the mirror –

On the other side of the mirror where I'm still standing with my hands and face up to the glass –

Up at the glass, the mirror –

Until –

Until the Yorkshire Ripper says: 'Yes.'

Noble: '*Yes*?'

The Yorkshire Ripper: 'Yes, I'm sure.'

'Sure it wasn't you?'

'Yes.'

Noble: 'Let's move on then?'
The Yorkshire Ripper: 'OK.'
Noble: 'To the ones you did?'
The Yorkshire Ripper nods.

Sixteen hours later, in the dark room –
 The dark room on our side of the glass –
 Our side of the mirror –
 Drowning, we're drowning here –
 Drowning in here in his bloody sea –
 The bloody tide in –
 His bloody tide high –
 The bloody things he's said –
 The bloody things he's done –
 Noble: 'Joyce Jobson?'
'I saw her in the Oak. She annoyed me, probably in some minor way. I took her to be a prostitute and I hit her on the head and scratched her buttocks with a piece of hacksaw blade or maybe it was a knife. I'm sorry, I can't remember. But it was my intention to kill her but I was disturbed by a car coming down the road.'
 Noble: 'Anita Bird?'
'I asked her if she fancied it. She said not on your life and went to try to get into her house. When she came back out, I tapped her up again and she elbowed me. I followed her and hit her with a hammer. I intended to kill her but I was disturbed again.'
 Noble: 'Theresa Campbell?'
'She was drunk and laughing at me and said, come on get it over with. I said, don't worry I will and I hit her with the hammer. She made a lot of noise and kept on making a lot of noise so I hit her again. I took a knife out of my pocket and stabbed her about four times.'
 Alderman: 'It was more than that.'
'It might have been.'
 Alderman: 'It was fifteen to be exact.'
'I know.'
 Alderman: 'Why'd you stab some of them in the heart?'
'The ones that wouldn't die, I stabbed them in the heart. You can kill them quicker that way.'

Noble: 'Joan Richards?'

'She was wearing very strong and cheap perfume and I pushed a piece of wood against her vagina to show how disgusting she was.'

Noble: 'What did you stab her with?'

'A screwdriver.'

Noble: 'How many times?'

'Quite a few.'

Alderman: 'Fifty-two times.'

'That many?'

Alderman: 'That many.'

Noble: 'Ka Su Peng?'

'She went behind some trees to urinate and then said we should start the ball rolling on the grass. I hit her once on the head with the hammer, but I just couldn't bring myself to hit her again. For some reason I just let her walk away and I went back to the car and drove home.'

Noble: 'Marie Watts?'

'I used the hammer and a Stanley knife on her. As she was crouching down urinating on the grass I hit her on the head at least two or three times. I lifted up her clothes and slashed her abdomen and throat.'

Noble: 'Rachel Johnson?'

'She took a long time to die, that's all I can remember.'

Alderman: 'You remember how many times you stabbed her, Peter?'

'No.'

'Twenty-three times.'

Noble: 'Elizabeth McQueen?'

'I went back to cut off her head, make that one more mysterious.'

Noble: 'Kathy Kelly?'

'She was dirty and just talked about sex and so I hit her but she still wouldn't shut up so I stuffed some filling from a sofa in her mouth. But then a dog started barking and I had to leave her.'

Noble: 'Tracey Livingston?'

'She was another one I heard using foul language. It was obvious why I picked her up. No decent woman would have been using language like that at the top of her voice in the street. When I had killed her, I picked her up under the arms and hoisted her up on to the bed.'

Noble: 'Candy Simon?'

'She undid my trousers and seemed prepared to start sexual intercourse straight away in the front of the car. It was very awkward for me to find a way to get her out of the car. For about five minutes I was trying to decide which method to use to kill her. She was beginning to arouse me sexually. I got out of the car with the excuse that I needed to urinate and managed to persuade her to get out of the car so that we could have sex in the back. As she was getting in I realised that this was my chance but the hammer caught on the edge of the car door frame and only gave her a light tap. She said, there's no need for that, you don't even have to pay. I expected her to immediately shout for help. She was obviously scared but just said, what was it? I said, just a small sample of one of these and I hit her on the head hard. She just crumpled making a loud moaning noise and then I realised what I had done was in full view of two taxi drivers who had appeared and were talking nearby. So I dragged her by the hair to the end of the woodyard. She stopped moaning but was not dead. Her eyes were open and she held up her hands to ward off blows. I jumped on top of her and covered her mouth with my hand. It seemed like an eternity and she was still struggling. I told her that if she kept quiet she would be all right. As she had got me aroused a moment previous, I had no alternative but to go ahead with the act of sex as the only means of keeping her quiet. It didn't take long. She kept staring at me. She didn't put much into it. Then the taxi drivers left and I went back for the hammer but she got to her feet and ran for the road. This was when I hit her heavy blows to the back of the head. I dragged her to the front of the car and threw her belongings over the wall. But she was still obviously alive so I took a knife from the car and stabbed her several times through the heart and lungs. I think it was the kitchen knife. It's in the cutlery drawer at home.'

Noble: 'Doreen Pickles?'

'I had the urge to kill any woman. The urge inside me to kill girls was practically uncontrollable and it still dominates my actions. Following Pickles the urge inside me remained dormant, but then the feeling came welling up. I had the urge to kill any woman. It sounds a bit evil now. There I was walking along with a big hammer and a big Philips screwdriver in my pocket ready for the inevitable but I have been taken over completely by this urge to kill and I cannot fight it.'

Noble: 'Noorjahan Davit?'

'She was walking slowly like a prostitute and wearing tight jeans and I hit her on the head with a hammer. I dragged her down the road and her shoes were making a scraping noise. I apologised to her and took her shoes off and put them over the wall with her handbag. Then I stabbed her.'

Noble: 'Joanne Thornton?'

'It had been a long time since the last one. I realised she was not a prostitute. I had to try and convince her she was safe with me and I said, you can't trust anyone these days. I used the Philips screwdriver, the big one.'

Alderman: 'You put it up her, didn't you? In her vagina?'

'I think I waggled it about two or three times, yes.'

Alderman: 'This one, this one here with the sharpened point?'

'Yes. I used it on Joanne Thornton and on Dawn Williams.'

Noble: 'Tell us about Dawn Williams?'

'I took her to the back of the house before I stabbed her, that's all. Before doing it, with any of them I had to go through a terrible stage each time. I was in absolute turmoil. I was doing everything I could to fight it off, and I kept asking why it should be me, until I eventually reached the stage where it was as if I was primed to do it.'

Alderman: 'Twenty-eight times?'

'I honestly can't remember.'

'I'm telling you, you stabbed her twenty-eight times.'

'I believe you.'

Noble: 'Tessa Smith?'

'I attacked her because she was the first person I saw. I think something clicked because she had on a straight skirt with a slit in it.'

Noble: 'Prudence Banks?'

'I changed my methods here because the press and the media had attached a stigma to me. I had been known for some time as the Yorkshire Ripper and I didn't like it. It isn't me. It didn't ring true. I had been on my way to Leeds to kill a prostitute when I saw Prudence Banks. It was just unfortunate for her that she happened to be walking by. I don't like the method of strangulation. It takes them even longer to die.'

Noble: 'Laureen Bell?'

'The last one I did. I sat in the car eating some Kentucky Fried Chicken, then I saw Miss Bell. I decided she was a likely victim. I drove just past her and parked up and waited for her to pass. I got out of the car and followed about three yards behind her. As she drew level with an opening I took the hammer out of my pocket and struck her on the head. By this time I was in a world of my own, out of touch with reality. I dragged her on to some waste ground. A car appeared and I threw myself to the ground, but the car passed by. I can't imagine why I was not seen. She was moving about, so I hit her again. Then I dragged her further on to the waste ground as a girl was passing by. I pulled most of her clothes off. I had the screwdriver with the yellow handle and I stabbed her in the lungs. Her eyes were open and she seemed to be looking at me with an accusing stare. This shook me up a bit so I stabbed her in the eye. I just put it to her lid and with the handle in my palm I just jerked it in.'

Sixteen hours of this in the dark room –
The dark room on our side of the glass –
Our side of the mirror –
Drowning, we're drowning here –
Drowning in here in his bloody sea –
The bloody tide in –
His bloody tide high –
The things he's said, the things he's done –
Sixteen hours in the dark room –
Sixteen hours and six years –
In dark rooms –
In silence –
Silence and tears.

Up the stairs –
Sleeping coppers on every desk –
On every desk, face down –
Faces down in ash and cans –
Snoring, farting, belching –
The cans, the dog ends, the wretched smell –

We're all back in the upstairs office –

Sergeant Ellis in full flight, swing whatever –

Me all ears –

Only me –

'Took one bloody look at him, didn't I. And I said to lads, he's an odd one this one, I did.'

Me: 'Time? What time?'

'Minute they bloody brought him in; nine o'clock.'

Me: 'So what'd you do?'

'Called Ripper Room, didn't I? Bloke nicked with false plates and prossie in a red-light area – I'm straight on him. Dialled Millgarth before his arse even touched a seat.'

Me: 'Who'd you get at Millgarth?'

'Bob Craven,' he says –

'Where is Bob?' I ask.

'Fuck knows,' says Ellis. 'Anyway, I says to Bob, you want to clock this one and Bob's like, keep him sweet and Jim Prentice'll be down for a butchers.'

Me: 'Kept him sweet did you?'

'As bloody sugar – talking ten to dozen, he was: telling us how he's always up Sunderland, over Preston way, how he takes a size eight Welly, all the different passion wagons he's had – Corsairs and Rovers and Escorts and you-bloody-name-it he's had it.'

Me: 'Mention Ripper did you?'

'Just what Bob said to tell him, routine when a bloke gets pulled with a slag.'

Me: 'What did he say?'

'Fine. No sweat. Said he'd been seen half a dozen times already.'

Me: 'What'd you say to that?'

'I'm rubbing my bleeding hands, aren't I? But I say, is that right? You've got nowt to bloody worry about then, have you? And he says, only bloody missus. But I tell him she's already phoned and she thinks it's just about some dodgy plates and you'll be right.'

Me: 'What time she phone?'

'About ten minutes after he got here.'

Me: 'Then what?'

'Jim Prentice gets here after lunch, been up Bradford way for some funeral or something. Takes one look at our man and he's like: know him, seen by John Murphy about that fiver, clocked in Bradford, Leeds, and Manchester, and last time they did all local engineering firms. So Jim goes in and has a bit of a chat and he's in there twenty, thirty minutes, and he comes back out and he says, Mike I'm not happy. And I'm like, fuck we've screwed up and I say, why – what's up? But Jim's like, not happy about Peter David Williams and he goes gets Millgarth on blower.'

Me: 'What time's this?'

'Be about three o'clock.'

Me: 'And what did Dick Alderman say?'

'Test him.'

Me: 'And what did Williams say when you went down to test him?'

'Wasn't me, it was Jim Prentice, – but apparently he goes, what if it's same one you're wanting? And Jim says, calm as can be like, you Ripper are you? And feller he just says, no. Then you're all right then, aren't you laughs Jim.'

Me: 'So he's in the frame by now?'

'Oh aye. And then when test comes back and it's B – well then it was pints all round, waon't it?'

Me: 'What time was that?'

'Test results? Actually I can't remember which was first: Chainey finding hammer and knife back in Sheffield or blood type. Any road, must have been gone twelve.'

Me: 'Midnight?'

'Yeah, cos then Dick Alderman turns up, Pete Noble – and I mean no-one's going home, we're all just hanging around.'

Me: 'All night?'

Ellis nodding: 'Once in a lifetime thing, this. I mean, all night they're having top-level meetings, planning it all out.'

Me: 'Who?'

'Brass: Noble, Alderman, Prentice – and phone never bloody stopped.'

Me: 'And what they doing with the suspect?'

'Suspect? He's bloody sleeping like a baby, isn't he? First thing though when he woke – he must have noticed something was up.'

Me: 'Why's that?'

'Well minute he's had his breakfast – there's Alderman and Prentice and me sat there.'

Me: 'You?'

'Oh aye, first interview today I was taking it all down.'

Me: 'What'd he say?'

'Nowt much, they were just trying to get him relaxed, you know.'

Me: 'How?'

'Talking about cars, sex.'

Me: 'Sex?'

'Aye, Alderman was asking him all about him and his missus – how often they have a bit, because he'd been on to them saying like she was always nagging him and stuff like that. But he reckoned they were at it regular – nowt kinky mind. Said they forgot about rows and all that minute they went to bed.'

Me: 'Getting a bit personal then?'

'Oh aye, but he didn't seem to mind. Dead relaxed, he was. Best bit was when, this was lunchtime, – just before you and George Oldman got here. Jim Prentice says why don't we send out for some fish and chips and Ripper, he's a cocky bastard, he grins at him and says, I'll go if you want – but I reckon they might be a bit cold by time I get back.'

Downstairs I go –

Through the double doors and down the stairs –

Downstairs –

Underground –

Until I come to a corridor –

Bright lights overhead –

Walls half green, half cream –

Floors, black and polished –

Come to the cells –

Eight cells –

Four in a row on the right –

Four in a row on the left –

Doors open –

No-one –

No guards, no coppers –

No-one.

I walk down the corridor –

Looking left, then right –
Left, then right –
Left then right –
Until I come –
Come to the last two cells –
And I look to the left –
No-one –
And I look to the right –
And –
And there he is –
The Yorkshire Ripper –
The Yorkshire Ripper asleep on the bed in the cell –
His back to the door, curved –
Curved in a blue sweater, grey trousers –
Alone –
No-one inside the cell –
No-one outside –
And I stare at the back of the Yorkshire Ripper –
The back of the Yorkshire Ripper moving up and down, in
and out, ever so slightly –
Ever so slightly under that blue sweater –
And then I hear footsteps –
Footsteps on the black polished floor –
And I turn –
Turn and there they are –
Alderman and Murphy, John Murphy –
A shotgun each –
A small woman between them –
A small woman with black hair.
And the three of them –
Alderman, Murphy and the woman, they stare –
Stare until Murphy says: 'What you doing here, Pete?'
'After your hundred quid, are you?' snorts Alderman.
I say: 'There was no-one on. There should have been
someone.'
Murphy: 'They're short. We just went to get Mrs Williams
here.'
But Mrs Williams here –
Mrs Williams isn't looking at me –
She's looking past me into the cell –

And I turn back –
Turn back to look into the cell –
And there he is –
Upright on the edge of the bed in the cell –
The Yorkshire Ripper, upright.
And she goes past me –
Past me and into the cell –
And she says: 'Have you had anything to eat?'
And Alderman shouts after her: 'Oi, we're not bloody inhuman you know?'
And she's holding his hand, asking him about his clothes –
And I'm walking backwards away from them –
Walking backwards away from them, when he says –
The Yorkshire Ripper says: 'It's me.'
And she says: 'Is it Peter? Is it really?'
And he nods and she lets go of his hand.
She turns back to Alderman and Murphy and me, standing in the corridor with the guns, and she says –
The wife of the Yorkshire Ripper says: 'My priority is to let my parents know. Not on the telephone, face to face.'
Alderman: 'I wouldn't advise you to do that.'
'Why?'
Alderman: 'The press will get you.'
'What on earth are you talking about?'
Alderman: 'We've had a press conference. They're all waiting outside.'
And I'm saying –
Saying for her: 'What? You've done what?'
Looking at Murphy, turning, walking –
I'm walking away –
Walking away, then running –
Up the stairs –
Running.

to intensify the anguish for the tears they first wept knotted in a cluster and like a visor made for them in crystal filled all the hollow part around their eyes o lord break off these hard veils and give relief from the pain that swells my heart and rains down blows upon my flesh where then new tears freeze again his body in the world above for whenever a soul betrays the way he did a demon takes possession of his body controlling its maneuvers from then on for all the years it has to live and e who am dead must lead thee through this hell these scenes of blood and wounds for memory and vocabulary are not enough to comprehend the pain the bodies ripped from chin to arse between their legs their guts spilled out with the heart and other vital parts the dirty sacks from inside hear another with her throat slit her nose cut off as far as where the eyebrows start she steps out from the group and opens her throat which runs red from all sides of her wound and says bring back to those on earth this message of the things you have seen take back this from those who stained your world with blood your world now containing approximately five pounds in cash all this and heaven too missing a lorry driver called peter who drives a cab with a name beginning with the letter C on the side he lives in bradford in a big grey house elevated above the street behind wrought iron gates with steps leading up to the front door number six in its street peter committed crimes before and is connected to the containerbase at stourton he will kill for the last time in leeds on wednesday the tenth of december nineteen eighty the thirteenth and last transmission one final picture from the atrocity exhibition from the shadows of the sun out of the arc of the searchlight laureen bell in headingley leeds eating kentucky fried chicken e saw her and followed her and e took hammer from my pocket and e hit her and then e dragged her to some waste land and she was moving about and e pulled most of her clothes off and e had the screwdriver with the yellow handle and e stabbed her in the lungs her eyes still open she seemed to be looking at me with an accusing stare which shook me up a bit so e stabbed her in the eye the taste of the chicken in my mouth the taste of salt everything salt in my mouth clueless e scream the weather is letting me down again for e am not ripper e am the streetcleaner locked in the red room poor old oldman looking for the wrong man noble but no choice misled by a voice release of drury arouses fury preston was not me but just you wait and see sheffield will not be missed next on the list my nails already dead of colour this exegesis complete and illuminated e stand upon souls fixed under ice some bent head to foot shaped like bows the distorted jackknife postures their bras pushed up now the time has come this the place where no light is e cannot write e cannot tell memory and vocabulary not enough here neither dead nor alive before the king of the vast kingdom of grief once as fair as he is now foul all grief springs from him one head wearing three faces one red one white one blue beneath which two mighty wings stretch out not feathered wings but like the ones you would expect a bat to have and he flaps them constantly keeping three winds continuously in motion saying over and over and over again and again and again this is the world now containing approximately five pounds in cash all this and heaven too missing from the deceaseds handbag one edge sharper than the other this is the world now the weather letting us down again and again and again in a yorkshire way he says this is the world now this is the world now this is the world now this is the world we be

Chapter 21

New Year's Eve, 1980:
> Dawn or dusk, it's all fucked up –
> *The End of the World* –
> Fucked up and running –
> Running from Dewsbury Police Station –
> Dewsbury Police Station –
> Modern lies amongst the black –
> Crowds gathering –
> Posters out:
> *The Ripper is a Coward* –
> Defaced:
> *Hang him!*
> The homemade nooses, the studded wristbands –
> The skinheads and their mums, the mohicans and their nans.
> Running to the car park up the road from the police station,
puddles of rain water and motor oil underfoot –
> The car park already full –
> Journalists, TV crews, the word spread –
> Birds overhead, screaming –
> Rain pouring –
> The clouds black above us, the hills darker still –
> Hills of hard houses, bleak times –
> Warehouse eyes, mill stares –
> Unlocking the door, running –
> Engine running, *running scared* –
> *The North after the bomb* –
> *Murder and lies, lies and murder* –
> *War.*

M1 into Leeds –
> Radio on:
> *'A Bradford man will appear before Dewsbury magistrates later
this afternoon in connection with the murder of Laureen Bell in Leeds
on December 10. The man was arrested by officers in Sheffield on
Sunday night in connection with the theft of some car number plates.
A jubilant Chief Constable Ronald Angus told reporters:*

' "This man is now being detained in West Yorkshire, and he is being questioned in relation to the Yorkshire Ripper murders. He will appear before Dewsbury magistrates later today. We are all absolutely delighted, totally delighted with the developments at this stage. The officers who detained the man in Sheffield were outstanding police officers; these lads are real heroes, who have my heartfelt thanks. They did a wonderful job. We know the girl the man was with when he was arrested and she's very lucky indeed. She could easily have been his next victim."

'When asked if the hunt for the Yorkshire Ripper was now over, Chief Constable Angus said:

' "You are right. The hunt for the Ripper is being scaled down."

'Meanwhile a crowd of almost 4000 people has already gathered outside Dewsbury Town Hall in the hope of catching a glimpse of the man whose five-year reign has brought terror to the streets of every Northern city. A reign that would now appear to be at an end.'

Radio off, thinking –

What looks like morning, it is the beginning of the endless night.

Leeds, fucking Leeds:

Medieval, Victorian, Concrete fucking Leeds –

Decay, murder, hell –

Dead city:

Just the crows and the rain –

The Ripper gone –

The crows and the rain, his meat-picked bones –

Leeds, fucking Leeds –

The King is dead, long live the King.

I park under the dark arches with the water and the rats –

Out of the car, coat up –

Running up through the arches, past the Scarborough –

Into the Griffin –

Ringing the bell, waiting –

Fuck it –

Snatching the key from behind the desk –

Into the lift –

Pressing 7 –

1,2,3,4,5,6 –

Out of the lift –

Down the corridor –

Tripping –

On the dark stair, we miss our step:

Room 77 –

Key in the door –

Into the room –

Checking my watch, radio on, picking up the phone, getting a dialling tone, pulling the numbers round –

Ringing, ringing –

'Joan?'

'Peter? Where are you?'

'Leeds.'

'Is it true? They've caught him?'

'Yes.'

'You coming home?'

'Home?'

'Here.'

'Yes.'

'Now?'

'Yes, why?'

'I had that nightmare again – the girl . . .'

'I'm coming now, love.'

'Oh be careful, Peter.'

'Yes.'

'Please – '

Phone down –

Sweeping the *Exegesis*, the loose notes, *Spunk*, the photographs –

Sweeping everything into the carrier bags –

The pages from the *Holy Bible*, the *Exegesis*, *Spunk* –

Everything in bags, everything ready –

One last look around –

Opening the door –

Opening the door and there she is:

'Helen?'

Hair tied back, raincoat still dripping, she asks: 'Can I come in?'

On the dark stair –

'Yes,' I say and hold open the door.

She steps inside and I close the door behind us.

She undoes her raincoat and takes out an envelope –

Flat and manila –
She holds it up –
In slanting black felt-tip pen:
Photos Do Not Bend.
I'm nodding, asking her: 'When?'
'Boxing Day.'
'Boxing Day?'
'By hand.'
'Who?'
She looks up to the ceiling of the room, sucking in her lips,
trying not to let the tears in her eyes –
Trying not to let the tears –
The tears in her eyes –
She says: 'Bob Craven.'
'What?'
She nods, the tears in her eyes.
Me: 'How?'
She pulls open the envelope, taking out the photographs –
And she throws them down onto the bed:
Photographs, four of them –
Four photographs of two people in a park:
Platt Fields Park, in wintertime.
Photographs, black and white –
Black and white photographs of two people in a park by a
pond:
A cold grey pond, a dog.
Four black and white photographs of two people in a park –
Two people in a park:
One of them her.
'How?' I ask.
But she looks up at the ceiling again, sucking her lips, the
tears in her eyes –
The tears in her eyes –
The tears –
And she reaches into the envelope again, taking out a piece
of paper –
A piece of black and white Xeroxed paper –
And she holds it up –
Holds it up in my face:
A piece of black and white Xeroxed pornography –

Skinny and ginger, legs and cunt –
Cunt shaved –
Her cunt shaved –
Her –
Helen Marshall.
Across the top of the page, in black felt-tip pen:
Spunk, Issue 3, January 1975.
Across the bottom, in black felt-tip pen:
Manchester Vice?
Across her face, in black felt-tip pen:
A line, a line across her eyes.
She throws the paper onto the bed –
Onto the bed, next to the photographs –
And I'm reeling –
Reeling:
'Helen who?'
'From her Vice days. Tell her I said hello.'
Reeling until –
Reeling until I say: 'You should have said something.'
But she looks up at the ceiling again, sucking her lips, the
tears in her eyes –
The tears in her eyes –
The tears –
Tears –
Tears, tears, tears, until –
Until she says: 'Why?'
'Because – '
'Because what? Because you fucked me?'
'Helen – '
'Fat lot of good that did me.'
'Helen, please – '
'Fat lot of bloody good screwing the boss did me, eh? Preg-
nant and wide open to this shit.'
'Pregnant?'
'Oh, don't worry. I got rid of it.'
On my knees: 'What?'
'All bloody water under the bridge now.'
'When?'
'When what?'
'When did you – '

'Sunday.'

'Where?'

'Manchester. Why? Why do you want to know?'

*I catch him, stop him murdering mothers, orphaning children, then
you give us one, just one –*

I look up at the ceiling, the tears in my eyes –

The tears in my eyes –

The tears –

Tears –

Tears, tears, tears, until –

Until I see her –

See the tears in her eyes –

The tears –

Tears –

Tears, tears, tears, until –

Until I say: 'Where is he?'

'Who?'

'Craven.'

'Why?'

'This has got to end.'

'You can't – '

But I have her by her coat, my wings outstretched, shouting:
'Where?'

And she's shaking –

Shaking and looking up at the ceiling, sucking her lips, the
tears in her eyes –

The tears in her eyes –

The tears –

Tears –

Tears, tears, tears, until –

Until she whispers: 'The Strafford.'

And I'm gone –

Wings outstretched –

Wings outstretched and running, praying –

One last deal:

*I catch him, stop him murdering mothers, orphaning children, then
you give us one, just one more –*

My last deal –

Last prayer.

*

Down the stairs –
   Into the rain –
   Under the arches –
   Into the car –
   Hit the radio:
   ' . . . asked him, "Are you Peter David Williams of 6 Park Lane, Heaton, Bradford?" to which Williams replied, "Yes, I am."

   'The Court Clerk then told Williams, "You are accused that between 10 December and 11 December 1980 you did murder Laureen Bell against the peace of our Sovereign Lady the Queen. Further, you are charged that at Mirfield between 6 December and 27 December, you stole two motor vehicle registration-plates to the total value of 50p, the property of Cyril Miller."

   'Williams was then asked if he had any objection to the remand in custody and whether he wanted reporting restrictions lifted. Williams replied, "No" on both counts . . .'

   Punch the radio –
   Out the city –
   Onto the motorway –
   To the end, thinking –
   Know the way, know the time –
   Know the place, know it well.

The End of the World:
   Wednesday 31 December 1980 –
   Dawn or dusk, the whole thing fucked:
   River brown, sky grey –
   Seven shades of shit –
   Wings, my wings on fire –
   Into Wakefield city centre –
   Sky blood, city dead –
   The Bullring –
   The End of my World:
   The Strafford.

Everyone gets everything they want –
   The Strafford –
   The first floor, boarded up:
   Closed.
   I drive past and turn left –

Drive slowly round the back of the buildings –

Round and into a car park, dark under a row of first floor rooms –

Empty upstairs rooms, back rooms –

Blind eyes out onto a rotten, uneven car park –

A car park deserted but for puddles of rain water and motor oil –

Deserted but for one dark green Rover.

I park, waiting –

Watching –

Watching the row of rooms up above –

Their boarded glass, their blind eyes –

Knowing he's near, here.

I get out of the car and open the boot –

I take out a hammer –

Take out a hammer and put it in the pocket of my raincoat –

Then I take out a can of petrol –

A half empty can of petrol –

And I close the boot of the car –

I walk across the car park –

The rotten, uneven car park –

Puddles of rain water and motor oil underfoot, heading for the stairs and a door –

A door to an upstairs room –

A door banging in the wind, in the rain –

I climb the dark stone stairs one at a time and stop before the door –

The door banging in the wind, in the rain –

I pull open the door –

The backdoor to the Strafford –

The backdoor to a passage –

The passage is dark and I can smell the stink of a shotgun –

The stink of bad things, the stink of death –

The stink of the Strafford.

I step inside –

A rotting, eaten mattress against a window –

I walk down the passage to the front –

To the bar –

I pull open another door –

The door to the bar –

The walls of the bar tattooed with shadows, tattooed with pain –

Maps, charts, photographs of pain –

The pain of the photographs –

Joyce Jobson, Anita Bird, Theresa Campbell, Clare Strachan, Joan Richards, Ka Su Peng, Marie Watts, Linda Clark, Rachel Johnson, Janice Ryan, Elizabeth McQueen, Kathy Kelly, Tracey Livingston, Candy Simon, Doreen Pickles, Joanne Thornton, Dawn Williams, and Laureen Bell –

Across the maps, the charts, and the photographs –

Across them all –

Swastikas and sixes –

Shadows, swastikas and sixes –

Across every surface –

Six six sixes –

(Out of the shadows).

I put down the can of petrol and try the light switch –

Nothing, only darkness –

Darkness, shadow, pain.

I step further inside –

Underfoot smashed furniture and splintered wood, stained carpets and shattered glass –

Behind the bar, the broken mirrors and the optics –

The jukebox in the corner, the silent bloodstained pieces –

Beneath the boarded windows, the long sofa full of holes –

A low table pulled out into the centre of the room –

On the table, pornography –

Spunk –

Pornography and a portable tape recorder –

A cassette case:

All this and Heaven too.

I walk towards the table –

Walk towards the table and see him –

See his boots –

On the floor, between the table and the bar –

His boots, him –

Him –

Lying on his face between the table and the bar –

Bob Craven –

His head blown off, a shotgun across one leg –

I look away –
Look up –
Two holes in the ceiling, above the bar –
Look down –
The head blown off –
Kneeling, I reach down between the table and the bar, reach down and turn him over –
Head off, face gone, beard gone –
Blood across the wall –
Across the shadows –
Across the swastikas and across the sixes –
Six six sixes –
(If the shadows could talk).
I pick up the shotgun from off his legs and I step back –
Step back beside the table and the portable tape recorder –
Machines the only survivors –
I press play:
Pause, hiss –

'I'm Jack. I see you are still having no luck catching me. I have the greatest respect for you George, but Lord! You are no nearer catching me now than four years ago when I started. I reckon your boys are letting you down George. They can't be much good can they?

'The only time they came near catching me was a few months back in Chapeltown when I was disturbed. Even then it was a uniformed copper not a detective.

'I warned you in March that I'd strike again. Sorry it wasn't Bradford. I did promise you that but I couldn't get there. I'm not quite sure where I'll strike again but it will be definitely some time this year, maybe September, October, even sooner if I get the chance. I am not sure where, maybe Manchester, I like it there, there's plenty of them knocking about. They never learn do they George? I bet you've warned them, but they never listen.'

Thirteen seconds of hiss, count them:
One two three four five six seven eight nine ten eleven twelve thirteen seconds of hiss, then –

'Take her in Preston, and I did, didn't I George? Dirty cow. Come my load up that.

'At the rate I'm going I should be in the book of records. I think it's eleven up to now isn't it? Well, I'll keep on going for quite a while yet. I can't see myself being nicked just yet. Even if you do get near

I'll probably top myself first. Well it's been nice chatting to you George. Yours, Jack the Ripper.

'No use looking for fingerprints. You should know by now it's as clean as a whistle. See you soon. Bye.

'Hope you like the catchy tune at the end. Ha. Ha.'

Then –

'I'll say your name –

'Then once again –

'Thank you for being a friend.'

Silence –

The tape still turning –

Still turning in the portable tape recorder –

The portable tape recorder on the table –

The table –

Between the table and the bar –

Bob Craven –

His head blown off –

Head off, face gone, beard gone –

Blood across the wall –

Across the shadows –

Across the swastikas and across the sixes –

Six six sixes –

(The shadows talking).

Beside the portable tape recorder, the tape still turning:

Pause, hiss –

HISS –

Piano –

Drums –

Bass –

'How can this be love, if it makes us cry?'

STOP.

HISS –

Cries –

Whispers –

Hell:

'How can the world be as sad as it seems?'

STOP.

HISS –

Cries –

Whispers –

More hell:
'How much do you love me?'
STOP.
HISS –
Cries –
Cries –
Cries:
'Spirits will kill Hunter!'
STOP.
Silence –
Tape over.
Silence –
Between these walls, silence –
Walls tattooed with shadows silent, silent pain –
Maps, charts, photographs of pain –
The silent pain of the photographs –
Grace Morrison, Billy Bell, Paul Booker, and Derek Box –
Across the maps, the charts, and the photographs –
Swastikas and sixes –
Shadows, swastikas and sixes –
Six six sixes –
(Silent shadows, silent sixes).
Sat among the silence, sat upon the table –
The smashed and splintered, stained and shattered table –
Sat upon the low table in the centre of the room –
Wings, huge and rotting things –
Big black things that weigh me down, heavy –
Stop me standing –
Sitting on the table, his shotgun on my knees –
Staring at the sixes –
Silent sixes, waiting –
Six six sixes.
Across the sixes –
Across the swastikas, across the shadows –
Across them all –
The blood across the wall –
Head off, face gone, beard gone –
His head blown off –
Bob Craven –
Between the table and the bar –

Bob Craven, silent –
Tape off.
Silence –
Silence until –
Until outside I hear car tires on the car park –
The rotten, uneven car park –
Puddles of rain water and motor oil under wheels –
Car lights illuminating a door –
A door to an upstairs room –
A door banging in the wind, in the rain –
The car lights stop before the door –
The door to an upstairs room –
The door banging in the wind, in the rain –
More doors banging, slamming –
Car doors slamming –
Boots across the car park –
The rotten, uneven car park –
Puddles of rain water and motor oil underfoot –
Boots upon the dark stone stairs;
I look down at the shotgun across my knees –
Sat among the silent sixes, on the table –
On the table –
Wings, huge and rotting things –
Big black raven things that weigh me down, heavy –
Stop me standing –
Sitting on the table, the shotgun on my knees –
Staring at the sixes –
Silent sixes, waiting –
The door banging in the wind, in the rain –
They open the door –
Two figures in the doorway at the end of the passage –
Two shotguns –
The passage is dark and they can smell the stink of another
shotgun –
The stink of bad things, the stink of death –
The stink of the Strafford.
They step inside –
A rotting, eaten mattress against a window –
They walk down the passage to the front –
To the bar –

They pull open another door –
The door to the bar –
The last door –
Two figures in the doorway –
Two shotguns –
Two figures and two shotguns:
Alderman and Murphy –
Richard Alderman and John Murphy –
The shotgun across my knees –
The silent sixes, the shadows –
Wings, huge and rotting things –
Big black raven things that –
That weigh me down, heavy and burnt –
That stop me standing –
That stop me –
Stop me –
– *a shot.*